TRESPASSING
HEARTS

TRESPASSING HEARTS

JULIE ELLIS

G. P. PUTNAM'S SONS
New York

G. P. Putnam's Sons
Publishers Since 1838
200 Madison Avenue
New York, NY 10016

Library of Congress Cataloging-in-Publication Data

Ellis, Julie, date.
Trespassing Hearts / Julie Ellis.
p.   cm.
ISBN 0-399-13738-6 (alk. paper)
I. Title.
PS3555.L597T74   1992   91-42074 CIP
813' .54—dc20

Designed by Rhea Braunstein

Printed in the United States of America
1   2   3   4   5   6   7   8   9   10

This book is printed on acid-free paper.
∞

For Sally Ollivierre—
and Siobhán and Shane

CHAPTER ONE

Tense and uncomfortable in the humid June heat, lovely auburn-haired Betsy Bernstein sat among the 1941 graduating class of New York City's Hunter College, pretending to enjoy the organ solo. Perspiration left her dress clinging damply between her shoulder blades beneath the traditional black gown, stained the hairline that framed her oval face. When would the exercises be over? she wondered restlessly.

This should be the happiest night of her life, she thought, her luminous blue-green eyes darkening with frustration. But how could it be when Aunt Celia—who'd worked for and dreamed of this day—wasn't here?

In a corner of her mind, she heard her aunt's voice when she was about to leave the apartment: *"You're not to worry about me, Betsy. I'm not truly sick—just exhausted from these last weeks of teaching. After the graduation exercises I want you to go out with Emily and your friends to celebrate. I'll be fine."*

Betsy smiled tenderly as she remembered how proud Aunt Celia had been that her high school average was high enough for admission to Hunter. With the Depression at last behind them, Aunt Celia was convinced the Board of Education would be hiring more teachers.

How was she to tell Aunt Celia that she didn't want to teach? School was over now—she had to face the real world. How was she to explain the dreams that filled her head these last months?

At last, the exercises were over. Hordes of people spilled out of the auditorium onto the sidewalks. The atmosphere was electric with the excitement of graduation eve.

"It's so hot," Emily complained when at last she and Betsy joined the milling horde outside. Many seemed loath to end the evening. "Let's walk over to the cafeteria instead of taking the crosstown bus."

After congratulatory moments with Emily's proud parents—now en route to their subway—the two girls had decided to go for coffee and danish at their favorite cafeteria on Broadway in the Eighties rather than join a cluster of students bound for more festive celebration.

"It isn't as hot out here as it was inside." Betsy breathed in the night air with murmurs of appreciation. "But yes, let's walk."

They headed west toward Fifth Avenue, where they'd be able to cut through Central Park to the West Side of Manhattan, still full of the thrill of having earned their bachelor's degrees.

When they'd entered Hunter in the fall of '37—in the midst of the Depression—that had seemed a daring effort. But there were no jobs to be had then—and tuition was free.

"I can't believe school's behind us," Emily said, and Betsy nodded in agreement.

"It's scary," Betsy added. "Now we have to face the real world."

"The real world is a lot better than it was when we started Hunter," Emily acknowledged. "If it wasn't for my mother's job, we'd have been on the WPA. I went through junior high with two sweaters, two blouses, two winter skirts, and one summer one. My shoes were half-soled till the tops fell apart. Yeah, we're doing better these days."

"We were worried about money all the time." She and Aunt Celia had scrimped to get by, but they'd been better off than Emily's family. Emily's mother's salary had to cover herself, her husband, two kids, and Emily's grandmother. "But what's happening in Europe isn't any better. When we were born—only months after Armistice Day—people were saying we'd fought the war to end all wars."

"Let's not be morbid tonight," Emily ordered, pausing at the corner of Fifth Avenue to inspect the array of expensive apartment houses that lined the east side of the avenue. "Wow, wouldn't you like to live in one of those?"

"You will one day," Betsy predicted with a quick smile. She knew Emily's impatience to be rich and famous. Emily wasn't beautiful, but her shoulder-length near-black hair, gray-green eyes, a Rita Hayworth mouth, and slightly tilted nose gave her a striking attractiveness. That was important to a girl who wanted to be a Broadway star. "And I'll say—'I knew her when.' "

"Oh, yeah." Emily laughed. "You just saw that in your crystal ball." She frowned now. "I feel so guilty about not going on home to Brooklyn with Mom and Dad." Emily lived in a two-family house in Borough Park. Betsy shared a studio apartment in a brownstone on West 82nd Street in Manhattan with her aunt. "But I couldn't. Not tonight."

"Your mother understood," Betsy consoled.

"She wasn't happy that both the invocation and benediction were given by Reverend McDonell of the Catholic Charities," Emily drawled affectionately.

"She wanted to know why there couldn't be a rabbi, too," Betsy guessed. Emily's mother was one of her favorite people. She thought about Mrs. Meyers' oft-repeated declaration: *Hunter College is to poor Jews what Barnard is to the rich. But giving New York girls a free education is not just a gift to them. It's a gift to the city, too. Who makes a better teacher than a bright Jewish girl?*

"Mom's not terribly happy about my sleeping over at Colleen's. She's never met Colleen—she's just seen her the time she and Dad came into the city for our performance at the settlement house down on Delancey. She said Colleen was too 'brassy'—she didn't trust her. You she likes," Emily said with a chuckle. There was no way, of course, that Emily could stay with Aunt Celia and her, Betsy thought ruefully—not in a studio apartment. "She teaches and your aunt teaches—that's a real bond in her eyes."

"I wish Aunt Celia could have been at the graduation exercises." Her aunt had been her only family since her parents died in a car crash when she was ten. "She keeps insisting that she's just tired. She won't go see a doctor." Betsy felt a surge of frustration. "You know how proud she's always been of never missing a day of school. This year she's been absent a dozen times."

"She'll have the whole summer to rest up," Emily comforted. "And in another two years she'll be retiring."

Cutting through Central Park—the air fragrant with the scent of recently mown grass—they talked about the commencement exercises, dissecting all the happenings of the evening: the speeches, the performances of the college choir, the two organ solos.

"Didn't you want to kill Mr. Tead when he started talking about how 'many of you will soon embark on careers of happy family life'?" Emily grunted in disgust. "As though every girl in the graduating class is dying to get married. I have no intention of getting married before I'm at least thirty. What's the rush? Times are good now. Let's enjoy life before we settle down." She clucked in reproach. "You didn't hear a word I said. You're still worrying about Aunt Celia."

"It's just that she's never been sick until this year. It's scary," Betsy admitted.

"Look, instead of going to the cafeteria, why don't we pick up some danish and take them to your apartment?"

"She'd be upset. She kept saying she wanted me to go out with you and some of the other girls from school and celebrate. Besides, she's probably asleep by now."

On Broadway they turned north and headed for the cafeteria. They were not surprised to find it crowded. With so many people moving into defense jobs and working on round-the-clock shifts, the cafeterias were busy at all hours.

Busboys were clearing away dishes in the brightly illuminated cafeteria with its acre of utilitarian tables. Patrons were lined up at the serving counters. Aromas of coffee, freshly baked danish, hot rolls, blended with those of spicy pastrami and corned beef and noodle pudding.

Betsy and Emily collected silverware and napkins, gazed about for an unoccupied table.

"There's a table in the back." Emily pointed in triumph. "Let's nab it."

Their table staked out, they headed for the counter. The coffee line seemed endless. On nights like this people came in just for coffee because it was cool in the cafeteria.

"Are you worried about the license exam?" Betsy asked as they waited to be served. "I wish it wasn't so soon."

"You're not worried about passing?" Emily derided. "You with your *magna cum laude?*"

"Even if we pass and make the list, it'll be probably six or eight months before the list is published." She'd take any job that came along until then—even though it meant giving up her cherished part-time job at The Sanctuary. Aunt Celia had carried the burden of supporting her all these years, she reminded herself conscientiously. Yet her soul rebelled at the prospect of settling for a teaching job. Since her first days at The Sanctuary—almost seven months ago—she'd known she wanted to be an interior decorator. For her walking into the shop was like walking into heaven. Selling wasn't exciting—but being around the beautiful things in the shop, trying to guide customers into buying what was right for them filled her with satisfaction.

"There's going to be hell to pay at home when Mom finds out I'm serious about theater," Emily said when they were seated. "Not movies. Broadway," she emphasized with relish. When she'd first joined "the group"—as the members called it, she'd told her mother she was there to improve her diction and to build up self-confidence in public speaking. "Mom adores the movies, but to her every actress—except maybe Shirley Temple—is slightly immoral. She still talks about the Fatty Arbuckle scandal and the William Desmond Taylor murder. And actresses kiss strange men on stage. If Mom knew I'd already gone beyond the kissing bit, she'd have a stroke."

"So you had a fling with Joel in the group. Don't make it sound as though you were sleeping around like Colleen." She herself had never even had a real date, Betsy thought self-consciously. In an all-girl college the opportunities were limited. Besides, between school, studying, and a part-time job, when did she have time to date?

"I'll have to get a job right away," Emily said and Betsy nodded in agreement. "I'm not ready to cope yet, anyway, with making theater rounds. Let's try Macy's or Gimbels. The big department stores like college graduates. Even after the list is published, we might wait a year to be hired. By then—with luck on my side—I might have a two-line part on Broadway. Even a walk-on. Just so it's theater—not clerking in Macy's or Gimbels or teaching."

"To your mother and Aunt Celia teaching is like a trust fund," Betsy said somberly.

"So the money's lots better than it was fifteen years ago. It still stinks."

"Aunt Celia always talks about how great the vacation time and holidays are—but she was always trying to find a summer job." Which hadn't happened until last summer, when all at once jobs became available again. "And of course she loves teaching."

"Mom and your aunt Celia grew up on the Lower East Side, with parents who still spoke with foreign accents—but the two of them went to college and became teachers. It was a terrific step up the ladder. Now Mom forgets how she's always griped about what tyrants most of the principals are, and how she almost got fired when her principal found out she was married. And then she had the nerve to get pregnant." Emily rolled her eyes eloquently. "It's just as bad now. The minute you show, you're banished from the classroom. I suspect they really believe that kids from first to sixth grade think the stork brings babies."

"We'll both be at Macy's employment office on Monday morning." Betsy's smile was wry. "Along with half the graduating class. The other half will be signing up for civil service jobs or heading for the defense plants."

It had been wonderful to meet Emily that first day of their freshman year at Hunter. She'd been scared to death at starting college. College wasn't like high school. Everybody there was a stranger. Right away she'd known that she and Emily would be friends forever.

Reluctantly they decided to call it a night when they'd finished their danish and coffee. Emily would walk Betsy to her corner, then head two blocks south for Colleen's apartment. Both Betsy and Colleen lived between West End and Riverside Drive.

Waiting for a light to change, they ignored the good-natured efforts of a pair of Marines to pick them up. All at once, it seemed to Betsy, Emily was depressed.

"Let's move," Emily said with unexpected sharpness. "We've got the light now."

When they were on the west side of the wide Broadway crossing, Emily turned to Betsy. "I didn't mean to sound so nasty," she apologized. "I've been trying not to think about it—I wanted to forget about it for tonight—but Mom told me just before she and Dad went down into the subway that Bert received his draft notice this morning."

"Oh, Emily—" The war situation had long weighed on their minds, but until now it hadn't touched them personally. But now Emily's brother would be in uniform.

"Mom hadn't meant to tell me tonight. She said she didn't want to spoil graduation for me. It just slipped out."

"That doesn't mean Bert is going off to fight," Betsy told her. "We're not in the war." Still, people worried. Just two days ago the *Times* ran an article about Governor Lehman calling for the immediate organizing of civilian volunteer air-raid "spotters." That was scary. *Did the Governor expect New York City to be bombed?*

"Mom's furious because Bert and Rheba didn't push up their wedding plans when draft registration began last October. You know how couples are rushing to get married because everybody says married men are sure to be deferred."

"It seems so unreal to think that we might get involved in the war. It all seems so far away from us—"

"My father's convinced we'll never be attacked," Emily said. "But that doesn't mean we won't be dragged into the war. Bert could be shipped to Europe to fight. But let's stop being so pessimistic." She was determined to change the subject. "Aren't you glad I met Colleen at the group? You'd still be working at Woolworth's on Saturdays instead of for Mark at The Sanctuary."

"That was a real break." But now she'd have to walk away from that. Why couldn't she have afforded to go to Parsons instead of Hunter? Of course when she'd started Hunter she hadn't discovered the wonderful world of interior decorating.

"All those beautiful things that Mark sells at such fantastic prices." Emily laughed. "Can you imagine somebody paying seven hundred dollars for a spindly little chair?"

She'd told Emily about the chair Mark had sold to Mrs. Forrest—one of his rich customers. She'd bought it to go with the Spanish writing tables in one of her guest rooms. She'd made her son come down to the shop and sit on it to be sure it would be comfortable for a man. He'd hated having to do that, Betsy remembered sympathetically.

What was his name? She squinted in thought for a moment. Paul—that was it. He was so good-looking—and so friendly. His mother was kind of intimidating—maybe because she wore those gorgeously expensive clothes and always looked as though she was annoyed about something.

"Betsy, you're dreaming again." Emily punctured her introspection.

"I was thinking about the shop. Mark's really building up the business. Of course he doesn't sell a chair for seven hundred dollars very often. At least not yet."

"Can you imagine the house that woman must have?" Emily sighed. "Like a movie set, I'll bet."

"Mark's been there a couple of times," Betsy told her. "He says it's very elegant. It's a wide, five-story limestone townhouse with an elevator and half a dozen fireplaces." Like Mark and Eric, a window-dresser at Saks with ambitions to become a stage set designer, she had a passion for fireplaces. The kind they treasured were the usable ones, not those like the one in their brownstone studio that had been sealed off even before Aunt Celia moved in. "He said the entrance foyer is almost as big as his apartment."

Mark and Eric—who shared an apartment—spent every Sunday driving all over northern Westchester and Putnam counties in search of antiques they could restore. More and more wealthy women were wandering into The Sanctuary, many willing to pay top dollar for antique finds. Betsy sighed. It hurt to think that she would have to give up her part-time job there.

Daddy had thought he was leaving plenty of money for her to

grow up and be whatever she wanted, Betsy remembered tenderly. Those had been his last words, Aunt Celia said, then—not long after he and Mom died—the stock crash came. Almost everything was wiped out. And what little had been left was lost when Daddy's bank failed. Like banks all over the country in that awful period.

"Damn, I have to go to the bathroom like crazy," Emily complained as they approached Betsy's corner. "All that coffee. But I'll make it to Colleen's."

"Come into the apartment with me. We won't wake Aunt Celia—she's a heavy sleeper."

"That'll be good." Emily giggled with relief. "You know, when we first started at Hunter, I used to wonder how you could stand living in the city in just one room. I thought it was sweet the way you and Celia loved that big tree outside your windows and the tiny garden the people in the basement apartment tend so seriously—but how could you live in one room? After that first year of commuting to Hunter, I decided it would be sensational to live in Manhattan. Even in a broom closet."

"Once you have a job, maybe you can move into the city," Betsy encouraged.

"All I could afford would be a hall bedroom." Emily grimaced in distaste. "But even that would be better than a forty-minute schlep on the BMT twice a day."

Betsy and Emily turned in at the neat brownstone that had been home to Betsy for eleven years, walked up the steep stoop and into the foyer. Betsy unlocked the door and they started down the narrow, dimly lit corridor to the rear apartment.

"There's a note on the door," Betsy said in astonishment. Oddly disturbed. "Did Aunt Celia go out?" When she felt too bad to come to graduation?

"What is it?" Emily asked while Betsy squinted to read the tiny, scrawled message.

"It's a note from Lois next door. She wants me to knock on her door when I'm home." All at once her heart was pounding.

The two girls hurried to the front apartment. Betsy knocked on the door. In an instant it was opened. As though Lois had been waiting for her, Betsy thought anxiously.

"Oh, I'm so glad you're here!" Lois pulled Betsy into her apartment, barely acknowledging Emily's presence. An ex-chorus girl, Lois usually loved to talk to Emily about theater.

"Lois, where's Aunt Celia?" Betsy asked, her face taut with alarm.

"Now don't panic," Lois pleaded. "I was having a cup of coffee with Celia, and all of a sudden she had this terrible pain in her chest. She said it went right down her arm—"

"Where is she?" Betsy's voice soared in fear.

"In the hospital," Lois said. "It happened about two hours ago. I called for an ambulance. St. Clare's responded. I went with her to the emergency room. She'd had a heart attack," Lois explained gently. "She was worried about your coming home and not finding her here. She sent me home to tell you. She said to tell you not to worry."

"You said she had a heart attack!" Betsy was cold and trembling. "Is she—"

"It could be a mild attack," Emily said quickly. "We'll go right over to the hospital."

"It's very serious," Lois said after a moment. "They won't let anybody see her except next-of-kin. I can't believe it." Lois's voice broke. "One minute she was saying how much better she was feeling and scolding herself about not going to your graduation— and the next minute she was clutching at her chest."

"She'll be all right," Betsy insisted. *She had to be.* Aunt Celia was all she had in the world except for distant cousins somewhere in California. Once a year—at Rosh Hashanah, the Jewish New Year—they exchanged cards. "Emily, will you come with me?"

"Give me two minutes to go to the bathroom," Emily said apologetically and scurried in that direction.

"Take a taxi," Lois ordered. She turned to reach for her purse on a table near the door. "I have money here."

"I have enough—" Betsy said quickly and waited for Emily to

return. Her mind in turmoil. She forced a smile while Lois murmured encouragement.

The two girls hurried out of the house and into the street. At West End Betsy hailed a taxi. Why had Lois insisted they take a taxi instead of the subway? *Was she afraid they'd be too late?*

CHAPTER TWO

The taxi pulled up before St. Clare's Hospital. Betsy shoved bills at the driver—she was too distraught to worry about the change—and thrust open the door. In a corner of her mind she was remembering the desperate rush to Bellevue Hospital with Aunt Celia eleven years ago.

Aunt Celia had tried to be encouraging about the car accident that had summoned them there, yet she had seen the terror in her aunt's eyes—the kind of terror she felt now.

"We'll go straight to the emergency room," Emily said. She reached reassuringly for Betsy's hand. "You know how dramatic Lois always is. It's probably not as bad as she thinks."

That might have been true, but Lois had said that only the next-of-kin could see Aunt Celia. That had to mean she'd suffered a serious heart attack.

At the emergency room they were told that Celia had been taken upstairs to a private room.

"She's on the critical list," a nurse told them. "One family member at a time may see her."

"We're her nieces," Emily said, calmly lying. "Betsy, you see her first." She turned to the emergency room nurse. "Can I go up and wait outside her room?"

"There's a waiting room on the floor. You can stay there," the nurse told Emily.

"Thank you." Betsy tried to smile. Her whole world was in chaos. *Aunt Celia was on the critical list.* "Emily, let's go."

On the designated floor Betsy and Emily went to the nurses' station.

"I'd like to see my aunt. Celia Bernstein." Betsy fought to keep her voice even. "The nurse in the emergency room told me I could see her."

"Yes." The nurse offered an impersonal smile, but Betsy read compassion in her eyes. "But please don't stay more than five minutes. The doctors want her to have complete rest."

"I won't," Betsy promised. "What room number, please?"

At the door to her aunt's room, Betsy paused to gear herself for the meeting. She didn't want her aunt to see how anxious she was. She opened the door slowly, careful not to disturb the quiet. With heart pounding, she approached her aunt's bed. She noted the other bed in the room was unoccupied.

Celia lay with her eyes closed, hands folded atop the coverlet. How pale she was, Betsy thought in anguish.

"Aunt Celia—" Her voice was shaky.

"Betsy?" A tremulous smile lifted the corners of her aunt's colorless mouth. Now—as though any movement were an effort—she opened her eyes.

"Aunt Celia," Betsy whispered with determined optimism, "you're going to be fine."

"We have lots to talk about, Betsy." Celia's voice was thin and unsteady. "I—"

"Don't talk," Betsy pleaded. "Let me just sit here and hold your hand."

"We have to talk, my darling," Celia said with unexpected strength. "My will is in my bottom desk drawer—though I hardly think it's necessary." A glint of wry amusement lighted her eyes.

"You mustn't talk," Betsy said desperately. "The doctors want you to rest." She struggled for a semblance of calm. "When you're well again, we'll talk."

"Betsy, my savings account book is in the middle desk drawer. The money is in trust for you. There'll be enough to handle—

everything, plus a few dollars to carry you until you're working. I'm so proud of you. As your father and mother would have been." Tears filled her eyes, but Betsy understood these were happy tears. "I promised your father—and myself—that I would see you through college. And I did." But the triumphant glow in her eyes was suddenly replaced by pain. "You've been the light of my life, Betsy—like my own child."

"Aunt Celia!" Terror welled in her as she saw her aunt grappling with pain. She reached for the buzzer that lay on a corner of the bed and pushed the button.

She saw Celia's hand lift up as though reaching for hers and instantly took it in her own. Moments later the room was invaded by a pair of nurses. A doctor followed.

"You'll have to wait outside," a nurse told her gently, prodding her toward the door while the doctor and the other nurse hovered above her aunt.

Fighting panic, Betsy waited outside the door. Then she spied Emily hurrying down the hall toward her.

"I knew they were coming to Celia," Emily explained and reached to draw Betsy into her arms. "We'll wait here together."

Though the passage of time before the door opened was only minutes, to Betsy it seemed an interminable period.

"I'm sorry," the doctor said. "We couldn't save Miss Bernstein."

Shaken—too stunned to cry as yet, Betsy walked to the elevator, rode down to the main floor.

"The nurse said we have to stop by the business desk downstairs," Emily told her. "I'll talk to them."

In a daze, Betsy saw a hospital official walk toward them. He offered to put them in touch with a funeral home.

"We'll handle everything," Emily said crisply. "But thank you."

An arm about Betsy in comfort, Emily prodded her toward the door that led to the street. Emily found a taxi and gave directions. Inside the darkness of the taxi Emily reached for Betsy's hand.

"I'll stay with you tonight," she promised. "I'll call Mom. She'll come down first thing in the morning and take care of everything.''

Not until they were inside the apartment—the apartment where Aunt Celia would never come again—did Betsy give way to convulsive sobs. She had been terrified when her parents died—but Aunt Celia had taken her in and made her feel safe. Aunt Celia was gone—and she'd never feel safe again.

Betsy and Emily talked far into the night. Betsy spoke about the years of living with her aunt.

"She was so determined to make me feel we were still a family," Betsy said in pain. "Even though there were just the two of us, we observed all the Jewish holidays. Before every Passover we cleared the kitchen of bread, and during Passover we ate matzo. For Seder night she made chicken and matzo balls in chicken soup and *tzimess.*" Tears blurred Betsy's eyes. "She made almond macaroons because she knew how much I loved them. For Purim she always made *homentashen.* At Hanukkah—when I was growing up—there was a little gift for each of the eight nights."

Then Betsy's mind darted back to poignant memories of the years when her parents were alive. She remembered winter outings when Central Park was covered with snow, and her parents took her there with her bright red sled. She remembered trips on the subway to Brighton Beach.

"Mom and Daddy always took me to the beach before the summer season arrived, when there was only a sprinkling of people on the beach or on the boardwalk. I remember all the rides— though some were not yet open—and being allowed a frank at Nathan's. I remember the first time they took me to the public library—it was the week I started kindergarten."

She talked nostalgically about the trip to London and Paris when she was nine. All these years later she could visualize the huge ship they had boarded at the New York pier.

"It was the *Aquitania.*"

Tom Mix—along with Tony, his "wonder horse"—had been aboard that trip. It had been so strange and exciting to see Tom Mix leading Tony along the companionways of the ship.

"Emily, that was such a wonderful trip!"

She had shared her parents' delight in roaming about the streets of London and Paris, not knowing then that those three weeks aboard ship and in the two magical cities would nurture her soul for years ahead.

At last—from exhaustion—both girls slept. Before eight in the morning Mrs. Meyers was at the apartment door. Betsy moved through the next forty-eight hours in a daze, unaware that Emily's mother slipped sedatives into her coffee at regular intervals. Nothing was required of Betsy except to go to the bank to acquire the funds left in trust for her.

Later Betsy realized that it was Mrs. Meyers who had handled all the necessary arrangements at the hospital, at the funeral parlor, at the cemetery. In accordance with the Jewish faith, Celia Bernstein had to be buried within forty-eight hours of her death.

The following morning Betsy and Emily left for the funeral parlor, where the services were to be held. The casket was closed, as Celia Bernstein had wished. Betsy was grateful for this. She wished to remember her aunt as she had been in life.

Betsy was astonished by the number of people who arrived for the services. Neighbors, a cluster of teachers from her aunt's school, several huddles of students who clung together—their eyes wet as they tried to accept the death of their teacher. The rabbi took Betsy in his arms and expressed his sadness.

From the services at the funeral parlor Betsy, Emily, and Mrs. Meyers drove to the cemetery. Betsy remembered the sad journey to the same Brooklyn cemetery eleven years ago, when she sat hand-in-hand with Aunt Celia. Now she alone remained of the family.

At the cemetery Betsy sat with Emily and Mrs. Meyers in the limousine rented for the occasion and waited until it was time to go to the grave site. Only now did she understand the reason for the button with its swatch of black cloth attached to her dress at the funeral parlor services.

"The rabbi will cut it as a symbol of your grief," Mrs. Meyers explained gently. Betsy had no recollection of this custom at her parents' funerals, which had been separated by only three days.

Then the three of them approached the grave site. Betsy was grateful that Emily and Mrs. Meyers each held one of her arms. She closed her eyes as the rabbi spoke. *It was Aunt Celia who lay there in that plain pine coffin.* Then there was the mourner's Kaddish: Yit-ga-dal ve-yit-ka-dash she-mey ra-ba. . . .

Then—according to tradition—Betsy threw the first shovelful of earth upon the coffin. She saw none of it; her eyes were blurred by tears.

On the ride back to the apartment on West 82nd, Betsy sat between Emily and her mother and tried to think of the future. She had a vague awareness that the hospital and funeral expenses had been shockingly high. But before she could plan for the life that lay ahead of her, she must sit *shiva* for Aunt Celia.

When they arrived at the apartment, Betsy was astonished that so many people were crowded into the tiny area. Several of Aunt Celia's colleagues, Lois, a pair of students accompanied by the parents of one. Oh yes, she thought gratefully, Aunt Celia had been loved. Mark and Colleen emerged from the tiny kitchen to embrace her.

"I have to leave for the shop in a few minutes," Mark told her apologetically, "but Colleen's staying to serve the food."

"He and Eric were cooking all last evening," Colleen reported. "You know Mark and Eric when they're in a kitchen. We're keeping everything warm."

"Oh, I'm glad you're here—" She hugged them each in turn. What could compare with good friends? She felt a little less alone.

"Look, I know this isn't the time to talk about it," Mark began self-consciously, "but Greta's quitting at the end of the month." Greta was his full-time assistant. "I'd like you to take over. You don't have to make a decision right now," he added. "Just think about it."

"Mark, I don't have to think about it." Tears spilled over onto her cheeks. "I'd love to have the job. Thank you."

"You're sure you don't mind if I go out for a while?" Emily asked Betsy anxiously on Monday morning. "I'll just run down to the employment office at Macy's and Gimbels and make out an application. Then I'll be right back."

"I'll be all right," Betsy assured her.

"Okay. I'll make us breakfast and head downtown. And I expect you to eat," Emily warned.

"You sound like your mom." Betsy managed a shaky smile. "She's been wonderful."

Betsy forced herself to eat the scrambled eggs and toast Emily made for them. She clung to a second cup of coffee while Emily went into the bathroom to brush her hair. Moments later Emily emerged.

"Do I look all right?" she asked Betsy with a nervous glance at herself in the mirror that hung above the nonworking fireplace.

"You look great," Betsy told her.

"You've got a job already," Emily reminded, striving to sound cheerful. "Now I'd better find one. Wish me luck!"

Betsy sat motionless, nursing her second cup of coffee—which was already growing cold. She was prodding herself to be practical. The rent on the apartment was paid up until the end of the month. She couldn't afford to stay here after that. She'd have to look for a furnished room somewhere in the neighborhood.

What would she take with her? she wondered, wincing at the thought of what she might have to leave behind. Certainly she would keep her mother's crystal vase that had stood on their dinner table on Friday nights—and her mom's candlesticks. When Mom and Dad died after that drunken driver had run them down, Aunt Celia had had to sell all the furniture in that beautiful house they'd had for a little while out on Long Island, but she had kept those treasures.

"We'll keep the brass candlesticks your grandmother gave your mother as a wedding present—and the crystal vase your daddy gave your mother when you were born. Part of them will always be with us."

With a fresh rush of grief, Betsy reached for the pair of brass candlesticks. Every Friday night she would light the Sabbath candles—as Mom had done and, later, Aunt Celia. And Mom's crystal vase would always be where she could see it the moment she walked into whatever furnished room was her home.

Reverently she deposited the candlesticks and the vase on Aunt Celia's desk. The moment her period of *shiva* was over, she must search for a place to live. It was an unnerving prospect. This had been home for more than half her life.

CHAPTER THREE

For Betsy the seven days and nights of sitting *shiva*—the traditional mourning period of observant Jews—dragged on interminably. Each day seemed a lifetime. She was grateful for Emily's almost constant presence, for the arrival in the evening of friends.

Memories of her aunt flowed through her mind. Aunt Celia had been such a warm, gentle woman. A compassionate woman, she thought with pride. Aunt Celia had always told her that compassion was important both to the receiver and the giver. *"Always remember, my darling, to consider other people's feelings. And you'll feel better for the doing."*

She remembered Aunt Celia's kindness toward a neighbor disliked by everyone else. *"But Betsy, she had such a terrible childhood. Her mother beat her. Her father was an alcoholic. We have to understand what made her this way."*

Emily had been hired to work at a candy counter at Gimbels, but she would not start until the following Monday. While she was pleased to have a job, she was upset that yet another member of her theater group had withdrawn to take a swing-shift defense plant job.

"I don't know how we're going to replace him," Emily wailed, just home from yet another rehearsal with missing cast members. "We're having to postpone for now the three performances we've scheduled for settlement houses. We're all so desperate Eric's been trying to persuade Mark to join the group."

"Will he?" Betsy asked sympathetically.

"Not Mark. He said he'd die of stage fright. He says he's good at selling one-to-one, but he'd never remember a line with a whole audience out front. Oh, will you cue me tonight? One character in the play—male, of course"—she sighed in frustration—"has been cut. Plot lines are picked up by the rest of the cast."

"Sure," Betsy agreed.

"Oh, I didn't tell you the big news," Emily said with a spurt of effervescence. "About Colleen."

"What about Colleen?"

"She's going out to Hollywood next week. We've got double casts for the female parts, so that's no problem," Emily added quickly.

"She has a studio contract?" Betsy asked in astonishment.

"Not exactly. Her boyfriend is going out to work in a studio makeup department. She's going with him. He keeps telling her she's the Hollywood type—that something is sure to turn up for her. Her mother, of course, is throwing a fit. She wants Colleen to stay here and try for a government job. That pays better than clerking in Gimbels." Emily paused. "Even with my salary at Gimbels I might be able to afford a furnished room in Manhattan."

"Would your mother let you?" All at once Betsy was alert. "I mean, move into Manhattan?"

"I'm twenty-one, baby. Almost twenty-two. And I have a job. I can make that decision. And let's face it—if this job doesn't work out, I'll find another." There was an expectant glint in her eyes.

"Would you want to share this apartment with me?" Her mind juggled figures. "Together, I think we can afford it."

"I was going to bring that up next week," Emily confessed. "I didn't know if you'd feel like talking about it just now."

"I couldn't share this place with anybody in this world except you," Betsy said tenderly. Relief flooded her. *She wouldn't have to leave the apartment.*

"I can move in over the weekend—if you don't think that's too soon." She smiled ruefully. "Mom's going to have a shit fit—but she'll get over it."

"Aunt Celia would be so pleased that we'll be together," Betsy told her softly.

"Okay, let me put up coffee—then you can cue me on those new lines."

Betsy was grateful for the full-time job at The Sanctuary. Mark was more than her boss. He was a warm friend. Both he and Eric were her good friends, she told herself. She'd been thrilled when Mark offered her the Saturday job at The Sanctuary. Now she was his full-time assistant. She could learn so much from him. It would be almost like going to Parsons.

To placate her mother, Emily signed up to take the teachers' exams, though with no enthusiasm. Betsy felt guilty at intervals because she had abandoned all thoughts of teaching, even though Aunt Celia put so much stock in that. But she'd never wanted to teach. Now there was no reason to.

"I would sell my soul to go to the Neighborhood Playhouse or the American Academy of Dramatic Arts," Emily said with a wistful sigh over dinner at the Automat the following Saturday evening. They each splurged on an individual beef pot pie and coffee for twenty cents. "Or to take evening classes with Stella Adler. But where will I ever get the money for that?"

"I'd love to take some night courses at Parsons." Mark had studied at Parsons and at a school in Paris.

"You've got a foot in the door," Emily pointed out. "You said you're learning so much from Mark."

"From Mark *and* Eric," Betsy told her with satisfaction. "Eric's talented, too."

"Don't you love what they did with their apartment?" Mark and Eric lived in a tenement in the West Forties, but to open the door and walk inside was to discover a totally different world from what was expected. "Those dark green walls and all the white cushions."

"Mark said the dark green walls are his tribute to Elsie de Wolfe—that's one of her trademarks. He said she *invented* interior decorating. He said that when he was in Paris, a friend took him to one of her Sunday gatherings at the Villa Trianon. It was one of the most exciting moments of his life." Mark was thirty and he'd seen so much, Betsy thought wistfully.

"You know she's Lady Mendl in private life," Emily reminded. "She's married to Sir Charles Mendl. He's Jewish."

"She's rich and he has a title. It sounds like a plot for a Hollywood movie." Betsy laughed. Then all at once she was somber in recall. Aunt Celia had been such a movie fan. She'd adored the Jeanette MacDonald and Nelson Eddy movies and screwball comedies with Carole Lombard.

"Let's go to a movie tonight since we can't get second-balcony seats for anything playing at the theaters." Emily was restless, Betsy understood. It looked as though her drama group would be disbanded at any moment. The director had been drafted.

"What's playing at the Loew's?"

Emily spied a Saturday *Times* left at the next table and reached for the section that carried the movie ads. "I wish to hell we'd gone to a coed school. We have no men in our lives. Look at all those girls up at Barnard. I know"—she stopped Betsy's imminent comment—"Barnard isn't coed. But there are all those Columbia boys practically on the same campus."

"Look for a movie," Betsy ordered. "Let's get in before the Saturday mob arrives."

The summer was rushing past. On hot weekend nights Betsy and Emily cooled off on walks along the Hudson or by sitting on the benches that lined Riverside Drive. When the weather was especially humid, they took a ride on the Fifth Avenue bus that ran on Riverside Drive. They always rushed to seats on the upper level. The Fifth Avenue buses—ten cents rather than a nickel— were particularly popular in summer.

The newspapers kept talking about how great the economy was—how jobs were out there now for anybody that wanted one.

It was weird, Betsy thought, how in two years the whole country had turned around. But it was sad to realize this was happening because of a war—with so many people dying.

Late in the afternoon on the Thursday before Labor Day weekend, Mrs. Forrest—one of Mark's most important customers—phoned the shop. Betsy answered.

"Put Mark on immediately, please," Mrs. Forrest ordered after identifying herself. Like a royal summons, Betsy thought, as she summoned Mark to the phone.

Betsy stood by while Mark talked with Mrs. Forrest.

"Yes, of course. I understand how important it is that the drapes pick up the colors of your Aubusson." He pantomimed exasperation, but his voice was charmingly warm. Often Mrs. Forrest was difficult. Still, he respected her insistence on perfection. And with her, price was never a problem.

"I can't leave the shop myself," he apologized. "I have someone coming in for a consultation at any moment. But I'll send Betsy over immediately with swatches. Keep whichever batches you think might be right and take them out with you to the Southampton house."

"Darling, I hate to put you through this," Mark apologized to Betsy when he was off the phone, "but she's leaving for that showplace of a house she has out in the Hamptons—Southampton—in the morning, and she wants to order drapes for the dining room and living room out there when she returns. It could be a *big* order. I don't know why it's such a rush when they're closing the house up anyway in two weeks, but her Royal Highness has spoken. She understands I can't leave the shop, even for her."

"What do I have to do?" Betsy felt a tingle of anticipation at the prospect of seeing the inside of the Forrest mansion. Mark said it was like nothing he'd ever seen—but then Mrs. Forrest was his richest client. So far. Betsy thought again of Mrs. Forrest's son, who'd come to the shop with her to "try out the chair" a few weeks ago. Paul Forrest, she recalled his name with guilty pleasure. He had dark hair with golden glints, features that reminded her of Tyrone Power, warm brown eyes.

"Just take over the swatch books. Oh, tell her you decided on your own to bring along the book that just arrived this afternoon—that the bolts won't be delivered for another six weeks because of the bloody fighting in Europe," he added in sudden inspiration. "If she thinks she's latching on to something special, she'll insist that's what she wants. And that delivery delay will buy me time. The fabrics are gorgeous—but they'll be so expensive." He beamed with approval. "Take a taxi over. She'll keep you forever," he warned. "She always does—so just go on home from there and bring back the batches she doesn't keep when you come in tomorrow."

In a flurry of excitement Betsy left the shop, found a taxi, and headed up to the Forrest house, on Fifth Avenue in the high Sixties. Emily would want to know every detail about the furniture. She wished wistfully that she was wearing something chic and beautiful from Saks or Bergdorf's—which she knew only from the exterior. She and Emily lacked the *chutzpah* to walk past those elegant portals when they knew they couldn't afford to buy even a lipstick there.

Arriving at her destination, Betsy paid the taxi driver and paused at the curb to gaze at the imposing, five-story limestone townhouse. Mark had told her it had been built almost sixty years ago for the first James Paul Forrest and his bride. Struggling to appear poised in her Klein-bought printed dirndl and white peasant blouse, Betsy rang the bell. When the door was opened, she explained her mission to the houseman.

"Mrs. Forrest will see you in the library," he told her. "This way, please."

She walked into the huge marble-floored foyer, subconsciously admiring the exquisite Waterford chandelier that hung from the ceiling, the gleaming mahogany staircase that led to the upper floors. She followed the houseman down the wide, wainscotted hall and guessed that the pair of area rugs were fine old Caucasian rugs from Russia.

"In here, Miss." The houseman indicated an open door. "Mrs. Forrest will be with you shortly."

The Forrest library was triple the size of her apartment, Betsy thought humorously. The paneled bookcase walls were interrupted at one point by a tall, marble-faced fireplace. Betsy recognized the furniture as Elizabethan revival. A carved wood chandelier hung from the beautifully beamed ceiling. It looked like a Hollywood movie set.

Betsy's mind darted back through the years to the beautiful house she had lived in with her mother and father at Sands Point, out on Long Island. They'd lived there only a few months before the accident. It was nothing compared to the Forrest mansion, of course—but Mom and Daddy had been so proud of that house. It had been lost along with all of Daddy's stocks.

"Hi." A warm, friendly masculine voice punctured her reverie.

Betsy swung about to face Paul Forrest, hovering in the doorway to the library in beat-up blue jeans and a rumpled red sportshirt.

"Hi." She smiled spontaneously.

"You're from the decorator shop," he pinpointed with an air of triumph. *He remembered her!* "You're waiting for my mother—"

"That's right."

"Don't let her scare you," he advised with a grin. "She does that to a lot of people."

"I won't," Betsy promised.

"Paul, must you walk around in those awful clothes?" Mrs. Forrest appeared beside him. She was slim and patrician in her starkly simple black dress and pearls. Her makeup was beautifully understated, her dark hair perfectly coiffed. She would be a beautiful woman, Betsy thought, if she didn't always seem so discontented.

"I came over to pick up the rest of my books," Paul explained. "I don't need a dinner jacket for that." His eyes teased his mother. Clearly *he* was not intimidated by her.

"You'll stay for dinner," she began.

"I can't. A buddy's coming over to help me put up bookshelves in the apartment. I should be there already—"

"Then get your books and run," Mrs. Forrest said fretfully, yet

Betsy understood she adored her son. "I don't know why you can't drive with us to Southampton in the morning."

"School deals." He shrugged. "I'll phone you out there over the weekend." He bent to kiss his mother—careful not to muss her hair, Betsy noted—waved a hand in farewell, and strode from the room.

"Take care of yourself," his mother ordered. "Do remember to eat decently, darling." Now Mrs. Forrest turned to Betsy. "All right. Show me what Mark has come up with this time." Her faint smile told Betsy that Mark was in favor.

With the deference displayed to Sanctuary clients, Betsy brought out the various swatches. As Mark had instructed, she explained about the delivery delay they expected to encounter regarding the last sample.

"Shipments from out of the country are taking much longer than usual to arrive because of the war in Europe," she apologized. True—but this was a ploy to buy time. At the moment they were very busy—and it was increasingly difficult to meet schedules. So many workers were going into defense jobs.

"How much longer?" But it was clear that Mrs. Forrest was intrigued by the material. The most profitable for the shop.

"Mark expects delivery in about six weeks."

"These might do," Mrs. Forrest said after a moment. "But I must check with my rug. It's so easy to make a mistake—and I like everything to be just right. I'll take these swatches out with me to the house," she decided. "Though I don't know why I'm making all this fuss about drapes when I just may redo the whole house next spring." Betsy's eyes lighted. Mark would love to hear that! "Tell Mark I'll call him when I return from Southampton."

"Thank you, Mrs. Forrest." Betsy collected the samples that Mrs. Forrest had rejected and said a polite farewell. She'd stop at a pay phone and call Mark, she decided as the houseman ushered her down the hall, across the foyer to the front door. From the glint in Mrs. Forrest's eyes, she was sure this was a sale.

She hurried out into the still bright sunlight of the city with a sense of returning to the normal world. She paused in surprise as

Paul Forrest emerged from a gray Packard parked at the curb and walked toward her.

"Let me give you a lift back to the shop with those," he said casually. *He'd been waiting for her.* "That's too much for you to lug around all by yourself."

"I'm not going back to the shop," she told him. Almost apologetically. "I'll take these home with me."

"Then I'll drive you there. Just point me in the right direction."

Betsy allowed Paul to scoop up the swatches and lead her to the car. He helped her into the front seat, dumped the swatches on the backseat, and circled around to the driver's side.

"What about our having a hamburger and a Coke before I take you home?" he coaxed. "They make a great hamburger up at the West End Bar, across from the Columbia campus." His eyes told her he was eager to expand this casual meeting into something of greater duration.

"Sounds like fun." She tried to sound casual. "But I live up on West 82nd Street—"

"I've got the buggy." He shrugged and grinned. "Inherited from my mother. And we don't have gas rationing—yet."

"Do you think we will have it?" Not, she thought with a flicker of humor, that it would affect her life.

"My dad is sure it's coming." All at once Paul was somber. "And he's sharp about those things." Betsy sensed he was proud of his father.

"I can't believe so many countries are fighting a war. I know we're safe from attack here—at least I think so—but it's awful to remember that every day—maybe every hour—people are dying."

"I'm registered for the draft, of course—I'm twenty-two. But as long as I'm in law school, I'll probably be exempt."

"Are you excited about law school?" Betsy asked while they waited for a traffic light to change to green.

"I hate the thought of it." His face tensed in rejection. "But the family's leaning on me." His *mother* was leaning on him, Betsy suspected sympathetically.

"What do you want to do?" she asked softly after a moment of hesitation.

"Write plays," he said. Seeming self-conscious at this admission. "I suppose that sounds nuts—"

"No," she said. "What's wrong with being a playwright?"

"My mother's father was a lawyer. Her grandfather was a lawyer. Her brother—who died in the World War—left law school to enlist." Paul's face was taut. "All products of Harvard Law. There was a real battle at home when I refused to apply to Harvard Law. I insisted on Columbia." His smile was wry. "You know why?"

"Because it's in New York, and you'd be close to the New York theater," she guessed.

His eyes swung to her with a glint of approval.

"Hey, you're all right."

"My best friend wants to be an actress. On Broadway—not in the movies," she told him. "Of course, her family's no happier than yours is about her goal. Partly to please them she went to Hunter and just finished taking the teachers' exams." Betsy felt a sudden closeness to him. They shared the bond of co-conspirators rebelling against parental rule.

"What about you?" he probed.

"I want to be an interior decorator. I went to Hunter, too—my aunt wanted me to teach."

"Why do they try to tell us what to do with our lives?" he demanded in what Betsy sensed was recurrent frustration. "That should be our decision to make!"

"My parents were both killed in an accident when I was ten," Betsy explained. "My aunt raised me. She'd been a teacher. She felt teaching offered a lot of security." Her expression grew tender at the memory. "She died last June."

"I'm sorry."

Betsy could tell Paul's sympathy was sincere.

"What about you?" Betsy tried to emerge from the wave of fresh grief that threatened to inundate her. "Are you finding time to write?"

"I've got the rough draft of a first act, but with school opening up it'll have to go on a back burner. God knows when I'll find time to write—the first year of law school is the toughest. I'll go through law school, I suppose," he admitted, "but I won't ever work at it.

I tell myself that by the time I graduate I'll be able to prove to my parents that I can write a play—and be able to make a living at it. Maybe I won't make the kind of money my father makes—but I don't need that." Betsy knew from Mark's comments that Mr. Forrest was an investment banker and that Mrs. Forrest had inherited a fortune when her father died years ago. "I need to work in the theater," he said earnestly. "I need to write plays and see them performed on a stage." He paused. "Have you seen *There Shall Be No Night?*"

"No," Betsy told him. "But I hear it's wonderful."

"Robert Sherwood wanted to make Americans understand the implications of the fighting in Europe. I want to write plays like that." His face radiated determination. "Plays that have something important to say."

"You'll do it," Betsy said softly. "Because it means so much to you."

"It's going to be hell once I'm in the school grind—"

"You'll manage," Betsy predicted.

"Half the city will be away for the Labor Day weekend. If I can get tickets for the Sherwood play for tomorrow night, would you go with me? We could grab dinner somewhere first."

"I'd like that." All at once she was trembling with anticipation. Emily would understand if she went out with Paul instead of to a movie with her. "Yes," she said. "It sounds great."

Aunt Celia would have been upset that she was going out with a fellow who wasn't Jewish, she thought guiltily. But it wasn't as though they were serious, she told herself defensively. They were just going out to dinner and to the theater. Dating didn't imply marriage.

Over hamburgers, French fries, and coffee Paul spoke of his growing-up years, particularly about his mother and father.

"When you're an only child, you're kind of in a spot," he said, striving to pin down his feelings. He didn't know that she, too, was an only child, Betsy realized. "I know my mother means well. She wants the best for me. She's sure she's making the right decisions for me. I'm the only child she had and she pins all her hopes and dreams on me. Her grandfather was a Congressman. Her father was a judge. Her brother—who died in the World War—had been expected to go into politics. I'm supposed to follow in their footsteps."

"Only if the footsteps are right for you," Betsy told him with sudden intensity. "What you do with your life is your decision to make."

"You're good for me." Paul's voice was light, but his eyes telegraphed a disconcerting message. *He found her very special.* "Maybe with you around, I'll even make it through law school."

CHAPTER FOUR

With dizzying swiftness Betsy and Emily found themselves swept up into a new circle of friends. Through four years of college they'd been so embroiled in school work and their respective part-time jobs that they had not formed new friends. Only when Emily joined her theater group had their social lives expanded.

Now—in addition to Mark and Eric—their clique included Paul, Doug Golden—Paul's buddy at Columbia Law and his next-door neighbor, Sara Miller—a Barnard senior whom Doug had known since kindergarten, and her Columbia grad-school boyfriend, Frank Churchill. It quickly seemed as though they'd all known one another for years.

Midweek they were individually absorbed in school or work. But on weekends they spent every waking hour together. Betsy relished this new camaraderie. It helped assuage her grief for her aunt.

It was tacitly understood that she was Paul's girlfriend. The relationship marked a new distinction for her. During her high school years she'd been too shy to date. In college she'd been too busy. This past year Emily had drawn her into the social life of the theater group, but with the draft the boys were in and out with poignant speed. More often than not, the boys they knew from the group were more interested in other boys than in them.

In the middle of each week Paul called Betsy at the shop. She'd explained that often her home hall phone went unanswered. *"God, I hate school. I need your special brand of resuscitation,"* he would say. *"Just talk to me, Betsy."*

Emily was searching—futilely—for another theater group. The draft, plus well-paying swing-shift defense jobs, was siphoning off would-be young actresses and actors. Betsy spent her midweek evenings devouring the latest book on interior decorating loaned to her by Mark. There was no doubt in her mind that one day she would be a recognized interior decorator. She was gearing herself to look for a part-time evening job—to be able to put away a little each week toward a night class at Parsons.

Their group spent weekend evenings at the West End Bar, often exchanging lively conversation with other students who—like themselves—made the West End their favorite off-campus hangout. From there they usually retired to Paul's small one-bedroom apartment near the Columbia campus, furnished with ill-matched castoffs from his parents' beach house.

Sometimes they traveled to Times Square to see a French film at the Apollo. One Friday evening Paul—far more affluent than the others—produced four tickets to the new Lillian Hellman play, *Watch on the Rhine,* and he and Betsy and Doug and Emily spent an absorbing evening at the theater. But the four of them were somber on the drive uptown after the performance. The play brought the war into sharp focus.

Twice they went down to West 52nd Street to hear live jive. Twice they went to a hotel to hear Tommy Dorsey and then Benny Goodman. Mainly they listened to records on Paul's impressively fine phonograph and argued good-humoredly over whether Helen O'Connell or Martha Tilton or Marion Hutton was the best female vocalist. Often—particularly after listening to Billie Holiday or Duke Ellington or Lionel Hampton—they talked about the treatment in America of Negro musicians.

"Can you believe that Duke Ellington wasn't allowed to appear at the Paramount or the Strand?" Doug said with disgust on a night when they had listened with rapt attention to Ellington's latest record release. "Only Loew's State came through."

"It's awful for them on road tours," Sara—who planned to become a social worker—said. "I read somewhere that Billie Holiday has to go into hotels where she's singing by the back door—and leave the same way."

"I love the way Eleanor Roosevelt arranged for Marian Anderson to sing before the Lincoln Memorial when the DAR refused to allow her to sing at Constitution Hall." Betsy glowed with admiration for the First Lady.

"But in the whole United States Army," Paul said with contempt, "there are only two Negro officers—and not one in our Navy."

"Look, they're not alone in being subjected to bigotry." Doug's voice was low-keyed, but Betsy felt his anger. Of their group he was the one who always managed a semblance of calm, yet she was always aware of his inner compassion, his deep emotional capacity. "I know—even if I graduate *summa cum laude*—there are law firms that won't hire me because I'm a Jew. The Nazis don't have a monopoly on Jew-baiting. Here it's just less blatant—and less physically violent. But it hurts."

"Don't leave out the Catholics." Normally gentle and soft-spoken, Eric exuded a bitter frustration now. "We've been kicked around plenty through the years by the white, rich, Republican Protestants." All at once he grinned. "Present Protestants excluded, of course." They were all subconsciously aware, Betsy thought, that Paul came from a different, rarefied world.

"We have to admit that what's happening to the Jews in Germany—and wherever the Nazis invade—is the most shocking thing we've ever encountered in our lifetimes," Doug pointed out. "I'm furious when I hear people say that the stories about the Hitler atrocities are either exaggerated or untrue. Just this past July the New York Yiddish dailies reported on the hundreds of Jewish civilians who were massacred by Nazi soldiers in Minsk, Brest-Litovsk, and other places as they moved into Russia. The Polish government-in-exile told about the machine-gunning of thousands of Jews in eastern Poland and the Ukraine. Late last month the *New York Times* wrote that 'reliable sources' revealed that the

Nazis had slaughtered ten to fifteen thousand Jews in Galicia." A pulse hammered in Doug's forehead. Involuntarily Betsy thought about her aunt. She would have liked Doug. She would have appreciated his capacity for compassion.

"Look, let's catch the late movie at the Loew's," Paul said, striving to puncture the current mood. "Who votes with me?"

"Okay," Doug approved. "Screw the fancy law firms." He picked up his earlier declaration of anti-Semitism in the legal profession. "Who needs them?"

"Come on, Doug," Mark kidded. "You know that sooner or later you'll run for governor—or maybe senator. But we promise not to hold that against you."

On the Wednesday evening before Thanksgiving, Betsy and Emily lingered over a cheap dinner at the Automat on 14th Street. They were gearing themselves for the madness of shopping at nearby Klein's basement. Tonight Betsy and Emily would take the subway to Borough Park, sleep over, and have Thanksgiving dinner at the Meyers' house. While they ate, Emily bemoaned her celibate state, since the boys in her theater group had taken off for defense jobs, were drafted, or had enlisted.

"I might eventually have gotten serious with Joel," Emily considered. "We had a lot of fun together. We were both twenty-one and hot, so what was wrong?"

"You were the gal who didn't want to get married before she was thirty," Betsy reminded.

"I don't." Emily grinned sheepishly. "But I do miss fooling around."

"Sometimes when we kiss goodnight in the car I know what Paul's thinking," Betsy said softly. "But I can't. And he doesn't ask," she added.

"He just looks," Emily said. "I've seen those looks."

"I know a lot of girls *are* doing it these days," Betsy said. "With so many boys going into service—and everybody scared they'll be fighting in Europe—I suppose it's natural." Sometimes—when Paul held her in the darkness of the Packard and kissed her with such urgency—she wanted to take him up to her room and make love "all the way." But she'd been brought up to believe "nice girls" didn't. "Anyhow, Paul's deferred because he's in law school." At least for now, she thought involuntarily.

"Mom would die if she knew I'd ever slept with a guy. Her generation waited until they were married. But she doesn't know." Emily refused to be ruffled. "What she doesn't know can't hurt her. Anyhow, she's never liked my 'theater friends,' " Emily mimicked. "To Mom people in the theater all have 'loose morals.' She doesn't understand that times are changing," she pursued with vigor. "The whole country's changing. *The Depression is over.* People want to enjoy life. And for people our age that means sex. And it's for free." She giggled. "The hookers must be having a rough time."

"I think I'd be scared. At least the first time." Betsy analyzed her emotions. "It'd be different if we were married—" The prospect sent ecstatic shivers through her. Of course that couldn't happen. Paul had almost three years of law school ahead of him—and there was the difference in their religion. She could never convert. She felt a recurrent surge of guilt. Aunt Celia would be so upset that she was seeing a boy who wasn't Jewish.

It was crazy to think this way, Betsy scolded herself. Paul hadn't said a word about their getting married. But what would she do if Paul did ask her?

"You know, sometimes I'm sure Doug is secretly wild about you," Emily intruded on her troubled thoughts. "He's so good-looking—with those gorgeous blue eyes and olive skin. Sara said if she wasn't in love with Frank she could really go for Doug."

"Doug doesn't think about me that way." Color touched Betsy's cheeks because sometimes she glanced up to find Doug's eyes fastened on her with a disturbing intensity. "He knows about Paul and me."

"Anyhow, only the 'working class' gets married young," Emily flipped. "Not us middle-class college kids."

On Sunday, December 7, Betsy and Emily stopped off on Broadway to pick up fresh bagels, then headed by bus for breakfast with Paul and Doug at Paul's apartment. The morning was cold and raw, the sky overcast. They walked swiftly, eager for the warm comfort of the apartment.

When Betsy and Emily arrived, Paul was arguing good-humoredly with Doug about what kind of omelets to make. Already the pungent aromas of strong coffee filled the apartment. The heat was coming up in the radiators.

"All right," Paul challenged Doug. "Put it up to Betsy and Emily. Cheese omelets or 'whatever's-in-the-fridge' omelets?"

"Let's live dangerously," Betsy told him. This morning—here with Paul and Emily and Doug—the world seemed a fine place to be. "Whatever's in the fridge."

Doug took on the making of the omelets while Betsy put the bagels into the oven for a brief warmup. Paul and Emily were arguing about the merits of the newest production on Broadway while they set the table. Betsy remembered that starting Monday evening she'd be relief cashier at a restaurant just three blocks from the apartment. She'd work two evenings a week, which meant she'd be able to save for a class at Parsons.

While they dawdled over second cups of coffee, Doug warned Betsy and Emily that he and Paul must settle down for three or four hours of concentrated study this afternoon.

"Everybody says the first year of law school is the hardest." Doug grimaced. "I believe them. We've really got to plug for that exam tomorrow."

"Hey, they're dumping us," Emily complained to Betsy. "There's a new Jean Gabin film on 42nd Street. Why don't we run down and catch it?"

"We'll make dinner when you come back," Paul promised. "My famous James Paul Forrest spaghetti."

"Shall we do the breakfast dishes for them?" Emily consulted Betsy.

"Let's," Betsy agreed. "Crack the books, you two!"

With the dishes washed and dried, the two girls headed downtown on the IRT. They found a long line waiting at the theater box office for the first showing. They joined the line, drew coat collars about their throats against the raw chill of the day.

"Weren't the boys cute, sitting there all wrapped up in their textbooks?" Emily said indulgently while they waited to buy tickets. "Wow, am I glad we're out of school."

"I won't mind going to Parsons—when I have the money," said Betsy. "But that's far ahead."

"I wouldn't mind studying at the Neighborhood Playhouse." All at once Emily was serious. "I'd love it. But why kid myself? Where would I ever dig up the money? I can't settle for just a course."

"The results of the teachers' exams should come out soon," Betsy pointed out. "If you get called for a job, what'll you do?"

"I won't take it." Emily was firm. "I know—it'll pay more than what I'm getting at Gimbels. But it'd be a trap. Once I was teaching, I'd never get out."

Finally they had their tickets and were moving into the slowly filling movie house. Both Betsy and Emily were fascinated by French actor Jean Gabin. When the movie was over, they walked out with a sense of well-being.

"It's early," Betsy noted as they headed toward Broadway. "You feel like walking?"

"That's a long walk," Emily clucked, "but if we get too bushed, we can hop on a bus."

At Broadway they became aware of clusters of people staring with an air of numbed shock at the news bulletin being flashed around the Times Building, spelled out in a bolt of electric light bulbs. They lifted their eyes to read the message.

"Oh, my God!" Betsy clutched at Emily's arm. "Pearl Harbor's been attacked by the Japanese! *That means we're in the war.*"

The two girls hurried to the IRT—impatient to share the traumatic news with Paul and Doug. The train was crowded. They had to stand. From the convivial mood of most of the subway riders on the uptown train, they sensed that the news about the Pearl Harbor attack had not yet been widely circulated.

"I never had it so good," a male straphanger was boasting to his companion. "It was rough, you know, when I was workin' for the

WPA. But now with the shipyard runnin' around the clock, I'm packin' in the dough. If they keep fightin' over there another year or two, I'll stash away enough to buy myself a car." He laughed raucously. "If they're comin' off the assembly line."

Betsy and Emily winced, made an effort to move away from the man so pleased to prosper via death in Europe. And now the war was moving in from the Far East, a threat to their own West Coast, Betsy thought with anguish.

The two girls were relieved to be out of the subway and hurrying through the dank cold to Paul's apartment. They talked in an aura of disbelief about the attack on Pearl Harbor—little of the details known to them as yet.

"Do you suppose there's news on the radio?" Betsy asked Emily while they waited for Paul to buzz them into the building.

"That's probably all that's on the air," Emily guessed. "I still can't believe it—"

They arrived at the apartment to find the door had been opened for them. Paul and Doug were slumped over textbooks, with empty mugs of coffee on the floor at their feet.

"How was the movie?" Doug asked with an absentminded smile. Still engrossed in study.

"You haven't heard the news!" Betsy accused. Paul and Doug gazed at her questioningly.

"I'll turn on the radio—" Emily crossed to the small radio that sat atop an end table, switched on the dial.

"Pearl Harbor has been attacked," Betsy blurted out, an instant before the emotional voice of a newscaster began to discuss the Japanese attack. *"We're in the war."* Her voice had dropped to a shaken, incredulous whisper.

The four huddled about the radio. The only sound in the room now was the voice of the newscaster. They listened to the meager details that were coming through after the initial report of the attack.

"They're censoring the news," Doug pounced in fury. "What the hell is going on out in Hawaii?"

"All we actually know," Paul said grimly, "is that the United States is at war."

"I'll make coffee," Emily said. "I think it's going to be a long evening."

Paul lowered the volume of the radio to a level that would alert them to fresh bulletins without intruding on their somber conversation. It had been awful, Betsy thought, hearing about what was going on in Europe ever since the invasion of Poland on Labor Day weekend, 1939. Before that they'd heard unbelievable stories of the Nazi treatment of the Jews. Over 1,000,000 had died in the Spanish Civil War—and that had been awful. But all at once the war was frighteningly personal.

Betsy gazed at Paul and Doug and turned cold with fear. They could be sent to fight in Europe—or out there in the Pacific, where the Japanese had launched a second war area. *They could die.* What they'd all grown up believing could never happen again was happening: a second World War.

The radio kept repeating what little news was coming through.

"I'll bet you," Doug prophesied, "that the radio stations are getting calls from listeners complaining that the reports of the football game at the Polo Grounds are being interrupted by all these bulletins."

"Doug, you're so cynical," Betsy protested. *How long would it be before Paul and Doug would be pulled into service?*

"The world should have known this would happen—back when Hitler started brutalizing the Jews," Emily said bitterly. "When the Japanese moved in on China, and Mussolini seized Ethiopia. Why didn't we stop them then?" Betsy knew that Emily was scared to death for Bert. He was in uniform now.

"This isn't unexpected." Paul suddenly looked exhausted. "We knew it was a matter of time before we'd be dragged in. Despite all the ranting by isolationists like Lindbergh and Henry Ford and Senator Borah."

Without switching off the radio, they settled down to a dinner of canned soup, canned baked beans, and cold cuts. Tonight dinner was no more than an automatic reflex.

While they listened to the latest reports, Mark called—and moments later Sara. Their generation was the one that would fight this war.

"I'd better call home," Emily decided. "My folks must be terribly upset."

She talked briefly to her mother, trying to calm her.

"Mom, I'm coming home," she said after she'd been silent for a while. "Yeah, I'm leaving right now."

"I'll walk you to the subway," Doug said. He knew Emily was upset about her brother.

"I'll drive Betsy home later," Paul said. "There may be some fresh news coming through." He turned to Betsy for confirmation. She nodded in agreement.

Moments after Emily and Doug left, the phone rang again. Paul's mother was calling. Mrs. Forrest was talking so loudly—on the edge of hysteria—that Betsy could hear her.

"Paul, it's insane that we've been dragged into this war! But you can't be drafted while you're in law school!"

Paul sighed, closed his eyes in silent protest while his mother continued to wail. Feeling herself an intruder, Betsy went into the kitchen to check the coffee percolator. There was enough there for two more cups, she decided, and turned on the gas burner beneath. By the time the coffee was hot again, Paul had managed to get off the phone.

"My mother and father drove down from Boston this afternoon, then went out to dinner. They didn't hear about Pearl Harbor until they were at the restaurant," Paul said tiredly. "My mother is a nervous wreck."

"Do you think you'll still be exempt from the draft after what's happened today?" Betsy asked, her eyes searching Paul's.

"For a while maybe. But with the country at war, being in college won't mean a damn." The atmosphere in the small apartment was heavy with their unspoken fears.

"I've reheated the coffee." Betsy tried to keep her voice even. "Would you like some?"

"Sure," he said gently.

Betsy brought the two mugs to the coffee table, managed a tremulous smile when Paul reached to pull her close.

"I know we realized we were sitting on a keg of dynamite," he conceded, "but it's still one hell of a shock when the keg explodes."

"The war will be coming at us from two directions." Betsy's throat was tight with fear. "The Japanese on one side and the Germans and Italians on the other."

"I doubt that we'll see fighting in this country," Paul tried to comfort her. "We can be thankful for that."

"But our soldiers will be fighting and dying—" Betsy's voice broke as she was assaulted by terrifying visions of Paul and Doug in battle on foreign soil. "Oh, Paul—"

"Betsy, don't go home tonight," he pleaded urgently, lifting her face to his. *"Not tonight."*

"I won't," she promised, managing a shaky smile. She understood the full implications of this.

His mouth came down to fuse with hers in a mutual hunger. Both were only too conscious that in the last few hours their lives had been brutally changed. Nothing could ever be the same again.

"Betsy, you're the greatest thing that ever came into my life," he said at last. He rose to his feet and pulled her along with him. "I never thought I could love anybody so much."

"That goes for me, too." She'd felt so alone since Aunt Celia died—until she met Paul. He'd turned her life around.

It seemed natural to walk with Paul into the small bedroom. The reheated coffee forgotten now. The bedroom was dark except for a sliver of light intruding from the living room. A radio disk jockey was playing a record of "I'll Never Smile Again." If anything happened to Paul, Betsy thought in anguish, she'd never smile again. She wouldn't want to live.

"It's chilly in here," Paul apologized as he helped her out of her sweater. "With the price of oil going up, the landlord keeps turning down the heat earlier and earlier."

"I don't mind," she murmured, though she was momentarily startled by the coolness of his hands as they found the hook of her bra and released it.

"I knew you'd be beautiful." His voice was hushed while his hands caressed the lush spill of her breasts.

Again his mouth came down on hers, and his hands simultaneously rushed to free her of her remaining clothes. She'd thought she'd be nervous, she remembered subconsciously. But she wasn't. This was Paul, whom she loved.

He lifted her onto the bed, still unmade from the night before, and slid beside her. Rumpled bedclothes brushed to one side. His mouth burrowed between her breasts while his hands moved with growing passion.

"It'll be wonderful for us," he promised while he lifted himself above her.

"Yes." It wasn't wrong when they loved each other this way, she told herself with giddy defiance. *And nobody knew what tomorrow held for them. It was their generation that would go to war.*

For one poignant instant she stiffened as he moved to enter her.

"Betsy?" He hesitated in uncertainty.

"Paul, yes," she said exultantly. "Oh yes, yes!"

She felt tears in her eyes when they clung together in climax, heard the soft sounds of pleasure that escaped her—and heard Paul's grunt of satisfaction. No matter what happened to them, they would always have this to remember.

CHAPTER FIVE

In the two days after the bombing of Pearl Harbor New York City had three air raid warnings. One occurred at the heart of the rush hour. There was chaos at the sound of the first sirens, but on the second New Yorkers searched the sky, saw no enemy planes flying overhead, and dismissed this as unworthy of notice.

Word came through that all windows were to be darkened at night. It was reported that Macy's was running out of percale—going at 27¢ a yard. Patriotic yard goods shops were marking down $15-a-yard drapery fabrics to $7.50 to help meet the need.

Before the attack on Pearl Harbor the country had been sharply divided about participation in the war. At a luncheon just a week before, President Roosevelt had said he wasn't sure that Congress would declare war even if the Japanese invaded the Philippines. But since their very country had been attacked, sentiment to fight back ran high. Three days after the United States had declared war, Paul and Doug were discussing the situation over coffee in Paul's apartment.

"Remember, there've been a lot of college students across the country who've vowed not to fight if we got into the war," Paul pointed out. "We have a group right on campus."

"That was before Pearl Harbor. The whole scene has changed." Doug's face tightened. "We have no choice now. We have to go in and knock the shit out of the Japs and the Axis."

"I heard this morning that a couple of guys have already dropped out of school. To enlist." Paul shook his head in frustration. "We're doing lousy in Europe. Now we've got the Japs breathing down our necks. What in hell has happened to us? We're supposed to be the great world power."

Doug squinted in thought. He hunched his shoulders as he cradled his coffee cup between his hands. Paul waited for him to speak.

"Look, it's a matter of time before we're drafted," he said at last. "We're the prime age group. We're the ones who have to fight this war."

"With this country helping the Allies, it'll end fast," Paul predicted, with more bravado than conviction.

"We hope it'll be over fast." Doug was grim. "We still don't know what really happened at Pearl Harbor. The censors are keeping us all in the dark—you know that. Too many crazy, conflicting rumors are circulating. I don't believe the official communiqués," he scoffed. "This crap about how only 'one old battleship and a destroyer' were sunk—and that Japs suffered heavy casualties. It doesn't add up that way."

"And what's going on in the Philippines?" Paul challenged. "We know the Japs have been bombing American bases—"

"In the Pacific and in Europe the bastards are winning. They've got to be stopped." Doug paused. "I'm thinking hard about pulling out of school and enlisting."

"Jumping the gun on the draft?" Paul was startled.

"At least if I enlist, I can choose where I serve. I'm thinking in terms of the Air Force. I never was enthralled by the infantry."

"You're serious," Paul realized all at once.

"Yeah." Doug managed a lopsided smile. "I'm going home for dinner tonight. I have to prepare my folks first. They'll be upset."

"I hate the thought of going into military service." Paul flinched at the prospect. "I know—that sounds rotten in the face of what's happening. I wish the hell I was fifteen years older or ten years younger—"

"Hey, this is our war," Doug repeated with fatalistic calm.

"With luck I'll come home, go back to law school, live a productive life. Or I'll die somewhere in Europe or the Pacific."

"We don't have much choice in the matter," Paul said after a moment. "Unless we're 4-F or working in a defense factory."

What kind of a world had they brought about when men went out to kill other men?

Though he knew Doug meant to drop out of school and try for the Air Force, he was upset when Doug knocked on his door a few days later to say he'd joined up.

"I report for induction in three days," Doug explained. "My mother is having a shit fit, but my father understands. What's the point of hanging around campus until I'm grabbed? With luck they might allow me to finish the school year. Big deal."

"We'll have to have a blast." Paul tried for an air of conviviality. "Tomorrow night. My place. I'll round up people."

Between classes and studying for finals—because the end of the semester was approaching—Paul made phone calls. He was encased in an air of unreality. Draft registration carried a whole new meaning now.

Doug was right, of course—he was just jumping the gun a little. Every guy who was registered for service knew he could be called up at any time. If the situation got bad enough, college attendance would mean nothing.

God, it was hard to feel like celebrating, he thought in distaste while he shopped the following afternoon for cold cuts and beer in a neighborhood grocery. *What was to celebrate?*

Walking up the last flight to his apartment, he spied Betsy sitting on the landing and clutching a bakery box.

"Mark told me to leave work half an hour early," she explained, "to help you with the fixings." She relieved him of his parcels so he could unlock the door. "Mark and Eric will be here around seven. Oh, the box of cookies is from Mark."

"They won't have to worry about being drafted," he said with an unexpected trace of cynicism and swung the door wide. "Their lives won't be turned upside down." Because of their life-style both were classified 4-F.

"Eric's leaving his window-dressing job to go into a defense plant." Betsy's voice was faintly reproachful. "He says he can't just go on as though we weren't at war."

"That was a rotten crack," Paul apologized. "I like Mark and Eric—they're both bright, talented guys." He shook his head tiredly as he flipped on the wall switch. "I can't stop feeling guilty that some students are dropping out of school to enlist and I'm not. Like Doug says, by enlisting he can select where he wants to serve." He reached for the parcels again, opened the refrigerator door.

"Paul, don't rush to enlist," Betsy pleaded, helping him unload the bags. "Maybe it'll all be over before you're drafted."

"I feel like scum," he admitted. "Sitting back and waiting to be grabbed."

"Let's have as much time together as we can," Betsy whispered, "before you're drafted."

"I'm not afraid of dying," he said quietly. "I recoil from killing." He reached to pull Betsy into his arms. "I want to be able to build a whole life with you. I want us to grow old together."

"That's what I want, Paul—"

He glanced at his watch. "The others won't be here for a while." His eyes clung to hers. "I need so much to love you—" For a little while let them forget the horror that had descended on their world.

"There's time."

Hand in hand they walked into his tiny bedroom. Beside the bed he kissed her gently, then helped her undress. He knew what he was going to do tomorrow night—when he was scheduled to have dinner with his parents. He was going to tell them about Betsy and how much he loved her. He was going to tell them Betsy and he were going to be married. She wouldn't refuse to marry him because they were not of the same faith, would she? Now anxiety intruded.

"Paul?" Betsy's voice broke into his troubled introspection. "Did you take the phone off the hook?"

"We just won't answer," he promised and pulled her down onto the bed with him. "If it's one of the crowd, they'll think we went down for beer or something—"

"Paul, I think I'll die if you enlist," she whispered. "I don't care that I sound unpatriotic. It's just that I love you so much—"

"And I love you, baby—"

She wouldn't turn him down.

Betsy struggled to join the air of conviviality—forced, she knew—that filled Paul's living room. It was awful to realize that Doug was going into service. *Maybe to die.* She glanced about the room at the faces of the others. Except for Emily, she'd known them only a few months, yet it seemed as though they'd been friends for years.

"No news tonight!" Doug called out as the radio broke off in the midst of a recording of "Please Give Me Something to Remember You By" to issue a news bulletin. "Turn to another station."

But despite the general effort to keep the mood festive, talk eventually focused on the war. In the Pacific, Guam had surrendered to the Japanese. More than 56,000 Japanese troops had landed on Luzon in the Philippines, where General MacArthur commanded American and Philippine troops. The Luftwaffe continued to bomb London at regular intervals, though it was clear the Germans would never beat the British from the air. The Russians were battling furiously to defend their homeland in the worst winter in 140 years.

"Look, we're going to win this war," Paul said with reckless confidence. "This country has never lost a war."

"The last war the Japanese lost," Doug pulled from his memory, his blue eyes somber, "was in 1598. This war is not going to be a picnic."

"No war is a picnic," Betsy said softly. "No one ever wins."

There was an effort to regain a festive air, but the atmosphere in Paul's small living room was heavy with apprehension. Mark and Eric left shortly. Betsy knew they felt uncomfortable in the knowledge that they were not apt to be drafted. Moments later Sara and Frank left.

"Come on, Betsy, let's wash the dishes," Emily ordered. "You guys, pick up the glasses and empty the ashtrays."

Doug was relieved when Betsy and Emily insisted there was no need to take them home. Right now he just wanted to be alone. Seeing Betsy with Paul, Sara with Frank, made him realize he was going off without leaving a girl behind to miss him, love him, write to him.

"We'll just hop on the Broadway bus," Emily said breezily. "It's too cold to walk. Aren't you lucky? You just go next door."

"Take care of yourself, Doug," Betsy told him while he lingered with them at the landing on his floor and Paul lounged in his own doorway.

"I'm not going off to war yet," he drawled. "I'll be home on a pass after basic training."

"Take care anyway," Emily ordered and reached up for a good-bye kiss.

"Write us if you have time," Betsy said gently, and lifted her mouth to his. Doug was special.

Doug paused a moment before unlocking his door. He'd seen the glint of a tear in Betsy's eyes. That fleeting farewell had unnerved him. He'd been in love with her since the first evening he'd met her. But she was Paul's girl. You didn't make a play for a buddy's girl.

Concentrate on what lay ahead, he ordered himself. For a while—nobody knew how long—the Army would be doing his thinking for him.

Paul sat stiffly at the table in the elegant Georgian dining room in the Forrest townhouse and tried to gear himself for what must be said. Always appearing so fragile, his mother gazed at him in reproach because he'd just refused to go down to Palm Beach for part of the school's winter "break."

"But Paul, why can't you come down for at least a week? I've rented a beautiful house right on the water for the month of

January. You've always loved the beach. And your father's coming down for two weeks."

"Alice, maybe he has other plans," his father said cautiously. Dad usually agreed to whatever Mother said, he thought in rare rebellion. Everybody always talked about how devoted they were to each other. And Dad forever worried about her health. "Give Paul a chance to tell us."

"As a matter of fact, I have." Paul forced a smile. All right, this was the moment to tell her about Betsy. "There's a girl I'm see-ing—"

"Oh, darling," his mother interrupted tenderly, "you're seeing Doris again."

"Mother, I've never 'seen' Doris." He felt himself growing more tense. His mother and Doris's—his mother's best friend—were forever trying to throw them together. "I like Doris, but we're not interested in each other. Not in the way you mean."

"Oh." Alice Forrest exchanged a swift glance with her husband. "Then who is she?" She was trying to appear eager to know, but Paul sensed her alarm. He knew she harbored dreams about his marrying "the right girl" from a "good family." Someone from her own social circle.

"You've met her." He struggled to sound casual. "Betsy works at that shop you like. You know," he stammered. "The Sanctu-ary." He avoided mentioning Betsy's last name. Later she'd learn that Betsy was Jewish. Not that she was a bigot, he told himself. She would be upset—just at first—because he was marrying out of his faith.

"That little girl who works for Mark?" All at once her voice was shrill. "You hardly know her!"

"I've known Betsy for months. She's—"

"Are you out of your mind?" his mother broke in. She gazed at him in disbelief, then swerved to his father. "You know what she's after. Our money!" She turned back to Paul. "There're so many girls around like that. All after young men in your position!"

"*Betsy's* not like that," he said, pale but determined. "I want to marry her. If she'll have me."

His mother winced, lifted one hand to her throat as though in anguish. Then she seemed to be striving for calm. She managed an indulgent smile.

"You can't rush into something so serious. Darling, I'm thinking of your future. You're so young. Too young to be talking about marriage. You're—"

"I'm twenty-two, Mother. I'm a man."

"You're a boy," she protested. "And that sly young girl knows that. The world is full of girls determined to marry into rich families. And you met her here," Alice moaned. "I brought you together."

"Alice, you mustn't get upset," her husband said urgently. "You know it isn't good for you."

"Paul, you're my only child." His mother's face was devoid of color, her hands trembling. "I live for you. I'd be a dreadful mother if I didn't try to protect you. Promise me you won't talk marriage to her. Take time out to think about this."

"It won't matter, Mother." He tried to keep his voice even. Already he felt sick with guilt at upsetting her this way. He remembered those anxious periods during his growing-up years when she disappeared for weeks in discreet private sanitariums. "Even if I say nothing for a time, I'll still want to marry her."

"Alice, why don't you go up to your room and lie down?" his father coaxed. "You know you shouldn't get overwrought this way."

"My heart's palpitating insanely," she whimpered. "I feel just awful."

"Elise!" Mr. Forrest called loudly to the maid. "Elise! Phone Dr. Raymond. Ask him to please come to the house immediately."

"I can't stay, Dad," Paul stammered, pushing back his chair and rising to his feet. "I'm sorry Mother feels this way about Betsy."

He hurried from the dining room, down the hall to the front door, painfully conscious of the uproar he had created. Before he charged out of the house into the crisp, cold night, he knew his next step. He'd enlist. That was the only way to escape his mother.

CHAPTER SIX

Paul sat tense and unhappy in the tufted, burgundy leather armchair before his father's office desk. He was bracing himself for an explosion. Instead, his father seemed to age before his eyes.

"Paul, how will I tell your mother that you've enlisted?" he agonized. "You know what this will do to her."

"I'm just jumping ahead of the draft." Paul tried to sound rational. "You know I'll be called up as soon as the school year is over."

"Damn it, that's half a year away! We have important connections—we could have wangled a job for you in Washington. Don't think your mother and I were not already talking about that." He sighed in frustration.

"Dad, I don't want special treatment." How many times had he said this already?

"You did this because of your mother's reaction to that girl," his father accused. "She'll blame herself for your enlisting."

"Maybe that was part of it," Paul conceded. "But I need a chance to go out and be a man in my own right." His eyes pleaded for understanding. "I can't allow Mother to run my life for me."

"Your mother is a fine woman." His father was terse—from anxiety, Paul realized. "She thinks only of your own good. You mean more to her than anything in this world."

"I'm sorry, Dad. *I had to enlist.* I could never settle for a safe little job in Washington. Not when my friends are going into service. I hate the prospect of fighting—" He paused for an instant. "But it's something I'll have to learn to do."

"We didn't get into the last war until the very end." His father seemed suddenly exhausted. "As a husband and father I was exempt. But I would have loathed going into battle. I can only pray that the war is over before you're shipped out. Or that you'll be stationed here at home for the duration."

"That's not likely," Paul said after a moment. "We need every man we can get in uniform in both Europe and the Pacific. You hear the news every night. You know the Allies are in serious trouble. This is a war that has to be fought, Dad. We have no choice."

"Will you come home tonight?"

"I think it'll be better if I don't." Paul rose from his chair. "I'll come home on my first leave." He hesitated again. "Will you tell Mother? It'll be better that way—"

"I'll tell her," his father agreed. "It'll be a terrible blow."

Betsy hurried from the subway to Paul's apartment. Christmas was a week away and the streets were jammed with shoppers. The store windows festively decorated. Finals were over—Columbia students on their winter break.

Something in Paul's voice when he'd called her at the shop and asked her to come for dinner tonight had troubled her. They'd become so close in these few months—she could sense his every mood. He was upset about something.

She hadn't expected to see him tonight. He'd told her last week that he'd reluctantly agreed to go to the opera with his parents tonight.

The downstairs door to Paul's brownstone was unlocked. She hurried inside and up the dark stairs to his floor, all the while fighting against a feeling of foreboding.

Paul opened the door at her first ring.

"We're eating Italian," he told her with a flourish. "My one culinary talent."

"I'm starving." She lifted her mouth to receive his kiss. *Why did she have this fear that something awful was about to happen?* "I hope you're heating Italian bread?"

"Heating the bread and chilling the wine," he said, holding her close.

"Paul, is something wrong?" She felt the tension in his body as he held her.

"Promise me you won't be upset," he pleaded, trying for a jocular tone. He pulled her down on the sofa with him. "Because this will have a happy ending." He paused, took her hand in his. "I've enlisted."

"Oh, Paul—" She was suddenly cold, trembling.

"I had to enlist. I'd be drafted soon anyway. But I had to do it now—it's the one way to make a clean break with my mother. I'll go wherever the Army sends me—and when I come back, I'll be a free man. To hell with law school! Betsy—" His voice was deep with tenderness. "When I come back from service, will you marry me?"

"Oh, Paul, yes." All of her earlier misgivings—when she had allowed herself to think about this—disappeared. What did it matter that they were of different faiths when Paul was going off to fight in the war?

"I tried to talk to my mother about you. She went into one of her spells." Betsy knew that Mrs. Forrest suffered a nervous collapse when he had been born—after four miscarriages—and that she was subject to attacks of nerves. "I couldn't handle it. I walked out."

"Paul, I'm so sorry."

"As soon as this lousy war is over and I'm out of service, we'll be married. For now," he said wryly, "my mother thinks she's broken us up. We'll let her believe that. She's in bed under sedation—she fell apart when Dad told her I'd enlisted." He forced a smile. "I'm to report in three days for induction. Three days seems to be the magic number."

"I didn't want this to happen." Betsy's voice broke. "I'll be frightened every moment until you're home again."

"Ask Mark if you can take off the next two days. We'll go away together." He brought her hand to his mouth while his eyes made love to her.

"How can I leave him alone in the shop?" Betsy protested. Yet how could she not go away with Paul? When would she see him again after he was inducted?

"Call him," Paul urged. "Explain the situation. These are special times. He'll understand. You phone Mark," he ordered, "and I'll bring dinner to the table."

Betsy went to the phone. Mark would still be at the shop, she surmised, and called him there. When he answered, she haltingly explained the situation. Mark wouldn't be shocked that she'd go away with Paul before they were married. He knew how often this was happening in these hectic times.

She heard the compassion in Mark's voice when he told her to take the time off. He'd persuade Eric to call in sick, he said, and come in to the shop to cover for her.

"And if I know Eric," Mark said gently, "he'll be lighting a lot of candles for Paul."

"In the morning we'll drive out to Sag Harbor," Paul told her while they ate. Betsy knew that—like herself—he barely tasted their food. "You'll love it."

"Isn't that on Long Island?" Farther out than where she and her parents had lived, but the name rang a bell.

"It's a small fishing village where I went a few times with my father. At this time of year it's almost deserted. The air is clean and sweet. I phoned out already and arranged to rent the tiny cottage where Dad and I stayed. We'll rough it," he warned. "No heat except for a Franklin stove in the kitchen, fireplaces in the bedroom and the living room. But we'll be blessedly alone."

"It sounds wonderful!" She wouldn't think about when they returned—only about the two days alone with Paul. Maybe the war would be over before he could be sent overseas, she thought rashly. She would pray for that.

"We'll head back for New York around six A.M. You'll be back in time for work—and I'll make my date with the induction center."

"I'll have to go back to my apartment to pack," she said unsteadily. If Paul hadn't talked to his mother about them, she wouldn't have carried on that way. *He wouldn't have enlisted.* But she found a poignant—momentary—joy in knowing he'd made this effort. "What should I take along?"

"A warm sweater and slacks, walking shoes with heavy socks," he instructed. "And don't look so scared," he chided. "I'll be fine. It'll probably be months before I'm shipped out—and with luck on our side, the war will be over by then."

But Paul didn't believe that, Betsy thought with fresh anguish. He was convinced this would be a long war. At home they'd be safe—but a lot of Americans would die before the war was over. *Not Paul. Please God, not Paul.*

After dinner Betsy and Paul went to her apartment so that she could pack. She fought against a surge of self-consciousness as they walked together down the narrow, dark hall—hoping they wouldn't encounter her landlady, who would not approve of her taking a man to her apartment. Their landlady knew Emily had taken leave from work to go with her family for a cousin's wedding.

Back at his apartment, Paul set his alarm for five A.M. He and Betsy retired early and slept fitfully in each other's arms. Before the alarm went off, Paul gently disentangled himself and left the bed.

"Stay under the blankets," he told Betsy. "It's freezing in the house. I'll light the oven in the kitchen, then make coffee for us."

Before six they were in the Packard and crossing the Queensboro Bridge, the interior of the car deliciously warm via the car heater. They spoke little on the drive out to Sag Harbor. They were content with the nearness of each other, with the feeling that they were grasping a precious parcel of time that excluded the rest of the world.

Arriving in the small, picturesque village, they sought out a restaurant for breakfast, found a grocery store where they shopped for food, then headed for the cottage.

"It's tiny," he apologized. "Smaller than my apartment. But the nearest cottage is a city block away—and that one is probably empty this time of year."

The two days and nights seemed pitifully brief, yet simultaneously were packed with beautiful moments Betsy would treasure. Through constant feeding of the Franklin stove and the two fireplaces, they kept the cottage comfortable. They cooked, they made love, they walked through the lovely old village.

"Some of these houses are marvelous," she said with awe as hand in hand they weaved in and out of the narrow streets. "The ones along here must be a hundred and fifty years old."

"It's like living in another century," Paul mused as they returned to Union Street. "You walk into this town and you escape the whole Manhattan ratrace. Dad wanted to buy a house here several years ago, but my mother was horrified. Southampton is fine—but not Sag Harbor."

"Oh, Paul, look at that church!" Betsy paused to inspect the Whaler's Church.

"That's the pride of Sag Harbor," Paul told her. "It was dedicated in 1844 and cost a fortune to build. One of the local ladies told me that when it was dedicated, the minister compared it to the temple of Solomon."

"It's kind of Egyptian, isn't it?" Betsy said with surprise.

"You're the decorator," he teased. "I wouldn't know. But the church lost its steeple in the hurricane of '38. Dad and I came out the following spring, and we couldn't believe it was gone. It had been built—135 feet high—so that Sag Harbor whalers could see it when their ships rounded Montauk Point."

"I'll bet there are some wonderful antiques to be bought out here." Betsy's face glowed in anticipation. "Eighteenth- and nineteenth-century furniture," she guessed. "Dishes, bric-a-brac, antique quilts. I'm going to suggest to Mark that he and Eric come out here and look around. They've scouted mostly in Putnam and Westchester counties. Do you know when this town was built?"

"You can't get away from business, can you?" he joshed. "According to the local historians, the area was first inhabited by white men in 1707 and became the village of Sag Harbor in 1770. Of course the Indians had been here for many years before that. I know because Dad was fascinated by the history of the town."

"We have clients that would kill for the antiques that are probably still in use in some of these houses." Some of them were mansions. She could visualize the fine early Duncan Phyfe pieces, the sculpturesque tables by Charles-Honoré Lannuier, furniture by Hepplewhite and Sheraton.

"Tell Mark you expect a finder's fee," Paul joshed. "It's funny," he said with affectionate amusement. "Mom wouldn't even drive out here to look at the houses when Dad talked about buying—all she could think about was Southampton. But she brightens up like Times Square before the dimout when anybody talks about authentic antiques."

Mrs. Forrest had not been interested in Sag Harbor because it wasn't fashionable, Betsy interpreted. Wealthy New Yorkers had been going to Southampton since the turn of the century.

"You know what I have a yen for?" Paul grinned in anticipation.

"I have a strong suspicion—" Betsy lifted her face to his. Her eyes were lit with tender humor.

"Besides that?" He slipped an arm around her waist.

"I can't imagine." Her eyes mockingly reproachful.

"Hot apple pie with a chunk of ice cream on top."

"All right, let's find a café."

They sought out a café they'd noticed earlier. A motherly waitress agreed to heat up slabs of apple pie for them.

"You'll have to settle for chocolate ice cream," she warned, while beneath the table Paul's knee sought out Betsy's. "The vanilla's all gone."

"We'll make do with chocolate," Betsy said gaily.

After pie à la mode and coffee, they left the café to head for the near-deserted waterfront. A sharp wind swept in as they strolled beside the water. In warmer weather, Paul told her, the area was colorful with small fishing vessels.

"Dad said it made him wish he was an artist so he could capture its special quality," he reminisced. "We supposedly came out here to fish—but for Dad it was much more than that. It was an escape into another world."

Too soon they were closing up the cottage and climbing into the Packard for the drive back into New York. Betsy sat with her head on Paul's shoulder, dreading the separation that lay ahead of them.

Around seven they turned off the highway to search for a café where they could have breakfast. Betsy wished with painful intensity that they could turn the car around and drive back to Sag Harbor. Stay there in the beautiful winter quiet of the village. *Forget the war.*

Seated at a rear table in the small café—occupied except for themselves by a cluster of workmen in high spirits—Betsy struggled to hide her growing anguish. After this morning, when would she see Paul again?

"I'll hold on to the apartment," he told her—sensing her mood. "And I'll keep the phone connected. Stay there with Emily on the weekends," he urged. "Somehow I'll manage to phone you." The hall phone at her apartment often went unanswered. "After basic training—on my first weekend leave—we'll stay there." He hesitated. "Would you want to move into my place? The rent'll be paid—"

"Paul, I couldn't." She felt color flood her face. That would be like being kept.

"But you'll stay there weekends?" he persisted. "I need to be able to visualize you there—and remember our wonderful times together."

"Every weekend," she promised. She'd feel close to Paul there. "You'll write to me?"

"Every chance I get." He reached for her hand. "We'll see this through together. And after the war we'll build the kind of life we want."

"Oh, yes, Paul!"

He would be a playwright and she would be a decorator. And they'd be husband and wife. His mother couldn't stand in their way.

While a car behind the Packard honked raucously for him to move on, Paul kissed her good-bye with a poignant urgency.

"I don't know where they'll send me, but there are sure to be phones," he said huskily. "I'll call you, baby."

Betsy left the car and stood at the curb. She watched while Paul drove on. Tears blurring her eyes, she watched until the Packard was out of sight. Now she crossed the sidewalk and climbed the stoop that led to the entrance of her brownstone.

Change and rush to the shop, she ordered herself. If she didn't dawdle, she'd be there by the time Mark arrived to open up.

CHAPTER SEVEN

Betsy waited impatiently to hear from Paul. Mark told her it was unlikely there'd be phone booths in the barracks where Paul was receiving basic training.

"Honey, they've got those guys in total isolation—to drum everything they can into their heads in the next thirteen weeks. And be glad for that," he added gently.

"Paul said he'd phone," Betsy insisted, yet she realized it was childish to cling to this promise. "I don't even know where he is!" Did his mother and father know? But she couldn't call them.

At last a brief letter arrived from Paul. He was in Virginia.

"Please write," he urged. "I miss you."

"Now you'll stop being so grumpy," Emily joshed. "You know where he is."

On Christmas Eve—after dinner at the Meyers' home in Borough Park—Betsy and Emily holed up in their apartment. There was little real Christmas cheer in the city this year. Mark and Eric had driven out to spend Christmas with Eric's family in Sussex, New Jersey. Sara was down in Washington on a government job, and Frank in the Marines.

On Christmas day Betsy and Emily went to a neighborhood theater to see *Mrs. Miniver*. They clutched hands and handkerchiefs at crucial scenes.

"Why doesn't Paul write again?" Betsy demanded of Emily for the dozenth time while they dawdled over coffee and danish at the neighborhood cafeteria. "Surely he can find a piece of paper, an envelope, and a stamp!" She tried to push down frightening fears that Paul had suffered a change of heart about her.

"Uncle Sam's got first call on his time," Emily reminded. "When he can write, he will. And you know how slow mail is this time of year."

When Betsy was exhausted from nights of insomnia—another letter arrived from Paul. *"No chance of a pass until I'm out of basic training. Baby, I can't wait to be with you! But for now I'll write every chance I get—and you write me."*

Every night she sat down to write to Paul. For a fragment of time it was as though she and Paul were together. She tried to sound cheerful about the changing scene in Manhattan. When rationing began in January, she wrote amusingly about the new little books and stamps that stipulated how much food or gas they could buy—and how everybody complained about it, though they understood it was necessary.

"Mark is having fits that his card limits him to three gallons of gas a week. He has to hoard up for an occasional Sunday of antiquing. I read somewhere that at Selfridge's in London things in the windows don't list the price—just how many coupons are needed!"

She told Paul that they'd heard from Doug—that he was out in Texas. She gave him Doug's address so that he could be in direct contact and told him she and Emily had given his address to Doug.

As Paul had urged, she and Emily were staying at his apartment on weekends. Each time the two girls walked past what had been Doug's apartment, they were painfully conscious of his absence.

"It's scary to think of Doug flying a bomber over Germany or France," Betsy said on one of those occasions.

"If he makes it into the Air Force," Emily said with a wry smile. "I hear the dropout rate is awful."

"Doug will make it," Betsy predicted. "He'll make it at whatever he chooses to do."

"Let him make it home safely through this war. Let Paul and him come through safely," Emily said, and it was like a benediction.

* * *

The lights of New York—usually visible sixty miles at sea—were dimmed now. The Broadway theater marquees were dimmed. Strangers in the city were made immediately aware of the war. On weekend nights girls roamed about Times Square and the adjacent side streets in pairs or groups. Their lives devoid—except for a lucky few—of masculine companionship.

Dreading the day when Paul might be shipped overseas, Betsy tried to bury herself in work. With Emily obligingly in tow, she wandered on Sundays about the exhibits of the city's great museums. Mark had taught her to learn through these trips. To pick up ideas for room treatments, unconventional color combinations.

"God, our whole life-style stinks," Emily mourned on a Saturday evening in early February while they went about preparing dinner. "From Hunter graduation to Pearl Harbor everything was great. Except that the group folded for lack of men," she conceded. "But with Paul and Doug in uniform, Eric working sixty hours a week in that aircraft plant out on Long Island, Mark getting all worked up over becoming an air raid warden, we've got no social life."

"We're having dinner with Mark and Eric tomorrow night," said Betsy.

"And we'll probably go down to 42nd Street to a movie," Emily added. "I want more excitement in my life than that!"

"We're in the middle of a war," Betsy said. Her words were sharp, but her eyes were sympathetic.

"Damn, why couldn't we keep the group together?" Emily sighed. "Don't answer that. It's the perennial problem these days—no men in our lives."

"Maybe you ought to try to take a few days off from work and make 'rounds,' " Betsy said, trying to sound casual.

"I'm not ready for that." Emily was instantly defensive. "I don't have Colleen's brand of *chutzpah*. I know I need more experience with an experimental group. Or classes—" But they both knew she couldn't afford classes on her salary.

In Emily's eyes, Betsy thought, *she* had it made. She was in love with Paul and she had a job that fascinated her. But she wished she could afford night classes at Parsons. She was already restless in the job—she wanted to be able to be more creative, to move ahead as an interior decorator.

She clung to her image of life after the war. Paul would write plays for the Broadway theater. She'd develop her own clients as a decorator, make revolutionary changes in the field. As a successful playwright, she thought tenderly, Paul could help Emily. She was convinced that Emily had genuine talent.

"Let's go to a movie tonight," Emily suggested, turning off the gas beneath the percolator. "I wonder what's playing at the Loew's?"

"We'll check after we eat." Movies were the great escape. Lines at the box offices on Saturday nights were heavy.

"I don't want to hear any more news bulletins about the war tonight," Emily said. "That's all I hear when I go home. Dad rushes out of the house every time he hears a newsboy yelling 'Extra!' He hangs on to every word of Kaltenborn and Ed Murrow. Mom's all upset because the schools have to teach the kids what to do in the event of air raids. She says kids shouldn't have to worry about something so awful."

"Kids in Europe have to deal with them." Betsy was somber. "Those who haven't been sent out of London spend their nights in air-raid shelters! The children in the countryside live in terror of the German raids."

"The lucky kids are those who've been sent over here," Emily said.

"But you know they cry for their parents." Now Betsy considered the safety factor in New York. "Remember that article in *Newsweek* back in late December?" Paul's subscription hadn't run out yet. "How they told us that 'Germany and Italy can bomb New York if they so desire'?"

"I wish the magazines and newspapers wouldn't say those things!" Emily's eyes darkened in rebellion. "I can't see how German planes are going to cross the Atlantic to bomb us. Our planes would mow them down!"

"Okay, no more war talk tonight," Betsy said.

"And no talk about men," Emily added.

"You'll survive until the war's over," Betsy told her. But she understood Emily's discomfiture.

"Look, all through Hunter I was an earnest, virginal student." Emily giggled in recall. Forgetting her order not to discuss men. "Then I joined the group—and boy, I grew up fast! I was getting it regularly. I miss it," she said with her usual candor.

"The hamburgers are done. Let's sit down and eat." Betsy tried to divert the conversation.

"What about you?" Emily pursued, pouring the now-hot canned peas into a bowl. "Don't you miss making love?"

"Yes." She hadn't realized how much she would miss it, Betsy thought. "But Paul's down in Virginia and I'm here. I can't wait till he's eligible for a weekend pass."

"I look at girls hanging on to their soldier and sailor boyfriends in the street and I wish to hell there was a man in my life. I'm not like you, Betsy. I don't have to be in love to go all the way. I just have to like the guy a lot."

"Emily, be careful." Betsy inspected her with simmering alarm. She knew how restless Emily was these days. "You can't go out and just pick up anybody."

"Look at all the girls who're hanging out at bars these days," Emily challenged. "They're not there because they're thirsty."

All at once Betsy felt an overwhelming loneliness. When would she see Paul again? Would he feel differently when he came home on leave? It was a frightening possibility.

"Where's the paper?" she asked Emily. "Let's see what's playing at the Loew's."

On an unseasonably warm early April morning Betsy walked into the shop just as the phone began to ring. Mark hurried to pick it up. His face lighted. He beckoned excitedly to Betsy.

"It's Paul!"

Her heart pounding, Betsy raced to reach the phone.

"Paul?" Her voice was resonant with joy.

"Baby, I have a weekend pass," he told her jubilantly. "I'll be arriving at Penn Station somewhere around six P.M. Can you meet me?"

"Of course I'll meet you!"

"I have to run now—about a hundred guys are lined up behind me waiting to use the phone. Somewhere around six P.M.," he reiterated. "I'm not sure of the exact time."

"I'll be there," she promised. Her face incandescent. "Even before six."

"'Bye, baby—" His voice was a caress. Then there was silence. Betsy turned to Mark.

"Paul has a weekend pass. He wants me to meet him around six o'clock at Penn Station." Her eyes were questioning. Shop hours were ten A.M. to six P.M.

"Get out of here by five," Mark ordered, "in case there's a delay on the subway going to the station."

"Thanks, Mark." How wonderful to have friends like Mark and Eric.

"Don't come in tomorrow," he said after a moment. "I'll drag Eric in to cover for you."

"Doesn't Eric work on Saturdays?"

"Not this Saturday—he's been working nine straight days, so they're giving him off tomorrow. If he falls asleep in the shop," Mark said with a grin, "I'll wake him up."

The rest of the day every moment dragged. Betsy debated about dashing home at lunchtime to change into a more festive dress, rejected this because she felt guilty already about leaving the shop early, taking off Saturday. She'd run over to Nedick's for a frank and coffee.

Would Paul want to go directly home or would he like to have dinner somewhere? Anxiously she checked her wallet. Paul had made wry cracks about his "twenty-one bucks a month" Army salary. Were his parents sending him money—or was his mother punishing him for enlisting?

By five-forty she was in Penn Station, waiting for Paul's train to be announced. One train after another arrived and disgorged its passengers to exuberant, joyous cries of welcome. The area was colorful with uniforms of every branch of service. She'd never seen Paul in uniform, she remembered now.

Her smile grew strained as almost an hour went past without Paul's train arriving. Had she misunderstood? *Was she at the wrong station?* Was he coming in at Grand Central?

Then—while she fought off panic—she saw his train chalked in on the Arrival board. Rapturously impatient, she hurried forward to the escalator that would bring down the passengers from the Virginia train. Like dozens of girls and women around her, she gazed upward with a welcoming smile already on her lips.

There he was! In his Army-private uniform, his hair cut short—though not as badly as he had warned. He spied her and waved, his smile brilliant. Each pushed through the churning horde to reach the other.

How much of the weekend would they have together? She was wistful at the prospect of losing even an hour. But Paul would have to see his parents while he was on leave.

"Baby, you look wonderful," he crooned, swaying with her. His face against hers. "Now let's find a taxi so I can kiss you properly."

"It may take awhile," she laughed. "Everybody has the same idea." But more than one couple were locked in passionate embrace right here.

With a chuckle of triumph Paul snared a cab for them within minutes. He gave the address of the apartment to the driver, turned to pull Betsy into his arms.

"I used to dream about this every night," he whispered, his mouth reaching for hers.

They kissed with the passion of endless hungry nights, each reluctant to release the other.

"Should we stop off for dinner somewhere?" Betsy asked when at last his mouth released hers. "Was there a dining car on the train?"

"Honey, I was grateful to have a seat. There were soldiers standing in the aisles for the last three hours of the trip. But no," he said gently. "Let's not stop for dinner. Or maybe we could get off on Broadway and pick up deli to take home with us."

"When do you have to go back to camp?" she asked.

"Sunday afternoon. But from now till tomorrow afternoon belongs to *us*. I'll have to go home for one night—I can't not do that, Betsy—" His eyes were anxious.

"I know," she said quickly. She mustn't be greedy.

Now Paul talked about life at camp, his gaze straying toward the passing scene at intervals—as though to reassure himself that he was in Manhattan. He was striving to sound amused by the daily discomforts they encountered. He wasn't sure where he would be stationed, but rumors said they'd be heading for a camp in Massachusetts.

"Bets are that we'll eventually be shipped to Europe," he told her, and all at once she felt cold and scared. "Probably England," he guessed, "since we'll be on the East Coast. But with things so rotten in the Pacific, who knows?" Early in January the Japanese had seized Manila, and MacArthur's Philippine army had withdrawn to Bataan. Then only a week ago MacArthur and his army were forced to escape from Bataan and were en route to Australia.

"The deli's just ahead," Betsy said.

"Drop us at the next corner," Paul told the cabdriver and reached for his wallet.

They bought hot pastrami and corned beef, potato salad and apple strudel.

"God, after Army chow, this is gourmet heaven," Paul laughed.

"Let's pick up eggs and bagels and lox for tomorrow's breakfast," Betsy said when they emerged from the deli. Paul clutched the brown paper bag in one arm, the other encircled her waist.

"That's smart thinking," he approved and grinned. "We'll just get out of bed to eat. Or maybe you'll bring me breakfast in bed."

"I just might." Her smile was dazzling. *Don't think about his having to go off to some camp in Massachusetts. Don't think about his going to fight in Europe or the Pacific.*

Halfway up the stairs to his apartment Paul paused, deposited his parcels on the floor, and reached to kiss her passionately.

"Baby, you don't know how I've missed you!"

"Tell me all about it in the apartment."

With astonishing speed they put away the food, tossed aside their coats, and headed for the bedroom. They both shared the same thought. They clung together in the darkened bedroom, savoring the touch of each other.

"Betsy, all I thought about every night was coming home to you—"

"I wish we could stay here this way forever," she whispered, feeling the heat of him hard against her pelvis.

"Sssh," he scolded and reached to pull her sweater over her head. His hands—cold against warm skin—rushed to release her bra, then caressed her breasts. Then his mouth was at her ear while her hands tightened around his shoulders in response.

She closed her eyes while his mouth burrowed between her breasts and his hands shucked away her skirt and coaxed it to the floor. He swore softly as he fumbled with her garter belt, then guided her stockings down her long, slim legs.

"I missed you so much," she told him as he lifted her from her feet and carried her to the bed. "Every day seemed like a year."

"We'll make it up," he promised, stripping beside the bed. "Once this lousy war is over, we'll never spend a night apart."

He lifted himself above her, moving between her eager thighs. Her hands reached to fondle his chest as he thrust himself within her. Nothing could ever equal what they found together in moments like this, she thought exultantly.

Paul lay in luxurious idleness in the bed while Betsy, in a plaid flannel robe she kept at the apartment, went about preparing a breakfast tray for them.

"I should have run down to pick up the *Times,*" she said as she entered the bedroom with tray in hand. It would be a hearty breakfast: lox and eggs, bagels heated in the oven, strong black coffee in the huge mugs Paul liked.

"No," he rejected. "That would be an intrusion. Just the two of us here. No news. Nothing."

"What time do you have to leave?" Betsy asked, trying to hide her wistfulness.

"*We* have to leave in about two hours," he told her. "We have an appointment for blood tests." She gazed at him in bewilderment. "We'll need them when we go for our marriage license." *Their marriage license?* "Not this time," he conceded, "but on my next leave. If it's long enough—you know about the three-day waiting period—we'll be married then. Otherwise we'll have to wait till I can get down here again."

"Oh, Paul—" Her heart was pounding, her hands trembling.

"Now don't spill the coffee," he ordered in mock reproach. "I don't want to make love in a puddle."

"First we'll eat," she decreed, her face luminescent. "I slaved over a hot stove to make those scrambled eggs and lox." *Paul and she were going to be married soon. They wouldn't wait until the end of the war!*

Betsy was unnerved when Paul explained that his mother's doctor—Dr. Raymond—was coming in to his office expressly for their blood tests.

"But won't he tell your mother?" she stammered. Not that his mother could stop them, she thought defiantly. But she would try, instinct told her. She recoiled from the prospect of an ugly situation.

"He can't do that." Paul was matter-of-fact. "A patient is entitled to confidentiality. He'll do the blood tests, get the reports for us. And when I come down again, we'll go to City Hall and apply for our marriage license. You're on your way to becoming Mrs. James Paul Forrest the Third."

Would Aunt Celia have been upset that she was marrying out of her faith? Betsy asked herself, feeling a fresh surge of guilt. Possibly, but she would have loved Paul: his warmth, his sweetness, his compassion. She remembered Paul's anger—like Doug's—at the segregation in the armed forces. He had such sensitivity, such feeling for others. Oh yes, Aunt Celia would have loved Paul!

Betsy understood that Dr. Raymond was uncomfortable at being a part of their covert plans, but medical ethics demanded his silence. Still, he was polite and assured them no word of their plans would reach Paul's mother.

"I hope you young people aren't caught up in this war hysteria," he said gravely. "So many of you are rushing into marriage without thinking of all the implications."

"Dr. Raymond, we're not rushing into marriage," Paul told him. "We've thought about it for many months."

They left the doctor's office—with Paul's telltale Band-Aid hidden beneath his shirt. His mother would not suspect, Betsy told herself. And Dr. Raymond wouldn't tell her.

"I'll have to go to the house now—" Paul was torn. He wanted to stay with her, Betsy understood—but he wanted to see his parents, too.

"Call them first," she said while they stood before the posh Park Avenue building where Dr. Raymond had his offices. Only a few minutes' walk to the Forrest townhouse. "Maybe they're not home," she said with a rush of hope, clinging to his arm. She cherished every moment of Paul's weekend pass.

"I called while you were in the shower. Mother and Dad were out. Elise said they were having lunch at the Colony. I should have known. Mother's so tradition-bound. They always go to church services on Sunday morning, then to the Colony for lunch." He glanced at his watch. "They're probably home by now."

"Will I see you again before you return to camp?" He'd said he'd come back to the apartment, but she needed reassurance.

"I'll be at the apartment no later than two o'clock tomorrow. I have to make the four-oh-five train. It's the last one that'll get me back to camp in time." He sighed. "I wish I could sneak out tonight and be with you—but Mother would be terribly upset if I didn't stay at the house at least overnight."

"What's going to happen when she discovers we're married?" Betsy asked after a moment. She and Paul lived in two different worlds. Emily said his mother would think she was trying to marry into a rich family. *Marrying rich is a plus—don't knock it.* Once they were married, would his mother refuse to see him again? Would he be disinherited? Her heart began to pound at the possibility. She didn't want to be responsible for that. "Paul?" Betsy lifted her face to his.

"She'll be upset," he conceded. "She thinks I'm too young to get married." *But not if he were marrying some wealthy society girl,* *Betsy forced herself to recognize.* "She's terribly protective of me."

"Paul, you're not a little boy."

"I know." He smiled sheepishly. "But she's gone through a lot in her lifetime." He hesitated. "She's been emotionally fragile since she was a little girl. She had an older brother whom her mother adored. He was killed in a freakish accident when he was fourteen and she was eleven." Paul's eyes were dark with compassion. "She heard her mother say to her father, 'If we had to lose one, why did it have to be him?' "

"Oh, Paul—" What an awful thing to happen to an eleven-year-old. The vision of that little girl was heart-wrenching. She herself had faced tragedy at ten, she remembered—but she'd had Aunt Celia to see her through.

"She grew up in boarding schools and summer camps—lonely and scared and feeling unloved. I don't think she ever got over that."

"We'll work things out," Betsy told him.

"Still, I can't let my mother run my life for me," he said. "Hell, if I'm old enough to fight in a war, I'm old enough to choose my own wife."

"I'll be waiting for you tomorrow," Betsy told him.

"What'll you do tonight?"

"Emily and I will go out for a Chinese dinner." Chinese was always cheap. "Maybe go to a neighborhood movie. Then we'll buy the *Sunday Times* and go up to the apartment." The *Sunday Times* was always available late Saturday night.

"I'll put you in a cab," he said. Before he did he pulled her close for a quick kiss. To passersby it no doubt looked like just another GI and his girl saying a reluctant farewell. But Betsy knew their romance was not one of the many inspired by the exigencies of war.

* * *

Betsy sat huddled in one corner of the cab and clutched the bills Paul had thrust into her hands for the fare. Why did she have the awful feeling that he would see his mother and he'd not be able to break away again until it was too late to come back to the apartment?

Not until Paul and she were married would she feel truly safe from his mother's hold over him. Not until they stood before the judge down at City Hall and he said the words that made them husband and wife would she believe Paul's mother could not come between them.

CHAPTER EIGHT

Paul had barely touched the door-bell when he heard his mother's voice in the foyer.

"I'll get it, Elise," she called, sounding elated. "It's probably Paul." He heard the staccato click of her heels as she hurried down the hallway and to the marble-floored foyer. He was eager to see her, yet that eagerness was tainted by apprehension.

She opened the door and gazed up at him with a warm, welcoming smile.

"Hi, Mother—" She looked well, he decided in relief. She was handling his enlistment okay.

"My baby," she murmured and held out her arms to him.

"Some baby," he chuckled, towering above her. "It's great to see you." He bent to kiss her and then was conscious of her eyes focusing on his insignia.

"Darling, we must do something about getting you a commission," she said indulgently as she drew him into the foyer. "Paul's here!" she called to his father.

"Mother, I don't want a commission." Already he was tensing up, gearing himself for a battle.

"That's nonsense!" Her voice was sharp. She gazed in distaste at his enlisted man's uniform.

"Son, you look fine." His father pulled him close for a moment.

"Your father has excellent connections in Washington," his

mother reminded him. "With your background there's no reason why—"

"Mother, don't try to tell the Army what to do." He smiled, but his eyes flashed a warning.

"Are you hungry?" Alice Forrest lapsed into a show of maternal solicitude. "I'll have Elise bring a tray into the library."

"I had lunch on the train," he lied while he walked with his parents to the library—the informal family room, where a fire had been lit earlier. For a moment his mind darted back to the small, modest fireplace at the cottage in Sag Harbor, where he and Betsy had spent a precious parcel of time. He wished they could have stayed there forever.

"When do you have to return to camp?" his mother asked.

"I have to make a one-forty train tomorrow afternoon," he said, uncomfortable in this lie.

"So soon?" His mother sighed in disappointment. "You come all the way up from Virginia and they expect you back by tomorrow evening?"

"We're on twenty-four-hour passes, Mother," Paul said, improvising. "But once I'm transferred—hopefully to Massachusetts—passes should be for at least forty-eight hours." He was actually hoping for a three-day pass. That would allow Betsy and him to go down to City Hall for their marriage license. *He didn't want to think about telling his mother he and Betsy were married.*

"Let's sit down and have coffee. I want to hear everything that's been happening to you. But why, Paul," she reproached tenderly, "did you let your barber scalp you like that?"

"Alice, he has no say in the matter," her husband said dryly. "That's what is known as the GI haircut."

Paul came awake with startling suddenness. For a moment he wasn't sure where he was. Then his eyes settled on the bedside clock. Oh, God, it was almost noon! He sat up, trying to clear his head. He'd slept around the clock.

Take a fast shower, he ordered himself. Then he would go

downstairs for a leisurely breakfast with Mother and Dad. They must have been sitting downstairs waiting for him to surface.

He thrust aside the covers, hurried into the bathroom. Finding fleeting pleasure in the luxury of a private shower after Army camp facilities. Fighting guilt that he slept away the morning while his mother was anxious to spend time with him.

Fifteen minutes later, after a hasty shower and shave, he was rushing down the stairs and to the library. He heard his mother's strained voice as he approached.

"Paul, please, no more news today. I've come to loathe the radio."

Dad was anxious about what was happening on Bataan, Paul sympathized. And the way the German submarines, roaming the Atlantic like wolf packs, were sinking freighters within sight of the American mainland.

"Sorry I slept so late," Paul began as he charged into the library with a brilliant smile. "After all those weeks of a five A.M. reveille I guess I'm making up for lost time."

"Darling, I'm glad you were able to get a decent night's sleep." His mother lifted her face for his kiss. "If you'd be sensible and allow your father to pull some strings, you could forget about five A.M. reveille. You'd be able to settle down at a comfortable job— either here in New York or in Washington."

"Mother, it's too late for that." *He didn't want to fight with her today.* "And even if it wasn't, I couldn't. I can't hide behind Dad's contacts when my friends are all in uniform."

"Let's go in to breakfast." His father's eyes were sending warning signals to his mother. "Everything is in warming trays on the dining room buffet. We weren't sure when you'd be awake."

Paul took his mother's arm as they walked toward the dining room. He felt an urgent need to comfort her, even while he knew that she must share the pain of other mothers with sons in service. Dad couldn't protect her from this.

"I told Peggy to prepare those sausages you especially like," his mother told him. "She's made scrambled eggs and potatoes and corn muffins and cinnamon danish—"

"If I eat all that," Paul laughed, "I'll pop right out of my uniform."

"I don't know why you have to be so stubborn," she pursued. "If you'd just listen to reason, then—"

"Alice, Paul says he has to leave here at one-thirty," his father interrupted. "Let's make this a cheerful breakfast."

"If you're stationed in Massachusetts, do you suppose it'll be near Boston?" Mrs. Forrest asked Paul while he pulled out a chair at the dining table for her.

"Probably." But the likelihood of their staying there long was doubtful, he thought. Men were being shipped out as fast as possible.

"Then perhaps I could run up and find a comfortable apartment for you," she said eagerly. "A little place where you could—"

"We're not allowed off-base," Paul broke in. "Whenever I can wangle a pass, I'll come home."

"Have you thought about applying for admission to the new Officer Candidate School down at Fort Benning?" His father was trying to appear casual.

"No." Paul walked to the buffet. "Everything looks great." *Why did everybody think that sons of families with money must be officers?*

Paul ate with a show of gusto, meant to reassure his mother that he was enjoying this brief time at home. Lingering over his third cup of coffee, he managed a glance at his watch. Betsy was expecting him at the apartment by two o'clock. He needed these last two hours alone with her to see him through to his next leave. Let it not be his last leave, he thought with sudden apprehension. Before his company was shipped out, he wanted to know he was leaving his wife behind.

"I'll tell William to have the car out front by one-thirty." His mother had intercepted his checking on the time. "Dad and I will go with you to Penn Station."

"No, I'd rather go alone," he said quickly. "I'll catch a cab. I'd like to say good-bye right here at home."

"Oh, Paul—" Her voice broke. "I can't believe this is happening."

"You're not to worry about me," Paul ordered gently. He rose to his feet and moved to her with a resolute smile. "I have to come home. I have so much living to do. I want you just to sit here at the table with Dad. That's the picture I want to take with me."

He bent to kiss his mother, turned to embrace his father.

"I'll write as soon as I can," he promised. "As often as I can. I love you both very much."

His eyes rested on them for a last poignant moment. Then he turned and walked from the dining room and down the hall to the door. Please God, let him find a taxi right away. Betsy was waiting for him. How long would it be before he'd see her again?

Paul was impatient as his taxi followed a bus across town through the park. The first signs of spring were all around him. Clusters of forsythia were pushing into golden bloom, buds on the trees. *Why the hell didn't that bus move faster?*

Betsy pulled the door open at his first knock. She stood there— small and beautiful in the plaid bathrobe. Even before he pulled her into his arms, he knew there was only Betsy beneath the robe.

"Oh, baby, I missed you," he whispered. "I couldn't wait to get back to you—"

At the latest possible moment they left the apartment and went down to the street to look for a taxi to take them to Paul's train. In the taxi—after urging the driver to rush because he had to make a train—Paul drew Betsy into his arms, his face nuzzled against hers.

"Hold on to our blood tests," he told her. "On my next leave we'll go down to take out our marriage license."

Please God, he silently prayed, don't let the company be shipped out before Betsy and I can be married.

CHAPTER NINE

Late in April Betsy received a phone call from Paul at the shop. He was stationed now at a camp near Boston.

"Honey, move into my apartment," he told her. "That way I'll be able to reach you whenever I can get to a phone—which is usually at night, when you're not at the shop." It was impossible to get a residential phone installed. "Ask Emily to stay with you—she'll understand. My mother will keep paying for my apartment until I'm shipped out."

"I'll talk to Emily." She didn't want to think about Paul's being shipped out. "Is there any chance of your getting a pass for Easter?" she asked wistfully. Last night Emily told her Bert was coming home for the first night of Passover.

"I doubt it, baby. We've just got here. But I'm sure to get a pass soon," he comforted. "Even if it's just a twenty-four-hour pass, it'll be a snap for me to come down from Boston." His voice dropped to a passionate whisper. "Betsy, I love you so much."

"I love you, too." Why did she always feel like crying when he phoned her? Was it because each time she was terrified he was calling her to say he was being shipped out?

"Once I know the routine here you'll be able to come up to meet me here in Boston for the day. It's a long haul for one day," he said, "but we could spend a few hours together."

"Anytime you say," she told him. "Even if I have to stand the whole way, it'll be worth it." Trains were notoriously over-crowded. But would they be able to find a hotel? These days they were usually booked to capacity. "Oh, this Sunday Emily and I are driving out with Mark and Eric to Sag Harbor—providing they can round up enough gas coupons. Mark wants to see the houses and ask questions about tracking down antiques. I want to go," she confessed, "and yet I dread being there without you."

"Honey, did you receive our blood test reports?" he asked.

"We're both all right. No venereal disease," she said with a laugh. "It's legal for us to get married." But fiercely objectionable to his mother, she remembered with recurrent misgivings.

"Next time I get out of here, we go down to City Hall for our marriage license." His voice was jubilant now.

"Will you receive the letters I sent to you down in Virginia?" she asked.

"Mail's being forwarded," he said reassuring her.

They talked for another moment and then the operator inter-rupted with a request for more change.

"Betsy, I'll have to hang up," he said hastily. "There're a ton of guys in line for the phone. 'Bye for now."

On Sunday morning Mark and Eric drove over to pick up Betsy and Emily for the drive out to Sag Harbor. The day was cold and dank for early spring. Mark and Eric grumbled about the weather—both loved the summer. The girls had checked the radio for a weather report, wore warm slacks, sweaters under their jack-ets.

"We'll stop somewhere along the road for breakfast," Mark said as they settled themselves in the car. "Eric and I didn't bother eating, and I figured you two would just have coffee this early."

"I hope we have enough gas to get back to the city." But Eric seemed unconcerned, Betsy noted. "I'll probably sleep all the way out." He smothered a yawn. "I worked thirteen hours yesterday."

"Nobody can say you're not doing your patriotic duty." There was an undertone of defiance in Mark's voice. Both he and Eric were self-conscious about not being in uniform.

"Did I tell you guys I passed my civil service exam?" Emily asked. Betsy already knew, of course. "Hey, I may be a government girl any day now."

"I couldn't believe it when Betsy told me you'd taken the exam," Mark clucked. "I expected you to be out there making theater rounds soon. It's a shame there're no groups to join."

"I have to wait until I have some real money stashed away," Emily said. Only Betsy knew that Emily had called in sick one day last week with the determination to go out to "make rounds." She'd spent an hour getting ready, changing outfits three times, concentrating on makeup, as always unaware that she was unusually attractive. She'd bought herself a copy of *Variety,* gone over to slide on a stool at the Astor drugstore, and ordered herself a Coke. She'd listened to the others seated on stools at this hangout for would-be actors and actresses—and she froze. *How did she know if she was good enough? She wasn't gorgeous and sexy like some of those gals.* "But working for the government won't be like teaching," she continued with a touch of bravado. "Teaching is a trap. This new job as a government clerk will be over the minute we're at peace."

"Let it be a short job." Betsy's smile was wry. "That's one I'll be happy to see you lose."

About an hour out of the city Mark turned off the highway to search for a café where they could have breakfast. In sudden anguish Betsy remembered driving to Sag Harbor with Paul, her head on his shoulder for most of the trip. She remembered breakfast in the cozy little place they found in the village. It had been so wonderful to be there with Paul—for that little while cut off from reality.

"Eric, wake up—" Mark took one hand from the wheel to jog Eric into consciousness. "What do you two think?" he asked the girls while he pulled up before a small café on the main street of a village off the highway. "Shall we give this joint a try?"

"Let's," Betsy approved, inspecting the steamed-over window, which was somehow inviting. At least it would have a ladies' room, she told herself. That was becoming an imminent necessity. She'd felt uncomfortable at asking Mark to look for a gas station with washrooms.

They had scrambled eggs and bacon, tall homemade-style biscuits, and fragrant, strong coffee.

"With coffee so hard to get, I can't walk past any place that serves it without running in for a cup." Eric seemed more relaxed now, Betsy thought. Mark said his job was a killer. "Though I hear that—like gas—there's plenty out there on the black market." The black market was something the four of them considered contemptible.

In high spirits they left the restaurant, returned to the car, and headed for Sag Harbor. Mark entertained them with stories about Elsie deWolfe—now Lady Mendl—and Syrie Maugham.

"Syrie Maugham—you know, she's married to Somerset Maugham—came to New York when Paris fell. The story is that she stayed at the River Club for a while, charging everything to her husband's publisher until he balked. Then she moved into the Dakota and sold antiques from there. Oh God, I'd kill to live in the Dakota." He sighed.

Because she had been in Sag Harbor before, Betsy was appointed their official guide. Like herself and Paul, the other three loved the charming old houses. They admired the imaginative monument erected in Oakland Cemetery on Jermain Avenue back in 1840 to commemorate the death of a twenty-eight-year-old skipper of a whaleboat in an encounter with a sperm whale. They visited the stone lighthouse built at the entrance to the harbor in 1868.

It would have been a beautiful day, Betsy thought nostalgically as they headed back for the city, if she had not been so embarrassed at having to search for a ladies' room every two hours. Emily said she was probably coming down with a cold.

She was grateful that no cold developed. Still, she was absurdly sleepy, she scolded herself in the following days. Even Mark teased her about constantly yawning.

"I know," he joshed, "you're trying to keep up with Eric." With his long work week—and much overtime—Eric was forever sleepy.

By the end of the week frightening suspicions were tormenting Betsy. Not until she and Emily were in the apartment on Friday evening and sitting down to a quick spaghetti dinner did she confide her suspicions.

"I've got a weird feeling that I might be pregnant," she said while Emily sprinkled fresh-grated parmesan over the spaghetti.

"Oh, God!" Emily's hand froze in midair. "You're late?"

"Almost two weeks. And you know me. I'm never late." Betsy's throat was tight with apprehension. "And I've been so tired and sleepy. And always running to the bathroom. I read somewhere those are sure signs."

"The last two maybe," Emily conceded. "The first, yeah."

"I always thought we were careful." The spaghetti sat untouched on plates.

"Nothing's sure except abstinence," Emily reminded. "And you and Paul haven't been abstaining. But you've planned on getting married, anyway. You've already taken your blood tests."

"But, Emily, Paul's in the Army. I don't know how I'll manage—"

"There're ways of not having the baby," Emily said after a moment. "My mother has a neighbor. She was forty-eight and pregnant last year—after four grown kids."

"Emily, I couldn't." Betsy stared at her in shock. "If I am pregnant, this is our baby—Paul's and mine. I—I love it already," she whispered.

"Write Paul tonight," Emily ordered. "It's his baby, too. Look, between the three of us we'll handle this. You're not to worry. But write Paul tonight. He'll have your letter by Monday."

"Do you suppose he'll be angry?" He'd taken it for granted she wouldn't get pregnant. *He hadn't planned on this.*

"Honey, it takes two to start a pregnancy. And no," she added gently, "Paul won't be angry. Upset at first, maybe—but not angry."

"It would be wonderful if we were married already and Paul was home with me. But Emily, I don't know when he'll be shipped out! I'll be here alone to have our baby."

"You won't be alone," Emily said resolutely. "You have me and

Mark and Eric. And Mom will help in any way she can. But maybe," she said with a compassionate smile, "we ought to know for sure if you *are* pregnant."

"You mean go to a doctor?"

"There're labs who do the 'rabbit test.' Usually, I understand, it's done through a doctor's office. But I'd guess that if you call up and say you want a test, they're not going to turn down your five bucks—or whatever it costs."

"Then I won't write Paul until we're sure," Betsy resolved. "If I'm not pregnant, I'd just be worrying him for nothing."

At nine A.M. sharp on the morning the lab promised to have a report on her pregnancy test, Betsy dialed their number. She was trembling with apprehension yet conscious of a strange exultation. She might be carrying Paul's baby, the ultimate symbol of their love.

Moments later a lab technician was checking on the results. Betsy waited to hear.

"Oh, yes, Mrs. Forrest, I have it right here." She had given her name as Mrs. Betsy Forrest—which she would be any day now. "The result is positive." The technician's voice told Betsy she considered this fine news.

"That means I'm pregnant?" In this moment her whole life was changing.

"It sure does."

"Thank you. Thank you so much." She understood the lab customarily gave such reports to physicians, but these were unusual times. A lot of girls in wartime were too impatient to wait to consult an obstetrician.

On her lunch hour she wrote a letter to Paul and mailed it. At moments she was attacked by fears that Paul would be upset. What if he were sent overseas before the baby was born? She could work for another few months, but how would she survive after that? Not on an Army wife's allotment check. Not in a city as expensive as New York.

She and Paul had their blood tests—they could be married as

soon as they acquired the license and went through the three-day waiting period. When would Paul get a long enough leave? *Would he be upset about the baby?*

Emily met her after work. Ever conscious of money, they decided to have dinner in the apartment. They'd moved seasonal clothes and daily necessities into Paul's apartment as he had asked. Now her mother's candlesticks sat on Paul's small dining room table and the crystal vase on the night table beside his bed. It was as though, she sometimes thought poignantly, she had brought her world into Paul's private world. The world away from his family.

Over dinner Emily tried to divert Betsy's thinking from the present crisis.

"I can't believe I'll be out of Gimbels in two weeks and working for the government. And instead of the $1,220 a year I expected, I'll be earning $1,400. I seemed to hit it off with the guy who was interviewing me. I feel absolutely rich!"

"How does your mother feel about your not waiting for a teaching job?"

"She figures I'm doing my patriotic duty, and when this bloody war is over I'll go into teaching." Emily grimaced. "That's what Mom thinks. By then I'll have money stashed away. I can afford to take some classes. Okay, maybe not two years at the American Academy, but enough evening classes to give me some confidence."

"You're awfully good, Emily. You stood out in every group production."

"I'm chicken," Emily admitted. "I don't have the guts to answer the casting calls. I can't get past an agent's door. Now forget about me," she ordered. "How're you feeling?"

"I can't believe I'm pregnant." Betsy managed a wisp of a smile. "Remember how we used to say we didn't want to get married before we were thirty? But that was before I met Paul—"

"We'll work this out." Emily radiated optimism. "After all, you're carrying my niece or my nephew." Emily had immediately designated herself the baby's aunt. "The minute you let me tell

Mom, she'll be knitting up a storm. Booties, sweaters, caps. And scolding me because it's not me that's pregnant."

"I don't think she'd be happy at the sequence." Betsy chuckled. "First you get married, *then* you get pregnant."

"You've got your blood tests already. That shows intent. And stop playing with your dinner. You're eating for two now."

Two mornings later Paul phoned Betsy at the shop.

"Paul, are you upset?" she asked instantly.

"Honey, how can I be upset? It takes two to make a baby—and I'm proud of our partnership."

"Can you get down here soon?"

"I've made an appointment already to talk to the chaplain," Paul told her. "I'll explain I need a four-day furlough so we can get married. And if the chaplain can't pull it off, then I'll talk to the rabbi," he said with an effort at humor. "We'll be married long before the baby comes."

Five hours later Paul phoned again. He had a four-day furlough beginning Friday morning. Betsy was to meet him at the train, and they'd go directly down to City Hall for their marriage license. On Monday they'd be married.

"Paul, what about your parents?" she asked, her voice unsteady.

He hesitated a moment. "We'll tell them afterwards. But this furlough belongs to us. Do you suppose Emily and Eric will be our witnesses? I know Mark can't leave the shop."

"It wouldn't be legal without at least two of them there."

"Everything is going to work out fine," he promised. "I just wish I could be there with you all the time. How do you feel?" His voice betrayed his anxiety.

"Wonderful. Except that I'm tired and sleepy a lot of the time," she admitted. "But Emily says that's typical."

"We'll have to find you a doctor," he began, serious now. He was worrying about the money for this, she suspected. "I want you to have the best."

"First let's get married. Then we'll be practical." Just take one day at a time, she ordered herself.

Paul's parents would be furious. It would be awful if they cut themselves off from him because he'd married her. Not just because of the money. They were his father and mother—his *family*. He loved them.

On Friday Betsy left the shop in time to meet Paul's train from Boston. She was grateful when the train arrived on schedule. They paused for a quick sandwich and coffee at a luncheonette, then headed to City Hall via subway. They were startled by the long lines at the Marriage License Bureau.

"Everybody's got the same idea," Paul teased, an arm about Betsy's waist.

Finally, their marriage license tucked away in Betsy's purse, Paul helped her into a taxi. His solicitude brought tears to her eyes.

"Paul, it's only two months," she reminded. But already her skirts and slacks were tight at the waist!

"Is it going to be all right for us to—to make love?" His voice dropped to a whisper out of deference for the cabdriver's presence.

"For a long time yet—" She lifted her eyes to his. *By Monday this time she'd be Mrs. James Paul Forrest III.*

Betsy and Paul spent the weekend in blissful solitude. The others made a pact to stay away until it was time to go to City Hall for the ceremony. On Saturday morning Betsy and Paul emerged from the apartment to look for a neighborhood jewelry shop where they could buy a wedding band.

"Later I'll buy you something beautiful," he promised while the jewelry store owner went off to inscribe their names and Monday's date inside the simple gold band.

"This one is beautiful," she insisted. Radiant.

With the wedding band in Paul's wallet, they walked down to Riverside Drive, sought out the pedestrian promenade along the Hudson. The day was gloriously warm and sunny. They walked until they were exhausted, then headed for Broadway and the Tip Toe Inn for lunch.

"This is our honeymoon," Paul pointed out while they dawdled over hot apple strudel and coffee. "Enjoy."

"What does it matter that we're doing things backwards?" she asked humorously.

"Should we try for theater tickets tonight?"

"Not unless you really want to go to the theater." She sensed he'd prefer to be alone with her. *When was he going to tell his parents?* "Let's have dinner at the apartment and then just relax." *He was worried, wasn't he, about how his parents would react?*

"Right after the ceremony at City Hall, I'll have to go home to talk to my mother and father." He said this somberly—as though he were reading her mind, she thought. "If I'm shipped out, I want to know they're here to take care of you."

"I'll be all right," she said quickly. She recoiled from the thought of any close association with his parents. Betsy didn't want to think that Paul might not be with her when the baby was born.

"I have to know they're watching over you," he said. "Over their daughter-in-law and grandchild."

"If they don't want it that way"—Betsy sought for the words to put Paul's mind at rest—"then we'll manage. I can work right up to the seventh month—Mark won't mind. He's always saying I'm good for the business. And I'll have my government allotment checks." She'd be the wife of a GI. "Emily's mother said there are great maternity clinics in Manhattan—"

"You're not having our baby in a clinic," Paul interrupted, almost terse. "I still have money left in my college account." His smile was wry. "Mother was always worried I might be short—she was forever giving me checks beyond what I needed. Before we go to City Hall Monday, we'll go to the bank and make it a joint account. It's only about eleven hundred, but that'll help."

Only eleven hundred, Betsy thought indulgently. The way she and Paul regarded money was so far apart. To her that was a small fortune. To Paul it was play money. *How would he feel if his parents disinherited him?*

Paul grew up in the Depression without ever being a part of it. He went to a private school, then to Harvard for a year, until he switched to Columbia, and then to Columbia Law. He never worried about the cost of a new pair of shoes or looked to save a few cents on items in the grocery store. He rode in a chauffeured limousine or drove his own car—while she debated about saving a nickel by walking instead of taking a bus or a subway. Would he come to hate her when he discovered what it was like not to be rich?

Today Paul spoke again of his childhood. His mother had long obsessively feared for his well-being. She saw danger in every sport. Only because his father had insisted was he allowed to learn to swim.

"I remember Dad pointing out that knowing how to swim might one day save my life. That's when Mother consented to swimming lessons. I was never sent off to summer camp like the other kids. Mother and Dad bought the house out at Southampton, and I spent the summers there. I was the center of her life."

His mother had tyrannized him all his life, Betsy thought angrily. She'd made him feel guilty about every independent thought. And even as she thought this, she herself was suffused by guilt. At errant moments she remembered the eleven-year-old girl who'd heard her mother say, *"If we had to lose one, why did it have to be him?"*

Late that evening, while Betsy lay in Paul's arms after making love, she forced herself to bring up the subject that had been causing her much anxiety in these last weeks. Paul had been raised as a Protestant. He'd told her that to his mother the church was an important part of her life. Wherever they had been—Palm Beach, Bar Harbor, Paris, London—on Sunday morning she sought out a church.

How would he respond to her own determination to raise their child in the Jewish faith? It was Jewish tradition for a child to follow the faith of its mother.

"Paul, do your parents know I'm Jewish?" she asked softly.

"I didn't see any need to mention that." His arms tightened about her. *He worried about that.*

"I want to bring up the baby in my faith—" Her heart was pounding. But Paul had to know this. "It's terribly important to

me." Because it would have been important to her parents and
Aunt Celia.

"We'll raise our kids any way you like," he promised. "Jews are
a minority," he pointed out. Betsy flinched, remembering how the
Nazis were intent on wiping them out. "So we'll raise one more
Jewish kid. The church can deal with that," he said with an effort
at gentle humor. "What's that crack Doug used to make? 'Why do
some Christians persist in thinking Jews dislike Jesus? He was one
of us.' "

"You won't regret that later?" She suspected his mother would
be furious. "You're sure, Paul?" Her eyes searched his.

"Honey, we're all descended from one set of parents. Underneath we're all sisters and brothers. I'm not saying that makes all
marriages incestuous," he said with a laugh. "But we're all members of the human race. I don't love you because you're Jewish—
and you don't love me because I'm Christian. Love transcends
religious faith. I love you because you're you. And I'll love our son
because he's our child."

"Ah-ha," Betsy said with a hint of laughter, "you're hoping for
a son!" But her heart pounded in pleasure because religious faith
would not be a barrier between Paul and her.

"Son or daughter—or both," he told her, his face radiating
tenderness, "I'll be happy."

On Monday morning—as scheduled—Betsy and Paul went first
to his bank and then with Emily and Eric to City Hall. In a
moment of sentimentality Emily had stopped at a florist shop to
buy a tiny bridal bouquet of red roses—Betsy's favorite flower—
and a corsage of pink rosebuds for herself. Now the four sat in the
crowded waiting room until they would be summoned into the
judge's chambers for the marriage ceremony. Here and there
other brides-to-be clutched floral bouquets.

"Betsy, you look beautiful," Emily murmured. "The radiant
young bride—like in those stories Mom loves in *Ladies' Home
Journal.*"

"Business here is booming," Eric said ebulliently but with an undertone of self-consciousness. A number of the prospective grooms wore uniforms. "Remember, when we get out of here, we're going up to Peacock Alley at the Waldorf for a wedding breakfast." Mark and Eric insisted on hosting this—though of necessity Mark had to be an absentee host.

Betsy sat with her hand in Paul's while they waited to be called. She wondered anxiously if she "showed" in the simply cut sea-green velvet shift she'd chosen for her wedding dress. She was unaware of the furtive admiring glances from a pair of young men attending other marrying couples, of how flattering the green velvet shift was to her luminous blue-green eyes and lush auburn hair.

Her throat constricted with alarm as she tried to envision Paul's encounter with his parents later. Just before they left the apartment, he'd phoned his father.

"I'll be in town for a few hours today," he'd said, lying yet again. "I have something important to tell you and Mother. Could you be at the house around one?" He'd paused, then rushed to reassure his father. "I'm not being shipped out, Dad. It isn't that."

She knew how Paul dreaded this confrontation. She could imagine how upset his mother would be about their marriage, especially when she learned about the baby. Emily was right. Mrs. Forrest probably regarded her as a gold digger, out to marry rich. But she mustn't allow his mother to ruin their wedding day, she exhorted herself. This was the most important day of her life.

"Have you heard from Doug?" Paul gazed from Betsy to Emily. "The way we've both moved around, we seem to be losing touch."

"A couple of short letters," Emily reported. "It looks like he'll be flying for the Air Force."

"That's what he wanted." Paul smiled reminiscently.

Then Betsy and Paul were called—with their witnesses—to follow the previous couple into the judge's chambers. With dizzying swiftness the judge performed the marriage ceremony. *She was Mrs. James Paul Forrest III.* Moments later they were being ushered out.

"I don't think the ceremony took more than two minutes,"

Emily said in amazement as they headed out of City Hall to search for a taxi. "That didn't hurt at all, did it, kids?" she teased the bride and groom.

Sitting at their table in the Waldorf's legendary three-hundred-foot-long Peacock Alley—favored by society and well-heeled tourists alike—Betsy allowed her mind to dart back through the years to the time when Mom and Dad were alive. Oh, how she wished they—and Aunt Celia—were here with her today! They might be concerned that she was marrying out of her faith, but they would love Paul. They would love their grandchild.

She saw Paul's furtive glances at his wristwatch. Poor darling, he was dreading the encounter with his parents. She was to wait in a small coffee shop around the corner from his family's townhouse until he had told his parents about their marriage, and about her being pregnant.

Maybe he should wait to tell them about the baby until later, she thought. But these were frightening times. He was solicitous about her welfare. They both knew he could be shipped out at any moment.

"I hate to break up this party," Paul announced finally. "But if I'm not to go AWOL, I have to get moving."

Emily and Eric saw them into a cab. On the brief drive to the coffee shop near the Forrests' townhouse, Betsy and Paul sat in tense silence, hands clasped. She was Paul's wife, Betsy defiantly told herself. *His mother couldn't change that.*

CHAPTER TEN

With a final smile at Betsy from the entrance, Paul walked out of the cozy coffee shop and headed toward the family townhouse. The glorious morning sun had given way to ominous clouds. A chill in the air penetrated Paul's Army uniform. He hadn't brought his overcoat. This time of the year was so unpredictable, he thought. But his mother was very predictable, he remembered with apprehension.

Dad must suspect what he had come to tell them, he told himself with shaky confidence. It shouldn't be a total shock. Had Dad dropped some hint to Mother?

At the house he was admitted by William, effusive in his welcome.

"Where are they, William?"

"In the library," William told him and he sprinted down the hall.

"Hi, Mother—" He forced a smile as she turned toward the door. She hadn't heard the doorbell. "Dad—" He crossed the room to the sofa, where his mother sat.

"Paul, why didn't you call from camp and let us know you were coming into the city?" Mrs. Forrest scolded indulgently while she held up her face for a kiss. But already she was upset, Paul sensed.

"There were things I had to take care of before I came home." He struggled to appear casual. "Dad, sorry to pull you away from the office—" He exchanged a warm embrace with his father.

"What is this all about?" His mother was lacing her hands in that nervous gesture he knew so well. "You sounded so mysterious."

"Now take it easy, Alice," her husband urged. "Give Paul a chance to catch his breath."

"Paul, are they shipping you out?" Her eyes darkened in alarm. "Is that what this is all about?"

"No, Mother," Paul rushed to reassure her. "I'm not being shipped out. At least not yet." He paused, took a deep breath, then plunged ahead. "There's no easy way to tell you—" His eyes pleaded for understanding. "Betsy and I were married this morning. At City Hall. We—"

"You've been seeing her all along," his mother said with a gasp.

"Yes," Paul admitted. "I didn't want to upset you until it was absolutely necessary. I—"

Again his mother interrupted him.

"You let me believe you weren't seeing her anymore!" Mrs. Forrest was pale and trembling.

"We didn't discuss it," Paul hedged agonizingly. *She'd* decided he wasn't seeing Betsy anymore—he'd said nothing like that. "Betsy and I love each other very much. I want to spend the rest of my life with her."

"Darling, you're just infatuated! That's all it is. What could you possibly have in common with her?" Her voice was shrill. "You come from two different worlds. But we understand, Paul. It's because of this awful war—you're not thinking clearly." Her words were tumbling over one another. "We'll find a way out. You can have the marriage annulled."

"No, Mother." Paul was resolute. "Betsy is my wife. That's what we both want." He hesitated. His eyes swung to his father in a plea for support. "I have to return to camp this afternoon. I want to bring Betsy over to meet you."

"No." For an instant his mother closed her eyes in anguish. "I can't face that." But she wasn't falling apart, Paul recognized in shaky relief. Dad must have made sure she'd taken one of her pills. "I can't believe you did this to us. I've looked forward to the day you'd marry—when you were older, of course. I envisioned a beautiful church wedding, where you'd be married in the eyes of God. To some fine girl of your own kind."

"Mother, whom I marry is not a family decision," he said gently. "It's my decision."

"Paul, what about her family?" His father was trying to be matter-of-fact. "Where are they from?"

"Betsy's parents were killed in a tragic accident when she was a little girl. The aunt who raised her—a schoolteacher—died just recently."

"They're nobodies!" Alice was growing distraught again. "It would never have happened except for this awful war!"

"What is—" His father hesitated, glanced warily at Alice. Looking for a way to lessen her shock, Paul understood. "What was her name?"

"Betsy Bernstein." He waited for this to sink in.

"She's Jewish?" His mother gaped in disbelief, a hand at her chest. "How will I ever explain to our minister that you've married out of the church?"

"Betsy and I are not concerned about that. We love each other—that's all that matters."

"This could ruin your law career," she reproached. "When we have such fine connections!"

"I have more news," he began warily, dreading her reaction. "Betsy's pregnant."

"You see what's happening?" Alice turned to her husband. "It's what I told you. This girl is some sly fortune-hunter." Her eyes swung back to Paul. "When she was afraid she couldn't hold you, she used the oldest trick in the world. She managed to get pregnant!"

"Alice, take it easy." His father was pale but composed.

"We went for our blood tests weeks ago—before Betsy knew she was pregnant," Paul said defensively. "But once we knew, we pushed ahead the wedding."

"I'm going to my room." Mrs. Forrest rose to her feet. Her eyes avoiding Paul. "I can't talk about this anymore. I'm too upset."

In silence the two men watched Alice Forrest slowly walk to the door and disappear down the hall. Now her husband crossed to the door and closed it.

"You'll have to give your mother time," he told Paul. "It's been a shock. You can't expect her to accept this in moments."

"Dad, Betsy's pregnant," Paul emphasized. "I don't want to be shipped out without knowing you'll look after her." He'd been praying for a miracle—but it hadn't happened. "She's carrying your grandchild." He knew how much his parents wanted grandchildren. Only his wife—Betsy—could give them that.

"I promise you, your wife will be taken care of." His father's face was grave. "But you must give your mother time to accept this. She'll come around. You can't expect her not to be upset," he reminded. "You know how fragile she is emotionally. Meanwhile, I'll contact Dr. Raymond. He'll refer—" The senior Forrest hesitated a moment, managed an awkward smile. "He'll refer your wife to a topnotch obstetrician. The bills will come to me."

"Do it now," Paul said. "Let me go back to camp with peace of mind."

Twenty minutes later, without saying good-bye to his mother, Paul was striding toward the coffee shop where he had left Betsy. Angry with himself that he had to ask for help from his family. But at least he knew that Betsy would be in the care of an excellent obstetrician. And with luck *he* would be with her when the baby was born. But he felt a surge of helplessness and frustration that he must depend upon his parents for financial assistance.

Betsy's face brightened as she saw Paul approach the coffee shop entrance. But almost immediately she knew that the meeting had been disappointing. Paul's strained expression was eloquent.

"Paul, we're going to work things out," she said urgently as he slid into the booth. She couldn't bear seeing him so anxious.

"We figured there would be trouble with my mother. But Dad understands," he added with a forced smile. "He says we have to give Mother time to digest everything. But meanwhile he called Dr. Raymond and was referred to an obstetrician Raymond knows well. You're to call this number and make an appointment." Paul reached into his jacket pocket for the piece of paper with the necessary information. "The bills will go to Dad. I'm not happy about that," he conceded, "but there's a war going on and there's not much I can do about it."

"I've been talking to Mark." Betsy struggled to sound confident. "He says I can work at the shop as long as I want. 'Just make sure the baby isn't born here,' he said." Her laughter was shaky but defiant. "And afterwards I can bring the baby to the shop. I'll set up a crib in that little room in the back—and I can be as close as I need to be. Paul, we'll manage by ourselves. I don't need a fancy obstetrician. The city has terrific maternity clinics."

"You'll go to this doctor," Paul insisted quietly. "Dad suggested it himself. But it'll take a while until Mother accepts the fact that I'm married. She had it all worked out in her mind that I'd marry the daughter of her best friend. Neither Doris nor I ever had any such ideas, though both mothers kept throwing us at each other. Betsy, I knew right away—you were the only girl for me."

"How soon do we have to leave for the station?" She wished they could go back to the apartment for a little while. She needed Paul to hold her in his arms and comfort her.

"In about forty minutes. Remember," he said, "we had the honeymoon first."

"Have something to eat," she encouraged. "You'll be hungry on the train if you don't."

"That's right." He reached for her hand. His eyes gently teasing. "The prospective father has to keep up his strength."

Betsy read and reread Paul's letters, always hoping for some indication that his mother was ready to accept her. There was no indication of this. Still, Paul was relieved that he had managed a reconciliation of sorts with his mother. They'd talked by phone several times—though, he admitted, she pointedly ignored his marriage.

Betsy soon realized that Mrs. Forrest was boycotting The Sanctuary. She was plagued by guilt—she had caused the loss of the shop's best customer.

"Betsy, don't mope about it," Mark ordered when she tried to apologize. "We're doing great. And you're a real asset to the shop. Those color combinations you suggested to the Carsons for their master bedroom drapes and upholstery were sensational. We've picked up two new customers already because they were so pleased."

"It was just an idea that came to me when Emily and I were at the Metropolitan one Sunday." But she was delighted by his approval.

"Keep going," Mark ordered ebulliently. "You've got a sharp eye. Dorothy Draper, look out! Betsy Forrest is in town."

Betsy waited wistfully for Paul to receive another weekend pass. She wrote him every night, trying to amuse him with reports on the baby's growth. After a month of using safety pins to accommodate her growing waistline, she had capitulated and bought her first maternity skirt and dress.

"At this rate I'll be enormous in another three months," she wrote Paul. But she felt a little less alone because she carried Paul's baby within her. On nights when she found it difficult to sleep, she lay in bed with her hands resting on the small protuberance that was their child. And she prayed that Paul would be able to come to her when the baby was born.

She was grateful for Emily's presence in her life. Emily was the sister she'd always yearned to have. Emily's family was the closest thing to her own family she knew. Already Emily's mother and grandmother were knitting and crocheting for the baby.

Every Sunday Betsy and Emily went to a museum, where Betsy made copious notes about the furniture on display. She was learning to identify various periods, to distinguish between a cabinetmaker's earlier and later designs. She studied the endless procession of books on decorating that Mark lent her or that she borrowed from the public library.

She was ever enthralled by being surrounded by beautiful furniture in the shop, by dealing with the finest of fabrics. She felt a joyous excitement at visualizing—designing—elegant interiors and at bringing together unexpected yet dramatic colors.

Now Mark was teaching her how to identify an antique as real or fake. "You must learn to recognize old workmanship," he repeated regularly. "It's like handwriting—very identifiable once you learn. You have to understand how the old cabinetmakers worked, what kind of tools they used. You won't find a genuine Early American piece that doesn't have toolmarks on it."

Betsy and Emily followed the war news on radio and in the newspapers with apprehension—as did most Americans. It was clear the war was going badly for the Allies, both in Europe and in the Pacific.

Emily's brother, Bert—now a Marine and married to Rheba— was somewhere in the Pacific. Those at home knew the fighting there was ferocious. On May 6 General Wainwright had been forced to surrender Corregidor. Word was coming in now—just a month later—about an important American victory at Midway. American forces had repulsed an effort to take the island—sinking seventeen Japanese ships and bringing down 275 Japanese planes. But everybody knew this was only a first painful step toward victory in the Pacific.

After having gone to Borough Park to have Friday night dinner with her family, Emily returned to the apartment to report to Betsy that her father and mother had both enrolled in the Air Warden Service.

"I'm surprised they waited this long." Emily chuckled indulgently. "Now Mom's saying she'll go to work in a defense plant as soon as school closes." Many teachers and students, they knew, were making this same decision.

"Mark told me that an antisubmarine patrol has been set up along the Atlantic seaboard. It's scary to think that German subs come that close to us." Betsy flinched at a mental vision of this. "But then merchant ships are being torpedoed almost every night right off our coastline."

"I kind of feel glad that we have a Civil Air Patrol base right near us—at Atlantic City." Light planes from the base patrolled the coastal waters from New York Harbor to below Cape May. "The whole country knows that New York City is Enemy Target Number One." Emily giggled. "Mom says she can handle that. What bugs her is all the waiting in line we do these days. At the dentist's office, at the movies, at the auto repair shop."

Consumer goods were disappearing from the shelves as the war continued. Thousands of small businesses closed for lack of merchandise, and their owners and help had to search for jobs in unfamiliar occupations. In May sugar rationing began. For Emily—who adored sweets—this was a real deprivation.

Mark was now admitting to worries about the survival of The Sanctuary. Betsy had suspected for months that he was anxious. He'd confided, even before Pearl Harbor, that he was grateful he'd had the foresight to take out a loan in order to stock up on fabrics not long after Hitler invaded Poland.

"I'm strapped for cash," he admitted, "but we've got inventory on hand for a while."

"We'll make it, Mark," she vowed. And again she felt guilty that she had cost the shop its best customer. And Mark had hoped that Mrs. Forrest would bring her friends into the shop.

" 'From your mouth to God's ear,' as Eric would say. Anyhow, nobody works harder than us."

But Betsy understood his anxiety. Some people predicted that decorating shops—and interior decorators—would be forced out of business until the war was over. There was no silk coming from Japan, no china from Peking, no Irish linen or English chintz. Furniture production was way off.

She prayed Mark could hold on. While she knew she would be able to find another job in these times, she dreaded the prospect of not working at The Sanctuary. This wasn't just a job to her. It was the gateway to the career she yearned to embrace.

CHAPTER ELEVEN

Mark was jubilant when—despite the war—he received a delivery of fine English chintz. It had been arranged for him through a former classmate at Parsons who now lived in London.

"Betsy, isn't it gorgeous!" he gloated as they uncrated the bolts of fabric when the store had closed for the day.

"Exquisite," she agreed. Both she and Mark almost reverent as they lifted the first bolt out of the crate.

"It'll make beautiful drapes. And the same material can be used for slipcovers. Oh, and can't you just visualize this as a bed canopy?" He glowed with a surge of creativity. "Thank God that Carla and her crew are still sewing for us!"

"Mark, put the chintz into the display window," Betsy suggested.

"I thought I'd call some of our regular customers," he reproached. "I can charge astronomical prices." His smile was dazzling. "That'll help lift us out of the red."

"Mark, save a bolt for regular customers," Betsy agreed. "But put a length into the display window. It'll bring in customers. Even if they think this is too expensive, they may buy something else." She paused, her mind charging ahead. "I know this is supposed to be a bad time for interior decorators," she conceded, "but don't you think it's time you put a small sign in the window saying, 'Mark Jamison, Interior Decorator'?"

Mark's face grew luminous as he considered this.

"Betsy, do I dare?" he asked.

"Of course you dare. You don't need a license. And I'll be your assistant. Mark, you can do this." The thought had been germinating in her mind for weeks. Mark had talent—and an ability to handle the wealthy women who came into the shop. He should be doing more than selling pieces. He should be doing rooms, apartments.

"But I have to be here in the shop," he said. "You know how demanding those women are. I could be dragged away for hours on end—"

"I can handle the business here if you're off on consultations. And once you're set with a lineup of clients, you can afford to hire somebody to come into the shop," she forged ahead.

"We'll give it a try," he said after considering for a moment. The atmosphere in the shop was electric now. "But you have to remember how bad it is right now for interior decorators. Do you know how many have folded already?"

"You have the shop," she reminded. "This is a side campaign. Mark, let's try it!" It was important for both of them, she told herself. *They needed this breakthrough.*

"The chintz goes into the window the moment I can have the sign made up," he agreed after a moment of deliberation. "But God knows when we'll be able to get another delivery of fabrics from overseas—"

"We'll improvise," she said ebulliently. "And Emily said her father is willing to give us his gas coupons so we can do more scouting for antiques. Just pray"—she laughed—"that a client doesn't show up who adores modern furniture!"

As they anticipated, the display of the truly magnificent English chintz brought customers into the shop. Most winced at the price Mark had set. A couple of women ordered drapes with an air of euphoria at acquiring such a find. And then, on a dreary rainy afternoon, a tall, dark-haired, fiftyish woman with a strong Spanish accent strode into the shop. Her expensive attire, her jewelry, her air, indicated great wealth.

"Darling, I love that chintz in the window," she announced as

Mark approached with a charming smile. "How soon can you have drapes made for me?" She didn't bother inquiring about price. "I have three windows in the master bedroom of my apartment in the Waldorf Towers. I've never liked what the decorator hung there five months ago. He whined," she said distastefully, "about how impossible it was to get attractive fabrics."

"I'll have to come up for the measurements," he said, making mental calculations. "We'll hang the drapes within a week," he promised.

Hovering close by, Betsy understood that other orders would be briefly waylaid. Now on impulse she moved forward.

"Excuse me," she said with a diffident smile. "We still have another bolt uncrated," she reminded Mark. "There's enough to cover a chair to match or even add a canopy to the bed."

"Oh!" Their new customer looked from Betsy to Mark with an air of discovery. "That's right, you're interior decorators." She reached into her huge crocodile purse to pull out a card. "I'm Felicia Goulart. Let's set up a time for a consultation."

Mark and Betsy were launched as interior decorators. Felicia Goulart ordered her entire bedroom redone, which meant a frantic search for a headboard, a dressing table, a night table, a slipper chair to replace the ones installed by a less imaginative decorator. Mark combed through the antique shops in New York. He and Betsy—with Emily's father contributing the necessary gas coupons—drove to Duchess County on Sunday to follow a lead about available antiques. He'd cautioned Felicia, who was leaving shortly for her primary home in Rio, that this would take time. Clearly money did not concern her.

"Darling, I want you and Betsy to come to my cocktail party on Friday," she ordered at a meeting with Mark. "I love having young people about," she confessed flirtatiously. "And who knows, I may decide to have you redo the drawing room as well while I'm away."

Mark and Betsy considered the invitation with mixed feelings.

"How the hell can the both of us be away from the shop at the same time?" he fretted.

"We can't afford not to go," Betsy pointed out. Increasingly she

realized that she was the more practical. "First, we can't antago-
nize Felicia. And secondly, we might pick up another client."
Mark and she realized that to operate as interior decorators they
needed more than one client. "Why don't we ask Emily and Eric
to take the afternoon off from work to cover for us?"

Mark brightened. "They could handle it. Eric's been working
like a dog—he can call in sick one day."

"And Emily has a lot of leave piled up—she'll ask for Friday
off." At a time when business was so awful in the field, could she
and Mark pull off this move?

Mark insisted that the shop would pay for a cocktail dress for
Betsy.

"Go to Saks," he ordered grandly. "We're going to a cocktail
party at the Waldorf Towers."

"To Lane Bryant," she corrected, her eyes dropping to her
expanding waistline.

"Okay. Lane Bryant. Buy something expensive. We have to
look *très* successful." He lifted an eyebrow in a gesture of triumph.
"You know who're Felicia's neighbors? Cole Porter and his wife!
They usually spend the fall in New York, but they're here now
because of his new play. They're coming to the party."

"Where do they spend the rest of the year?" Betsy asked. Cole
Porter's new musical—*Something for the Boys*—had opened in
January. It was a smash hit.

"Oh, we're beginning to move in fancy circles," Mark drawled.
"The Porters spend the fall at their forty-first-floor apartment at
the Waldorf Towers. Then they divide their time between a country house in Massachusetts and a mansion in Hollywood." Mark
sighed rapturously. "Wouldn't you love to redo their houses?"

Betsy took Emily with her to Lane Bryant. Both girls winced
after furtive glances at price tags in the Maternity Department.

"It's a business investment," Betsy declared as she inspected
dresses on the display racks. "We might pick up a prospective
client."

"Do you think Cole Porter will really come?" Emily vacillated
between awe and doubt.

"Felicia said he was going to 'drop by,' " Betsy recalled. "She's known him for years. She told us about his mansion in Paris. One room had platinum wallpaper—it was the talk of Paris. The floors and some of the walls were covered in zebra hide."

"To remind him of El Morocco?" Emily quipped. El Morocco was one of the New York nightclubs favored by café society and which Emily yearned to visit.

"She was at fabulous parties at his *palazzo* in Venice—Elizabeth and Robert Browning once lived there." Betsy paused and took a dress from the rack.

"Let me try on this one. Paul loves to see me in soft yellow—"

Betsy struggled to hide her nervousness as she walked with Mark to the entrance to Felicia Goulart's apartment. She felt faintly self-conscious at going to a cocktail party when she was already "showing"—but people didn't care about that these days, she reminded herself.

"Did I tell you that we received a postcard from Doug with his APO address? He's with the Air Force in England."

"At least three times," Mark said with a chuckle. "Does Paul know?"

"He called me last night. He got a card, too." Some of her earlier conviviality fizzled away. "Paul said he almost wishes his company would be shipped out and have it over with. Except that he wants to be here when the baby's born."

"Everybody says the Allies are plotting a second front," Mark said somberly. "Nobody can figure out where it'll be—"

Arriving at the door, they heard laughter and music inside. Somebody was at the piano. Two women were singing.

"Darlings, come in." Felicia greeted them with outstretched arms and corraled them across the foyer into the huge drawing room. "It's going to be a wonderful party."

Betsy and Mark smiled dutifully as Felicia introduced them to a cluster of young people around their own ages and moved on. They all had bit parts in Broadway plays. They radiated a professional charm, but Betsy noted the way their eyes strayed about the irritatingly ornate eighteenth-century drawing room. They were all here, she suspected—like Mark and herself—to make connections.

With a shock she recognized the two women hovering over the piano and singing "Begin the Beguine." They were Ethel Merman and Tallulah Bankhead. Merman was starring in Cole Porter's new musical, and Bankhead was appearing on Broadway in *Clash By Night.*

"Don't you think Cole Porter is just the bravest man in the world?" a statuesque young blonde cooed to Betsy and Mark as the others in their group focused on individual conversations. "After all those operations on his legs—and he's always in pain— he still writes such gorgeous music and lyrics."

The short, dark man in the wheelchair at the piano was Cole Porter, Betsy realized in shock. Paul would be so excited when she told him. He'd said that while Cole Porter was in college he'd had a show on Broadway. Paul couldn't wait for the war to be over so he would write *his* play. Even now he kept making notes.

Betsy made a pretense of listening to the conversation between Mark and the blonde, but she was really focusing on what suggestions Mark might make to Felicia about redoing her drawing room.

Now Betsy eavesdropped on an older couple who appeared to be viewing the guests with condescending amusement.

"Darling, Felicia only has show business people at her parties," the woman said arrogantly. "Now she's on a patriotism trip. Of course, all three of her husbands were Americans—"

All at once Betsy's mind leaped into action. Felicia was on a patriotism kick. Then let them suggest she redo her drawing room in Early American! Mark had a couple of fine pieces in inventory. For the right price, she guessed—and with Felicia that was no problem—Mark's contacts up in Putnam and Duchess counties would come up with others. Perhaps that man they'd talked with up in Sag Harbor . . .

Felicia was at the door again, welcoming a large, rather ugly woman in a flamboyant cocktail dress.

"Elsa, how sweet of you to drop by." But an undercurrent of tension in her voice indicated she wasn't happy about this.

"That's Elsa Maxwell," the blonde whispered, her eyes avidly glued to the new arrival.

"Cole's leaving," the blonde said disappointedly. "He and Elsa Maxwell are mortal enemies now. They used to be great friends." Her face lighted up as his small entourage came within a few feet. "Mr. Porter, what are you going to do next?" she asked with an ingenuous smile. "I just adore the new musical. I saw it before I went into rehearsal of my play—"

"I'm starting soon on a musical for Mike Todd," Porter told her. "It'll be based on the Cinderella story. Not quite right for Ethel." He laughed and turned his head to wave to Merman.

Mark improvised a consultation with a client to cover their early departure. He'd come to realize that the young men invited to Felicia's parties were supposed to be charming to the older, unattached women. The attractive young girls—and they were all attractive—were a diversion for the older, unattached men.

"Oh, Mark, you and Betsy are the best-kept secret in New York," Felicia teased. "And don't expect me to spread the word around. I want to know you're there for me." She paused, her eyes mischievous. "And what do you think of my drawing room?"

"Mark has a wonderful idea for it." Betsy shot a warning glance at Mark not to interrupt. "We were talking about it just now. What would you think of Early American? It's so fitting for these times."

"Darling, that's fabulous," Felicia said enthusiastically. "Let's talk about it tomorrow."

Doug and Stan Morino—the bombardier of Doug's Air Force crew—sauntered on this dreary July evening into a restaurant in Soho. They'd been in London almost three weeks. They were chafing from inactivity, impatient for action.

"Remember, Stan, no hamburgers," Doug kidded while they settled themselves at a table. They had early discovered that beef had been replaced in long-suffering London with horsemeat. In London those with cash ate in restaurants to compensate for the onerous rationing. "But all the coffee you can drink." The English preferred their traditional tea, and coffee was plentiful.

"What I wouldn't give for some fresh fruit." Stan sighed. "Or white bread that wasn't gray."

"You know what they keep telling us," Doug joshed. "Don't eat bread—eat potatoes."

"When are we going to get moving?" Stan challenged. The RAF had been making massive raids over Germany since April. On May 30, 1,000 RAF bombers hit Cologne. "From rumors, I suspect the RAF will bomb the Continent by night and we'll handle the day shift. But when?"

"Soon," Doug consoled.

"Remind me to mail my letter to Jean," Stan said. "God, it's great—the way she writes me every night."

"Yeah," Doug agreed. His expressive blue eyes looked wistful.

Mail call was the big moment of every day when you were in the service. He was grateful for the letters from Betsy and Emily—it was like touching home to hear from them. But in his mind he wrote endless letters to Betsy, telling her how he truly felt about her. In his mind he said the things he couldn't say to his best friend's girlfriend—now Paul's wife.

"Wow, that's something nice," Stan murmured.

Doug's eyes followed Stan's. His throat tightened as he inspected the beautiful young redhead pausing at the door. She was obviously searching for someone.

Her resemblance to Betsy was startling. The same lovely features, the same gorgeous hair. She smiled, and it was almost Betsy's smile.

"Hell, we're out of luck." Stan sighed in exaggerated regret as a young RAF officer rose to his feet and gestured to her. "Oh, shit!" he said a minute later as the sirens began to wail. "They're starting early tonight."

They joined the orderly exodus toward the shelter. Involuntarily Doug's eyes sought out the girl who so resembled Betsy.

CHAPTER TWELVE

O n this steamy late August night Betsy trudged up the stairs to the apartment with a wry awareness that she was less agile this far into her pregnancy. When Paul phoned last night, she'd told him the baby was beginning to kick.

"Paul, I was so excited! It was like the baby's tiny foot or fist was saying, 'Mommie, I'm fine.'"

She paused at the landing, deriding herself for being awkward, then walked to the apartment door and unlocked it. She remembered that Emily was going to her parents' house for dinner. She'd have the chicken left over from last night and a vegetable. She was ever conscious of the need to follow the proper diet in pregnancy.

"Emily—" She stared in shock. Emily sat curled up at the end of the sofa. Her face was white and anguished. Her eyes puffy from crying. "What's happened?" Betsy asked in alarm.

"Mom called soon after I got to the office this morning. I rushed right out to Borough Park. She had just heard from Rheba—" Emily paused to take a deep breath. "Rheba received a telegram from the War Department. Bert's missing in action. Somewhere in New Guinea—"

"Oh, Emily—" Betsy hurried to her side. "But that doesn't mean he isn't all right," she said forcefully. "He could be in hiding on the island. Or a prisoner of war. Don't think the worst." But she was cold with fear—for Bert, for Paul, for Doug. *How long before Paul would be on a fighting front?*

"Mom and Dad are both wrecks. Now Mom's lambasting Rheba for not marrying Bert earlier and getting pregnant right away. She figures then he wouldn't have been drafted. I stayed most of the day, then I came back here. Mom's furious because I said I was going in to work tomorrow. What good will it do for me to sit around the house and listen to Mom cry?"

"It's important for you to be at your office," Betsy said. "You're part of the war effort."

"I want to join the WACs, Betsy." Back in May the Women's Army Auxiliary Corps—now called the WACs—had been authorized. "I have to do something!" A vein in her neck was distended.

"You are doing something." Betsy gazed at her in dismay. "You're working for Naval Intelligence. That's an essential job."

"I won't enlist before the baby's born," Emily said quickly. "You know I wouldn't do that."

"Listen to me, Emily. You're as much a part of the war effort as all those Naval officers you work with every day. Some of them are young enough to be fighting out in the Pacific," she pointed out. "But they're not walking around saying, 'I'm not doing something for the war.'"

"They're part of Naval Intelligence—they have skills. Millions of girls could fill my job. When I think of Bert out there—" Emily's voice broke.

"There's a good chance he's all right," Betsy said. "He could be hiding out from the Japs," she suggested. "Or maybe he's a prisoner of war. But you're doing as much as those girls who're going into the WACs or the WAVES. You're part of a vital military service."

"I'll sign up for a course in shorthand," Emily said after a moment. "These days they're set up to fit in with all kinds of crazy work schedules. I'll be more useful if I know shorthand."

A few evenings later Emily went to her first shorthand class. Her mother, Emily reported, had returned to her teaching. She clung now to the conviction that Bert was in hiding.

"I guess that's necessary for her survival," Emily rationalized, her eyes somber. "We all have to believe that."

The news of Bert's missing-in-action status had brought the tragedies of war appallingly close to Betsy. She prayed that Paul would be among those lucky ones who would remain on duty within the United States. It was selfish, she thought defiantly, but she prayed Paul would never leave U.S. soil.

Betsy and Emily received an occasional letter from Doug, stationed somewhere in England with the Air Force. He spoke with deep respect about the way the English continued their daily lives despite horrendous conditions. With censorship what it was, he could say little about his own daily life, but when he talked with nostalgia about New York delicatessens, Betsy and Emily chipped in to buy a salami to ship to him.

Betsy waited hopefully for Paul to wangle another weekend pass, but summer gave way to autumn and still this didn't happen. Mark insisted now that she come into the shop half an hour later and that she leave half an hour earlier in order to miss the rush hour traffic, though with wartime working hours these were irregular.

She was pleased that Mark kept telling her she could work as late in pregnancy as she wished. He was taking it for granted that she'd come back to the shop soon after the baby was born. She wasn't ready to handle that yet, she confessed to Emily.

"Paul told you his parents would see that you were all right if he couldn't be with you," Emily reminded. "That means you won't have any money problems." Emily was unabashedly delighted that Betsy had married into a wealthy family. "You'll be able to hire somebody to look after the baby while you're working."

"Everything's so—so unsettled." Yet she knew she'd be miserable if she couldn't continue working. If she and Mark became successful decorators, they'd make a lot of money. She could support Paul and the baby and herself while he wrote his play.

"Take one day at a time," Emily coaxed. "We'll work things out between us."

"Actually things are slow at the shop right now—what with all the shortages. If we hadn't landed the assignment to do Felicia Goulart's bedroom, we'd be in serious financial trouble. Of course, now we have the problem of doing her drawing room." Felicia had left for Rio, leaving only a 20 percent deposit on the new assignment. Mark had to lay out all the costs until the job was completed, she remembered uneasily.

"That woman is so rich!" Emily's eyes glistened with envy. "Mark should have made her pay up front for the whole deal."

"He didn't dare. He said it would look unprofessional. Still, I think he should have worked out arrangements to be paid in segments. Mark has to lay out cash for everything. But we'll be able to show her bedroom and drawing room to prospective clients," she said with a show of optimism. "That means a lot." Mark had told her he wanted to raise her salary—*"Betsy, you deserve it"*—but that would have to wait.

On a late October evening—with Emily going to her parents' for dinner—Betsy tried to deal with setting a date to leave the shop. Paul worried that she was working so close to her due date. Though she never said a word, he guessed that she was tiring easily now. It was difficult for her to sleep.

She started at the sound of the phone, rose awkwardly to walk across the room. That would be Paul, she thought joyously. Right now Emily was on the BMT, en route to Borough Park.

"Hello—" She was faintly breathless.

"How are you, baby?" Paul's voice was a tender caress.

"I'm fine," she told him, questions charging through her mind. Paul never phoned this late at night. It was almost lights-out time in the barracks. "Are you all right?"

"Yeah," he soothed. "I'll be home tomorrow—I'm taking a very early train. I have to be back by five the next morning."

"What time will you arrive?" she asked, churning with anticipation.

"Don't meet the train. I have to see Dad, then I'll come right to the apartment." *Why did he have to see his father?* "I should be there around noon. Mark will let you off, won't he?"

"I'll make sure Eric will cover for me. Paul—" All at once her heart was pounding. "Is your company on alert?"

"We'll talk when I get there," he hedged. She understood. He couldn't say that on the phone. *His company was on alert. They were shipping out.* "You're sure you're feeling okay?" he asked again.

"I'm great." She laughed shakily. "And great in size. Emily's mother said she never saw anybody pop out so much."

"I love you," he told her. "I can't wait to see you. Pat the little guy for me."

"I promise."

"I have to run. See you tomorrow." She heard good-humored grumbling on the other side. As usual a line was waiting to use the phone, she understood.

Betsy sat immobile by the phone. The time she had dreaded was arriving. How would she survive the days and nights—never knowing when Paul was in danger, asking herself agonizing questions each time there was a delay in V-mail? Was he wounded? Had he been taken prisoner? How did wives and mothers live through those times? But a handful of maniacs had thrown the world into chaos, and this was how they must live now.

Paul wouldn't be with her when the baby was born. It was a terrifying realization. But she wasn't alone in this, she rebuked herself. Thousands of babies would be born to fathers who were halfway across the world, fighting for a better world for themselves and their families. *Don't feel sorry for yourself. You can handle this.*

She could understand how Paul's mother would feel when she learned he was being shipped out. It was a pain they shared. But his mother wanted no part of her. Paul kept insisting she'd change, that she would love their baby as she loved him.

But she would never have a night of undisturbed sleep, Betsy warned herself, until Paul was safely home again. Paul would come home to her and their child. She would not allow any other thought to take root in her mind.

But one thing she vowed—Paul's mother would never dominate her grandchild's life the way she had dominated her son's. *Her* child would never be subjected to the kind of guilt that forever haunted Paul. That was too high a price to pay for love.

* * *

Paul sat at the edge of his chair, drawn close to his father's desk. Morning sunlight poured through the window of the large corner office.

"Dad, I have to know that Betsy will be with you at the house," he said earnestly. "She has no other family in the world. I know she insists that she'll manage on her own—but I'm scared for her."

"Your mother will be terribly upset when she learns you're shipping out," his father warned somberly. "She'll be terrified for your safety. As for Betsy coming to live in our house, you know how she feels about your marriage—"

"Betsy is my wife." A nerve in his eyelid quivered, betraying his anxiety. "She's carrying my baby. Your *grandchild.* Can't Mother understand that I have to know that Betsy's not alone at a time like this?"

"I'll make sure she comes to live with us," his father said finally. "That we're with her when the baby is born. Give me two or three weeks." His eyes were apologetic. "I'll need that time to get through to your mother. Betsy will have your room. The baby will be in your old nursery," he said more strongly. "That I promise you, Paul."

"I'd hoped to bring Betsy to the house while I'm here." Paul's smile was rueful. "But two or three weeks will do."

"Dr. Raymond tells me he speaks with the obstetrician regularly. Dr.—" He frowned, straining to recall the name.

"Dr. Jacoby," Paul told him. "Betsy likes him very much."

"I understand she's fine. No problems anticipated," his father comforted.

"Yeah." *God, he hated the thought of Betsy giving birth without his being there. He ought to be with her.*

"Paul, you can't leave without seeing your mother." His father brought him back to the moment. "I know you want to go to Betsy—but see your mother," he pleaded. "Spend fifteen minutes with her."

Of course he wanted to see his mother before he sailed. God only knew when he'd be home again. *If* he'd be home. Yet he dreaded the confrontation.

"Is she at the house?" Paul hedged.

"At this moment she's probably sitting down to breakfast. We'll go there together—" Mr. Forrest hesitated. "I know you can't say anything, but do you have some idea where you're headed?"

"We don't know," Paul said somberly. "But from the gear we're receiving, it looks like somewhere hot."

"The Pacific?" His father lifted his eyebrows in astonishment. "When you're here on the East Coast?"

"We won't know until we're aboard ship and headed for our destination. All kinds of rumors circulate, but nobody knows."

"All right, let's go to the house. Paul, don't say anything to your mother about Betsy," he ordered. "I'll handle the situation later. She's going to be distraught that you're on alert."

"She'll have to cope, Dad," Paul said gently. Thousands of mothers—and wives—did.

In the taxi en route to the house they talked about the fighting in the Pacific. While the gear being issued his company hinted that Paul might be soon bound in that direction, he was skeptical about this.

"I can't believe we won't be headed for Europe. There's a lot of talk about a second front, but nobody can figure just where that'll be."

Paul felt himself gripped in tension as they walked into the house, the servants delighted at his unexpected arrival.

"Your mother's in the family dining room," Elise told him warmly. "She'll be so pleased you're home."

"Paul?" His mother's surprised voice drifted down the hall toward the foyer: pleasure almost immediately overshadowed by anxiety. Oddly, to his mother *he* was Paul. His father was Paul Jr. if they were present at the same time.

"Yes, Mother," he called, trying for a convivial note. "This is just a quickie."

Wearing one of her elegant black dresses and pearls, she was at the door to welcome him. She was straining to smile, but Paul saw the fear in her eyes. Her face told him she understood the meaning of this unexpected visit.

"How are you, darling?" She held up her face for his kiss.

"Probably more fit than I've ever been," he said with a chuckle. "Army life does that."

"What did you mean about this being a quickie?" she asked with an air of reproach.

"I can stay only long enough for a cup of coffee," he said warily. "I have to—"

"You're going overseas!" A faintly shrill quality in her voice now. "Oh, Paul, why couldn't you have listened to me? You could have had a safe job here or in Washington!"

"Alice, take one of your pills." Paul Jr. gestured to Elise, hovering at the door. "You know what Dr. Raymond told you."

"Why don't we all have a leisurely cup of coffee together before I have to leave?" Paul cajoled.

"When are you leaving? Right away?" Alice Forrest was making an effort to regain her poise. "Tomorrow?"

"We don't know," Paul told her while they settled themselves at the dining table. "Just that it'll be soon—and this is our last time to go home before we ship out." When would he be here again? How long before this damn war was over? Why couldn't he have stayed home another few weeks—to be here with Betsy when the baby was born? It was scary for her to go through that alone.

His father made an effort now to appear optimistic about the Allies' progress in the war.

"We're clearly turning the tide," he said with determined confidence. "For the first time the Allies are on the offensive in the Pacific. The fighting's fierce, but we'll gain control of the Solomon Islands and push right through to Japan. And Allied bombers are making almost daily raids over Nazi-occupied Europe."

"I have a buddy from Columbia who's flying one of those bombers," Paul said quietly.

"You'll write, Paul?" His mother took the pill bottle from Elise, brought to her along with a glass of water. "You know how anxious we'll be."

"I'll write," he promised. "Every chance I get." How often could that be if they were in action?

"I'm giving a lot of time to the Red Cross," Mrs. Forrest told

Paul. "I'll be more active than ever now." She intercepted his furtive glance at his watch. "You didn't mean that about being here just fifteen minutes?"

"Not much longer than that," he said apologetically. He knew she suspected he was rushing off to be with Betsy—though she pretended their marriage didn't exist. "For a while," he lied, "I thought I might not get home at all."

Lingering longer than he intended, trusting Betsy would understand, Paul finally rose to his feet, kissed his mother, embraced his father, and told them he had to leave.

"Stay right here," he ordered them. "I want to go away remembering the two of you here together. I'm going to make it through this war," he said gently. "I've got so much living ahead of me."

Betsy lay in the curve of Paul's arms, both of them conscious of the passing hours.

"It was all right?" he asked again. "The doctor said it was safe to make love this far along?"

"We're just under the wire," she told him.

"This will have to last until I'm home again," he whispered, his mouth brushing her cheekbone.

"It's getting late," she said wistfully. "I'd better dress."

"I don't want you to go to the train with me at this hour," he told her, his eyes seeming to photograph her face. "I want to take with me the image of you here. I want to cling to the image of you, warm and radiant after making love."

"Paul, tell me you won't take unnecessary chances," she pleaded, her eyes searching his. *When would she see him again?*

"Betsy, I may spend the rest of the war miles behind the fighting lines as a supply sergeant or a pencil pusher." He fondled the lush spill of her hair. "But remember, Dad will call you about moving into the family house. Stand by for that."

"Paul, I'll hate it," she whispered. "Why can't I stay here? I can manage." For a little while she wouldn't be working, but there was money in their joint bank account. She'd have her allotment checks.

"Hang on to this place. Come here now and then," he urged.

"But I have to know you're being cared for. And once my mother sees the baby," he said softly, "she'll be in love with it. I have to know you'll both be safe till I come home again." He paused. "Betsy, try to understand my mother. Be compassionate toward her. She's been through so much. She's so fragile."

"I will, Paul," she promised. She'd known she'd have to capitulate—she couldn't let Paul go off worrying about her and the baby. "And when you come home, the baby and I will be there at the house waiting for you." In his own room at the Forrest house, she remembered. The baby in the nursery that once was his.

"Oh, I bought a little present for you." Paul leaned across the bed to reach into the pocket of his jacket, draped across the back of a chair. "I saw this in a jewelry store window in Boston." He drew out a tissue-wrapped parcel and gave it to her.

Lovingly Betsy folded back the tissue, opened the box, and inspected the exquisite brooch that lay against a black velvet bed. A collection of gleaming, tiny garnets set in the form of a rose.

"Oh, Paul, it's beautiful," she whispered.

"I know how you love red roses."

"I'll wear it always." Her eyes were luminous with tears. "Until you can bring me red roses again."

CHAPTER THIRTEEN

A lice Forrest sat at the Chippendale carved mahogany tea table, set before a master bedroom window that looked down on Central Park—austere and gray this morning, her breakfast forgotten because moments ago Elise had brought her the first V-mail from Paul.

Simultaneously joyous at hearing from him and fearful in the knowledge that he was on a fighting front, she reread the tiny writing section of the V-mail, made available last June to speed up correspondence between the armed forces and their families. He could say so little, she fretted—but at least she knew he was all right.

She reached with one fragile hand for the Wedgwood coffee cup, lifted it to her mouth. Why had Paul been so stubborn? He should have allowed them to pull strings, arrange a safe job for him in Washington or right here in the city.

Paul didn't have to be off fighting a war. Georgette's son was smart, she thought with envy—he was in a job with his father down in D.C. Both came home at least one weekend out of a month. She'd never have a moment's peace until Paul was safely home again.

Why did Paul Jr. have to be out of town today? she asked herself impatiently. She wanted so much to share this letter with him. But he'd be home tonight—and he'd be so pleased that they'd heard from Paul.

Once this awful war was over, life would return to normal. Paul would go back to law school. He'd forget that nonsense about being a playwright. He'd realize he'd made a dreadful mistake in marrying that girl. He'd divorce her. She blotted out of her mind the knowledge that Betsy was pregnant.

With a longing to share her thoughts, she left the table to cross to the bedside phone. For a moment she remembered Georgette's dislike of morning interruptions.

"Oh, I just hate when anyone calls me before noon. The morning is my private time, just to relax in bed and plan my day."

But Georgette would understand if she called now. After all, they'd been best friends since their first year at boarding school. She sat at the edge of her oversized canopied bed and reached for the phone.

"Hello—" Georgette Adams' voice revealed her annoyance at this intrusion.

"Georgette, I've just received my first letter from Paul. Just that skimpy little V-mail, but it was so good to hear from him." All at once she was fighting tears. "Paul Jr. says he must have been part of that huge North African invasion—and that the war can't go on much longer with that kind of force in the fighting." But what about the casualties before the war was over? No, she mustn't think like that.

"Darling, I know how awful this is for you," Georgette sympathized. "But you just have to bear up. We're both working so hard for war relief, aren't we? Our afternoon a week at the Red Cross, and that fund-raising committee for families of servicemen. We're doing our share here at home," she said virtuously.

"I wish Paul could say more in his letters." Alice sighed in frustration. "It's so sweet the way he wrote in that tiny little scrawl—so as to get as much as possible in the allotted space. Usually he has this large, sprawling handwriting—"

Georgette murmured sounds of comfort while Alice confided her fears, her conviction that she would never have a decent night's sleep until Paul was home again.

"Alice, you need to get away and unwind," Georgette interrupted solicitously. "We haven't been away from the city in months."

"How can you talk about going away at a time like this?" Alice was affronted.

"You can't change anything by sitting home and upsetting yourself. I don't want to see you have another breakdown. Of course traveling is so difficult these days. Remember how we had to drop our plans to run down to The Greenbrier for a few days last month?"

"I can't believe they're interning German diplomats in that charming place!" Alice churned with fresh indignation. "I think it's outrageous to coddle them that way when American soldiers are living in hovels and tents!"

"The Japanese diplomatic corps is at The Homestead," Georgette reminded. "It makes me ill just to think about it. But, Alice, you do need to get away," she prodded. "It's important for your health."

"It seems so callous for me to be vacationing when Paul's fighting in North Africa—"

"We won't stay long. We'll make sure we're back before Christmas. Maybe we could run down to Sea Island. That's always so lovely. Oh no," Georgette suddenly rejected this. "I'd be scared to death down there. Remember how they closed the Jekyll Island Club last spring after that German sub torpedoed a tanker right in St. Simon's Sound?"

"Perhaps a week or two at Palm Beach," Alice considered to give in. She couldn't bear the thought of all those pre-Christmas parties in town. *When Paul's life was on the line.* "Just maybe—" she said. All at once her heart began to pound. Paul Jr. said that girl—she wouldn't allow herself to think of her as Paul's wife—expected her baby shortly before Christmas. *How did they know it was Paul's child?* "Yes, Georgette—Palm Beach for two weeks—" Alice clutched at this escape. "If we can get reservations somewhere before the Army turns all the resorts into detention camps or barracks or training compounds."

"I'll start calling right away. But we may have trouble getting flight reservations," Georgette warned. "I couldn't survive twenty-four hours on a train."

"Paul Jr. can handle plane reservations." He'd been doing it ever since the war broke out in Europe. Two weeks in Palm Beach would be a blessing—she wouldn't have to listen to his craziness about bringing that girl into the house.

"It'll just be for the two of us," Georgette said. "We won't take a maid along this trip." Normally they shared one between them. "And Doris, of course, is in school."

"What's she doing now?" Alice remembered wistfully how she and Georgette had always thought Paul and Doris would marry one day.

"Darling, I've told you a dozen times. She's going for a master's in social work. At Columbia." Georgette sighed. "I still can't get over her refusing to make her debut at the conventional time. Sometimes I think she's ashamed that we have money. Thank God, Ron has his feet on the ground. He won't let her squander away her inheritance when Carl and I are gone."

"We'll go to Palm Beach." Dr. Raymond kept telling her she must learn to relax. It was easy for him to say. "Georgette, I know I'm going to have to bring that girl into the house. That common little fortune-hunter." Her voice broke.

"I told you before, Alice," Georgette repeated. "Threaten to disinherit Paul—I'll bet she'll leave the baby and take off for good."

"I couldn't do that to Paul," Alice reproached with shock. "You should know that. He's my whole world."

"We'll go down to Palm Beach for two or three weeks. You'll feel better. Let Paul Jr. cope with his daughter-in-law."

Betsy ordered herself not to be tense as she dressed for her dinner with Mr. Forrest. *This was Paul's father.* Still it was unnerving to realize she'd never even met him. He'd told her to ask for "Mr. Forrest's table" at the smart French restaurant he'd chosen for their meeting.

She understood the reason for this dinner. They were to schedule her moving to the house. It was what Paul wanted, she told herself. How did Paul's mother feel about this? Was it going to be an awful experience? How could it not be?

"I don't know what I'm supposed to call Paul's parents," she said nervously to Emily while she ran a brush over her hair and inspected her image in the mirror above the dresser.

"Rheba calls my folks Mom and Dad," Emily told her.

"They're total strangers to me," Betsy protested. "And I don't think they'd like me to call them by their first names."

"Avoid calling them anything for now." Emily smiled sympathetically. "Play it by ear."

Betsy glanced at her watch.

"I'd better run. Thank God he chose an early hour—there won't be many people in the restaurant. I feel like a small blimp now."

"A fashionable blimp," Emily flipped. The cape Betsy had bought at Klein's basement was a terrific markdown from Saks. "But treat yourself to a taxi," she urged. "You don't want to arrive windblown and breathless. And that cape isn't really warm enough on a bitchy cold day like this."

Settled in a taxi, Betsy focused on the imminent meeting. Once she would have been fascinated at the prospect of living in an elegant Fifth Avenue townhouse. Now she was intimidated.

At the small but charming restaurant she was shown to their table. Mr. Forrest had not arrived yet. She was relieved at this brief respite. Moments later an expensively suited man somewhere in his mid-fifties was being led to the table. Her heart began to pound. Instantly she knew this was Paul's father. How much the two men resembled each other!

"You're Betsy," he said casually, taking a seat across from her. "I'm Paul's father."

"You and he look so much alike," she said. "For a moment I was startled."

"So many people say that." He smiled, but his eyes were somber. He, too, was worried that Paul was in the fighting zone. "How are you feeling?"

"Fine. Except for wishing that Paul was here." Her eyes were wistful.

"Shall we order?" He reached for the menu. "Then we'll be free to talk."

Betsy soon understood—with shaky gratitude—that Paul's father was willing to accept her. He was regretful that their family was small.

"I have a married sister—childless—who lives in Dallas. I see her occasionally when I'm on business in Texas. Paul's mother had an older brother who died at fourteen." He hesitated. "Sometimes it may seem that my wife is difficult. Please understand—she's extremely high-strung. She'd desperately wanted children. She went through four miscarriages before Paul was born. He became her whole life. We'll have to be patient with her at times."

"Of course," Betsy agreed. She'd been touched by what Paul had told her about the eleven-year-old so desperate for love. How could any mother have behaved as Paul's grandmother had? Yet instinct told her it wasn't going to be easy to live in the same house with her mother-in-law.

It was arranged that Betsy would move into the Forrests' townhouse on Sunday. William, the family's longtime chauffeur, would come to her apartment with the limousine to move her belongings. And Mr. Forrest insisted it was time for her to stop working.

"You have your government allotment check," he said, seeming self-conscious at introducing the subject of money. "I imagine that'll care for your incidental expenses."

"Yes. Of course," she assured him.

She didn't tell her father-in-law that she would continue to keep Paul's apartment. It would be there for the day he came home, she'd promised herself and Paul. Emily was handling the rent on the studio. It had to be there for Emily when Paul came home. *"Nobody gives up an apartment these days,"* Emily had pointed out emphatically.

Later, she'd explain that she wasn't really working when she went into the shop to help Mark with the last touches on Felicia Goulart's apartment. Working meant selling in the shop. Mark had already hired somebody to replace her in that capacity. But there was no way she would abandon her tenuous hold on a decorating career. If things went well—and Mark and she were determined to be successful as decorators—that meant security for Paul and the baby and herself while Paul sat down to complete his first play.

On Sunday Betsy waited with apprehension for William to arrive at the apartment. A small, compact man close to sixty, he arrived on schedule, carried her luggage to the car, and helped her into the backseat. Betsy remembered Paul's saying that their domestic staff had been with the family "forever."

"Mr. and Mrs. Forrest are at church," William explained as he settled himself behind the wheel. Betsy was suddenly self-conscious about the difference in faith between her family and Paul's. It might not matter to Paul. It would to his parents. "They usually go out for lunch after church services. Elise will serve your lunch on a tray in the library."

"Thank you, William."

She was relieved that the Forrests would be away when she arrived at the house. For a little longer she could stave off the encounter with Paul's mother. Emily had offered to help her with the move, but she suspected it would be easier if she arrived alone. Emily would be with Mark and Eric today—they were going to a movie and then would have dinner at Mark and Eric's apartment.

"I checked with the movie schedule," Emily had told her. "We'll be at the apartment by six-forty. If you can get away, come to dinner with us."

At the house Elise, who had been with the family since Paul was a baby, showed her to Paul's third-floor room. A tiny elevator had long ago been installed.

"Anything you want, Miss Betsy, just tell me," Elise urged, her eyes brightly sentimental. "Mr. Paul's room was not planned for the needs of a young lady."

"It's lovely," Betsy said, glancing about at the fine antiques and subconsciously identifying them as Chippendale. The rug was an exquisite Aubusson. How different from Paul's off-campus apartment, furnished with discards from the family beach house!

It was difficult to envision Paul living in this formal bedroom, the drapes, the bed covering, the upholstered chairs beautifully coordinated. She gazed at the marble-faced fireplace and thought of the precious days with Paul in Sag Harbor.

Paul had slept in this room—in that bed—since he was old enough to be moved from the nursery. She remembered his telling her how as a small boy he'd stood at those windows to watch squirrels dart about the trees in Central Park. Oh yes, she would feel close to him here.

"Mrs. Forrest has kept Mr. Paul's private phone. The number's right there. And the bathroom is off through that door." Elise pointed to the left. "The other door leads to what used to be Mr. Paul's nursery. He was such a sweet child." Her eyes were bright with sudden tears. "I light a candle for him every week."

"Thank you, Elise," she said softly.

"I'll serve your lunch in the library in about an hour. Will that be all right?"

"Perfect." Betsy managed a smile. Elise would be a friend in this house, she thought, and was grateful. Instinct told her she would need friends here in the days ahead.

Alone in her room, she sat at the edge of the bed. One hand subconsciously stroked the smoky-blue comforter. Tonight she would sleep in the bed where Paul had slept. She would listen for a while to his bedside radio. For a poignant moment she felt his presence in the room. Living here in the house where he had grown up, she thought in a rush of prescience, she would learn to know him as never before.

She had always realized, of course, that Paul came from this kind of background. Their small group had known the Paul who lived in a sixty-dollar-a-month apartment near Columbia, who was addicted to beat-up clothes, scuffed loafers. The only hint of wealth had been the Packard he had inherited from his mother— but even Doug had inherited his family's old car, and Doug's parents were middle-class New Yorkers who'd scrimped to send their children to Ivy League schools.

Her eyes moved to the door that led to what had been the nursery. Her heart all at once pounding, she left the bed and walked to the door, then reached for the knob. Again, she felt Paul was close to her.

Her eyes widened in astonishment as she gazed inside the adjoining room. Nothing had changed in the years since Paul was a baby. His mother had kept it as a shrine, she thought. The realization made her uneasy. A pair of white, fuzzy rugs lay on the floor. A canopied crib was pushed against one wall, a youth bed on another. A double dresser, a toy chest, a rocker, an antique cradle were scattered about the room.

She turned eagerly to inspect the collection of framed photographs that hung above the dresser. Enveloped in tenderness— tears stinging her eyes—she gazed at the myriad snapshots of Paul. As a beguiling infant, a toddler, at his sixth birthday party. Ice-skating in his early teens. And now Paul's child would sleep in this room, play with the toys she knew instinctively remained in the toy chest.

She sat in the rocker, her hands folded over what Emily called "Junior Mountain," her eyes closed, feeling Paul's presence, yearning to reach out and touch him, to feel his arms about her. Not once had she admitted to anyone—not even to Paul or Emily—her increasing anxiety over the baby's delivery. *Nothing must happen to her.* She must be here to raise their child.

She remained there, oblivious to the passage of time, until Elise arrived to say a tray was ready to be served to her in the library.

After a pleasant lunch she went upstairs to her room. William had said the Forrests usually went out to lunch after church services. To the Colony, she recalled Paul's saying. There was no knowing when they would be home.

She was exhausted from the strain of the day. Uncomfortable in advanced pregnancy. Take a nap, she ordered herself. She tired easily these days.

She discovered Elise had unpacked for her. She tried to brush aside her embarrassment that Elise knew the limitations of her wardrobe. But Mom's brass candlesticks and her beloved crystal vase occupied a choice position on the mantel atop the marble-faced fireplace. Elise had admired them, Betsy surmised. She felt a touch of comfort at their presence in her bedroom. In moments she was dozing.

She awoke to the sound of a knock on her door.

"Yes?" She rose from the bed with her late-pregnancy awkwardness and crossed to the door.

"We thought you might like to join us for tea." Mr. Forrest stood there with a cautious smile. "I'm sorry we weren't here to welcome you on your arrival. Alice is tradition-bound. We always go out for a leisurely luncheon after church services."

"Paul told me." She managed a wisp of a smile. Here it came. The encounter she'd been dreading so long. "Yes, I'd like very much to have tea with you."

"If there's anything you need—" She read compassion in his eyes. He suspected her discomfort at living in this house with his wife hostile toward her. "Anything at all," he stressed, "just ask Elise. She's been with the family forever. She used to help Paul's mother spoil him rotten."

"Elise has been very sweet," Betsy said haltingly as she walked beside him down the carpeted hall to the elevator.

Her hair beautifully coiffed, her dress a deceptively simple black crepe that Betsy knew cost a small fortune, Alice Forrest sat at one end of a needlepoint-covered sofa before a Sheraton table set with a magnificent silver tea service and three Wedgwood cups and saucers.

"How do you take your tea?" Mrs. Forrest asked with no preliminaries. Her voice was polite, her eyes opaque.

"Plain, please," Betsy told her.

Immediately she understood the relationship her mother-in-law would accept. She was a slight acquaintance, foisted on them by some emergency. Breeding demanded politeness. She could expect nothing more.

CHAPTER FOURTEEN

Betsy quickly learned the household routine. Mr. Forrest was out of the house before eight A.M., returned around seven. His wife rarely emerged from the master bedroom suite until close to noon. William would drive Mrs. Forrest off to luncheon with friends or to a wartime benefit luncheon.

"Can't you imagine where she lunches?" Emily said with candid envy when Betsy mentioned this to her. "The Colony, '21,' Le Pavillon."

Alice Forrest's afternoons, Betsy learned from Elise, were devoted to volunteer work or shopping. She returned to the house in late afternoon to rest until dinner. Three or four nights a week the elder Forrests went out to small dinner parties or to charity affairs. But since Paul enlisted, they themselves did no entertaining.

Betsy came downstairs around nine, when she could have breakfast in solitude. On her first morning in the house she had insisted there was no need for Elise to bring a breakfast tray up to her bedroom. After breakfast she returned to her room to write to Paul, always striving to sound cheerful. She wrote daily V-mails, in hopes that they would reassure Paul of her well-being, as well as one long airmail each week.

Immediately after lunch each day she joined Mark at the shop to work out the last details for Felicia Goulart's drawing room. She was due in town in two weeks. They vowed that everything—

down to the last detail—would be ready. Their jobbers had agreed to work over the weekend to make sure all the curtains and drapes could be hung in time.

"If Felicia likes it, we're made," Mark told Betsy while they relaxed over cups of Earl Grey in the small area at the back that he considered the staff's lounge. "She'll probably throw some war relief bash to show off the new look." He grinned complacently. "And we'll be there to take the bows."

Mark wasn't happy with the girl he'd hired to replace Betsy in the shop.

"We have to make do," he conceded. "It's tough to get good help these days. Remember, we operate on two levels. We have a shop where we sell—and we have our interior decorating service. Donna just sells—and I'm breaking my back to show her how to handle herself. But you and I are a team—even if you're wearing small tents now," he teased. "You've become a decorator. Sometimes you amaze me. We can walk into a flea market or a roomful of junk—and you'll find something wonderful before I see it."

"I'll always be here for the decorating," she promised. "That's as important to me as breathing."

"You're great with our jobbers," he told her. "They all love you because you know what we want—and you don't make impossible demands. You understand we're in the midst of a war. A lot of decorators are throwing hysterics these days."

"That doesn't accomplish anything," she said with a laugh.

"Do you think you'd be up to having dinner with me and the Carsons tomorrow night?" he asked. "They're buying an apartment for her mother. We might just wangle the whole decorating deal. That's what we're after," he reminded. "Residential decorating. Let Dorothy Draper do the Carlyle and the Hampshire House and the Essex House. We want private houses. And Mrs. Carson was quite impressed with your ideas for their guest room." This was a recently completed project that Betsy had handled almost on her own.

"Dinner will be great," she said. Another night when she wouldn't be sitting down to dinner with her in-laws. It was childish, she scolded herself, but she dreaded that. Thus far since moving into the Forrest house, she'd had dinner each night with Emily. "But I'll have to run home and dress," reminded Mark. Since she wasn't on the selling floor now, she usually wore slacks and what Mark called her tents.

"Leave early tomorrow, take a cab back around six. On the expense account," he said. "We'll throw ideas around for a while. Oh, Mrs. Carson was so impressed when you told her you tried to design a room that's not only charming and reflects the taste of the occupant but that is also comfortable."

"That I learned from you," Betsy pointed out. "Where are we having dinner?"

"At '21,' " he told her. "They're paying."

The evening with the Carsons proved productive, though initially Betsy felt ill-at-ease in the main dining room at "21." The rough plastered walls with their decorative wooden plaques, the wainscotting, the red-and-white checkered tablecloths were not intimidating, but the knowledge of the wealth of those around her was. That plus the awareness of the designer frocks worn by the other women diners. Names such as Mainbocher—who'd fled Paris to open a shop last year on East 57th Street, Schiaparelli, Sophie of Saks Fifth Avenue flashed across her mind.

Gradually she relaxed, caught up in the excitement of selling the Carsons on the ideas she and Mark had formulated. Mark presented sketches. She described the color schemes with an enthusiasm that was contagious. Before the evening was over, she and Mark had the assignment confirmed. It was a heady triumph for them.

"You'll come back to the shop after the baby's born, won't you?" Mark asked as he drove her home. "I *need* you."

"After the first few weeks," she promised. "I'd die of boredom staying home." Paul agreed with this—he knew how important decorating was to her. And the baby wouldn't be short-changed. She would make sure of that. "Mr. Forrest told me Paul's mother insists on hiring a nanny. I don't intend to hand over the baby's care totally to anybody," she said defensively, "but I want to be involved with the shop." It ever amazed her how so much of her thinking went into the business. It helped her, she realized gratefully, not to dwell on her inner fears.

"We'll work it out," he said in high spirits, "though I doubt we'll need to set up a crib in the back room of the shop."

On Saturday Betsy and Emily went shopping for a layette.

"You've waited long enough," Emily said when they completed this task and were relaxing in a neighborhood coffee shop. "I was afraid the poor little kid would come home without even any diapers."

"I feel as though I've been pregnant forever," Betsy confessed. "These last weeks are the longest."

"I know it's awhile yet, but remember, Betsy. The minute you go into labor, call me. Even if it's during working hours, I'll manage to get away."

"Dr. Jacoby says anytime the baby decides to come, it's okay." She patted her stomach tenderly. "*I'm* ready, but he's not announcing yet."

"Are you scared?" Emily's eyes were solicitous.

"A little," Betsy admitted. "But mostly I'm full of wonder. I only wish Paul were here to hold my hand. You and Mark will have to stand in for him."

"I was supposed to bring in more loot today, but I forgot. Mom's finished another sweater and two more caps."

"The way she's knitting and crocheting I should be having triplets." Betsy chuckled, glanced at the coffee shop clock. "What time did you tell the guys to come up to the apartment?"

"I said around six—or right after Mark closes the shop," Emily told her. They were meeting at Paul's apartment for dinner. "The guys are bringing dessert and white wine."

"I'm glad Paul insisted I keep the apartment," Betsy confided. "It's a wonderful escape hatch."

"That's a hoot! You can run from that gorgeous townhouse on Fifth Avenue to a sixty-dollar-a-month apartment and call it a wonderful escape hatch!" But Emily's smile was understanding.

Emily and Betsy were involved in preparing the main course—

Country Captain chicken, via a recipe Eric's mother had brought back from a visit to a cousin in Georgia—when Mark and Eric arrived.

"If I fall asleep, wake me for dinner," Eric ordered, collapsing on the sofa. "I've been on another of my eight days of twelve-hour shifts."

"We'll wake you," Emily promised. "When I spend this much time on making dinner, you eat."

"Have you heard from Doug lately?" Mark asked, putting the bottle of wine in the refrigerator.

"Not for almost a month,". Betsy acknowledged. "The last we heard he was groaning about the prospect of having Spam for Thanksgiving dinner. All we know is that he's somewhere in England—and flying a lot of missions." He was probably too busy to write, she told herself. But at intervals she was anxious.

"London's probably far behind him," Emily guessed. "Unless the Air Force provides weekend passes now and then. Doug liked London."

"He wasn't happy with everything he saw," Betsy reminded. "It bothered him that money could buy so much more protection from the German bombs. The rich—who live in hotels like the Dorchester—go down into their basements, where neatly madeup cots with guests' names attached wait for them. Expensive West End restaurants have all-night shelters in case a raid begins in the middle of dinner. But over in the East End, Doug says, thousands crowd into unventilated, unsanitary shelters."

"You don't read about that in the newspapers," Mark pointed out. "They make it sound all 'stiff-upper-lip' and patriotic."

"Doug wrote that many of the Underground stations have become pestholes. He said they stink of sweat, urine, and carbolic acid. And fleas and lice are having a ball down there."

"Doug's always been a great worrier about the poor and helpless," Emily reminded. "Like Paul."

Betsy started at the sound of the phone. No one ever called her here, since Paul went overseas, except Emily. Almost warily she hurried from the tiny kitchen to pick up the receiver.

"Hello."

"Betsy, may I talk to Emily?" It was Emily's mother, seeming elated.

"Of course, Mrs. Meyers." Betsy called to Emily. "It's your mother."

Emily emerged from the kitchen with an air of anxiety and hurried to the phone.

"Hi, Mom—"

Betsy returned to the kitchen to transfer the Country Captain into the oven.

"How long before it's ready?" Mark asked.

"Twenty-five minutes. I'll start the salad now."

"Oh, Mom, that's wonderful!" Emily's voice was joyous. "I told you it would turn out this way!"

Instantly the other three were alert, stopping all activity to eavesdrop.

"Bert's okay!" Emily bubbled. "He was wounded, but he's being flown to a military hospital. Rheba just received word. He's not critical, but he'll have a long convalescence."

"And by then," Betsy said prayerfully, "the war may be over."

For a little while there was an almost festive air in the apartment. Then talk became more somber, though there was a new sense of optimism about the progress of the war. Fifty ships and 400,000 troops had arrived in North Africa under the command of General Eisenhower. In Stalingrad Russian troops had trapped Nazi forces inside the city, and other German soldiers sent to break the siege were being thrown into retreat. In the Pacific, American soldiers were fighting bloody battles meant to lead them to Tokyo.

For a while this evening hope soared in the small apartment near the Columbia campus, though, in truth, much bitter fighting lay ahead.

Betsy suspected that Paul's parents were relieved that she was away from the house from Friday evenings to Sunday evenings. She explained that she was staying with her "best friend" at a West Side apartment. They asked no questions—she volunteered no further information.

"If the baby decides it's time to arrive, you'll notify us, Betsy?" her father-in-law had asked solicitously.

"Of course," she'd promised. He was so looking forward to this first grandchild, she thought, and was touched.

She was startled when she learned through Elise that Mrs. Forrest would be leaving very shortly for two weeks in Palm Beach.

"She's been worrying so much about Mr. Paul." Elise was defensive now. "Mrs. Adams persuaded her to go down there to rest up."

On the morning of Alice Forrest's departure her husband remained at the house to see her off. He was at the breakfast table, sipping coffee and concerned about the time, when Betsy came downstairs. He truly loved his wife, Betsy thought compassionately, despite all the torment she put him through. Somehow the knowledge made her feel closer to her father-in-law.

"I hope you're not upset that Alice is going to be away for two weeks." He seemed apologetic about this. *What difference would it make to her if his wife were here?* "I'll be at the house every night, of course. And Elise and William and Peggy. You won't be alone," he emphasized self-consciously.

"I know." Betsy managed a smile. She hardly expected her mother-in-law to rush with her to the hospital when she went into labor. They barely saw each other.

When Elise arrived with Betsy's breakfast, Mr. Forrest instructed her to go up to his wife's room and remind her they must leave within twenty minutes.

"Traffic to the airport will be heavy at this hour. If Alice and Georgette miss their flight, I won't be able to get them on another plane," he told Betsy.

Now he excused himself to make a business call. He drove himself so hard, she thought. Not that family finances required this—he was always trying to prove himself to his wife, she suspected. And perhaps it was a subconscious escape into a world he could control.

Betsy felt an odd sense of relief when Mrs. Forrest was hurried out of the house into the waiting limousine after only a perfunctory farewell between them. Some of the pressure of being there seemed to evaporate.

In a sudden rush of loneliness, knowing that any day now the baby would come, Betsy went up to the nursery. Here she felt so close to Paul. His childhood photographs seeming to speak to her.

She ran a hand along the railing of the crib—polished to a golden sheen in readiness for its new resident. She walked to the dresser, opened the drawers that contained the modest layette she had bought, along with the dainty sacques, caps, and booties that Emily's mother and grandmother had lovingly crocheted and knitted.

Where was Paul now? He could say so little in his letters. Careful though he was, she still encountered censorship. Chunks were cut out of his long airmail letters. She'd surmised he was still in North Africa when he talked humorously about a heavy black market in sheets.

The newspapers reported light casualties, but that was meager consolation. Any casualties were too many. She suspected, too, that reports were meant to bolster morale here at home. How many more men must die before the world was at peace again?

CHAPTER FIFTEEN

Betsy was tired and uncomfortable this late in her pregnancy. Each day seemed to drag endlessly. At Mr. Forrest's urging she had William drive her to the shop in the late afternoons now, and called for him to drive her home again. She was always mindful that William usually headed for Wall Street sometime between six P.M. and seven P.M. to bring Mr. Forrest home, and adjusted her hours accordingly.

Three evenings in a row she sat down to dinner with her father-in-law. She knew that he, too, was ever anxious about Paul's welfare. This was a growing bond between them.

With his wife away he seemed less formal. On the third evening he talked about his own family.

"My sister, Beverly—there were just the two of us—lives out in Dallas now. She and her husband have no children. I'm glad my parents lived to see Paul grow up. He was very precious to them. They died when he was sixteen—within three months of each other."

"Paul talked to me about them," Betsy remembered. "He told me about the fun he had on summer trips to their house."

"Out at Greenport—on the Island." He grew nostalgic. "We didn't see as much of them as I would have liked. My father ran a small grocery store and my mother helped out. They were very independent," he said with pride. So he had not always lived with wealth, Betsy realized in surprise. "And now Beverly's husband—

he's a pharmacist—owns a drugstore in Dallas, and she helps out."

"Your parents must have been proud of your success in business," Betsy said with a fresh vision of her father-in-law, a highly respected investment banker.

"Never stopped bragging." He chuckled in recall. "They struggled to put me through Harvard. That's where I met Alice. I was a senior—she was a sophomore at Radcliffe. She was a beautiful girl. Vivacious and charming."

"She's still a lovely woman," Betsy said. She would have been, Betsy mentally amended, except for that air of perpetual anxiety. Involuntarily she thought of Alice Forrest's bitter childhood. Aunt Celia would have said, "Be compassionate, Betsy."

"It's always bothered Alice that I didn't go on to Harvard Law like her father and grandfather."

"I don't know what Jimmy will be when he grows up," Betsy said softly, remembering Paul's tug-of-war with his mother, "but that'll be his decision to make. Jimmy—or Jenny," she added with a tender smile.

Mr. Forrest appeared startled.

"I thought Paul said that if the baby is a boy, he'd be James Paul Forrest the Fourth."

"Oh, he will be," Betsy said, reassuring him. "But we'll call him Jimmy. That'll make life a lot less complicated." Just as she was "Miss Betsy" to the domestic staff so as to differentiate her from Mrs. Forrest Jr. Only she and Paul would understand that the "Jimmy"—or "Jenny"—was in memory of her father.

Mr. Forrest glanced up in inquiry as Elise hovered in the doorway.

"I'm sorry to disturb you at dinner, sir," she apologized, "but there's a Mr. Campbell calling from Albany. He insists it's urgent."

"Thank you, Elise. I'll take it in the library."

Ten minutes later Mr. Forrest returned to the dining room. Elise was serving dessert.

"That was a call from a major client," he apologized to Betsy as he returned to his place at the table. "I'm afraid I'm going to have to go up to Albany first thing in the morning. He's up in arms about a new bill before the State Assembly. I may have to remain up there for a couple of days." His eyes were troubled. "I don't like leaving you—"

"I'll be all right," Betsy said quickly.

"If—if anything happens," he said, seeming uncomfortable in discussing her imminent delivery, "you're to call William immediately. He'll drive you to the hospital. Have Elise pack for you."

"Please don't worry about me." Betsy tried to be casual. "My friend Emily is standing by. All I have to do is phone and she'll be right here."

Betsy considered inviting Emily to stay at the house with her while both Forrests were away. Or she could stay with Emily. No, she discarded these possibilities. Paul wanted her to be here. She would stay. And Paul's father would be away just for a night or two. Why fuss about it? It wasn't as though she was alone—and Emily was five minutes away by taxi.

The following morning Betsy made a point of being downstairs for an early breakfast with her father-in-law. It would help put his mind at rest, she told herself. She knew he was upset about being away for a night or two when she was so close to delivering.

She wanted so desperately to feel part of Paul's family. She had no real family of her own now. She was ever envious of Emily's family. Emily had her parents, her brother, her grandmother—and aunts and uncles only a few hours away. It must be such a warm, loving feeling to be surrounded by family.

Mr. Forrest was touched and pleased when he found her at the breakfast table.

"Did you come down early to see me off?" he asked, his smile almost shy.

"I thought it would be nice." All at once Betsy was self-conscious.

"Paul used to do that when he was a kid—when he knew I had to run off on one of my business trips." He loved Paul very much, Betsy thought. "He always wanted to know where I was going and when I'd be back. Sometimes I feel I didn't spend enough time with him in those precious growing-up years." Her father-in-law sighed. "They go so fast."

"Paul used to talk about the times you took him fishing out at Sag Harbor." She didn't mention that Paul had taken her to the same cottage they had rented on those occasions. "He loved those trips."

"I'd gone there as a child myself," Mr. Forrest told her. "I grew up in Greenport. It's just two ferries and a quick drive across Shelter Island from Greenport to Sag Harbor. I took him to Sag Harbor," he recalled with an air of nostalgia, "when we wanted a change from the Southampton house. Greenport was a longer haul." Betsy sensed that in his mind he had moved away from the elegant Fifth Avenue townhouse to the modest home he'd shared with his parents in an earlier-day Greenport. He glanced at his watch. "I've got about another fifteen minutes. Then I have to head for Penn Station. With a little luck I might get a seat on the train."

Every train was jammed with passengers these days, Betsy remembered. She hoped he'd be able to get a seat.

Today Betsy decided not to go into the shop. The weather was raw and blustery. Ominous clouds were gathering together in the sky. Snow by midafternoon, she guessed. She phoned Mark and talked with him about the Carson assignment. The Felicia Goulart apartment in the Waldorf Towers was ready to be shown. Betsy and Mark were eager for her to return from Rio.

By noon snow began to fall in huge flakes, sticking to the ground. Within an hour the view of Central Park from her bedroom window was a Christmas card by Currier and Ives. She stood by the window, remembering how Paul had stood here as a child and watched the squirrels scampering about the trees below and the snow forming a white blanket over the earth. *Where was Paul now?*

She dropped a hand protectively about the huge mound that was their child. Her face lighted at a kick from within. Oh, this was an active one! Paul kept saying it didn't matter to him if she carried a son or a daughter. *"Just let it be healthy."* She surmised that, secretly, Paul's father was hoping for a grandson.

Tiring, she left the window to sit in the slipper chair beside another window. Later, she promised herself, she'd ask Elise to start a fire in the fireplace grate. And immediately her mind traveled back through time to that precious little while in the Sag Harbor cottage with Paul.

At Elise's summons she went downstairs for the lunch Peggy had prepared for her. She and Emily had planned on meeting for an early dinner at a small, inexpensive restaurant they'd discovered a few blocks east. But this was hardly the night for that.

After lunch she settled herself in the library and tried to read. Emily had loaned her a copy of *See Here, Private Hargrove*. *"Guaranteed to make you laugh, Betsy."*

A little after five Emily called from the office.

"I'll phone you later from the house," she promised. "The weather's so lousy I'll rush straight home. This is no night for us to be meeting for dinner."

Feeling restless, Betsy asked Elise to bring her an early dinner on a tray in the library.

"Maybe you'd like it up in your room," Elise suggested. "I'll bring up some wood for the fireplace. It'll be real cheery on a night like this."

"Thank you, Elise." She smiled gratefully. She would have dinner, listen to the radio or read until Emily called. And very early tonight she would climb into Paul's bed and write to him. A book of stamps was always there in her night table drawer.

By the time Elise arrived with her dinner tray, the chunks of wood in the fireplace had developed into a healthy blaze. Settled in the lounge chair before the fireplace, she watched the muted glow of color that crept into the room, enjoying the warmth, the crackling sounds from the grate.

"Elise, will you please turn off the lamps?" she said on impulse. "The firelight is so beautiful."

"Just as soon as I bring over a little table for your tray," Elise said. "And let me see you clean off your plate," she ordered affectionately, "or Peggy's gonna be hurt."

Long after she had eaten and Elise had taken away the tray, Betsy lingered before the fireplace. Only when she began to write to Paul did she turn on a lamp. The fire would smolder far into the night. She felt as though she were cut off from the rest of the world. The house was so quiet. There were few traffic sounds from below in deference to the weather.

When Emily called, they talked until she was attacked by a series of yawns. Betsy had refrained from mentioning that Mr. Forrest was out of town. Emily would worry.

"Honey, go to sleep," Emily ordered. "I'll talk to you tomorrow."

Betsy reread the long airmail letter she'd written to Paul, slid the fragile pages, filled with love and determined cheerfulness, into an envelope. Sleepily she prepared for bed, slid beneath the smoky-blue down comforter, and tried to find a comfortable position—an impossible task this late in her pregnancy.

The firelight was subdued now, the wood in the grate reduced to chunks of gray-edged charcoal, the embers beneath a glowing, jewel-like vermilion. In moments she was asleep.

She came awake with a startling suddenness, a feeling of falling through space. It seemed hours later, but a glance at the clock on her night table told her it wasn't quite midnight. Then she was conscious of a dampness beneath her—and she was jolted into total wakefulness.

She pulled herself to the edge of the bed, switched on a lamp. The bottom sheet and her nightgown were damp. She remembered what the doctor had said about the water "breaking." If that occurred before she went into labor, she was to go to the hospital. He was to be called. *"If that should happen, you're open to infection. I want you in the hospital."*

In a little while she'd call for William to drive her to the hospital, she promised herself. At the hospital a nurse would call Dr. Jacoby. She mustn't phone Emily yet, she decided. It would be awful to try to get across town in the middle of the night by bus, and Emily would never find a taxi in this weather.

She crossed to the window, her heart pounding now. She wasn't having contractions yet, but they were sure to start soon. Within the next few hours the precious infant within her would move into the world.

Exhilaration blended with fear in her. Why couldn't Paul be here with her? She wanted to hold his hand, to have him beside her as their child pushed its way into the world. Was it going to be awful, the way some women insisted? Would the baby be all right?

All at once she was transfixed. She felt a tightening in her stomach. *That was it.* Her first labor pain. Where was the clock? She was supposed to time the contractions. But they'd be far apart this early. Everybody said a first baby took its time in arriving.

She'd dress, then call William to drive her to the hospital—only minutes away from the house. But while she reached into the closet for a dress, she froze in a pain that was sharper than anything she'd ever experienced in her life. She stood still, clutching at a nearby chair, straining not to cry out.

The contractions were coming close together already. Get into clothes before the next one, she ordered herself. Fretting at her clumsiness and bracing herself for the next contraction, she dressed. She waited through the next contraction, aware of perspiration beading her forehead, trickling between her breasts.

Trembling, feeling an urgency to reach the hospital, she rang for William, then went to the closet to bring out her small valise—packed days ago—and her cape. She pulled the cape about her, fumbled in a dresser drawer for a kerchief for her hair. Then, with a surge of poignant sentimentality, she reached into the tiny velvet box that held the brooch Paul had brought to her that last night they were together before he sailed for North Africa.

For a moment she held the garnet rose in one hand while her mind swept back to those last hours together. Paul could not be with her now—but his heart was with her. And she would take the symbol of his love with her. Then she was caught up in another wrenching contraction, building to a crescendo that wiped her mind clear of everything except pain for its duration.

Her eyes swung to the clock. The contractions were less than five minutes apart now. *Where was William?*

CHAPTER SIXTEEN

Betsy rang again for William, waited in growing anxiety for him to appear. But she mustn't be so impatient, she reproached herself. He had to dress, to come down from his room at the top of the house. She'd give him her letter to Paul to mail tomorrow. *By the time Paul received it, he would be a father.*

Why was William taking so long? Then all at once she understood. He had gone to his parents' home in Queens this evening. The family was celebrating their wedding anniversary. He'd drunk a lot of wine and had come home to fall into a heavy sleep. He hadn't been awakened by the bell.

Fighting panic, she moved toward the phone. Call Mark. He'd come to the house and drive her to the hospital. With shaking fingers she dialed his number and prayed he'd respond. Mark always said he was a light sleeper.

"Hello—" Mark's voice, befogged by sleep.

"Mark, it's me—"

He was immediately awake. "Are you in labor?"

"Yes," she whispered. "And I can't wake William. I have to get to the hospital."

"I'll be there in minutes. The snow's stopped," he took time out to reassure her. "I won't have any trouble getting the car out. Can you wait for me in the foyer?"

"I'll be right by the door."

Clutching her valise, Betsy made her way down the night-darkened hall to the elevator, descended to the main floor. She paused for yet another contraction. Then, fighting against panic, she walked to the foyer. Later, she thought hazily, she'd call Emily. Or Mark would call her.

Betsy waited in the foyer. Each moment seemed endless. At intervals she pulled the door ajar to see if Mark's car was approaching. Fifth Avenue was blanketed with snow, the street deserted. Only a taxi moved slowly in the night. An eerie quiet hung about the city.

She remembered how Mark hated New York winters—but she'd known, of course, he'd come out for her. She grimaced as another contraction gripped her. *Where was Mark?*

A strangled sigh of relief escaped her when she saw the car approaching. Mark pulled to a crunching stop at the curb, emerged, and strode across the sidewalk to the house. She hurried awkwardly out into the raw night air and closed the door behind her.

"So you've finally got this show on the road." Mark was striving for lightness, but she saw the anxiety in his eyes. "How're you doing?"

"This kid is impatient." She tried to laugh. "Why do people always say a first baby is slow in arriving?" All at once she paused and reached for Mark's arm. "Ooh, that was a bad one."

"We'll be at the hospital in minutes," he promised. "Nobody's out on the street tonight except the guys on the snowplows. You're going to be okay."

In record time they were at the hospital entrance. With Mark hovering beside her, she was rushed in a wheelchair to the maternity floor. The nurses assumed Mark was her husband. When they'd changed her into a hospital gown, Mark was allowed to go to her in the labor room.

The contractions came one on top of another. She was vaguely conscious of Mark's anguish as she was swept up in a kind of pain she had never dreamed existed. Mark reached for her hand, and in a corner of her mind she was aware that he winced as she clenched at his hand with towering intensity.

Dr. Jacoby arrived. Mark was sent out of the room. Now Dr.

Jacoby summoned a nurse. Betsy was to be taken to the delivery room. She was conscious of a rush of activity, of being wheeled down the hall. In the brief minutes between contractions she tried to listen to what the doctors and nurses were saying to her. So many people fussing about, she thought fretfully. She cried out with each new contraction. She was aware of a compassionate intern stroking her hair in sympathy.

Then she was enveloped in merciful oblivion. She came awake slowly, conscious that she was in a small room now. Her hand moved involuntarily to her stomach. *She was flat.*

"Would you like to see your son, Mrs. Forrest?" a smiling nurse asked from the doorway. A tiny bundle in her arms.

"Oh, my God—" An exquisite blend of happiness and awe welled in her. There would never be another moment like this in her entire life. That was her child in the nurse's arms. Hers and Paul's.

The nurse gently placed the bundle in her arms. Her eyes searched the tiny face. Paul's features, she thought while tears blurred her vision. But she'd seen enough to know—he looked exactly like his father.

"Did you ever see so much hair on a newborn?" The nurse chuckled at the mass of dark hair that surrounded his face.

"Jimmy," Betsy whispered. "That's his name. James Paul Forrest the Fourth." She marveled at the tiny hands flailing free of the blanket, reached to hold one in her own. "He's all right?" she asked tremulously. "Everything as it should be?"

"Ten fingers, ten toes, all the standard equipment," the nurse reassured, as Betsy suspected she had done thousands of times before.

Betsy noticed the first streaks of dawn in the sky when she was finally wheeled into the private room reserved for her. Paul's father had insisted on this small luxury. Moments later Mark came in with a wide smile.

"I saw him," he told Betsy and bent to kiss her cheek. "The image of his old man. Even at this age."

"I wish Paul could know," she said with a sigh. "He wanted so much to be here with me."

"I don't think a cable would reach him." Mark's smile was humorous but compassionate. "You need to rest. I'll see you later. You did a great job."

She drifted off to sleep, to awake to see Emily seated beside her bed.

"You look terrific," Emily told her, "but the real star in this family right now is out there in the nursery. Betsy, he is gorgeous!"

"And he was in such a rush to greet the world." Betsy's smile was wan.

"It's over, honey," Emily said. "And he was worth it."

"What time is it?" she asked in sudden alarm. Her head still fuzzy.

"Almost eight—A.M., that is."

"When did Mark call you?"

"About six. He said he couldn't wait another moment. I rushed right over."

"Emily, phone the house for me," Betsy said in sudden urgency. "They don't know I'm here. I couldn't wake William last night." But, of course, Mark must have told her that. "Mr. Forrest is out of town, but the servants must think I'm asleep in my room."

"It was a hell of a time for him to be out of town," Emily flared. "Why didn't you call me? I would have stayed with you—or you could have stayed with me."

"It worked out all right," Betsy soothed. "Just call the house for me."

"Okay, I'll phone, then dash to the office. I'll be back after work. Now lie back and gloat. The baby is just beautiful."

In his Albany hotel room Paul Jr. finished the breakfast sent up by room service and reached for the telephone. First he'd call home to check on the New York household, he told himself. Then he'd phone Alice down in Palm Beach. After one more meeting and an early lunch he'd take a train back to New York. Everything had gone well, he thought with satisfaction as he asked the switch-board operator to put through his New York call.

Still, he'd felt guilty at being away from the city overnight when Betsy was so far along in her pregnancy—though she didn't expect to deliver for another ten days or two weeks. But Paul would be upset if he knew Betsy was alone in the house with only the servants there, he reproached himself.

William's voice interrupted his introspection. "Good morning—Forrest residence."

"I'm calling to pick up any messages that might have been left for me, William," Paul Jr. said briskly. "And when you've given me whatever messages you have, I'd like to talk to Miss Betsy." He glanced at his watch. She was always downstairs by this time.

"Mr. Forrest, she's in the hospital," William said with an odd air of self-consciousness. "She gave birth early this morning. It was a boy, sir. They're both doing well."

"That's wonderful news!" He felt a simultaneous rush of joy and relief. "Never mind the messages for now—I'll call back later."

Off the phone, he sat motionless, digesting the news William had given him. His son was a father. He was a grandfather. He felt awed and humbled—and joyous. He remembered the anguish when—four times—he and Alice waited so eagerly for the arrival of their first child, only to be disappointed. But that pain had not been inflicted on Paul and Betsy. God had been good to them.

He reached for the phone again. He couldn't wait to tell Alice that she was a grandmother. Despite her ambivalence about Paul's marriage, her pretended disinterest in Betsy's pregnancy, she would love Paul's child.

Moments later he heard Alice's voice on the other end of the phone line. Suddenly he was anxious. Was he being optimistic about her reception of the news? Would what he was about to tell her throw her into a bad emotional reaction?

"Yes?" Alice's slightly impatient voice came to him after her initial "Hello," which had brought no immediate response.

"Alice, wonderful news!" he said. "Betsy gave birth this morning. It's a boy. We have a grandson!" For a moment only silence greeted his announcement. "Alice?" he asked anxiously. "Did you hear me?"

"A boy?" Her voice was a barely audible whisper. "Oh, I can't wait to see him!" All at once she seemed electrified by happiness. "Paul, get me a return reservation immediately! My grandson," she said reverently. "Our son's child."

Betsy drifted in and out of slumber. At last she emerged into full wakefulness, to find Mark and Emily seated close by. A vase of red roses sat on the nightstand beside her. It was early evening, Betsy realized with a start.

"Oh, so you've decided to join the party?" Emily said. "We've just had a great visit with your son. The best-looking kid in the nursery."

"The roses are from Paul," Mark explained with a smile. "A long time ago he gave me instructions. *If I'm not around when the baby's born, you bring Betsy a dozen of the longest-stemmed red roses you can find.*"

"Oh, Mark, how sweet." Tears stung her eyes. How like Paul to do that.

"Eric will be over later, when he's off from work. He's bringing a camera."

"To take pictures of the baby?" Betsy's face was luminescent. "Oh, that's great!"

"Is the grandfather back in town yet?" Emily's voice was slightly acerbic.

"I don't know. He left me the phone number of his hotel—I suppose I should call him—" Betsy hesitated.

"He'll probably check with the house," Mark said. "One of the servants will give him the news."

She was relieved that her mother-in-law was out of town. Instinctively she knew she and Paul's mother would clash on endless decisions about the baby's upbringing. With Mrs. Forrest away she felt a precious sense of independence—though this, of course, would be short-lived.

But she would have to cope with Mrs. Forrest for only a little while, she consoled herself. When this awful war was finally over and Paul was home again, they'd move out of that house into their own apartment. They'd live a life that was not dictated by Paul's mother.

She glanced up in surprise when a smiling nurse brought in a beautiful bouquet of baby orchids.

"Oh, aren't they lovely!" Emily bubbled while Betsy reached for the card.

"They're from Paul's father," Betsy said. The card simply read: "From the proud grandfather." She was touched. Paul's father would truly love the baby. How she wished that her own parents were here—and Aunt Celia.

Moments later Eric walked into the room with an ebullient smile.

"I've been at the nursery already," he crowed after dropping a kiss on Betsy's cheek. "I've got two rolls of film to be developed."

"Oh, Eric, thanks!" Betsy glowed. "I can't wait to see them! I'll send them to Paul—he'll be so excited."

"What did he weigh?" Eric asked.

"Seven pounds seven ounces. He was one of the bigger babies of the night."

"He gave you a really rough time," Emily said. "But like I said before, he was worth it. My mother and grandmother will be over tomorrow. Now all I'll hear from Mom is, 'When will you get married and make me a grandmother?' " Emily sighed exaggerat- edly. She'd been hearing this for months. "Mom said if you want a *briss,* she'll make the arrangements for you. It would be easier if you had it here in the hospital. Of course that means you'll stay an extra day or two."

"I don't think Mrs. Forrest would appreciate a *briss* at the house," Betsy said humorously. "I thought I might have to ask Dr. Jacoby to circumcise Jimmy. I mean to raise him Jewish." Her face mirrored her determination. "Paul agreed. But if there could be a *briss*—" Her smile was radiant.

"Leave it to Mom," Emily said. "She'll handle everything."

Moments after Emily, Mark, and Eric left—with the warning bell for visitors having sounded—Paul's father arrived.

"Your flowers are beautiful," Betsy told him while he stood self-consciously by her bed. "Thank you."

"I've been standing out there at the nursery window for the last twenty minutes," he confessed. "I can't get over the miracle of birth. The baby is the image of Paul. I still remember—all those years ago—when I stood outside the nursery while a nurse held him up for me to see. After Alice's four miscarriages we finally had a son."

"I'm glad you did." Were those tears in his eyes?

"And now there's a fourth James Paul Forrest to face the world," he said with pride. "Thank you, Betsy."

"You'll love him?" she asked, still needing this reassurance.

"Alice and I will both love him," he told her. "When I called and told her the news this morning, she was so excited. She insisted on returning on the earliest available plane. Before she left for Palm Beach, she arranged for the nanny." He chuckled. "She gave the agency a dreadful time. She interviewed seven women before she approved of Miss Watkins."

"I mean to spend a lot of time with him," Betsy said, though she did plan to go back to the shop in two or three months. She wouldn't just turn her baby over into the hands of a nanny.

"Of course you will," he said. "As Alice did with Paul. She never sent Paul off to boarding school, as most of her friends did. He never went off to camp in the summers—he was with us at the Southampton house. When we traveled to Europe, Paul always went with us."

"I doubt that we'll be going to Europe for a long time. I suspect when Paul comes home from the war, he won't want to leave this country again for years."

Betsy was grateful for the private room the Forrest money had provided. She waited eagerly for the times when the baby was brought to her for his bottles. Those were precious moments— when she held him in her arms and he sucked at the nipple with such gusto.

On the following afternoon Emily's mother and grandmother made the trek from Brooklyn. Emily arrived while they were there. Mr. Forrest phoned earlier to ask about the baby and herself and to explain he was caught up in a meeting at the office that would keep him there until past visiting hours.

Her father-in-law seemed disappointed at not being able to see the baby tonight, Betsy thought, and remembered his poignant confession that he had not seen as much of Paul in his growing-up years as he would have liked. That was not going to happen with Paul and their son, she promised herself.

Much of the next day she steeled herself for the arrival of Alice Forrest. She reminded herself that Paul's mother had come to accept her presence in his life. There was no real reason for her to dread this meeting.

As planned, Emily stopped by for a quick, early visit so that Betsy would be alone when her in-laws arrived.

"Stop fretting," Emily exhorted, understanding Betsy's nervousness this evening. "You won't be living forever with Paul's mother. You can cope with her for a little while. So she'll fuss and fret over the baby—the way she did with Paul—but you're his mother. You'll make the decisions."

"I wonder how long it'll be before Paul knows about the baby?" Betsy asked wistfully.

"V-mail is fast," Emily reminded. "And then he'll get the snapshots Eric took. Wow, will that be a terrific moment for him!"

As her father-in-law had promised, he arrived with Alice at eight P.M. sharp. Betsy was startled by the tears she saw in her mother-in-law's eyes.

"He's wonderful." Alice's voice was hushed. She'd offered no preliminary greeting. But Betsy understood this was not meant as an affront. "He's the image of Paul. It was like turning the calendar back twenty-three years. It was the most wonderful moment in my life when I first held Paul in my arms."

"Yes," Betsy agreed softly. They were two women, linked together by the joys of motherhood.

"I gather from Dr. Raymond that Betsy had a rough time," Paul Jr. told his wife.

"Oh, but it was worth it." Again, Betsy saw tears well in her mother-in-law's eyes. "Wasn't it, Betsy?"

"Yes." This was the first time Alice Forrest had ever called her by her given name, Betsy realized. At last she felt truly accepted by Paul's mother.

"First thing tomorrow morning I'll go to Saks to buy his christening gown. I'll—"

"Paul and I agreed that he wouldn't be baptized," Betsy interrupted tensely. She saw her mother-in-law grow pale. "He's to be raised in my faith."

"I don't believe Paul would agree to that!" The room suddenly reeked of hostility. "My son wouldn't do that to me!"

"He's not doing anything to you, Mrs. Forrest." For the first time she called her mother-in-law by name, awkward though it was. "He's allowing the baby to be raised in his mother's faith. It's a tradition in—"

"He'll never be able to go to heaven!" Mrs. Forrest shrieked. "How can you do that to your child?" She turned to her husband. "Paul, make her understand! Tell her."

"Alice, this is something between Paul and Betsy," he said stiffly.

"I won't allow it!" Mrs. Forrest was trembling.

"Alice, you'll take one of your pills," Mr. Forrest ordered. He reached for the pitcher of water on the night table and one of several unused paper cups. "Get the bottle out of your purse."

"I won't stand for this, Paul!" Mrs. Forrest was fumbling with the catch of her purse. "It's unthinkable!"

Would she have to leave the Forrest house? Betsy asked herself. *How would she manage?* Her alarm grew as she watched Alice Forrest being coaxed into a chair by her husband. Once she was seated he stood over her, telling her to swallow the pill he'd put in her hand.

"You're going to be all right, Alice—" He spoke to her as though to a small child. "Just take your pill."

She would manage, Betsy vowed. She would handle the situation the way Mark had said when he first knew she was pregnant. He was dying to have her back at the shop. Maybe not right away, but in a month she could go back to work. Mark said she could set up a crib in the little storage room. She'd take a cab each way with the baby. *She would manage.*

CHAPTER SEVENTEEN

On the morning of the eighth day of Jimmy's life Betsy geared herself for his *briss*. He was so young to feel pain, she thought tenderly. Circumcision, she knew, was a rabbinic tradition that dated back to the time before Abraham. In the modern world it was widespread, having been approved by medical science.

Emily and her mother were both taking the day off from work to be here. According to tradition she herself would not be present when the *mohel* performed the very minor surgery. Mrs. Miller had assured her Jimmy would be just vaguely conscious of "the little snip."

"The *mohel* will give him a few drops of wine," Mrs. Miller had comforted, "and he'll be a little drunk."

In a flurry of excitement Emily and her mother arrived. Betsy was introduced to the rabbi who would offer the prayers and to the *mohel* who would perform the circumcision.

Betsy waited fretfully while Jimmy was taken off for the ceremony in a room close by. A faint moan of protest escaped her when she heard his reproachful cry. And then he was brought to her to cuddle and offer words of comfort. It was official, she thought with exhilaration. James Paul Forrest IV had been welcomed into his faith. He was a Jew.

That night Betsy slept little. The ceremony had reinforced her alarm about Mrs. Forrest's reaction to her statement that Jimmy was to be raised as a Jew. But what could Mrs. Forrest do? Paul had agreed, she reminded herself for the hundredth time.

She was just dozing off the following morning, after giving Jimmy his ten o'clock bottle, when her phone rang.

"Hello—" She tried to clear her head. She assumed the caller was either Emily or Mark.

"Betsy, I understand you're scheduled to be discharged from the hospital tomorrow morning." Mr. Forrest sounded unfamiliarly formal. *Was he calling to tell her she was no longer welcome in his house?*

"That's right." She fought for calm.

"I'll tell William to drive over to bring you home," he said. Betsy closed her eyes in a surge of relief. "And Miss Watkins—the nanny—will come along to help you. Alice isn't feeling well—she may not be up to coming over herself. But I'm sure Miss Watkins and William will see the two of you safely home."

"Thank you," she said softly. Would she have ever suspected that she'd be grateful to be going to the Forrest home? But she wasn't alone now—she had the baby's welfare to consider. "If possible, it would be good to have them here around eleven."

"I'll tell them. Eleven sharp." He hesitated, cleared his throat in that manner she'd come to recognize as a nervous gesture. "Alice and I won't be home for dinner tomorrow night. There's some Red Cross benefit. But I should think it would be better for you to have your meals served in your room for a few days. Until you've recovered your strength."

"Would it be all right if I have a friend over to the house tomorrow evening? My best friend, Emily—" She was conscious of an inner defiance, though she was polite in making the request.

"Betsy, of course. It's your home, too. Have your friend come for dinner," he encouraged.

"Thank you. I will."

Off the phone, she was startled to discover she was trembling. How much happier she would be if she were returning to the little apartment near Columbia! But it would be much better for the baby to be at the Forrest house. She wouldn't be terrified that the money would run out. She'd know that she and Jimmy would be secure while Paul was away.

Later in the day she attended a class for new mothers. They were given instructions about preparing formula and bathing the baby as well as hints about routine care. Most of the new mothers were involved in what was being told them. Only one—a sulky post-debutante, disliked by all the nurses—looked bored. She'd probably never touch her baby, Betsy surmised, except to show him off to friends. And all at once she felt self-conscious about being met by the Forrest chauffeur and the new nanny.

On sight Betsy liked Miss Watkins. She was a small, round woman with light-brown hair and warm brown eyes. Her white uniform was immaculate and perfectly starched. She radiated an air of friendliness. Betsy felt relieved that her mother-in-law had made this choice.

"He's a little love," Miss Watkins crooned, cradling Jimmy in her arms while a nurse pushed the wheelchair in which Betsy sat toward the elevator—in the hospital's tradition. "It's going to be hard not to spoil this one."

There was something special about a maternity floor, Betsy thought as they waited for the elevator, her small valise settled across her lap. It was such a happy floor. She and Paul had been blessed, she told herself with gratitude.

William hurried from behind the wheel of the limousine at their appearance and came forward with a sheepish smile. He was anxious about not having responded to her buzz the night she'd gone into the hospital, she realized. He understood what had occurred. She sought immediately to put his mind at rest.

"I hope it wasn't too much of a shock to discover I wasn't at home that morning Jimmy was born," she said, repeating the cover-up she and Mark had contrived earlier. "I was on a late-evening phone call with my friend when I realized the time had come to go to the hospital. He drove right over to the house to pick me up. There was no need to wake you up at that hour."

"That was most considerate, Miss Betsy," William said with

obvious relief. "And that's a fine-looking little fellow you're bringing home."

At the Forrest townhouse Alice was hovering about the foyer in her eagerness to welcome her grandson. Her outburst at the hospital was mercifully behind her, Betsy realized with relief.

"Are you sure he's warm enough?" she asked Miss Watkins. "It's such a raw day."

"He's fine, Mrs. Forrest. Just sleeping away." Miss Watkins pulled back the blanket from Jimmy's face.

"My precious little doll," Alice crooned. "Did he lose much weight in the hospital?" she turned to Betsy. "Of course they say all newborns lose a few ounces by the time they come home."

"Not Jimmy." Betsy laughed tenderly. "He gained three ounces. One of the night-shift nurses told me he was always hungry, so she'd slip him an extra bottle."

Alice frowned as she leaned over her new grandson. "Are you sure that was all right?"

"He gained weight and was checked out by Dr. Mitty as being in perfect health," Miss Watkins reported. "I spoke with her this morning as she asked me to do." Now she turned to Betsy. "Why don't we get Jimmy settled in the nursery and you in your room? Then you should have yourself some lunch. With all the excitement of leaving this morning I'll bet you didn't have a bite of breakfast."

"I had coffee," Betsy said, "but as you said, I was too excited for breakfast."

"I'll tell Elise to bring you up a tray," Alice said quickly. "Then I'll come up to the nursery to see my little precious."

At Miss Watkins' coaxing Betsy settled herself at the small table by the window, with the view of Central Park that Paul used to talk about, and waited for her luncheon tray to arrive. She was deliberate in allowing her mother-in-law some time alone with Jimmy in the adjoining nursery, sensing that Alice would relish this.

How long would it be before Paul knew he was a father? she asked herself for the dozenth time. How long before he received those first snapshots? She'd write Paul a long letter this afternoon, she promised herself. She wished with poignant longing that he could be here to stand with her beside Jimmy's crib. But until Paul could be home again, she must be mother and father to Jimmy.

As her father-in-law had suggested, she'd invited Emily to have dinner with her that night. Emily was eager to see the beautiful townhouse, after hearing detailed descriptions about various rooms. And why shouldn't she entertain her friends here? Betsy asked herself, faintly defiant. They were Paul's friends, too.

She had just given Jimmy his six P.M. bottle and deposited him, already half-asleep, in his crib when Elise brought Emily up to the nursery. She was alone with Jimmy—Miss Watkins had gone downstairs for her dinner.

"How's my number one boyfriend?" Emily asked exuberantly.

"Practically asleep after his bottle. Isn't he beautiful?"

The three women stood beside the crib and gazed at the tiny form oblivious to their presence.

"Mr. Paul wasn't much older than him when I came here," Elise said, her eyes alight with nostalgia. "And was he the spoiled one," she crooned. "His mother and I had many a fight with the nannies because we wanted to pick him up every time he cried." Elise turned now to Betsy. "Mrs. Forrest had lost four before him, you know." Her eyes made a silent plea for sympathy for her employer.

Betsy and Emily were served dinner on a small table set before a cozy blaze in the bedroom fireplace. Emily was candid about being impressed by the house. She loved the Aubusson rugs, the fine antiques, the beautiful paintings, the aura of luxurious living that permeated the atmosphere.

"Hey, I could get used to this kind of life real fast," she said.

"I've been kind of cut off from the news," Betsy said. "I didn't have a radio in the hospital. What's been happening?" Emily understood she referred to the war.

"Nobody seems to know what's really going on in the Pacific." Emily's voice was somber now.

"North Africa," Betsy pinned down. Paul was there. "What's happening there?"

"The Americans and the British are still fighting to drive out the

Germans. It's hot and dusty and dull, Mark surmises—but the Allies *are* driving the Germans back."

"It's so frustrating that they can't say much in their letters. But at least I know where Paul is."

"I can't believe it's just a little more than a year since Pearl Harbor." Emily sighed. "It seems like an eternity. It's been over a year since Doug enlisted."

"Have you heard from him again?" The last letter had arrived just before Thanksgiving.

"Nothing," Emily told her. "Do you think we should call his mother? He gave us her phone number before he shipped out," she reminded Betsy. "Maybe she's heard from him."

"Not yet," Betsy hedged. "He's probably flying a million missions over Germany now. No time to write." She was afraid for them to call Doug's mother. Right now, she thought, she couldn't cope with terrible news.

"I am so tired of living in a manless world." Emily sighed. "Life's so bloody dull."

"You ought to get involved with another theater group," Betsy said encouragingly.

"They don't exist," Emily said flatly.

"Then take classes," Betsy urged. "With your raise that just came through, you can afford it." Emily was good. She had an instinct for what worked onstage, Betsy felt. Her few performances with the group had proved that. She had a God-given talent that couldn't be acquired in any class, but she lacked confidence.

"I don't think I could take classes in the middle of the war," Emily admitted after a moment. "I know. Life goes on here at home. Two of the girls from the group work three days a week and make show-biz rounds the other two. I hear from them now and then. But I'd feel guilty. If Mom wouldn't carry on so, I'd probably join the WACs now that the baby's born. But after what she went through when Bert was missing in action, I couldn't do that to her."

"I wrote a long letter to Doug while I was in the hospital. I wanted him to know about the baby." Betsy smiled in tender recall. "I remember how gentle he was with the babies and the dogs we'd meet on Riverside Drive when we'd walk there on Sunday mornings. Before all this craziness—"

"It makes me so furious the way people are making fortunes because of the war! All the damn black-marketeering. I'll bet," Emily said softly, "you'll never see a shortage of coffee or sugar or meat in this house. I'll bet the Forrests never worry about running short of gas."

"Oh, Emily," Betsy protested.

"Come on, Betsy," Emily scoffed. "The rich don't expect the rules to apply to them."

"Their sons go to fight." Betsy was somber. "They—die." But she didn't want to think about that.

"A lot of them pull strings. Didn't Paul say his mother wanted him in a desk job here or in Washington? If he'd gone along with her, it would have happened." She frowned in thought. "Okay. Not just the rich want to stay out of the fighting. Mom tried to get Bert and Rheba to push up their wedding so he might not be drafted."

"If Hitler had been stopped earlier, Paul wouldn't be in North Africa. Doug wouldn't be flying missions over Germany. Bert wouldn't have been wounded at Midway. But with all that, people here at home are living in comfort—"

"Overlooking having to settle for one cup of coffee a day and with sugar as precious as gold," Emily broke in with an effort at humor. "Mom bitches about having to stand in line for so many things, and Dad complains about how so many small businesses are going under—though anybody who wants to work can find a job with good pay. Mom worries about how so many kids are dropping out of high school to go out and pick up fat paychecks."

"But everybody in this country is comfortable," Betsy said, her temper briefly flaring. "They're not dodging bullets or bombs. Remember all the hysteria last summer when those English-speaking Nazi spies turned up out on Long Island—and those in Florida?"

"A few people got upset." Emily shrugged. "Those jerks were caught right away."

"We eat decently," Betsy pushed ahead. "We go to the movies.

We go to bed at night without worrying about enemy bombers flying overhead."

"Of course the Army keeps telling us New York can be bombed," Emily reminded her.

"It won't happen," Betsy insisted. "We're safe when every other nation in the war is suffering so badly."

"You talk like Dad," Emily said. "He keeps quoting that article—in *Time*, I think—where some writer talks about how America is getting suddenly rich—everywhere, all at once."

"Paul says he can't wait for the war to be over and to be home again. Not here," Betsy emphasized. "The three of us in our own little apartment. But we'll be together, and Paul will be writing." She closed her eyes in sudden pain. "Sometimes I'm so scared for him."

"You know how my Dad hates the war—" Emily squinted in thought, seeming to search for words. "But he says this is a war that has to be fought. He said this even before the last Murrow broadcast." That had been a broadcast that shocked the civilized world.

"I think I'll remember that broadcast till the day I die," Betsy whispered. She tried not to miss any Murrow broadcast from London. "The whole world knows how the Nazis hate the Jews—but to resort to mass murder! When Murrow talked about the Warsaw ghetto, it's hard to believe we live in the twentieth century."

They sat in silence, each reliving the horror of the Murrow revelation of what had been happening for months in Nazi-occupied Warsaw. Starting last July, thousands of Jews were rounded up each day: men, women, children, babies. Some were murdered in their homes, others taken to the Jewish cemetery to be murdered, still others thrown into freight cars to be sent to camps that were slaughterhouses. In Poland the Jews were being exterminated.

Betsy tried to settle in to this new existence. Her life revolved around Jimmy. She tried to tell herself that her mother-in-law meant well in her constant fussing over him. She was sure Miss Watkins must be annoyed by the flow of anxieties expressed by Mrs. Forrest, though Jimmy's nanny showed commendable patience.

Betsy was ever conscious that it was Mrs. Forrest who was, in truth, Miss Watkins' employer. Still, she had chosen Miss Watkins over all the other candidates—she knew she had a prize in Jimmy's nanny. Alice's friend—Georgette Adams—was forever telling her that.

On those evenings when Alice and Paul Jr. were going out to dinner engagements, Paul's father made a point of dropping by her room to talk for a few minutes. Then they'd visit the nursery together.

He loved his grandson deeply, Betsy told herself. She was pleased. The whole household knew how Alice Forrest doted on her grandson, Betsy thought. But she wished that her mother-in-law wouldn't fuss the way she did. Was the nursery warm enough? Was it too hot? Did Jimmy look pale? Did he look flushed? Miss Watkins showed amazing patience, Betsy thought in gratitude— but she herself was uneasy in the tense atmosphere that Alice created.

She didn't want Jimmy ever to feel the tension that his grand-mother radiated, Betsy told herself. Let them be out of this house before he was old enough to feel that.

CHAPTER EIGHTEEN

Paul forgot the sharp chill of the desert night—in such contrast to the burning heat of the day—as he walked from the tent where a cluster of fellow soldiers were singing with gusto the Afrika Korps' marching song, "Lili Marlene." He was conscious only of Betsy's letter, its message etched on his brain. A kind of joy he'd never known warmed his body. James Paul Forrest IV—his son—had arrived in the world.

"Hey, how's the new daddy holding up?" a jovial fellow soldier called out.

"I'm hanging on," Paul told him.

"My kid's seventeen months old today," the other soldier said, a kind of hunger on his face that Paul understood. "He took his first steps on my last leave. Hell, I hope we get home before he starts to shave!"

Paul walked off into the darkness. Needing solitude. Thank God the war had not physically touched the world in which Betsy and Jimmy lived. He ached to hold his son in his arms. He felt a strange humility in knowing Betsy and he had created this child. *He had to get through this war for Jimmy and Betsy.*

He was grateful that their fighting thus far was mainly in the desert, away from innocent civilians who were helpless prey to death. And yet he sensed that he had grown into sudden maturity at his first encounter with the horrors of war.

He had felt so sick when he'd held a dying child in his arms and was unable to do more than utter words of comfort. He'd felt rage when he heard men from his company boast about taking "thirty Germans but coming back with no prisoners." He loathed the looting, the black-market dealings that were rampant.

When all this was over and he was home again, he would dedicate the rest of his life to writing plays that made the world understand another generation must never go into battle. He'd been in North Africa only months, but he felt a hundred years older.

Christmas and New Year's were quiet times in the Forrest household this year because Paul was overseas. Betsy devised a routine that kept her out of Alice's presence as much as possible. She knew her mother-in-law was still upset that she meant to raise Jimmy in her own faith. But Paul had agreed to this, she told herself repeatedly—he *understood.*

Before Alice left the house on her usual luncheon routine, she came into the nursery to fuss over Jimmy. When she returned in the afternoon, she went immediately to the nursery to see him. In the course of the evening she and Paul Jr. spent time with him. Betsy diplomatically remained out of the nursery at those times.

Now Alice shopped almost daily at Saks for Jimmy. Stuffed animals filled the nursery. Miss Watkins laughingly complained that she was running out of drawer space for the clothes that Alice bought for Jimmy.

"That's one young man who'll never lack for anything," she told Betsy as she showed off Jimmy's latest acquisition.

Early in January—with no announcement to her in-laws—Betsy returned to the shop on a part-time basis. She wasn't depriving Jimmy of attention, she told herself. Most of the time she was away he was asleep. And Miss Watkins was wonderful with him. He wasn't missing his mother's attention, she reiterated to herself in silence—all the while fighting guilt.

She wasn't dealing with selling on the shop floor now. She worked with Mark on the few decorating assignments that came in. Felicia had returned from Rio and was delighted with the new look at her Waldorf Towers apartment. They were waiting impatiently for the benefit cocktail party she promised to give for her favorite wartime charity, which would be a great showcase for them.

"I don't know whether to pray for more assignments or to be relieved that they're so slow in coming in," Mark confessed on a cold evening when they stayed late to go over the books. "It's harder by the minute to get fine fabrics. The prices on antiques— when we can latch on to them—are going sky high."

"But our clients aren't concerned with price," Betsy reminded. "Just thank God interior decorators aren't affected by the War Production Board rulings." The clothing industry was constantly being hit by new regulations.

Mark grinned.

"We're too low on the totem pole for that. But God, I wish we could do something about the dyes that are coming through."

"No bold, dramatic colors for now." Oddly Betsy wasn't overly disturbed by this. It was a challenge to create with delicate, dusky shades. "We can survive that."

Betsy devoured the newspapers and magazines that came into the Forrest house. She listened anxiously to news broadcasts. In mid-January Americans were hopeful when President Roosevelt went to Casablanca for a conference with Churchill and other Allied leaders and—at Roosevelt's insistence—it was agreed they would demand unconditional surrender from the Axis nations. The discussion of this generated an overly optimistic conviction among many Americans that victory was close at hand. Yet from Paul's letters Betsy sensed he didn't share this optimism. Still, he always tried to sound cheerful.

"Betsy, you'd love it here," he wrote. *"You'd be fascinated by the colors all around us—they're so strong they're almost violent. The Arabs in these parts have a proverb: 'The five senses of man are refreshed by pomegranates, silks, color, perfume, and women.' "*

In his next letter he wrote, *"There's something sensuous about the flowers everywhere. Yesterday I bought an armful of red roses from a vendor at the roadside and pretended I was going to lay them at your feet."*

Paul urged her to go to the theater and to tell him about the plays she saw. It was clear the war had not lessened his ambitions. Broadway was booming these days, she wrote him. She described the plays that she and Emily saw—always from the cheapest seats.

"God, I'd love to be rich," Emily sighed on a late January night as they climbed up to the second balcony for a performance of Chekhov's *The Three Sisters,* with Katharine Cornell, Judith Anderson, and Ruth Gordon. "Not ever to have to look at price tags. Take it for granted we'd have the best seats in the theater."

"The rich have their problems, too." Betsy remembered her mother-in-law's miserable childhood, which still governed her life. All the riches in the world couldn't make up for her hurt.

"They have silken problems," Emily derided. "Money cushions everything. Look, you're married to Paul—you'll never have to worry about money."

"Emily, that's not true," Betsy flared. "Paul and I don't intend to live off his parents. It's *important* to him to be independent."

"I'd marry Frankenstein if he was rich," Emily said flatly. "I went through high school with two blouses, two sweaters, and three skirts—two for winter, one for summer." It was a familiar complaint.

"We all did," Betsy protested.

"Not the rich," Emily said.

"Don't marry Frankenstein," Betsy ordered, chuckling. "Make yourself a successful career in the theater."

"The big money, of course, is in the movies." Emily squinted in thought. "But that's not for me. That's what Colleen's after. She wants a house in Bel Air and a Rolls-Royce in her garage. I just want to be a stage actress. For me it's the grand illusion."

"When are you going to do something about it?" Betsy probed.

"After the war," Emily said after a moment. "Who can think about anything else now?"

The following month the U.S. II Corps were beaten back at the Kasserine Pass in Tunisia by Afrika Korps tanks, with heavy casualties. Fighting with grim determination, American forces recaptured the pass five days later. To keep a toehold in Africa, Hitler ordered more troops and tanks into Tunisia.

Betsy clung to the radio, absorbing news reports with a mixture of terror and hope. Each morning she prayed there'd be a letter from Paul. Each night before she went to bed she reread his last letters. With her letters put away she went in to kiss her son goodnight. He was such a sweet, loving baby. How long before he would see his father?

Betsy and Mark tried to conceal their impatience with Felicia Goulart. She insisted she adored what they'd done with the Waldorf Towers apartment, but she stalled on setting up the promised benefit. Then late in February Felicia phoned the shop. Mark was out trying to speed up a supplier on a delivery.

"Tell him to come over to the apartment the instant you hear from him," Felicia ordered ebulliently. "Something's come up."

"I'll tell him," Betsy promised.

She waited impatiently for Mark to return. She was convinced Felicia was about to arrange the benefit. The publicity would be marvelous for them.

"Shall I phone her?" Mark hesitated when Betsy had blurted out the latest from Felicia.

"She said come right over. Go now," Betsy prodded. Normally she left about this time. But Mark—and she—were reluctant to leave Donna alone to deal with customers. "I'll wait till you get back."

"Keep your fingers crossed." He grinned. "We are about to enter a new dimension."

Twenty minutes later Mark was sitting with Felicia on the American Chippendale sofa he'd discovered in a house in Sag Harbor and had painstakingly restored and reupholstered. He was struggling not to betray his astonishment at her proposal that he go to Rio de Janeiro to redo her mansion there. All twenty-eight rooms!

"But, Felicia," he sputtered, his mind in chaos, "I'm not allowed to leave the country. I'm 4-F because of a heart murmur," he said, lying about the nature of his 4-F status, though he knew Felicia would not be fazed by the truth, "but I'm subject to call-up at any time." It was just a technicality—he was convinced he'd never be called up. Still, it had to be considered.

"I can take care of that," Felicia said grandly. "Brazil is a member of the Allies. Our ships keep the sealanes open along the south Atlantic. You will receive permission to go to Rio for three months."

"But how will we acquire furniture and fabrics down there?" Knowing Felicia's contacts, he suspected there'd be clearance from his draft board. But how could he leave the shop for three months?

"I have connections, Mark. Whatever you require, you will have." Now she mentioned the fee she was prepared to pay, and he felt a surge of excitement. "I will—how do I say it?" She squinted in thought. "I will pull strings."

Mark listened in a haze of disbelief while Felicia outlined her plans.

"You will be regarded as a member of the Brazilian Diplomatic Corps," she said with a laugh. "The United States wishes to keep Brazil happy—there's talk already about Brazil sending troops to fight in the war. No other South American country even considers this," she said with pride. "My new house will be important for entertaining on behalf of the government," she continued. "Everything must be in the grand style, yet—as Betsy always says—it must be comfortable and charming."

"I don't understand a word of Portuguese," he pointed out.

"Take your friend Eric along as interpreter," she told him. "He will be useful to you in decorating, also. So artistic." Felicia had met Eric twice at her parties. He recalled now how pleased she'd been to discover Eric's grandmother had been born and raised in Lisbon. From her Eric had learned Portuguese. "His Portuguese is close enough to ours for him to interpret for you."

"You can arrange for his draft board to release him, too?" Oh, God, Eric would go out of his mind to visit Brazil! But what about the shop? he asked again with mounting anxiety.

"It will take time," she conceded. "As long as a month, perhaps—but my government will make the arrangements with the State Department in this country. You will fly to Miami, from there to Trinidad, and on to Rio with just one stop in between. It'll be three fourteen-hour flight days from Miami. You'll have military priority," she promised.

"I'll have to think about it, Felicia," he said apologetically. The whole deal was mind-boggling, he thought. The money, the publicity that would accompany the assignment! Felicia would surely snare a layout of her newly decorated Rio mansion in *Vogue* or *Town & Country*—or both!

"And remember," Felicia said with a devious smile, "the climate is reversed in Brazil. It'll be glorious summer down there." She knew how Mark loathed winter.

To satisfy her feeling of guilt that she was not at home at the normal time, Betsy phoned Miss Watkins to check on Jimmy. She remembered Alice's shock at realizing just last week that she was at the shop again—though on a part-time basis. She wasn't depriving Jimmy. Her father-in-law understood. Paul understood.

"He's sleeping like an angel," Miss Watkins reported. "Oh, his grandmother bought the tiniest little baseball jacket you ever saw." She chuckled warmly. "Jimmy will be able to wear it when he's two. She said she bought it because she knew it'd please his grandfather."

"I'll be home in time to give him his next bottle," Betsy promised. She relished those times when she held Jimmy in her arms while he sucked noisily—almost greedily—at his bottle. She made a point, now that he was allowed cereal, to feed him his tiny portion of pablum each morning.

She left the phone to take over a particularly difficult customer—known for her efforts to chop down prices. The woman wore a mink coat and designer dresses, but she behaved as though The Sanctuary were some shop on Orchard Street.

"Thank you," Donna whispered gratefully and dashed away.

Her mind dwelling on the possibility that at last Felicia Goulart was about to arrange for the long-promised benefit, Betsy managed to convey to the would-be horse trader that The Sanctuary was not a fire sale. With a polite smile she walked with her to the door.

Betsy's face lighted at the sight of Mark charging toward her.

"Well?" she demanded as Mark, seeming breathless from his

brief stroll from the Waldorf Towers, joined her inside the shop.

"You won't believe what's happening," he said with a dazed grin. "Let's go in the back and talk."

In their private corner Mark gave her a concise rundown on what had occurred. He mentioned the fee, and Betsy gasped in disbelief.

"The problem is—" He paused, his eyes searching hers. "I can't take the assignment unless you come in full time to manage the shop. There's nobody else who can handle it."

"Mark, the baby's so little—" But her heart was pounding at this challenge.

"You'll hire another salesperson," he plotted. "You can run home at lunch to be with Jimmy. If Donna's absent, you'll still have someone at the shop. You're always saying how capable Miss Watkins is. At Jimmy's age he's sleeping most of the time—" His eyes implored her to accept. "You'll be with him every morning and every evening. All day Sunday."

"It's exciting," she admitted. Whatever decorating assignments came along, she'd handle alone. It would be a test, she told herself in exhilaration. But would it be fair to Jimmy?

"It'll only be for three months," he encouraged. "And Lord, can we use that fee!"

"But Mark, twenty-eight rooms in three months?" All at once she was realistic. "How can you do that?"

"I'll have Eric to work with me," he reminded. "We'll work our butts off. And Felicia has terrific influence down there—she'll even have special fabrics woven for us. She'll find us seamstresses, painters, plasterers—whatever we need. She'll provide us with an apartment and a housekeeper. Our expenses will be low—I should be able to send money to see the shop through the summer." They worried about the slowdown during the hot months, when most of their customers fled the city.

"All right," Betsy said in sudden capitulation. "I'll do it."

He uttered a long, relieved sigh. "Let me call Felicia right now and tell her it's okay. We're accepting the assignment."

Her mind reeling with this new development, Betsy hurried home to give Jimmy his six o'clock bottle. This was the routine time Miss Watkins went downstairs to have her dinner. Holding Jimmy in her arms while he rapturously chugged at his bottle, Betsy realized she'd have to change her schedule once Mark was off for Rio. She wouldn't be home by six.

Still, she'd have lots of time to be with Jimmy, she comforted herself. She'd come home at lunch every day while Mark was in Rio. And it would be only for three months. Hundreds of thousands of mothers with young babies were working a full shift at defense plants and at full-time office jobs, she reminded herself. Already, she thought in candor, she yearned to be back at work on a regular basis.

Jimmy was half-asleep by the time he finished his bottle. She gently pulled away the bottle, deposited it on the feeding table already set up in the nursery for the day when it could be used. He was so good, she thought lovingly as she sat with him in her arms. He was already sleeping through the night. She gave him his first bottle at a little past six A.M., while Miss Watkins went downstairs for her breakfast.

She'd have to pick up a cheap camera to take snapshots of Jimmy while Mark and Eric were away. Paul looked forward to receiving pictures. She couldn't wait to see the look on Paul's face the first time he took Jimmy in his arms. It was weird, she thought, the way government bigwigs were already talking about how to handle the postwar world while the fighting was still going on so viciously.

When Miss Watkins returned to the nursery, Betsy went to her room to freshen up for dinner. She wasn't meeting Emily—there was an aunt in town and Emily was going out to Borough Park. Tonight she'd dine alone with Alice, she remembered. Her father-in-law had a business-dinner conference. She and Alice would talk mainly about Jimmy. It was a household rule never to discuss the war.

Midway through dinner Betsy was astonished when Alice brought up the subject of The Sanctuary. She had ignored the shop all these months.

"Would you know if Mark has a Hepplewhite armchair that

would be right for the library?" Alice asked at a break in the conversation about Jimmy. "There's an area by one of the windows that just cries out for something like that."

"We don't have a Hepplewhite at the moment." Betsy had total recall of their inventory. "But I'll start looking for one if you like." She hesitated. "Mark will be in Rio de Janeiro on a major project for three months. He's asked me to take over the shop."

Alice's fork poised in midair.

"You're going back to work on a full-time basis?" She gazed at her in shock. "When Jimmy's so little?"

"It's just for three months," Betsy explained. But would she be willing to go to part-time when Mark returned from Rio? she asked herself realistically. "Miss Watkins is wonderful with him—" Her heart pounded.

"Miss Watkins is his nanny. You're his mother. I always had a nanny for Paul, of course—but until he was in school full-time I was always on hand during his waking hours. As his mother I felt that was my obligation. My *pleasure*," she added with a surge of sentiment.

"Miss Watkins will always be able to reach me." Betsy fought against guilt. "The shop is a few minutes from here by cab." But if she were on a decorating assignment, she'd be dashing all over town—to jobbers, to the apartment she was doing. Nothing was going to happen, she told herself with shaky resolve. Miss Watkins would be able to handle any emergency. But misgivings were eroding her initial exhilaration.

Had she made an awful blunder by agreeing to take over the shop? But this was such a wonderful career opportunity. It was important for the three of them as a family—Paul and Jimmy and herself—for her to be successful. Paul had no intention of going back to law school, though his mother clung to this belief. She must be able to earn enough to support the three of them while Paul concentrated on writing his play. Other wives saw their husbands through medical school and law school. She would see Paul through the writing of his first play.

She wasn't cheating Jimmy of anything! *Was she?*

CHAPTER NINETEEN

Within three weeks Mark and Eric were on the first lap to Rio de Janeiro. Betsy had hired another salesgirl, vacillated between euphoria and alarm. She knew that the situation for interior decorators remained in crisis. It was difficult even to acquire merchandise for the shop. Now the financial responsibility to meet The Sanctuary bills lay in her hands.

At agonizing intervals she questioned her wisdom in taking on a full-time job when Jimmy was not yet three months old. She was ever conscious of her mother-in-law's disapproval. Had Alice been right? Was she so elated about this progress in her career that she was short-changing her son?

Betsy waited impatiently for Mark's first letter. At last it arrived—pages of sprawling handwriting that described Rio with exuberance. He loved the elegance of Rio, the iron-grilled mansions, the black-and-white marble mosaic sidewalks, flowers—hibiscus, pyrocanthus, coleus—everywhere. He was rhapsodic about the endless stretches of sandy beach. Business in Rio was booming, Mark reported—"and how great to be able to drink all the coffee we want!" But despite Felicia's manipulations the trip had taken twice as long as they had anticipated.

"The city is loaded with rich Europeans," Mark wrote. "What a place to set up a shop! They've all come here to look for the luxurious life."

His next letter was more realistic, dealing with the horrendous problems of acquiring what they needed—though Mark conceded that Felicia knew where to offer the right "contributions" that eased their way somewhat. But already Betsy suspected that their three-month stay might have to be extended.

A week before Purim—the joyous Jewish holiday celebrating the delivery of the Jews of Persia from a plot to destroy them—Betsy was coaxed by Mrs. Meyers to join Emily in coming out to Borough Park for dinner and services at their synagogue.

"It's not just for family," Emily told Betsy. "Mom's invited four servicemen who're stationed at Fort Hamilton to be with us for dinner and to go with us to the synagogue afterwards. It's something her women's group out there is doing. You and I are part of the entertainment committee," she said with a giggle.

"I feel uncomfortable at leaving Jimmy alone all evening after being in the shop much of the day," Betsy confessed.

"You're not leaving him alone—Miss Watkins is with him. And this is your patriotic duty," she added in triumph. "These guys don't know when they'll be shipped out."

On Purim Eve Betsy and Emily took the subway to Borough Park. Before Mr. Meyers came to open the door at the two-family stucco house, they heard festive sounds inside. Appetizing aromas filtered out to them.

"Mom and Grandma are baking, of course. I'll probably gain three pounds tonight," Emily mourned, but her smile was brilliant in anticipation. "Wow, can they cook!"

Mr. Meyers welcomed them with his usual warmth and took them into the living room. Now Rheba took off for the kitchen, leaving them with the four GIs, who sat about the room with shy smiles. Immediately Emily put a record on the phonograph and invited one of them to dance.

It was so easy to talk with them. Three were from small towns in the Midwest, the fourth from Atlanta. All were Paul's age or a little younger, she guessed. All eager to share a Jewish holiday with families willing to receive them.

Rheba came into the living room to summon them to the table.

Mrs. Meyers and her mother were bringing platters of steaming food from the kitchen. Everyone ate with relish.

"I haven't had brisket like this since my last leave home," the Atlantan said nostalgically.

The GIs exchanged good-humored stories about Army chow, then one by one talked about their own families. They were lonely and fearful of what lay ahead. Betsy talked about Paul and passed around snapshots of Jimmy. One of the soldiers pulled out snapshots of his parents and younger brothers and sisters.

"All right, it's time to go to services," Mr. Meyers announced. "It's just a short walk from here."

By the time they arrived at the synagogue, the aisles were full of children in costume—the little girls all Queen Esthers. The Jewish Queen Esther had appealed to her husband—the non-Jewish King Ahasuerus—to save her people and he had complied. The atmosphere was joyous, as befitted the occasion. Within ten minutes the services began. Every time the name Haman—the evil prime minister who had plotted the massacre—was mentioned, the children twirled their groggers in noisy reproach.

After the services coffee and *hamentashen* were served in a room upstairs. Glancing about at the happy faces, Betsy thought that the war seemed so far away—but she knew that the four GIs with them could be on blacked-out ships on the Atlantic at any time. And she silently reiterated her vow that Jimmy would be raised in her faith. One day Jimmy would be old enough to be happily twirling his grogger on Purim Eve—as endless generations of Jewish children had done in the past.

A few days later Betsy suspected that Jimmy was cutting his first tooth. He was fretful, fingers moving constantly to his mouth.

"We must call Dr. Mitty," Alice decided. "It may be something serious. He's never cranky like this. Are you, precious?" She leaned over the crib to take one of Jimmy's tiny, flailing fists in her hand and murmured endearments.

"I don't think we should bother Dr. Mitty," Betsy said, demurring. Twice this month her mother-in-law had insisted on a house visit by the pediatrician—for what was a slight case of colic. "I'm sure he's cutting his first tooth."

"He's too young," Alice fretted. "Paul was almost six months before his first tooth pushed through."

"Nobody told Jimmy he was too young," Betsy said with a sudden luminous smile. "I can feel it!" There was the unmistakable indication that Jimmy's first tooth was trying to push through tender gums.

In April Paul was promoted to sergeant. "Tell Jimmy his old man is rising up in the world. And send more snaps of the two of you. I can't wait for this bastardly war to be over and to be home with you."

Betsy felt triumphant when she discovered on one of her frantic jaunts the perfect Hepplewhite chair for Alice. She was impatient at the delays in the restoration of the chair, but it was being handled by a craftsman who would understand Alice's insistence on perfection. She debated about price, then reminded herself that she was working for the shop. Price the chair as Mark would, she ordered herself.

Her new salesgirl left with one week's notice to join the WAVES, and Betsy searched frenziedly for a replacement. She had hoped that with Mark down in Rio she might acquire merchandise from down there, but Mark wrote that transportation was impossible.

She was simultaneously delighted and apprehensive when the Carsons brought in a client who wanted a country kitchen for their new apartment. She spent hours every evening—the door between her bedroom and the nursery ajar so that she could hear if Jimmy woke up—working out possible kitchens, ever mindful of the problems involved.

Mark wrote that he and Eric were going out of their minds trying to cope—"Everything takes ten times as long as we plan." Still, he relished what was being accomplished. "Felicia is euphoric," he wrote. "And nothing is too expensive—when it's attainable." He loved the rare Brazilian woods—*jacaranda* and *cerejeira*. He was ecstatic over some of the antique Portuguese furniture he had discovered. And, mindful that Mark and Eric must remain well beyond the original time, Felicia had upped their fee.

Betsy started a scrapbook with snapshots of Jimmy that she took almost weekly and the ones Paul sent home. Seeing a snapshot of him—early in May—on a beach in swimming trunks and darkly tanned—she understood he was somewhere along the Mediterranean.

On May 10 word flashed around the world that the last 20,000 Germans in North Africa had surrendered to the 2nd U.S. Corps in Bizerte. The terms were "unconditional surrender." But Allied leaders stressed that Germany was still strong, despite the loss of 750,000 men in the African campaign, that what happened in the coming summer would determine how long the war would last.

With the Germans out of North Africa, the Allies prepared for a land invasion of Europe. Betsy tried not to think about the casualties this would cost them. While censorship prevented her knowing Paul's exact locale, she guessed from his snapshots that he had been part of the final push to free North Africa from the Nazi assault.

On May 19 Winston Churchill spoke in the House before a joint session of Congress. That evening Betsy and her father-in-law listened to excerpts of the speech on a radio report—with the British Prime Minister referring to the *Führer* as Corporal Hitler, his rank as a soldier in World War I. Churchill pledged to fight to the end for the defeat of Japan.

"Some of those in Congress," Mr. Forrest remarked somberly, "are afraid Churchill is more anxious for victory over Germany— for obvious reasons."

The following evening Betsy met Emily for dinner at Paul's apartment. They came here at regular intervals. Here Betsy always felt closer to Paul. The apartment was permeated with precious memories.

Over dinner Emily told Betsy that, because she was coming home less often these days, her mother was convinced she was having an affair with some New York–based serviceman.

"Hell, I wish it was true," Emily said grimly. "I might as well be living in a convent for all I'm getting. Every other little teenager is giving it away. What chance have I got?"

"You're not exactly looking," Betsy joshed. "When would you—between your job, the shorthand class, and holding my hand?"

"I'll be done with shorthand this week," Emily said. "Maybe I'll give some time at one of the canteens. Oh, did I tell you I heard from Colleen?"

"No!" Betsy gazed at her in astonishment. "You had that one postcard from her after she went out to California."

"She's going out with a USO troupe. She says that with so many movie stars going into service she might make some great contacts. Tyrone Power is in the Marine Corps, Robert Taylor just went into the Naval Air Corps. Clark Gable, James Stewart—the list is endless."

"I wish we'd hear from Doug," Betsy said uneasily. "It's been so long."

"Maybe he's found himself a British girlfriend," Emily said. "Between that and flying missions, when would he have time to write?" She squinted in thought. "I suppose it's nutty of us not to call up his parents. They live just about twenty blocks below here. Should we?"

"Call," Betsy said. "Do you remember the number?"

"I don't have it with me, but they must be in the phone book. They're on West End Avenue. His father's name is Joshua."

"I'll put a light under the coffee. You make the call."

Betsy rose and went into the kitchen while Emily reached for the Manhattan phone book. With the coffee warming up, she returned to the living room. Emily was on the phone.

"We're friends of Doug's," Emily was explaining. "We haven't heard from him in quite a while and—" All at once Emily was silent. Her face ashen. "I'm so sorry," she stammered. "We didn't know—" She stiffened for a moment, then put down the phone. "His mother hung up."

"Emily, what about Doug?" Betsy was trembling.

"His mother said, 'My son gave his life for his country.' She said she received the telegram from the War Department this morning. She thought this phone call was some terrible joke."

"Oh, my God—" Betsy was dizzy with shock.

"I can't believe it," Emily whispered.

"Did she say 'missing'?" Betsy reached for hope.

"His plane was shot down somewhere over France. He's listed as killed in action." Emily's voice broke. "Damn this war! Damn it, damn it, damn it!"

They sat in silence for a moment, each trying to cope with reality.

"I'll never walk by Doug's old apartment without wanting to cry," Betsy said, her voice thick with tears.

"We had a lot of laughs together." Emily shook her head as though to brush aside the painful news. "He was a real friend. Part of our special world when we left Hunter behind us. I was going to be a Broadway actress and Eric was going to be a set designer and Paul was going to write plays. Doug was going to be the attorney who handled our contracts."

"Paul *will* write his plays," Betsy said with a stridency born of terror. She wouldn't allow herself to think anything else. "I won't write him about Doug. Later he'll have to know—"

"Maybe they're wrong," Emily said defiantly. "Maybe his plane went down but he parachuted to safety."

"Over occupied France? Not only an American flier but a Jew! What chance would he have?"

"My mother said two kids that I went to Erasmus High with— they lived on our block—died in the Pacific. Her closest friend lost a son last month on the first day of the North African invasion. Betsy, you're wrong," she said bitterly, "when you keep saying we're living in comfort here in America while so much of the world is in pain. We live on the edge of a nightmare. A nightmare that'll become a terrible reality over and over again."

Across the hall someone opened a door. The poignant strains of "You'd Be So Nice to Come Home To" drifted into the room.

"How will we survive?" Betsy asked in anguish. "How will we survive until it's over?"

CHAPTER TWENTY

The last week in May began disastrously for the shop. The Sanctuary's salesgirls both gave two weeks' notice. Donna was following her soldier-husband, stationed in Georgia. The new girl frankly said she wanted to pile up some of that "great defense-job money" while it lasted.

Betsy received an apologetic letter from Mark confirming her suspicions that there was no way he could be back early in June as planned. Despite his efforts to appear cheerful about the job, she sensed he was harried. And he admitted Felicia was slow in meeting their financial arrangements—"in the way of the rich," he'd added.

The payment situation was further exacerbated by the delay in finishing the assignment—much of this caused by transportation problems. There was a gasoline shortage, despite the fact that there was ample oil in Venezuela. It was impossible to ship the oil through the Amazon jungle. No Brazilian merchant ships were permitted on the high seas now, so lumber had to be transported overland. "The only good thing," Mark had written, "is there's no shortage of labor."

Actually, Betsy thought, it was good that the two girls had both given notice. She and Mark had counted on his sending funds to help pay the shop's expenses through the next three months. To see them through the summer. She'd try to manage with just a part-time girl. She could count on Emily to take a day's leave and come in to help out if she had to go out on a decorating assignment.

It wasn't just The Sanctuary that was hurting, she told herself conscientiously. Even the top decorators—including the great Dorothy Draper—were feeling the pinch. Draper was writing columns to teach war brides to furnish a house for $500. The new *Vogue* had an article by Syrie Maugham on "convertible rooms." She and Mark were lucky to have latched on to Felicia Goulart, considering the rough times.

Betsy was relieved when closing time arrived. The day had been unseasonably hot. She was tired and tense. It would be relaxing just to sit and hold Jimmy in her arms for a while. The mail had arrived late today—usually it was delivered by the time she arrived home for lunch. Perhaps there'd be a letter from Paul, she thought hopefully.

At the house she checked the hall table for mail. There was nothing from Paul. She was always anxious when letters were delayed.

"Miss Betsy." Elise came toward her with a smile. "Mrs. Forrest said she'd appreciate it if you could have dinner with her and Mr. Forrest tonight."

"Thank you, Elise. That'll be fine."

Betsy went upstairs to the nursery, eager for her time with Jimmy. Why had Alice asked her to be at dinner tonight? she wondered curiously. She'd been pleased with the Hepplewhite chair. Was she about to ask for another item?

Betsy chose a cool white peasant blouse and a flowered cotton skirt. After a moment of indecision she discarded her nylon stockings—her very last pair and almost impossible to buy these days. Usually she wore leg makeup by Elizabeth Arden, but today she'd had a meeting with a prospective client. She wore her nylons.

When she arrived downstairs, she found Alice and Paul Jr. in the library. Her father-in-law was drinking coffee. Where other men had a pre-dinner drink, Paul Jr. had coffee. Involuntarily she remembered Emily's jibe that there was never a coffee shortage in such households as the Forrests'—despite the one and one-quarter cup per day that coffee coupons allowed. Mark said one of the pleasures of being down in Brazil was that he could have all the coffee he wanted. *"Brazil used to send a third of its coffee to the Germans. They just have to make do with tea now."*

Immediately Alice ordered that dinner be served. Not until dessert did Alice reveal what she wished to discuss.

"Paul, I know we talked earlier about not going out to the Southampton house this season because of the war, but it's obviously going to be a hot, miserable summer." Her eyes turned to Betsy, already on alert. "It would be criminal to put poor little Jimmy through a Manhattan summer. I think we should arrange to move out to the beach house by the end of June at the latest."

"Alice, there's a gasoline shortage," Paul Jr. protested. Ever since the ban on pleasure driving began last January, he had given up on having William drive him to and from his Wall Street office. He traveled by subway. "You'll be stuck out there. You won't be able to drive into Manhattan whenever the fancy strikes you."

"William will arrange for gas when we need it. He's good about such things. And if not, the Long Island train is still running."

While her in-laws discussed the situation, Betsy grappled with sudden panic. She couldn't commute every day between Southampton and New York. She'd never see Jimmy except for a few minutes in the morning. And it'd be terribly expensive.

She gathered from the conversation between Alice and Paul Jr. that he would stay in Manhattan Monday through Thursday afternoon. William would drive into the city to take him to the beach house at the close of business on Thursdays.

"We *have* to go out to Southampton for the summer." Alice's voice was strident. "How can we allow Jimmy to be exposed to another infantile paralysis epidemic? I keep reading about how they expect this summer to be even worse than last."

Betsy froze in shock. She hadn't thought about that. Infantile paralysis struck terror into the heart of every parent.

"How can they know?" Paul Jr. scoffed. But Betsy saw the alarm in his eyes.

"Doctors are warning that we can expect a major epidemic,"

Alice reiterated. "How can we stay here with Jimmy? At least, out in Southampton we can keep him away from other children. Betsy, tell him," she commanded.

"How will Betsy manage with the shop?" Paul Jr. countered. He knew how important the shop was to her, Betsy thought gratefully—but her mind was in chaos. She remembered the horror stories of children stricken by infantile paralysis—what people were now calling polio. "It's a terrible commute."

"Betsy, aren't you expecting Mark back any day?" Alice challenged. "Or Jimmy could be at the beach house with me, and you could come out for weekends. Between Miss Watkins and me you know you wouldn't have to worry about him."

"I'll have to work out something," Betsy stammered. Alice was right. How could she expose Jimmy to an epidemic when there was a way to avoid it? He was so little and vulnerable. But how could she leave him with Miss Watkins and his grandmother during the week? Of course he'd be all right, she thought realistically—but she couldn't be away from him that way. She'd never have a moment's peace. "I'll work something out," she said again.

"Then it's settled," Alice said. "We'll move out to the Southampton house the last week in June."

Betsy paced about her bedroom, trying to come up with a solution for the summer situation. She was impatient to discuss it with Emily, but she'd have to wait. Recently, when there was an urgent call for volunteers, Emily had agreed to switch to the midnight-to-eight shift at the office. There was still no phone in the old apartment—you had to know the president of AT&T to get a phone these days, Betsy thought wryly.

At ten minutes past midnight she called Emily.

"What's up?" Emily asked anxiously. She knew Betsy called her at the office only in moments of deep distress.

"Alice has decided we should move out to the Southampton house for the summer. And she's got a strong point," Betsy admitted. "We can isolate Jimmy pretty much from other kids out there. The doctors are predicting a major infantile paralysis epidemic this summer—"

"Oh, God—" Emily's voice was hushed.

"Alice said I should leave Jimmy at the Southampton house with her and Miss Watkins and come out for weekends. But, Emily, I can't do that." She was shaken by the prospect.

"Look, I'll meet you for breakfast in the morning. That little restaurant around the corner from the shop. Around nine?"

"Great. Nine o'clock." As long as she was at the shop to open up at ten there was no problem. "I know Alice thinks I just ought to stop working for the summer—"

"How can you?" Emily asked bluntly. "God knows when Mark and Eric will finish with Felicia's house. Does Alice expect you to just close up the shop? Hey, I have to run," she apologized. "We'll talk at breakfast."

Betsy lay sleepless far into the night. Of course Jimmy must get away from the city for the summer. Parents went into hock to take their kids away. But she couldn't allow Jimmy to be separated from her for days at a time. Nor could she close up the shop.

By the time she arrived at the little restaurant where she was to meet Emily, Betsy felt herself wrapped in exhilaration. She knew how to handle the situation—with Emily's help. She prayed that Mark would understand and approve.

Emily signaled her from a rear booth. Betsy hurried back to join her.

"I had a cup of coffee already to keep me awake," Emily said. "Also, to clear the head." She strived for a light mood, but Betsy knew she was anxious. "Now let's order and get that over with," she said as a waitress approached their booth.

When the waitress left with their orders, Betsy repeated what she had told Emily last night.

"You can't close the shop!" Emily said again.

"I'm scared to death of exposing Jimmy to infantile paralysis," Betsy confessed. "There's no vaccine—nothing to protect kids." She took a deep breath. "I've worked out a possible plan. Mark may be furious with me, and I don't know if you'll be able to handle your part of it—"

"Tell me," Emily ordered. "If it's humanly possible, I'll do it."

"You know how slow business is in the summer." Mark said

that was inevitable. "I figured we'd keep the shop open only on Saturdays during July and August, provided you could juggle your schedule and cover for me." Emily knew a lot about the business now. And she was efficient and trustworthy.

"No sweat," Emily said with an ebullient smile. "There's always somebody happy to work Saturdays if I'm willing to take their Sunday shift. But that's not going to cover the shop's overhead," she said.

"I know it's terribly late in the season, but I want to look for a tiny store in Southampton and open up there for the resort trade. I'll put a sign in the window that we're open in Manhattan only on Saturdays during the summer, 'But if you're in the Hamptons, visit our resort shop at Southampton.' "

"Can you handle the money end of it?" Emily was dubious. "The rents at Southampton must be wild."

"I'll use my allotment checks," Betsy told her. "And I still have some money in my joint savings account with Paul." The only real expense she had was the rent for Paul's apartment. "I know Paul won't mind my putting up money for the shop."

"What do you think Mark will say? This is kind of revolutionary."

"There's no time to ask him." Betsy felt guilty at taking this on without consulting Mark, but mail was coming through slowly. A cable he'd sent had never come through. "I know it's a gamble," she conceded, "but it's the only way I can handle things."

"So where do we go from here?" Emily's eyes telegraphed her acceptance.

"We take an early morning train on Sunday to Southampton. And we start looking for a tiny shop. If it's available this late in the season," Betsy guessed with a flurry of hope, "the rent should be negotiable. I don't have to worry about stock." Already she was mentally stocking the proposed resort shop. "I'll bring out some of the most choice—most expensive pieces—in our inventory."

Early Sunday morning—with glorious sunshine drenching the city—Betsy and Emily went to Penn Station to take an early train out to Southampton. They took a cab from the tiny railroad station to the center of town and began to search for FOR RENT signs.

"You won't have to worry about getting around out here," Emily pointed out ebulliently. "Once the season opens, you'll have William and the limo."

"First let's find a vacant store." Betsy fought against infiltrating fears. Her earlier optimism was eroding as they walked about streets with picturesque names but no VACANCY signs.

Despite the war, they soon discovered, most space was already rented for the resort season. They discovered a pair of brokerage offices and inquired eagerly at each. What brokers offered were far beyond Betsy's means—though she had upgraded the amount she was prepared to pay.

"I can't believe the rents out here." Emily shook her head in dismay when they'd emerged from the office of the second real estate broker. "I know—I was the one who'd warned you they'd be high. But this is crazy!"

"Like the prices I'll ask." Betsy smiled determinedly. "When we find a place." They had to do it fast for her to be set up for business by the beginning of the July 4th weekend. That first weekend, she knew intuitively, would set the tone for the season.

"Let's find a place to have a sandwich and coffee," Emily said. "Not only am I starving—my feet are killing me."

They tracked down a small coffee shop that hinted at affordable prices and went inside.

"Oh, God, it feels good to sit," Emily said with a sigh, kicking off her pumps under the table. "We should have worn sneakers."

"Do you think I ought to phone home and ask about Jimmy?" Betsy squinted in indecision.

"Betsy, relax," Emily ordered. "You saw him this morning. Miss Watkins probably has him in the park on a gorgeous day like this. And you'll see him before he goes to sleep." She shook her head in mock reproach. "You're getting an obsession about being the perfect mother."

"I've got to find space out here!"

"Maybe you can rent part of a shop," Emily suggested, then paused as a friendly waitress hovered over their table.

"You planning to open a dress shop?" the waitress asked interestedly.

"I'd like to open a decorator shop," Betsy told her, managing a wisp of a smile despite her frustration. "I don't need much space, but what I've seen that's available is madly expensive."

"My sister-in-law rented a store for a linen shop. She had to take it because it was all she could find—but she has more space than she needs. She'd love to be able to cut down on her rent." The waitress exuded enthusiasm at this encounter.

"Can we talk to her?" Betsy asked eagerly.

"You sure can. Have your lunch, then go over to see Millie. I'll phone and tell her you're coming. She hasn't opened for business yet, but she's over there getting set up. Now, what would you like?" The waitress deposited a menu before each of them.

Betsy and Emily ordered grilled cheese sandwiches and coffee. The prices were astronomical compared to their usual Manhattan haunts. In silent agreement they finished lunch in record time, both conscious that this could be their last chance at locating space for the Southampton branch of The Sanctuary. Their waitress came over to direct them to her sister-in-law's store, was zealous in giving them directions.

The store was a brief walk from the coffee shop, but Betsy quickly realized it was off the main street of town.

"It's a little off the beaten track," Betsy conceded as they approached their destination, "but that should keep the rent low."

Emily seemed dubious as they stood before the small shop with two tiny display windows.

"Do you think you can get people over here?"

"If I can work out a deal with Millie, then I'll have to dream up some kind of promotion to bring them in." And that wouldn't be easy in this town, where some of the Old Society dowagers were mourning that they'd had to give up their footmen because so many men were going into military service. Of course the Forrests didn't live in that kind of grandeur, Betsy conceded—but those who owned summer houses at Southampton lived in a special world.

Betsy knew the minute she walked inside the store that she'd found her space. Millie was frank in admitting she'd bitten off more than she could handle. She was eager to share. Betsy haggled briefly, then agreed to a figure that was high, yet considerably lower than anything she'd encountered out here.

There were wall dividers stored in the back, Millie told Betsy and Emily. "It'll be no sweat to set them up again. My brother will come in and do it. It'll be like having your own place. And we'll each have a display window."

Before Betsy and Emily left for the railroad station, Betsy had signed an agreement. She'd made arrangements, also—after Millie made a phone call to her brother, available for various odd jobs—to come into Manhattan with a truck to bring out what Betsy planned to use for inventory.

There would be a Southampton branch of The Sanctuary this season. Her major problem, Betsy warned herself, was to figure out a promotion to bring in customers this far off the main line.

CHAPTER TWENTY-ONE

On the hot train ride back into Manhattan Betsy talked with Emily about the summer campaign, all the while trying to push down simmering anxiety about Mark's reaction to how she was handling the business. It was a drastic move to stay open only on Saturdays during the summer, but Mark always said the rest of the year had to carry the summer losses.

"I realize we're not in the best location," she conceded to Emily. There the rents were far beyond her limited means. "We'll have to advertise in the local paper, I suppose." She winced at the prospect of this added expense. "I'll call up tomorrow and find out their rates."

"I'll bet some of your customers go out to Southampton for the summer," Emily guessed. "Why don't you drop little notes to them?"

"I'll do that right away." Betsy nodded in approval. "I'll pick up some pretty notepaper, make it very personal—"

"Talk about personal, I'll bet Alice Forrest could circulate the word to the right people," Emily said pointedly.

"I couldn't ask her. You know how she feels about my working." Betsy frowned in thought. "But I'll write to everybody whose address we have on file." Their rich, steady customers.

"July 4th falls on a Thursday," Emily recalled. "Will you open that day? Or are people all involved in celebrating?"

"We'll close on the Fourth—the official opening will be on Friday, July 5th—" Instinct told her that her prospective customers would not be shopping on July 4th. She wasn't anticipating Southampton's Old Society, but there were the new, very rich who'd bought houses out there and could, hopefully, be acquired as customers, perhaps even hire her to decorate a room.

"I have a lot of leave coming," Emily said thoughtfully. "I'll take off for the long July 4th weekend so I can help you." She paused. "Oh, do you want the New York shop to be open on that Saturday?"

"No, we'll be closed—any prospective customer will probably be out of town anyway. I'll ask Alice if it's all right for me to bring you out to the house for that weekend," she decided with a daring born of desperation. "You can share my room."

"Wow, am I moving up in the world," Emily drawled. "Do you think the old girl will mind?"

"She's too well-bred to say no or make some excuse," Betsy said, her eyes lit with sudden laughter. "Besides, you'll probably never even meet."

"Right, we'll be at the shop most of the time—or walking on the beach," Emily said in pleased anticipation.

All at once Betsy realized there could be pleasure for her in Southampton. It wouldn't be all work. There was so little fun in her life these days. "But I need a gimmick to bring in business," she pursued. She must show Mark that The Sanctuary wouldn't be losing out by making the resort its main source of income. "Won't it be awful if nobody shows up?" The prospect was unnerving.

"Pray for rain on opening day," Emily said. "When it rains in a resort town, the women shop. Pray it rains all weekend."

"Mark says the people out there live a very hectic social life," Betsy recalled. "Even if some of them have had to give up their footmen because of the male shortage," she added in amusement.

"Footmen in knee britches?" Emily picked up Betsy's touch of levity.

"I wouldn't be surprised—though not at the Forrest house."

"Did I tell you," Emily said offhandedly, "that the new lieutenant at the office takes the same subway home as I do? He gets off at the West 72nd Street stop. Interesting, huh?"

"So you traveled home together," Betsy said. "When is he taking you out?" Emily was so attractive but refused to see it.

"As soon as I can reel him in." Emily squinted in thought. "We'll have to be careful though—I mean, I'm a clerical supervisor and he's an officer." She lifted an eyebrow in mockery. She and Betsy had both been furious when they learned that noncommissioned WAACs in London were ordered not to date American officers. "Nobody's ever said anything about it—it's one of those unspoken things. Diane—you know, the girl who's been writing to her darling Vinnie every night—"

"The Marine in the Pacific." Betsy nodded in recall.

"Well, she's seeing an ensign in the department now and keeping it very quiet. I don't think it's because she's afraid somebody will write to Vinnie out in the Pacific. I think she's afraid fraternization between the lowly office workers and Naval officers isn't approved of by the top brass."

"She's dumping Vinnie?" Betsy was shocked. For over a year Emily had been talking about Diane's devotion to her boyfriend overseas.

"She's trying to work her way up to writing a Dear John letter. I think she and the ensign want to get married."

"How awful for Vinnie!" How could any girl do that to a man at the fighting front? Yet stories kept circulating about the Dear John letters—letters to overseas servicemen who were being dumped by the girls they'd left behind. And stories leaked back about soldiers sleeping with girls wherever American forces were fighting. Not Paul, Betsy told herself with conviction. Paul couldn't wait to come home to her and Jimmy.

"I can kind of understand how it happens," Emily confessed after a moment. "Vinnie's been in the Pacific a year and a half. Before that they'd been sleeping together for almost a year. They were stalling on getting married until Vinnie's job paid enough to support them both—they wanted to have a baby nine months after

the wedding ceremony. But then Vinnie enlisted and—zingo—
she's sleeping alone. She's passionate. Not one of those gals who
pretend they're all hot and bothered. Come on, Betsy. Be honest.
Don't you miss making love?"

"Yes. So much—" How many nights she lay sleepless, clutching at memories. "I miss Paul terribly—and of course I miss that
part, too. I didn't know how much I'd miss it."

"You can cope with the waiting," Emily said gently. "Diane
can't. And she's not alone, sweetie."

"I couldn't sleep with anybody else. For me love and sleeping
with a man are tied together. So I'll wait till Paul comes home," she
said with an effort at lightness. But her eyes were somber. How
many more nights must she lie alone, aching for Paul's arms about
her? Aching to make love.

While heavy rain hammered against the dining room windows
and the May temperature slithered down to a raw chill, Paul Jr.
listened with relief as Betsy explained to Alice and himself that she
would be at the Southampton house for July and August.

"Oh, Jimmy has to be away from the city." Alice appeared
pleased with this decision, though Paul suspected she would have
preferred that Betsy be at the beach house only on weekends.
Then she would have felt completely in charge of Jimmy.

"I'm closing the shop for July and August except for Saturdays.
My friend Emily will be there then. Mark always says business is
dead in the summer." She paused. "I'm opening a tiny little place
in Southampton for the resort season."

"That's smart," Paul Jr. said. "You might pick up customers
out there that will follow you right back into the city." Betsy had
a sharp mind, he thought with respect. She looked small and
fragile, but she had real inner strength.

"When did this happen?" Alice's smile was brittle. She was
upset, Paul Jr. sensed uneasily.

"I was afraid it wouldn't," Betsy confessed. "Almost everything
was already rented out there—and the prices are so high. But I can
manage," she added. She didn't want them to think she was asking

for financial help, Paul Jr. interpreted. "I'm sharing a store with someone else. I found it when I'd just about given up hope."

"I talked with Georgette this afternoon about our going out to their house in Bar Harbor in August," Alice told Paul Jr. "Carl will be there at the same time, so you can't complain about being bored. I'll miss Jimmy." She turned to Betsy. "But you and Miss Watkins will be there with him. I'll phone every night."

"I can't wait to see Jimmy on the beach." Betsy's face lighted. "I know he'll love the ocean."

"He'll have the world's biggest sandpile right at his feet," Paul Jr. said affectionately. But the familiar glint of agitation in Alice's eyes disturbed him. She was upset because Betsy was opening a shop in Southampton. Did she expect Betsy to fall on her face?

Tonight Alice went directly up to the master bedroom suite after dinner. Paul Jr. went into the library with Betsy to listen to the news. At times like these he felt particularly close to his daughter-in-law. There was no doubt in his mind that she deeply loved his son.

In North Africa American troops had captured Bizerte. The British had taken Tunis. With Tunisia in Allied hands the North African campaign was over. Since Sicily was less than ninety miles away, many Americans assumed that would be the Allies' next destination. In the Pacific there was intense fighting in the Aleutian Islands, the casualties heavy on both sides.

Almost reluctantly Paul Jr. turned off the news.

"I guess that's it for the night."

He left Betsy in the library, where she was flipping through the collection of magazines to choose one to take up with her to her room, and headed for the master bedroom suite. Why was Alice stewing that way? he asked himself again. Why should she be upset that Betsy was opening a summer shop in Southampton?

When he walked into the sitting room of the master bedroom suite, he geared himself for trouble. Alice was sitting in a chair by one of the windows, an open but obviously unread book on her lap. When she stared out into the park that way, he knew she was brooding.

"You're upstairs early," he said warily, and she turned around to face him.

"I'm upset," she told him, rising to her feet. "She's trying so hard to push herself into our lives!"

He understood, of course, that she referred to Betsy.

"Alice, Betsy *is* part of our lives. She's Paul's wife, Jimmy's mother."

"I agreed to have her here in this house because Paul asked this of us. But once this dreadful war is over and he's home again, he'll understand what a mistake he's made. He'll divorce her, gain custody of Jimmy. We'll—"

"Alice, stop that!" he ordered tersely. He'd thought she'd gotten past that craziness. "Paul has no intention of divorcing Betsy. He's living for the day he can come home to Betsy and the baby. I can't understand why you're upset that she's opening a shop out in Southampton. I think it's quite enterprising of her." That was the reason for her brooding.

"She wants to use our name to promote that shop!" Alice's voice was shrill—a warning signal that Paul recognized. "Southampton is a small town—everybody knows us. I will not have her part of our social lives. And it'd be so embarrassing if somebody out there found out she's Jewish. You know how they feel about Jews—"

"I know how some people feel," he said grimly. "Not this family."

"Why can't you understand?" Alice's voice broke. "She's come into our lives and spoiled everything."

"She gave us Jimmy," he reminded.

"I don't want to talk about her." Alice began to sob. "And to think I'm responsible for their meeting—"

"I want you to take one of your pills," he said quietly. "It's not good for you to let yourself get upset this way."

"I'm tired of taking pills," she said querulously, but she was crossing to the drum table whose drawer held her bottle of pills.

"I'll get you a glass of water," he soothed.

He crossed to the bedroom en route to Alice's bathroom. He

saw the ivory satin and lace nightgown that lay across their bed. Once she took her pill and relaxed, she'd be the beautiful, passionate Alice he'd known in the first years of their marriage. Already he felt a stirring low within him.

Often—after one of the painful episodes with Alice—he asked himself why he remained devoted to his wife. But in that huge bed they shared, she was another Alice. For all her elegant, patrician exterior, in their bed she gave him the kind of joy that kept him forever at her side.

Betsy waited impatiently for mail from Mark—seeming slower than ever in coming through. She had written him about the Southampton shop, trying to sound optimistic. And with rising alarm she watched her savings account diminish as new expenses arose: ads for the Southampton shop, train fare and taxis because now it was necessary to go out to Southampton every Sunday to work on the shop, trucking costs to bring out inventory. Millie's brother performed necessary small services that required more cash outlays.

She'd decided to offer an afternoon tea on opening day. Emily had bluntly dispelled her thoughts of an inexpensive outlay for this. The Health Department had rules, Emily pointed out. They'd have to bring in a tea urn from a local restaurant. The wonderful petits fours that Emily's grandmother would be happy to make couldn't be served—they must be bought at a commercial bakery.

Millie was consulted. She made herself their unofficial assistant. On the Sunday before the shop opening, Betsy arranged Millie's display window, using an antique armchair that bore a small sign indicating it could be purchased through The Sanctuary, Southampton.

"Honey, that looks really elegant." Millie was enthralled. "And that's the word out here. That's why I'm stocking the most expensive linens. My husband keeps warning me we could end up with the classiest bathroom and bedroom supplies in Southampton— and a bank loan it'll take us three years to pay off. But what the hell, sometimes you have to gamble."

"Do you live here year-round?" Betsy asked curiously.

"I'm from Brooklyn," Millie drawled. "My mother-in-law and sister-in-law have been living out here for sixteen years. They like being near the water. Off-season, I like it better out here," she admitted. "When the summer people head for Palm Beach or wherever they go the rest of the year." She was contemplative for a moment. "Doesn't it make you wonder what kind of world they live in when Americans are dying every day in Europe and the Pacific, and they're out here living it up in their mansions and complaining about how hard it is to get cooks and maids and chauffeurs?"

"My husband's in North Africa," Betsy said somberly. All at once she realized that Millie didn't know that *she* would be living in one of those mansions. "He's been there since the invasion began."

"It's rough," Millie commiserated. "My husband's working in a defense plant further down on the island. He's just old enough to miss the draft. We never had kids, and sometimes—like now, I'm glad."

Betsy glanced at her watch. "I'd better head for the station or I'll miss my train. See you Thursday morning!" Her smile was warm and reassuring, but she was assaulted by doubts as the opening date for the resort shop approached. *Had she taken on more than she could handle?*

On Wednesday afternoon, July 3rd, Alice was driven out to the beach house along with Paul Jr., Miss Watkins, and Jimmy. William returned to the city to drive out Elise and Peggy, plus an assortment of luggage that couldn't be accommodated on the first trip. Betsy and Emily were taking a train out after the Manhattan shop closed for the day.

At lunchtime Miss Watkins had brought Jimmy over so that Betsy could be with him for a little while. It would be the first time that he'd go to sleep without her kissing him goodnight, she thought guiltily as she and Emily left the shop and headed for a Chinese restaurant in the West Forties for dinner.

"The city looks dead already," Emily commented. "People have been heading out since early this morning. Those that can take Friday and Saturday off. With the gas shortage some drivers have been hoarding for months to make the trip."

"It's so humid." Betsy sighed. "It's going to be like an oven on the train."

"You should have closed up early and gone out with the others." Emily clucked in tender reproach. "I would have found my way out by myself."

"I didn't want to close early, and I wanted to go on the train with you. But aren't you glad I arranged for William to take your luggage along with mine?"

"Yeah." Emily chuckled. "That means we'll be free to make a mad dash for seats." She hesitated. "You're sure the old gal isn't mad that you're *schlepping* me along with you?"

"No. She's mad that I'm opening the Southampton branch, though I don't see that it affects her. Oh, she doesn't say anything, but I see the way she looks—so pained—when Paul Jr. mentions it. He thinks I'm doing the smart thing."

"But she's not doing anything to help you."

"I didn't expect that," Betsy said. She had come to understand that Alice didn't talk to her friends about her and Jimmy. She spoke of them only to her very close friends, like Georgette Adams.

"I'm glad we staked out the house the last time we were out there." Emily giggled. "I wouldn't have been prepared for anything so lush. Not at the beach! But then the only beach I've known is Coney Island and Brighton."

The Forrest beach house, they'd discovered, was within comfortable walking distance of the Southampton shop. It was a magnificently landscaped, fourteen-room, white-brick Georgian colonial with wraparound verandas, one stretch of which faced the ocean. Tall hedges protected it from view on the other sides. Paul had talked casually about the "family's house at the beach." Betsy hadn't expected it to be a sprawling estate.

With an eye to the Long Island Railroad timetable, they ate hastily in the small, inexpensive Chinese restaurant west of Broadway in the Forties, then headed for Penn Station, gearing them-

selves for the mobs that would be descending on Long Island–
bound trains on the brink of the long holiday weekend.

Clutching Betsy's hand in hers, Emily pushed her way onto
their train, moving with determination toward a pair of empty
seats: a habit learned from years of subway commuting.

"We did it," Emily said triumphantly while they settled themselves. "I'd hate to stand all the way out there."

As prearranged, Betsy had phoned the house so that William
could drive to the station to pick up Emily and herself. He was
there waiting when the train pulled into the Southampton station. He informed them that Mr. and Mrs. Forrest had gone out
for dinner and that Peggy was prepared to serve them on their
arrival.

"Peggy thought you'd like dinner on the veranda," William
reported. "The view is beautiful. But you'd best wear sweaters.
There's a nice chill in the air."

At the house Betsy and Emily went briefly upstairs to what was
to be Betsy's bedroom for the summer. Elise told them that the
adjoining bedroom—there was a connecting bath—had been as-
signed to Emily.

"Where's Jimmy's room?" Betsy asked eagerly.

"Just across the hall," Elise explained. "It was Mr. Paul's
room," she added tenderly. "And Miss Watkins' room is right off
the nursery."

They looked in on Jimmy—fast asleep now—then hurried
downstairs to dinner.

"Oh, wow, is this the way to live," Emily whispered to Betsy
when they were alone at the table set up on the ocean-facing
veranda. "Remember what Sophie Tucker said? 'I've been rich
and I've been poor—and rich is better.' Sweetie, I agree!"

In the morning—the first to arise—Betsy and Emily had breakfast on the veranda. The ocean reflected the brilliant blue of the
sky. The surf was gentle this morning, the stretch of beach occupied only by a pair of sea gulls.

Betsy was impatient for Jimmy to wake up. She'd never been

away from him so long. Finally Miss Watkins brought him downstairs.

"Oh, how's my precious?" Betsy crooned, holding out her arms.

"He slept late because of the sea air," Miss Watkins said. "But he's had his breakfast and his bath, and I'll take him down to play on the sand in a while."

"May we take him for a walk first?" Betsy asked ingratiatingly.

Though she was anxious to get to the shop and to take care of last-minute details for the opening tomorrow, she relished strolling along the beach with Jimmy in her arms.

"He loves it out here," Emily decided while they paused to play with a town Labrador taking a solitary stroll. "He'll have a wonderful summer."

"Doggie!" Jimmy said rapturously. "Doggie!"

"You think I'm doing right?" Betsy asked, needing reassurance.

"Paul would be proud of you."

"Let's just hope I can make it with the shop." Betsy's smile was wry. "I have to show Mark I pulled through the summer without falling on my face."

When she and Emily prepared to leave the house, Betsy explained to Elise that Peggy was not to expect them for lunch or dinner. They'd be busy at the shop.

"Good luck, Miss Betsy," Elise said with an encouraging smile. "I saw your ad in the newspaper."

It seemed to Betsy that she would never be totally satisfied with the way she had displayed their merchandise. In late afternoon they went back to the house to spend time with Jimmy, then returned to the shop. Despite Emily's insistence that everything was perfect, she was rearranging until well into the evening. Finally they returned to the house, exhausted but pleased.

Promptly at ten A.M. the following morning Betsy and Emily were at the shop. The window looked attractive, Betsy told herself with pleasure. Millie's window, too, was attractive. But no customers appeared until early afternoon, despite the waiting tea urn and platters of petits fours.

Betsy realized that they were drawing tourists, who came in, admired, accepted tea that Emily served, chose a petit four—and bought nothing. Late in the afternoon Millie left her part-time salesgirl to come into their area.

"It's slow," she said. "It takes time, I hear, for the summer people to start looking. When they get bored with playing cards—" She rolled her eyes eloquently. "Or the weather is lousy."

Betsy and Emily closed up an hour later than planned in hopes of acquiring a last-minute sale. Millie, too, stayed late.

"Today was a dog. Tomorrow will be better." Millie tried to be philosophical. "It was so nice today everybody wanted to be on the beach."

Weekend sales were poor. Waiting with Emily at the station for the west-bound train, Betsy was upset about the state of business.

"I'll go over to the newspaper in the morning to run another ad, and I'll ask them if they'll do a story about the shop. You know, mention that Mark is down in Rio de Janeiro doing a twenty-eight-room castle for Felicia Goulart."

"You might mention that you're Mrs. James Paul Forrest the Third. The name carries a lot of weight around here," Emily said.

"No," Betsy said firmly. Paul approved of her opening the shop, she remembered with satisfaction. The V-mail she'd received Saturday was full of encouragement. But she would not trade on her in-laws' name.

"Stubborn," Emily jeered. "But I love you anyway." She reached to hug Betsy for a moment. The train was pulling into the station. "Call me at the office."

Emily dropped off her valise at the apartment and headed for the subway. Tonight would be a bitch, she warned herself. She'd slept on the train from five minutes out of Southampton until its arrival in Penn Station, but that wasn't much to see her through until eight tomorrow morning.

It had been a great weekend, she thought as she strolled through the hot night. As Betsy had predicted, they'd barely encountered the Forrests. Of course Betsy's in-laws obviously adored Jimmy. She was nuts not to use Alice Forrest's influence out there to help bring in customers. The situation with the shop did not look good, she thought uneasily.

"Hi, there—" Emily stopped short at the sound of a familiar male voice behind her. She swung around to face its owner.

"Hi." It was Oliver Mason, the new lieutenant in the office. He'd been wounded in the Pacific, shipped home to recuperate, and then reassigned to a desk job.

She wasn't the only one who thought he was awfully good-looking, she remembered. "Headed for work?" she asked casually.

"Another dull night." He shrugged. His eyes rested for a moment on the lush rise of her breasts. "I might survive if you agree to have breakfast with me when we get off."

"It would be unpatriotic of me to refuse," she countered.

"I'll meet you down in the lobby," he said with an air of anticipation.

"Sure." Nobody in the office had to know.

"What's that perfume you're wearing?" He sniffed appreciatively as he took her arm.

"The very last of my Chanel No. 5," she told him. It had been a birthday gift from Betsy. "There won't be any more till Paris is liberated."

All right, she thought jubilantly. Life was looking up. Instinct told her that Oliver Mason was looking far beyond breakfast. But for the summer, she warned herself, she was tied up for weekends. Saturdays she would be at The Sanctuary. Sundays at work. That was going to complicate seeing Oliver Mason.

CHAPTER TWENTY-TWO

On Monday morning Betsy left the newspaper office with a flurry of hope. She'd placed a larger ad, which made a painful inroad into her current allotment check, and there was promise of a small article about the shop in the same issue. She'd mentioned Mark's assignment in Rio, and then talked about Felicia Goulart's Waldorf Towers apartment.

She had been part of that. Mark wouldn't mind that she listed herself as joint decorator, would he? Wealthy socialities out here would know Felicia, of course. That might help bring women into the shop.

If she had not been so concerned about the business, she would enjoy being out here, Betsy thought. Early every morning she scooped up Jimmy and took him down to the beach with her. It was so peaceful, so beautiful at that hour of the morning. This was where Paul spent his growing-up summers, she remembered tenderly.

At sunset she walked along the beach again, feeling poignantly close to Paul, wondering where he was—how he was. His father was sure his company was headed for Sicily. Often she thought about Doug. How wrong that his life had been cut short this way!

She was disturbed when there had been no mail from Paul for almost ten days. He knew about the move to the beach house, she reassured herself—he knew to use this address. Every morning William went to the post office to pick up the mail from the family post-office box. Late in the afternoon he went again. Had Alice heard from Paul? She couldn't bring herself to ask.

Each day she arrived at the shop well before ten, the official opening hour. This morning she arrived just at ten. She'd waited for William to return from the post office. Still no mail from Paul. With no customer in sight, she sat down to write to him, then another letter to Mark. She still had received no reply to her last one.

Mark was upset by Felicia's cavalier attitude toward money. He'd expected to be sending her international money orders at regular intervals. *"But you know the rich. They don't understand people need to be paid on time. 'What's the problem?' they ask. 'You know we're good for it.' "*

Business continued to be shockingly slow. Millie, too, complained. Then when Betsy's new ad—together with the story about the assignments for Felicia—appeared, there was a sudden upsurge. Mark had been right, she thought joyously. Felicia Goulart's name as a client was magic.

But her pleasure in the shop activities was brushed aside in her concern at not hearing from Paul. As her fears mounted, she forced herself to ask her mother-in-law if *she* had heard from him.

"Not for almost three weeks," Alice confessed. "I'm just terrified."

"There's probably some unexpected problem in getting the mail through." Betsy tried to hide her own alarm. "We'll both probably receive a bunch of letters all at once."

Then radio newscasters and journalists broke the news that American, British, and Canadian troops had landed on the southeastern coast of Sicily. The Allied invasion of Italy was being charted. Nine days later word came through that 500 planes had bombed Rome—spared the past four years because of its religious significance.

Almost simultaneously Betsy and Alice received a flood of letters from Paul. For a poignant brief period Betsy felt a new closeness to her mother-in-law. Together they stood beside Jimmy's crib in relief that word had come from his father.

"He didn't have to go to fight," Alice said with tears in her eyes. "Why couldn't he listen to me?"

She didn't understand, Betsy thought with frustration. And she couldn't accept the knowledge that Paul wasn't her little boy anymore. He was a man, who made his own decisions. She wanted so much to be truly part of Paul's family, Betsy thought—but would his mother ever let that happen?

The weeks were rushing past now. Betsy was grateful that the shop was doing well. She talked regularly with Emily by phone, and made arrangements with her for Millie's brother to pick up items from the Manhattan shop and bring them out to Southampton.

In early August Mark wrote that he'd be returning within four or five weeks.

"We haven't been able to do the entire house, but all the major rooms are being wrapped up. Even Felicia admits that we can't do more at this time. She's very happy with the results. She promises to pay up everything that's due before we leave. And she expects to be in New York in the fall and will arrange a benefit cocktail party in the Waldorf Towers apartment. That should be a great break for us."

Alice and Paul Jr. were scheduled to leave to spend two weeks with Georgette at her house in Bar Harbor. At the same time Peggy and Elise were taking their vacations. A local woman had been hired to come in to cook. William would handle the cleaning.

"Betsy, feel free to invite friends to the house to stay with you," Paul Jr. encouraged. "It's been a rough summer for you, keeping the shop open seven days a week."

"Thank you." Betsy smiled gratefully. Emily had leave coming to her. She could come out after closing the shop on a Saturday and stay until the following Friday evening. Emily would love it.

Emily closed up the shop on this humid August Saturday and headed north for a bus home. Her pale blue shirtwaist dress clung to her back. Perspiration trickled between her breasts. She'd have time for a quick shower, she promised herself while she climbed onto a bus—mercifully not crowded yet, though city buses would soon be mobbed.

She dropped into a seat at the rear, near an exit and an open window. Wow, was she glad she'd agreed to stay indefinitely on the midnight-to-eight shift. If she hadn't, she might never have met Oliver. They weren't letting on to anybody at work that they were seeing each other outside. They'd had dinner twice at that snazzy restaurant in Greenwich Village. They'd seen a late movie at the Apollo—where his hands had wandered brazenly in the dark. Tonight they were having dinner at his apartment.

Twenty minutes later she stood gratefully under a lukewarm shower. She really ought to start dieting, she told herself. Her clothes were becoming a bit snug at the waist and across the bustline. But guys liked bosomy women. Oliver's eyes had a way of fastening themselves to that area.

She felt a pleasant surge of anticipation as she contemplated the evening. Sometimes when Oliver cornered her at the office, he'd softly whistle, "Please Give Me Something to Remember You By"—and she knew just what he meant. Tonight was the night, she thought ebulliently.

Out of the shower she redid her face and dressed quickly. She smiled in approval at the cleavage the dress provided. Oliver wouldn't waste much time over dinner tonight. Oh, cologne, she reminded herself. Her Chanel No. 5 was gone. Settle tonight for Elizabeth Arden's Blue Grass.

She left the apartment and headed south. Oliver lived in a brownstone house between Broadway and West End in the low '70s. She'd never been there before. Arriving there, she noted it was slightly more pretentious than those she knew. The foyer was well lighted, the foyer and stairs carpeted in a fading red that once must have been lush. The wall sconces on the stairway hinted at an earlier elegance.

Approaching the door to his apartment, she was aware that her heart was pounding. This might just be the real thing. Oliver was good-looking—and he was sharp.

Walking up the stairs to his fourth-floor apartment, Emily could hear his voice in her memory. *"I've got a picture of a little house with a white picket fence. Somewhere in the suburbs."* The house had to be close to a good school, he'd said—for the two kids he wanted. It wasn't quite the future she'd seen for herself back in high school, but right now it sounded great.

She heard the sound of the radio, blaring out the popular strains of "Mairzy Doats." Oliver was singing the crazy lyrics along with the record. He was probably hot as a pistol in bed, she thought while a pulse throbbed wildly within her. How had she gone all this time without sex?

No doorbell, she noted, and raised one fist for a jaunty knock. Moments later the door swung wide.

"Hi, gorgeous," he drawled, his eyes resting on his favorite part of her anatomy.

"It's a gorgeous night." Her eyes offered a heated invitation.

"Which we will shortly make more gorgeous," he promised, drawing her into the living room. "Shall we have dessert before or after?"

"That depends upon what you consider dessert." Being with Oliver, she thought dreamily, was like playing a role in a Noël Coward play.

"How's this for a starter?" He pulled her close, brought his mouth down to hers.

He kissed differently from other men she'd known. It was great, she decided. She was disappointed when he withdrew his mouth.

"Dessert first," he decided, his breath hot at her ear. "I can't wait—" He caught the tip of her ear between his teeth while a hand slid beneath the low neckline of her dress.

"So let's don't wait."

In silence, the apartment seeming charged with their shared passion, they walked hand in hand into the tiny bedroom.

"Take off your clothes," Oliver said.

"Persuade me," Emily told him. A girl had a right to expect a little romance.

With seductive skill Oliver undressed her and then stripped to the skin himself.

"You drive me nuts, you know?" He pulled her down on the bed with him. Emily abandoned herself to emotion. Knowing it would be fantastic for them.

"Oh, you are something, baby!" he muttered a few moments later while they moved together with soaring heat. "I figured that—"

Afterwards Oliver pulled her into the bathroom to shower with him. And underneath the stinging cold spray he kissed her passionately, his hands roaming about her moist body.

"Ever do it in the shower?" he challenged.

"No," she admitted, "but I'm willing."

"Okay, baby. Take a lesson from the master."

Oliver was older than the other guys she'd known. He was probably thirty-two or thirty-three—and much more sophisticated. She could see spending the rest of her life with him, she told herself when they'd had dinner and were doing the dishes. He'd made it clear he wanted to settle down, she remembered with jubilation.

Mom and Dad would be upset if she married somebody who wasn't Jewish. Dad always said mixed marriages brought problems to the kids of those marriages—*"They don't know who they are."* But these were different times.

She didn't know what Oliver's religion was—they never discussed that subject. But she was playing for keeps now. She wanted a guy of her own on a regular basis. She wanted that little house with the white picket fence that Oliver talked about. And yes, a couple of kids. Today that was the American dream.

Betsy waited at the Southampton railroad station for the late-Saturday-evening train from Manhattan to arrive. She'd been startled when Emily asked if she could bring Oliver Mason out with her. *"He'd come out with me on Saturday night and go back into the city Sunday night."* But how could she object? she asked herself guiltily.

She was taking a dislike—sight unseen—to Oliver Mason, and that was wrong. It was just that she worried about Emily, she told herself. Maybe because she was afraid Emily was discarding all her dreams of theater to focus on marriage and "a cute little house in suburbia." She wasn't afraid that Oliver would come between Emily and herself. She knew nothing could ever break up their closeness.

She rose to her feet as the train appeared in sight. It seemed so long since she'd seen Emily. Since their first year at Hunter it was rare for a day to pass without their seeing each other. Thank God for the telephone, she thought with a touch of humor—and her father-in-law's insistence that she not worry about the cost of long-distance calls.

The train pulled to a stop. Eagerly she searched for Emily and Oliver among the disembarking passengers.

"Emily!" she called out, spying Emily and a tall, good-looking man in Navy whites. "Over here!"

They greeted each other warmly, then Emily introduced Oliver.

"Say, it's great of you to have me out here," he told Betsy. "The city's an oven."

"William's waiting with the car," she told them and prodded them toward the parking area. "Peggy's temporary replacement made salad plates and a pitcher of iced tea. We can have a late snack on the deck.

"Oh, Oliver, it's glorious out here," Emily bubbled. "And on a night like this"—she glanced up at the star-splashed sky—"it'll be spectacular."

In the car Betsy and Emily discussed the Manhattan shop on the brief ride to the house. Betsy sensed that Oliver was impressed with what he saw. At the house William brought the luggage into the foyer, waited for directions.

"We'll take it from here, William," Betsy told him. "Good night."

Betsy and Emily took Oliver out to the deck, listened to his expression of admiration for the magnificent view, then headed out to the kitchen to bring out the food.

"You're probably bushed after the trip on the hot train," Betsy said while she pulled plates from the refrigerator. "After we've eaten I'll show you your rooms." She felt oddly self-conscious at playing hostess in the Southampton beach house.

"You won't mind if we sleep in one room and use the other for window dressing?" Emily drawled.

"I won't know anything about it." Betsy laughed, but she was inwardly disturbed. Was Oliver serious about Emily? She was so vulnerable. She *knew* Emily was serious.

"Jimmy's asleep, of course," Emily said with a wistful sigh.

"If you're up early, we'll take him down to the beach."

"I'll be up early," Emily promised. "I don't want to waste time sleeping out here."

"Oh, I'd better run upstairs and get a couple of sweaters for us," Betsy realized. "It'll be cool sitting out on the deck."

"It was ninety-one degrees and sweltering in the city," Emily murmured. "Baby, this is the life."

Betsy was relieved when Sunday night arrived and she and Emily went with Oliver to the railroad station. He'd been the perfect guest, she acknowledged. And these days it was considered a patriotic duty to be hospitable toward servicemen. Why did she distrust Oliver? she asked herself. It was because she was so afraid for Emily, she conceded inwardly.

Betsy enjoyed being at the beach house with Emily at her side. They rose early to walk on the beach at sunrise, strolled again at sunset. They worked together at the shop for long hours, yet spent cherished time with Jimmy. They talked with the kind of candor that exists only between two young women who recognize their friendship as special.

"Do you think men talk the way we do?" Emily asked curiously on her last night before returning to the city. "There's nothing *we* can't talk about." She giggled in retrospect.

"I'll bet they'd be shocked if they knew how much women 'best friends' share," Betsy said. "And I think that's kind of a safety valve for us."

"This has been a great week. Mom's dying to hear all about my vacation at the playground of the rich," Emily said laughingly.

"Some vacation." Betsy's smile was rueful. "You worked your butt off." But she understood what Emily meant. It had been a great week for her, too.

Then Emily was off to the city, and Betsy felt a sense of loss. She was happy, though, that the shop was doing well. The receipts from the Southampton shop, together with the Saturday business in Manhattan, after expenses, showed a profit. Mark had not expected the summer season to break even.

Then, the last week in August, Alice and Paul Jr. returned from Bar Harbor, both insisting that Bar Harbor was pleasant but that it couldn't compare to Southampton. And Betsy suspected that Georgette felt the same way about Bar Harbor in comparison with Southampton. All through the season she'd heard summer Southamptonites boasting about its superiority to such places as Bar Harbor and Newport and Tuxedo.

In need of help at the shop, Betsy self-consciously asked if she might invite Emily out over the long Labor Day weekend. The Manhattan shop would be closed that Saturday. She made a point of requesting this at the dinner table, when both Alice and Paul Jr. were present.

"Of course, Betsy," Paul Jr. approved instantly.

"Grady's coming out that weekend," Alice remarked, seemingly ambivalent about Emily's presence.

"Emily can share my room." Now Betsy felt uncomfortable about having asked.

"No need for that," Paul Jr. brushed this aside. "We have plenty of bedrooms. Georgette and Carl have decided not to come out," he reminded his wife.

"We'll both be out of sight most of the time," Betsy told them. "It's the final big weekend at the shop."

"You haven't met Grady, have you?" he asked Betsy. "Grady Harrison—"

"I've heard you talk about him," Betsy said. "And Paul talked about him, too."

"He was best man at our wedding." His eyes settled tenderly on his wife. "And I was best man when he married Nadine. Alice has known him since kindergarten," he told Betsy. "His wife died six years ago, after a long, tragic illness. He's become a terrible workaholic since then. We've been trying to get him out here all summer."

Paul Jr. was a workaholic, too, Betsy thought. She'd always envisioned the rich as spending much of their time at luxurious resorts, enjoying leisurely lives that included a minimum of work. That was true for the women, she'd come to realize—the men worked exhaustively. At least, those who were not part of the café society crowd.

Betsy saw Grady Harrison for only a few minutes during the entire weekend. He'd been "Uncle Grady" to Paul, she remembered—liking him on sight. A soft-spoken, slender man of Alice's age, with a distinguished air about him. Emily said he'd resembled "an ex-leading man in the theater. Past his prime but still good-looking."

Betsy learned from Paul Jr. that Grady was a highly successful banker. He owned a house in Nassau, an apartment on Park Avenue, and a rustic hideaway in Vermont. She gathered, also, that on occasions when Paul Jr. was tied up on business, Grady was Alice's escort to social events. In truth, Betsy mused, she knew little about Alice and Paul Jr.'s lives. She lived in their house a stranger, except for a growing closeness to Paul Jr.

The long weekend raced past for Betsy and Emily. Business at the shop was excellent. Betsy had lined up an assignment to redo a bedroom in the Sutton Place apartment of a couple who had a house in Southampton and another in Palm Beach. Mark would be pleased, she told herself.

She was relieved when the Forrest entourage returned to the city—despite steamy days and nights that continued well into September. Heeding Paul's written exhortations, she pushed herself to buy a few smart outfits because it was necessary to dress well for business. There were no doubts in her mind now that she and Mark were launched as interior decorators.

In the middle of the month—after Betsy and Emily had spent anxious days worrying about their whereabouts—Mark and Eric arrived in New York. Mark phoned from La Guardia.

"It's been wild," he said exuberantly, "but we finally made it! You won't believe what we went through to get home! Buy a bunch of cold cuts, a couple of bottles of soda, and meet us at the apartment for dinner when you close the shop. And try to round up Emily."

That night Betsy closed the shop promptly at six, hurried to meet Emily at the Stage Delicatessen. They shopped lavishly, deciding to splurge on a cab to Mark and Eric's apartment. They found the two men exhausted but jubilant to be home again.

"We won't be so thrilled in a month from now," Mark predicted after warm greetings. "We worked our tails off down there, but do the Brazilians know how to live!" He whistled appreciatively.

"Imagine us," Eric said with rapturous recall, "living in this gorgeous apartment looking down on white beach and blue sea. And we've got two live-in help just dying to fulfill our every wish." He exchanged a grin with Mark. "Now we have to worry about cleaning up this dive so it's habitable again."

"I want to hear about the Southampton shop," Mark told Betsy while Eric and Emily brought out plates and glasses, transferred delicatessen and salads from paper containers. "That was one bright move."

"I was a nervous wreck," Betsy confessed. "I was so scared you would be angry."

"Are you kidding?" He chuckled. "It gives us a special cachet to talk about 'our shop at Southampton last summer.' "

"Did Felicia come across with the check?" Betsy asked.

"We're all clear now. With a bonus for you for saving my neck this summer."

Betsy told him about the assignment to do the Bentleys' bedroom in their Sutton Place apartment.

"They're staying at their Southampton house until this coming weekend, but Mrs. Bentley will call us as soon as they're in town." She hesitated, all at once self-conscious about having taken on the assignment in her own name. "I'll introduce you to her once they're back."

"No need." His eyes told her he understood her concern. "This is your assignment. Handle it on your own. And please, God, let us be able to find what we need." Shortages still threatened all decorators.

Betsy and Emily listened avidly as Mark and Eric, interrupting each other in hilarious recall, reported on their months in Rio.

"Oh, but the weather!" Eric rhapsodized. "We'll miss that."

"Most important," Mark said with quiet satisfaction, "is that Felicia will be back in New York early next month. She's already planning the benefit at the Waldorf Towers apartment. She's promised to try for a spread in *House Beautiful* or *Town & Country*. Betsy, you know what that means. The Sanctuary will take off like crazy." His smile was dazzling.

"Mark, let's wait and see if Felicia really comes through," Betsy said. Felicia wasn't the most reliable of patronesses. But her heart pounded at the prospect of the shop—and their names—being mentioned in a top magazine. "You know Felicia—next month she could be tearing off on some new project that's come along and we're totally forgotten."

"Don't even think it." Mark shuddered eloquently. "Think positive, my darling. It's bad enough to have to face another New York winter—after those marvelous months in Rio. I'll die if Felicia walks out on us."

CHAPTER TWENTY-THREE

Betsy and Mark were both nervous wrecks as the day for Felicia's benefit cocktail party approached. They had spent long hours going over the Waldorf Towers apartment again to make sure every tiny detail was right. They'd brought in a few additional pieces that Felicia welcomed with her customarily extravagant approval.

At Mark's insistence Betsy had gone to Saks to buy a Sophie original.

"Look, we have to look as though we're making scads of money," he said over dinner with Betsy and Emily the evening before the benefit.

"You're doing great." Emily smiled brilliantly. "And even greater after this bash."

"Alice still doesn't approve of my working." Betsy's smile was wry. "She can't understand why I don't want to stay home and spend all my time with Jimmy."

"The rich have limited vision." Mark shrugged. "But they do provide us with some fascinating assignments."

"Paul approves of your working," Emily reminded. "That's what counts."

"He's so proud of me." Betsy glowed in recall. "Even when he comes home and becomes a successful playwright, he's willing for me to work. He knows how important it is to me." She cherished Paul's letters—as she knew he welcomed the flood of V-mails and regular letters that went out to him religiously—along with the stream of salamis and chocolate bars.

"Tomorrow will be a terrific breakthrough for us," Mark predicted with an air of triumph. "Felicia insists we'll have press coverage. Every ticket to the benefit has been sold. And every ticketholder is a prospective client."

"I just wish it didn't take so long for magazines to hit the newsstands. It'll be three months after the benefit before the public reads about it." Emily sighed, but her eyes radiated satisfaction. "Do you really expect *House Beautiful* to cover the benefit?"

"Stop fishing," Betsy told her. "You know their people will be there." But like Emily she was anxious to see the magazine's reporter and photographer at the benefit. Mark would die if they didn't show. *She* would die.

Betsy and Mark arrived at Felicia's sumptuous Waldorf Towers apartment half an hour before the cocktail benefit was to begin. Felicia had inveigled half a dozen of the season's favorite debutantes to serve as waitresses. Already they were circulating about the living room—tiny white aprons over their designer dresses. Felicia fussed over the flowers she'd ordered for the event.

"Mark, do the flowers overwhelm the furniture?" she asked in a flurry of nerves. "I want everybody to see what a marvelous job you and Betsy have done."

"Felicia, they're perfect," he soothed. "The party will be a huge success."

"It already is financially," Felicia conceded with rare practicality.

Within ten minutes after the first cluster of guests had arrived, Betsy knew that the party would be a tremendous career boost for Mark and herself. Even before the spread in *House Beautiful* appeared, they would be picking up exciting new assignments.

A week before Thanksgiving Alice Forrest explained to Betsy that it was family tradition for many years now for the Forrests to have Thanksgiving dinner with Georgette Adams and her family.

"You're invited of course," Alice began self-consciously. "I've told Georgette that—"

"Thank you," Betsy broke in, "but I've made arrangements to spend the day with my friend Emily and her family out in Brooklyn." She'd heard earlier from Elise that the Forrests always went to the Adams' for Thanksgiving. "I'm taking Jimmy with me. That way Miss Watkins can spend the day with her family."

"Do you think you should take Jimmy all the way to Brooklyn in this weather?" Alice was upset. "It's so uncertain—there's talk of rain or even snow. At Jimmy's age they catch cold so easily."

"We'll take a taxi," Betsy soothed. "He'll be fine."

"I hate not to be with Jimmy on his first Thanksgiving." Now Alice seemed ambivalent about going to the Adams' house for dinner. "I could ask Peggy and William to stay—"

"Jimmy will be fine," Betsy repeated, struggling to sound casual. Would she ever become accustomed to all this tension about every little detail? "We'll go out by taxi."

"No," Alice said. "I'll arrange for a limousine to pick you up and bring you back. I wouldn't have an easy moment at the thought of you standing out in the street with Jimmy and trying to find a taxi on a holiday like that. Just tell me when you plan to leave and when you'd like to come back."

Betsy arranged for Emily to be at the house to drive with Jimmy and herself to Borough Park. She was looking forward to the visit, though the holiday highlighted Paul's absence. What would he be doing today? Thinking of Jimmy and her, she knew. He would be wishing they could be together. The war didn't stop because it was Thanksgiving, she thought wistfully while the three of them settled themselves in the limousine. But to every American soldier, absence from home and family today would be especially painful.

"Back in Hunter did you ever imagine we'd be driving to Borough Park in such style?" Emily asked as the chauffeur pulled away from the curb.

"I keep asking myself what Paul's doing today." Betsy hugged Jimmy, deposited a gentle kiss atop his head. "One thing's sure," she added wryly, "he's not having turkey and dressing and cranberries and pumpkin pie."

"I'm a traitor—I don't like pumpkin pie," Emily confessed.

"But Mom always makes at least two pies—and one of them is sure to be pecan."

"Horse!" Jimmy announced exuberantly. "Horse!" A mounted policeman had appeared on the road, and he was ecstatic.

Within ten minutes Jimmy was asleep. He lay between the two women, with his head in Betsy's lap. She was going to enjoy today, Betsy told herself. Emily's parents always made her feel that she was part of their family. There would be ten at the table, including Jimmy. That would be such a warm, lovely experience.

At the house they were greeted with hugs and kisses, plus much affectionate fussing over Jimmy. It was a dramatic contrast to his grandmother's constant fretting, Betsy realized—a sense of warmth and love.

"Okay, Jimmy, let's get you out of that snowsuit," Mrs. Meyers crooned. "Betsy, I can't believe how he's growing!"

"She's saving all his clothes for Rheba." Emily laughed. Rheba—happily pregnant—was vowing she and Bert would have at least four children. "Your grandkids, Mom, will be dressed by Saks and Best!"

The house was filled with the aromas of cooking. The twenty-pound turkey had been in the oven for hours. Fresh coffee was perking on the range, scheduled to be ready for arrivals.

"Come out into the kitchen and I'll give you coffee," Mrs. Meyers said to Betsy and Emily while Rheba took over Jimmy.

"You made a pecan pie?" Emily asked, smiling.

"Don't I always?" her mother countered. "But no pie before dinner. Maybe a cookie or two," she stipulated.

When it came time to sit down to the early afternoon dinner, Mrs. Meyers brought out a borrowed high chair for Jimmy.

"We'll put you right next to Mommie," she told him, lifting him into the chair. Clearly he loved the attention he was receiving from all sides.

Please, God, Betsy thought, let Paul be home to celebrate next Thanksgiving with us.

* * *

Two days after Thanksgiving, while Betsy played with him in the nursery, Jimmy shakily pulled himself erect and took his first step.

"Oh, sweetheart!" Betsy glowed. "Come over here to Mommie," she coaxed, holding out her arms to him.

"Walk!" Jimmy announced in triumph. "Walk!"

She must take some snapshots of Jimmy on his feet, Betsy told herself. Paul would be so excited. But how sad that Paul wasn't here to share this moment.

Betsy was startled when Alice announced her elaborate plans for Jimmy's first birthday. The guests would include only family and the house staff—but a clown had been hired to entertain, a fancy cake ordered from Rumpelmayer's, a photographer engaged to take photographs, and champagne was to be served to all but the birthday boy.

Betsy never remembered so festive an occasion in this household as on the afternoon of Jimmy's birthday. His grandfather arrived home from the office at four, though he made it clear he must return to the office later. For the first few moments Jimmy was wary of the clown, but soon he was enthralled. The beautifully decorated cake was superb. With help from his grandmother Jimmy blew out the single candle. Betsy saw gratitude in Mr. Forrest's eyes that she allowed his wife to dominate the occasion.

For all her joy in Jimmy's first birthday, Betsy was ever conscious that Paul had missed a whole year of his son's life. He hadn't shared in the delicious discovery of the first tooth. He hadn't been there for Jimmy's first steps. Jimmy had yet to learn to say da-da—because his father was fighting a war in Italy.

Jimmy had been robbed of a father for all this time—and for how much more? Paul would be delighted, she thought tenderly, when he received the photographs of the party. She was sure her mother-in-law would send them on as fast as possible.

When Hanukkah arrived, Betsy took Jimmy to the Meyers' house for a first-night party. Fascinated, he watched while Mrs. Meyers placed the first candle in the menorah, lighted it, and said the appropriate prayer. In addition to the traditional potato latkes,

Emily's grandmother had made cookies in fanciful shapes, and Jimmy—who was rarely allowed sweets—was ecstatic.

Ten days before Christmas Alice and Georgette took off again for Palm Beach, with both husbands scheduled to join them for several days. Betsy was relieved to have the house almost to herself. For Christmas Eve and Christmas day—when the servants would be off—she would take Jimmy and stay at the apartment with Emily. There she felt a special closeness to Paul.

As the year drew to an end, Americans began to realize that the Italian campaign would not be swift and easy. The night before Paul Jr. was to leave for Palm Beach, they listened somberly to a late newscast.

"Most people thought once Mussolini was ousted and the new regime surrendered and declared war on Germany that the Italian campaign would be fast and easy." He shook his head. "No such deal. The Germans still hold two-thirds of Italy."

"Paul writes about all the mud, and climbing mountains with pinpoint turns," Betsy remembered with anguish. "And he says everybody curses the cold weather."

"Nobody expected the German resistance to be so dogged," Paul Jr. admitted. "The fighting is bitter and bloody."

"But we'll win," Betsy said, determined to be cheerful, refusing to consider the cost of the win. Please God, let Paul come through this bitter campaign.

CHAPTER TWENTY-FOUR

Betsy walked swiftly through the dreary late February twilight, her shoulders hunched in silent protest at the bone-chilling cold. The sky was a murky gray tinged with a reddish underglow that warned of imminent snow. She was meeting Emily for dinner at Paul's apartment. They hadn't expected snow tonight.

As usual she carried a briefcase filled with notes and an architectural textbook for bedtime study. She preferred to walk from the shop to the house rather than to shove her way into a rush hour subway or bus.

By the time she approached the Forrest house, silver-dollar-sized flakes were falling. Elise was at the door, talking with a Western Union messenger. He turned and strode past her with a jaunty smile.

"Bet we have six inches by morning," he threw over one shoulder. "That sky's just loaded with snow!"

Elise held the door wide for her.

"A telegram for you, Miss Betsy," Elise told her, holding out the yellow envelope.

"It must be for Mrs. Forrest," Betsy said.

"It's for you," Elise insisted, her eyes somber. "Mrs. Paul Forrest the Third."

"Thank you, Elise." All at once she was terrified. She stared at the envelope for a moment while Elise closed the door behind her. Her heart was pounding, her throat tightening.

She put her briefcase on the foyer table, forced herself to rip open the envelope, pulled out the brief yellow sheet of paper.

"No. Oh, God, no!" The words were wrenched from her as she read the War Department message. *"We regret to inform you that your husband, Sgt. Paul Forrest III, has been killed in action . . ."*

"Miss Betsy?" Elise hovered anxiously over her.

Paul dead? She'd had a letter just yesterday. He'd said how anxious he was to be home with her and Jimmy. He'd talked about the play he wanted to write. *"I've learned so much, Betsy, in this bastardly war. I know I can write a fine, meaningful play."*

The telegram fell from her hands to the floor. She swayed, her mind in chaos.

"Miss Betsy?" She was conscious that Elise had bent to pick up the telegram.

"No," she whispered. "Oh, God, no—"

She charged toward the door and out into the night, not heeding Elise's anxious exhortations to return. She walked without direction, the contents of the telegram echoing in her brain. *Paul was never coming home again.* He wasn't missing. He'd been killed in action.

Jimmy would never know his father. Her mother and father died when she was young, but she'd had ten beautiful years with them. Jimmy had never even seen his father. Her poor, poor baby.

She walked in anguish, unaware of the snow that was falling with increasing intensity, sticking to the ground. She tried to cope with ugly reality. All these long months—almost two years—she'd told herself nothing would happen to Paul. *He would come home to her.*

She walked until physical pain intruded on emotional pain. Now she paused and searched the street for an empty taxi. Her hand flailed the air as a taxi turned onto the avenue. The driver came to a crunching halt.

Her voice sounding strange to her ears, she gave the driver the address of Paul's apartment and settled back on the seat. She was impatient to be under the roof where she had been so happy with

Paul. As though, she taunted herself, she might reclaim those precious times.

At her destination she paid the driver and hurried across the sidewalk to the stoop, already searching for her keys. Her hand trembled so that she had difficulty unlocking the door.

"Damn! Damn!"

At last the door was open. She stumbled across the narrow foyer to the stairs. She was breathless by the time she arrived at her floor. Emily was there already. The radio was on. The plaintive lyrics of "I'll Never Smile Again" drifted to her. Paul had called it "our song."

She knocked clamorously on the door, too exhausted, too drained to struggle with the lock. Emily pulled the door wide. Her welcoming smile fading as she saw Betsy's distraught face.

"He's gone." Betsy's voice cracked. "Not missing in action. *Killed* in action. Oh, Emily, how am I going to survive?"

It was almost eleven before Betsy arrived back at the house. She was numb now and devoid of tears. She let herself into the foyer and walked with leaden feet to the tiny elevator. Emerging at her floor, she could hear the wails of her mother-in-law coming from the master bedroom suite on the floor below.

"Why, Paul? Why did it have to happen?"

"Alice, you've got to rest." Paul Jr.'s voice was hoarse. "The pill won't work if you carry on like this."

"Where's Dr. Raymond when I need him?" Alice whimpered.

"He's handling an emergency at the hospital."

"I need him!" Alice screamed. *"My son is dead!"*

"Reverend Ainsworth will be here soon," Paul Jr. soothed. "You don't want him to see you like this."

With a trembling hand Betsy opened the door to the nursery and walked inside. The sliver of light beneath the door of Miss Watkins' bedroom had told her Jimmy was alone. He was sound asleep. Thank God he wasn't hearing his grandmother. Everybody in the house must know that Paul was dead. Everybody except Jimmy—who had the most to lose.

Betsy hovered over the crib, her eyes clinging to the small

sleeping form. Her mind was fogged with grief. She reached for one tiny hand. What would happen to them now?

They mustn't stay in this house—Paul's mother would try to run Jimmy's life. He mustn't endure the smothering kind of love his grandmother would foist on him. *And he must be raised in the Jewish faith.*

She pulled up a chair beside the crib, sat in the darkness. So many questions plagued her. How did Paul die? Was it mercifully swift or did he suffer? Were there letters she had not yet received? There would be more word from the War Department, but answers would not lessen her pain.

Now the sounds from the floor below ceased. Little of the usual street noises intruded at this hour, in the midst of a snowstorm. She sat motionless beside the crib. One hand clung to Jimmy's tiny fist.

She started as the nursery door opened. In the spill of the hall light she saw her father-in-law standing in the doorway. His face was gaunt and haggard.

"Betsy—" He came toward her. "I was so worried. Elise said you'd gone out. I didn't know where you were."

"Tell me it isn't true," she pleaded, her voice choking with emotion. "Please tell me."

"You'll stay here with us," he said gently. "This will always be your home."

"I don't know," she whispered. "I have to do what will be best for Jimmy. He has to grow up with a normal life."

"Jimmy is all we have left of our son." He paused, fighting to keep his voice steady. "Please don't take him from us."

"I can't think straight," she whispered. "But I must do what's best for Jimmy." He understood she meant the suffocating atmosphere Paul's mother created in this household.

"This is your home and Jimmy's," he said strongly. "We're your family now. This is a terrible time for Paul's mother. For all of us," he added as Betsy flinched. "But together we'll come through this. Jimmy and you will lack for nothing," he promised. "One day Jimmy will inherit our estate." He hesitated. "You know that Paul would want you to be here with us."

"I'll try," Betsy said after a moment. She remembered Paul's last words to her: *"Betsy, try to understand my mother. Be compassionate toward her."*

Far into the night Betsy sat beside Jimmy's crib, reliving special hours with Paul. They'd had so little time. And now there was no more time. If Paul had been shipped out three months later, she told herself in anguish, he would have at least seen his son.

With the first light of dawn creeping into the sky, Betsy left the nursery to go into her room. Exhausted, she lay across the bed, then fell into troubled slumber. She awoke to the sounds of Alice's hysterical sobbing.

Elise knocked lightly, then came into the room with a breakfast tray. She shook her head in silence. Gently Elise coaxed her into drinking some coffee, then helped her change into a nightgown. Later she realized that the coffee had contained a sedative.

Early in the afternoon Emily called to try to offer words of consolation.

"Would you like me to come there after work?" Emily asked solicitously.

"I'll be at the apartment," Betsy told her. At the apartment she felt close to Paul. That was their *home*. "I'll be there by seven. After Jimmy's had his dinner." *Her poor baby, who would never know his father.*

CHAPTER TWENTY-FIVE

Three days later Betsy forced herself to go into the shop. She knew she must keep busy or she risked being swallowed up in grief. For Jimmy she must be strong. She fought against tears when Mark took her wordlessly into his arms. *Thank God for her friends.* They were more than friends—they were her family.

She followed the old pattern now, though insomnia was her constant companion. Night after night she left her bed at odd hours to go into the nursery to stand beside Jimmy's crib. To reassure herself that he was all right.

For ten days after the War Department telegram arrived, Alice remained secluded in her bedroom. There was a funereal air about the household. It seemed to Betsy that the servants were afraid to speak except in muted tones. Every day or two Dr. Raymond came to check on his longtime patient.

Then Betsy learned that late the previous evening Alice had been spirited away to the private sanitarium in Connecticut where she had recovered from earlier nervous collapses.

"I'll be driving up to see her most evenings," Paul Jr. explained. "Unless some business emergency arises. Please ask your friend to come to stay with you whenever you like. Remember, Betsy, this is your home."

Betsy was aware that often on his late-evening return from the sanitarium Paul Jr. crept on silent feet into the nursery to stand beside Jimmy's crib. She knew the pain he felt behind his quiet exterior.

It was so unreal, she thought endlessly—to know that Paul was dead in a faraway country. Endlessly she asked herself how it had happened. Was it fast? She prayed he hadn't suffered. Had he died on the battlefield or in a hospital?

He knew she loved him. She clung to this thought. He knew he had a son. At least he'd seen the stream of snapshots of Jimmy that she had sent to him. He must have died with them next to his heart.

Betsy struggled to involve herself in her work. That was the road to sanity. Betsy forced herself to notify Paul's landlord that his apartment would be available for another tenant at the end of the month. When he'd shipped out, he'd told his parents a friend was taking over and there would be no need to close it up. Now she'd arrange for the Salvation Army to pick up the furniture and whatever else remained.

Before notifying the landlord that the apartment was being vacated, she made one last traumatic visit. Her heart pounded as she unlocked the door for the last time. She was flooded by memories. She closed her eyes for a moment, feeling Paul's presence.

She'd take only some of Paul's records and a few of his books. With trembling hands she chose a handful of records. Eyes blurred by tears, she picked the recording of "I'll Never Smile Again."

All at once she was reliving that awful day when the telegram came from the War Department. She'd run to the apartment, where Emily had been waiting for her. And from behind the door as she knocked for admittance had come the music and lyrics— "I'll Never Smile Again. . . ."

Then—two weeks later—she became anxious about The Sanctuary. She realized that Eric—drained by the exhausting hours he'd spent on his defense job since the beginning of the war and frustrated by what seemed a death knell to his cherished ambitions—was trying to persuade Mark to sell the shop and

move with him to California. She'd heard Eric's earnest, eloquent pleas:

*"Mark, in California I have a chance to make it as a set designer.
How many plays a year come to Broadway? In Hollywood there are
hundreds of movies made every year."*

Colleen kept writing that in California she could introduce him
to the right people. *"Sweetie, contacts are everything out here."*

And both Eric and Mark hated New York winters. Betsy knew
California held magical promises for them—particularly after
their delight in Rio. Eric was blunt about not wanting to go back
to being a window dresser when the war was over. He wanted to
design sets.

Betsy prayed that The Sanctuary's growing success would keep
Mark and Eric in New York. Everybody was predicting the war
would be over soon—all their problems in acquiring materials
would be over. And the recognition she and Mark were acquiring
as interior decorators was exhilarating.

And all the while, Betsy nurtured a daring dream. If Mark and
Eric left for California, she'd try to buy the shop. She had Paul's
insurance money, she plotted, plus what she made a point of
depositing in the bank from her salary each month. The balance
she could pay off.

Late in April Mark returned from a trip to one of their suppliers
with a glow about him that instantly alerted her to some new
development.

"Betsy, I don't want you to be upset, because I'm sure things
will work out in your favor," he said cautiously. "Jim Taylor didn't
call me over just to see his latest shipment. He wanted to talk about
buying the shop."

"Oh, Mark!" Her initial reaction was alarm.

"I'm trying to make him understand that if the deal goes
through, he should take you in as a partner." But his eyes were
troubled.

"Taylor's not buying that," she guessed, fighting against panic.

"He wants to bring his daughter in to run the operation. But
she's a dilettante—she can't handle it," Mark said exasperatedly.

"I told him we're not just running a shop—we're interior decorators. *He needs you.* He said he'd have to think about it," Mark admitted. "But he's eager to buy. God, I want to move to California. Not just for Eric—for me, too. You know how I hate New York winters."

"Mark, sell me the shop," Betsy said. Her heart pounded and her throat tightened at the thought of what she was about to say next. "I can give you Paul's GI insurance money as a down payment. Pay off the balance on a quarterly basis. I—"

"Betsy, it's a tremendous responsibility," Mark said, interrupting her. Her offer had taken him off guard. "We're having such problems getting materials. We hope the craziness will be over soon, but we don't *know*. Think about it a few days," he urged. "I can hold up Taylor for a while. Be sure about this."

"Mark, I was never more sure of anything in my life." Her face glowed with conviction. "I want to buy the shop. This is what I want to do with my life. I'll give you Paul's GI insurance money as soon as—"

"I'm not worried about that," he broke in. "And every instinct tells me you'll be a big success on your own," he conceded. "But we're in the midst of such troubled times—"

"Let's work out a deal for me to take over," she said. "At whatever price Jim Taylor is willing to pay," she added.

"All right, you'll take over," he agreed after a moment of hesitation. "But there's just one stipulation." His tone was apologetic. "I'll want you to change the name of the shop. Not immediately— not until our regular clients know what's happening. But I'll be opening The Sanctuary on the West Coast. One day—with a lot of luck—I might expand into a chain. I'd like to hang on to the name."

"That's fine," said Betsy. Her mind was racing ahead. *She'd pulled this off.* "I'll call it The Oasis. How does that sound?"

"Great," Mark said.

"And, Mark, there's no reason to wait. We can change the name now."

Mark smiled. "You're right, Betsy—this is where you belong.

I'll talk to my lawyer about drawing up the papers. And I'll tell Eric we're moving to California."

Betsy said nothing to her father-in-law in the days ahead about her decision to buy the shop. She would tell him later. He had enough on his mind right now with Alice in the sanitarium, she told herself. But she was convinced he would approve.

With gratifying speed Mark moved to handle all the technicalities of the sale. He wrote to all their clients to explain that Betsy now owned The Oasis, formerly The Sanctuary, and that she would carry on as the shop's interior decorator on her own. He talked glowingly about her talents.

Together Betsy and Mark explained to their suppliers that she would carry on the business alone and that the name would eventually be changed to The Oasis. Betsy was upset that Felicia Goulart was sulking because Mark had not told her earlier about his planned departure. She refused to accept his explanation that it was a sudden decision. She hedged now about having Betsy take on the new house she had just bought at Southampton. All at once she was enthusiastic about Billy Baldwin.

"So you may lose a client here and there," Mark said. "Felicia likes to have a young male decorator in the wings. But she'll come back," he predicted. "She admires your skills."

Betsy was grateful to be so involved with business that there was little time to dwell on her grief. Still, the nights were painful. She read and reread Paul's letters, which she saved for the day when Jimmy could read and understand them. They would tell Jimmy so much about his father, she told herself.

At perilous moments she had clung to the possibility that there had been some terrible mistake and that Paul was missing in action rather than killed in action. But with the arrival of a small packet containing Paul's dog tags and a photo folder of snapshots of Jimmy and herself, she came to grips with reality.

With Mark and Eric preparing to leave for Los Angeles, Betsy learned from her father-in-law that Alice was coming home from the sanitarium.

"I'm arranging for a small welcome-home dinner party," Paul

Jr. told her. "Not actually a party," he said quickly. "The doctors feel it will be better for Alice—on her first night home—to sit down to dinner with a few people close to her. It'll be like family. You and I, Georgette and Carl, and Grady. You remember Grady?"

"We met at the Southampton house," Betsy recalled.

"Grady was 'Uncle Grady' to Paul. Grady and Alice grew up together. Grady's family owned the townhouse next door to her family's for many years. Grady sold it not long after his parents died and bought a smaller house divided into two apartments. He lives in one duplex."

"I remember Paul talked about a summer he'd spent with the Harrisons at Newport," Betsy said.

"That's right. You know Alice never shipped Paul off to camp in the summers—he was always with us. And we often shared vacation houses with Grady and Nadine. They never had children, so Paul was special to them."

At dinner with Emily that evening, Betsy confessed she dreaded coming face-to-face with her mother-in-law. They'd had no real meeting since the night before the telegram arrived from the War Department.

"You'd think that losing Paul would draw us close together," Betsy said wistfully. "That and our love for Jimmy. But I suspect she'll look at me and hate me for being alive when Paul's dead."

"You'll be a weird crew at dinner." Emily's smile was wry. "Everybody walking around on tiptoes not to upset Her Majesty."

"I know it's hard for her," Betsy said. "And I know Paul loved her." Paul's plea to her that last time they were together often echoed in her mind. She remembered Aunt Celia's ingrained compassion.

On the evening of the dinner party Betsy went directly to the nursery on her arrival home, as usual. Every moment she was all too conscious that Alice was somewhere in the house. When Miss Watkins went downstairs to her own dinner, Betsy settled Jimmy in his chair and fed him. This was her special time of day with her son. She would allow nothing to spoil it, she told herself defiantly.

With Jimmy in bed she read him a story, kissed him goodnight, and went into her room to dress. Would the other two women be dressing for dinner? she wondered anxiously. She knew that when Alice went to Georgette's home for dinner, she always wore a long dinner dress. Uncertain about this, she rang for Elise and questioned her.

"Oh, yes, Miss Betsy, if there's anybody outside the family at the dinner table, Mrs. Forrest dresses for dinner." Elise hesitated. "She seems to be bearing up well now."

"I'm glad to hear that, Elise." Betsy forced a smile.

For a moment, standing before the full-length mirror in the flattering yellow crepe dinner dress bought for special dinners with clients, she was assaulted by fresh grief. Paul had liked her wearing this particular shade of yellow. How could she be standing here this way and thinking about how she looked when Paul was dead?

Before going downstairs she went into the nursery again. Jimmy was asleep. She reached to take one tiny hand in hers for a moment. He was such a happy child, she thought tenderly. He didn't know what he had lost.

Approaching the library, she heard the radio, the volume low. Paul Jr. must be downstairs already. She felt a closeness to him now that she had never expected to feel. He hurt, too, though it was Alice who carried on so vocally. When he looked at Jimmy, held his grandson in his arms, she knew he was seeing Paul at that age.

He moved forward to switch off the radio when he saw her come into the room.

"Please don't turn off the news." He'd thought she was Alice. Talk of the war was forbidden in Alice's presence.

"The Allies seem to be making progress." He leaned forward to switch on the radio again. "The pundits are predicting Rome will fall by the end of the month."

Together they listened while the newscaster reported on activities, first in the European theater and then in the Pacific. At Georgette's appearance Paul Jr. switched off the radio and rose to his feet. He rang for Elise and asked her to tell his wife that Georgette had arrived.

"Jimmy is so adorable," Georgette gushed to Betsy. "Alice never stops talking about him. She can't walk into a toy shop without wanting to buy out the place."

"What's Doris doing these days?" Paul Jr. asked. Betsy remembered Paul saying that Doris was the only member of the Adams family his father liked. "We see her so seldom."

Betsy listened with a strained smile while Paul Jr. and Georgette talked about Georgette's daughter and son. Then she heard the doorbell. William was going to the door.

"That's probably Grady," Paul Jr. guessed with an anticipatory smile. "Do you know, he drove up to see Alice every week while she was away?"

"I was up twice," Georgette said defensively. "With all my war charities I couldn't do more than that."

Moments later Grady came into the room. Paul Jr. rushed forward to greet him.

"How's Alice?" Grady asked, his eyes solicitous.

"She's holding up," Paul Jr. told him.

"Grady, how do you manage to hang on to that marvelous tan?" Georgette asked.

"I run away to the sun at regular intervals." He smiled and turned to Betsy.

"I loved Paul," Grady told her. "I'll miss him very much."

"So will I," Betsy whispered, tears filling her eyes.

"You all must be starving," an imperious voice broke in. "I'll tell Peggy to serve dinner." Alice hovered in the doorway. She wore one of her deceptively simple black dinner dresses with her triple strand of pearls.

"Darling, you look lovely." Georgette moved forward to kiss Alice. "Welcome home."

Alice appeared pale but composed. Betsy guessed she was on medication and was touched by the tenderness on Paul Jr.'s face as he drew his wife into the room.

Alice placed Georgette and Carl on either side of herself at the dinner table. That left Betsy and Grady to flank Paul Jr. Betsy knew the conversation would be carefully monitored. Nothing must be said that might upset Alice.

Betsy opened up to Grady's warmth. She talked to him about the shop and was gratified by his show of interest. Then, midway through the main course, Georgette inadvertently triggered an emotional outcry from Alice when she mentioned her son Ron's "long hours at that awful job down in Washington."

"Georgette, how can you talk like that?" Alice sobbed. "Ron's alive and safe. He's not dodging bullets on a battlefield!"

Paul Jr. summoned Elise and asked her to bring Alice's pill bottle while Georgette and Carl tried awkwardly to calm her. Paul Jr. sat in anguished silence at the head of the table.

"Alice, why don't you and Georgette fly down to my house in Nassau and stay there for a while?" Grady suggested. "It's so beautiful and serene down there. It's a healing place. I can tell you that from experience." Betsy remembered the tragic early death of his wife. He must have sought refuge there, she guessed sympathetically.

"Alice, you've never been to Nassau," Paul Jr. reminded, speaking as though to a small, much-loved child. "It would be a wonderful change for you."

"Not Nassau," Georgette protested with a slight shudder. "This is the wrong season."

"There's no wrong season in Nassau," Grady said with a chuckle. "When George Washington visited the Bahamas in the eighteenth century, he declared them the 'Isles of Perpetual June.' The Bahamas sea breezes eliminate the kind of humidity that settles over other islands in the Caribbean."

"Alice, go," Paul Jr. entreated. "It'll do you worlds of good."

Betsy was touched by Grady's concern for Alice. When—over dessert—Alice finally agreed to go down to his Nassau house with Georgette for two weeks, he glowed with satisfaction. But how strange, she mused, that even in the midst of a world war the very rich could contrive to vacation in Nassau.

CHAPTER TWENTY-SIX

Grady Harrison was startled to realize that he was thinking constantly about Betsy over the next few days. She had the same delicate beauty, the same air of gentility that he remembered in Nadine in the early years of their marriage—before she contracted the devastating illness that attacked her when she was so young. Looking at Betsy, listening to her talk, he had a disconcerting sense of racing back in time.

Now, about to return to his office after a business luncheon at the Metropolitan Club, he made an impulsive decision. Stepping into his waiting limo, he instructed his chauffeur to drive him first to Betsy's shop.

"It's called The Oasis, and it's somewhere on Madison in the low Fifties," Grady directed.

He leaned back in the car now with an air of anticipation. The chauffeur drove away from the magnificent grayish-white Manhattan landmark, designed by Stanford White, and headed for his destination. So he'd get back to the office an hour later, Grady told himself self-consciously. He'd long needed a new lamp for the guest room night table. Sandra was always complaining, when she came down to visit, that the height was wrong. His sister was usually so amiable—he ought to indulge her in this.

He watched one side of the street and his chauffeur the other as the limousine made its way through the heavy lunch hour traffic.

"There it is," Grady said with a faint surge of excitement. "Just ahead, on the right."

It was absurd, he told himself, to take time off in the middle of the day to buy a lamp. Still, he'd enjoy a break in his daily—dull—routine.

He understood Betsy's grief. God, did he understand! He'd seen the pain in her eyes. Yet she was young and would bounce back, he thought. He admired her vitality, her involvement in her work. Let her be grateful for that.

Telling the chauffeur to circle around until he emerged from the shop, Grady approached the entrance. In his mind he framed the casual reason for his appearance. Then he spied Betsy off to one side, arranging flowers in a vase.

Her face lighted when she saw him. She hurried toward him with a reassuring warmth. He'd been subconsciously aware that she was lovely during the weekend at Southampton—though he'd seen little of her then. But at the dinner party for Alice he'd realized that Paul's young widow was a very special person.

He explained his needs to Betsy. "The room is used mainly by my sister when she comes down from Boston. She's an inveterate bedtime reader."

He was astonished by the care Betsy was taking to understand what would please Sandra. She apologized ingratiatingly for her limited stock.

"I hope to enlarge our inventory soon. Oh, but wait." Her face glowed. "I have a beautiful Tiffany lamp that will be just the right height. I haven't put it on display yet because I want to freshen it up a bit first, but I can show it to you."

"Please do."

He waited with disconcerting impatience for her to return. He smiled in instant approval as she approached with an exquisite Tiffany lamp in muted tones of mauve and gray.

"Sandra will love it," he said enthusiastically. "I'll take this one."

"Let me have it cleaned up. I'll have it sent over to your apartment tomorrow," she promised.

"That'll be great." He was disturbingly reluctant to leave. Reaching for his checkbook, he inquired about her efforts to expand. "You mentioned your limited stock," he said, reminding her almost shyly. "Have you considered a bank loan? The shop is doing well. It's a good risk."

"A widow with a small child and a large business overhead is not considered a good risk at the banks where I've applied," she admitted ruefully.

"That's nonsense. You obviously have a going business." He glanced around the attractive shop with respect. "Why don't you apply at my bank?" he said on impulse. He reached for his business card. This was Paul's widow—and so young to face such grief. "Go to this branch of my bank," he instructed. "I'll see to it that your application is accepted."

"Oh, that would be marvelous!" She was radiant. "It'll mean so much to me!"

"And this will be a confidential business matter," he said with a conspiratorial smile. "Alice and Paul don't have to know."

"I can't tell you how grateful I am." Her pleasure filled him with satisfaction.

"I know you'll do well. Come in whenever you like. Your loan will be approved." Now he retreated into a polite reserve. "I'm confident you'll ask for a loan that you can handle comfortably."

Betsy remained euphoric for the rest of the day. The next morning, before she opened the shop, she would be at Grady Harrison's bank to apply for a loan. She was impatient to report this unexpected windfall to Emily.

Once her nightly routine with Jimmy was over, she hurried to Emily's apartment.

"I can't believe it!" she said ecstatically when she'd told Emily about Grady's promise to see that her loan application was approved.

"How much did he offer?" Emily asked.

"He didn't. He just said he was sure I would ask for a loan I could handle comfortably."

"Hmmm-hmmm." Emily nodded knowingly. "He wouldn't have said that if you weren't young and pretty."

"Emily, you're all wrong," Betsy told her. "He was very close to Paul."

"What did the Forrests say about Grady arranging a loan for you?" Emily asked.

"We won't mention it to them," Betsy said. "Grady said there was no need to discuss the loan with anybody else. You'll like him. He loves the theater—and he's so knowledgeable about it. He sees almost every play that comes to Broadway." She remembered this from their dinner party conversation.

"So would I," Emily pointed out, "if I had his money. And I wouldn't be sitting in second-balcony seats."

"I think he's lonely." Sympathy welled in Betsy. She knew firsthand about loneliness. "His wife died six years ago after a long illness. He's approving the loan because he loved Paul. And stop being so cynical."

"What's happening with Alice and Nassau?" Emily asked.

"She and Georgette Adams have finally decided to go. They'll stay for at least two weeks."

"Great," Emily said, beaming with approval. "There'll be peace and quiet at Forrest Manor."

When Betsy returned to the house, she heard the faint sound of the radio in the library. That meant Alice was settled in the master bedroom suite for the evening. Betsy walked down the hall to the library.

Paul Jr. glanced up in welcome as she came into the room.

"Alice and Georgette leave in the morning for Nassau," he reminded her. "And in mid-June we'll settle in at the Southampton house for the summer. The doctors say it's best for Alice to be away from this house as much as possible for now."

"Of course." Betsy tried for a compassionate smile, but her mind was in sudden chaos. Up till now she hadn't thought about her summer schedule. Alice would expect Jimmy to be in Southampton for the summer again. The city was hot and uncomfortable—it would be good for him to be at the beach. But Betsy knew she had to run the Manhattan shop this summer. She had two major decorating assignments in town to be completed while the clients were away.

"I hope Alice enjoys Nassau." Paul Jr.'s anxious voice brought her back to the moment. "I understand Grady's house there is beautiful." All at once he seemed to sense she was troubled. "Are you having problems at the shop?" he asked sympathetically.

"I have to work out a practical summer schedule," she explained. "I don't like to keep Jimmy in the city, but I have to be here—"

"How did you handle it last summer?" Paul Jr. squinted, seemingly trying to recollect.

"Last summer I was at the beach house," she reminded. "I ran the branch shop in Southampton."

"Of course. How stupid of me not to remember." He smiled apologetically.

"The situation is different now. I have assignments that require my being in town." And she had the quarterly payments to Mark and her bank loan payments to meet.

"What about the two girls who work in the shop? Could they manage it?"

"They're not decorators. Just salesgirls." And not too good at that. But in the middle of the war they were the best she could find.

"Business is always slow in the city in July and August," Paul Jr. pointed out. "Could the shop be open for a short week? Say, Monday through Thursday? You could leave Jimmy with Miss Watkins and Alice at the beach house for four days out of each week, then join him for a long weekend. You know he'd be well cared for."

"I couldn't bear to be away from him for four days every week." The prospect was unnerving. "He's so little—he'd be frightened." Her mind searched desperately for a solution. "I could commute on Monday, Tuesday, and Wednesday. I could see Jimmy in the morning before I left. I could make myself available for personal consultations in Southampton on Thursday and Friday." She just might pick up some important assignments. "I have clients with houses out there." Now she was excited about this possibility.

"Betsy, that's a rough commute," Paul Jr. protested.

"I can work on the train both ways," she said, dismissing this problem. "I'll close the shop on Thursday and Fridays. Call it our summer vacation schedule. Emily's good—if she can arrange to be off from her job on Saturdays, like last summer, then she can run the shop on that day. It'll only be for ten weeks. I think that'll work!" She was suddenly jubilant.

Again Paul Jr. planned a small welcome-home dinner for Alice when she and Georgette returned from Nassau.

"There'll just be the same few at the table as last time," he told Betsy. "You'll be home for dinner that night, won't you?" His eyes pleaded for an affirmative reply.

"I'll be there," Betsy promised. She'd have an opportunity to thank Grady for seeing that her loan went through. With the new prestige she'd acquired from the publicity that followed Felicia's benefit cocktail party, it was important to be able to provide new clients with beautiful fabrics and fine antiques—available despite the war to an aggressive decorator willing to spend freely. With the loan she could do that.

On the evening of the dinner Betsy knew the moment she walked into the house that Alice had arrived on schedule. When Alice was home, there was a tense, watchful attitude on the part of the domestic staff. Still, she conceded, the servants were loyal to Alice. She could be difficult, but she was always generous. Paul had been proud of that, as though this were an indication that his mother possessed good qualities.

When Betsy walked into the nursery, she caught the scent of Alice's Chanel No. 5 lingering in the room. Jimmy was ecstatically clutching a new stuffed toy.

"His grandmother brought it back from Nassau," Miss Watkins reported. "Jimmy, show Mommie your new giraffe."

When Jimmy was at last drifting off to sleep, Betsy went into her room to dress for dinner. At least she knew now what to expect, she told herself with a touch of humorous relief. She'd be seated across from Grady. Already he felt like family. Paul's Uncle Grady was now Jimmy's Uncle Grady as well.

Arriving downstairs, Betsy found the others having cocktails in the library. At one side of the room Alice was reporting on Jimmy's latest activities while Paul Jr. stood by with a pleased smile. He'd said last night that it was Alice's devotion to Jimmy that was holding her together.

Betsy saw Grady's face brighten as he caught sight of her.

"You're looking lovely as always," he said, crossing to her side.

"Thank you." She was grateful for Grady's presence. She never felt at ease with Georgette and Carl Adams. For a man with an important post in Washington, D.C., Betsy thought, Carl Adams spent an awful lot of time in New York.

After a few minutes they left the library at Alice's instructions to go to the dining room. The seating arrangement was as Betsy had anticipated. Over dinner Georgette chatted about their two weeks in Nassau. Clearly she had enjoyed the trip.

"We met the Duke and Duchess of Windsor, of course." Georgette's smile telegraphed her pride in this. "The Duchess always dresses so smartly, though I'd hardly call her a beautiful woman. Still, she managed to grab off the King of England. She must have something."

"What was the weather like?" Grady asked with a reminiscent smile.

"It was dreadfully hot the last few days," Alice said, refuting Grady's insistence that there were no bad days in Nassau. "I don't know how civilized people stay in the Bahamas in the summer." Betsy intercepted Paul Jr.'s apologetic glance toward Grady.

"Darling, they don't," Georgette chided. "They go to Bar Harbor or Newport."

Betsy recoiled from Georgette's highly colored report on the murder of Sir Harry Oakes the previous summer and on the trial of his young son-in-law, Alfred de Marigny, for that murder. It had been sordid headline news—right beside the latest war bulletins.

"Poor Sir Harry." Georgette sighed in sympathy. "He must have known his son-in-law was no good—he'd disinherited both

Alfred and his daughter Nancy. Sir Harry was very close with the Duke and Duchess," she added.

"There are those," Paul Jr. reminded somberly, "who worry about the Duke's sympathies toward the Nazis."

"Paul, that's absurd," Alice reproved. "He's a charming man."

"Alfred was acquitted, of course." Georgette pantomimed her disgust at this. "Though local people didn't like him at all."

"Why not?" Paul Jr. asked. Betsy suspected he was merely concerned about keeping the conversation lively enough to distract Alice from brooding. For a moment, she sensed, he had reproached himself for mentioning the Nazis. But Alice had not been upset by that. "Why should they dislike the man?"

"He has no sense of tradition." Georgette sniffed. "He was involved in the building of several lovely apartment houses—and then he began to admit Jews." Betsy saw her father-in-law stiffen in annoyance, glance uncomfortably in her direction. Alice frowned, seeming to want to distract Georgette, but Georgette was unaware. "People were shocked."

Betsy understood that Alice had not told even her best friend that Paul's wife was Jewish. She'd overheard a disturbing inquiry about "Jimmy's delayed christening" from Georgette earlier in the evening. For Alice to admit that Jimmy's mother was Jewish would be to confirm that the christening would never take place, Betsy interpreted.

"That wasn't all," Georgette pursued. "He even persuaded some good clubs to admit Jews. And he wanted to waste taxpayers' money on improving the water supplies for the blacks during the dry months," she said contemptuously. "They'd only waste the water."

Betsy managed to conceal her rage, but she felt compelled to make one remark.

"I read about the murder. Sir Harry Oakes was a partner in that Nazi bank—the Continental in Mexico."

"Where did you read that?" Georgette flared.

"American newspapers and magazines," Betsy told her sweetly. "It's a well-known fact." Her eyes defied contradiction.

Sending her a cold stare, Georgette turned away from Betsy.

"Alice, I forgot to bring you that book everybody's talking about. I'm too busy with my committees to read it just yet, but I thought it might amuse you. It's called *Forever Amber,* and it's deliciously shocking, I understand."

Betsy heard little of the rest of the conversation at dinner. She was remembering little bits of Paul's letters. He'd hated bigotry of any kind. He'd seen it in the Army and Navy. He'd told her about villages in Sicily and Italy where the natives had never known a Jew or a Negro and harbored weird misconceptions about them. He talked about how the Red Cross kept "white blood" and "Negro blood" in different containers.

She was determined to see Jimmy grow up to share her values and Paul's. Was that possible in this environment? Could she be strong enough to instill her values in her son? Yet to remove him from the Forrest home would be to deprive him of his grandparents, and she wanted him to have a family. There was no doubt in her mind that Paul's parents loved Jimmy. She couldn't deprive him of that love.

CHAPTER TWENTY-SEVEN

It was becoming a habit for Betsy to join her father-in-law in the library late in the evening to listen to news of the war. It was as though they had to do this—for Paul. The library door was always kept shut, lest Alice realize they were listening to the news.

On June 4 Allied tanks drove the Germans from Rome. Two days later Betsy and Paul Jr. listened to the recap of the news of D-Day. The Allies had begun a massive invasion of the Normandy Coast.

"Betsy, can you envision this?" Paul Jr. leaned forward in excitement. "There are over three million men involved in this operation, five thousand large ships, and four thousand smaller landing craft."

"And eleven thousand planes," Betsy added, caught up in the enormity of this invasion. "Plus the paratroopers who went in to blow up the bridges and railroad lines and to seize the landing fields."

They heard how at six A.M. the first wave of infantry and armored troops had crossed the rough English Channel. By six-thirty, under cloudy skies, they were wading ashore along a fifty-mile front. Other troops landed on both sides of the Vire River, and still others pushed ashore near Caen.

"The weather is rough, the going rugged. For months the Germans—using slave labor—have been mining the coastal waters, erecting six-foot-thick concrete pillboxes and antitank obstacles," the newscaster reported. "It's feared that Allied casualties will be heavy."

"Oh, God—" Betsy tensed in anguish for all those who would die and for the grief of the families the dead would leave behind.

Eleven days later—in Southampton—she listened to the first statistics on the radio. Over 3,000 dead and more than 12,000 wounded. And ferocious fighting continued.

Additional Allied troops arrived in France. Meanwhile, London was under savage attack from the new V-1 rockets being launched from German-held sites in France and Belgium. When would it all be over? Betsy asked herself in anguish.

On July 10, Saipan finally fell to the Americans after twenty-five days of savage fighting. On July 21, U.S. Army and Marine forces landed on Guam. Listening to news reports on her bedroom radio, Betsy thought, as she had on so many previous occasions, that if the war in the Pacific did nothing else, it taught Americans geography they had never encountered in school. Islands like Midway and Wake and Iwo Jima were totally unknown to schoolteachers. Until now, they had been deemed beneath consideration.

Late in July Paul Jr. brought Grady Harrison out with him to Southampton for a long weekend. Returning to the house from a consultation with a client, Betsy was told by Elise that the two men were out on the veranda.

"Mr. Forrest told me to hold dinner until you came home," Elise reported. Normally Betsy had a tray on the veranda on Thursday evenings because Paul Jr. arrived from the city around ten.

"Thank you, Elise." Betsy smiled in anticipation. It would be pleasant to sit down to dinner tonight with Paul Jr. and Grady Harrison. It would be a tension-free evening since Alice was in Bar Harbor. "I'll be down in ten minutes," she promised.

Betsy washed up for dinner, changed into a colorful peasant skirt and a becoming white cotton off-the-shoulder blouse. A touch of Houbigant cologne, a quick brushing through of her hair, and she was ready to descend. Downstairs she went first to the kitchen to let Elise and Peggy know that dinner could be served.

She found the two men still on the veranda and engrossed in a discussion about the recent Democratic Convention in Chicago, which to nobody's surprise had nominated Roosevelt for an unprecedented fourth term.

"Betsy's happy about that," Paul Jr. teased after the three exchanged greetings. "FDR's her man."

"How do you feel about Truman as vice-president?" Betsy asked, gazing from one to the other. "I don't think I've ever heard of him," she admitted in candor. "I just now learned that he's a senator from Missouri."

"He was a dark horse," Grady conceded. "It took two ballots to nominate him. Henry Wallace went into the convention believing he would stay on the ticket. William Douglas and Alben Barkley—Washington gossip says—were each sure he was the President's choice. Truman planned on going into the convention to nominate Jimmy Byrnes. Then the word came through: the President favored Harry Truman."

"Funny how we all talk about the Democratic prospects," Paul Jr. said in amusement. "Hell, what chance does a Republican have this year? Financially we're seeing great times—and the public remembers Hoover as the man who couldn't handle the Depression. There's only one issue the Republicans have on their side." His face grew grave. "That's FDR's health. The anti-FDR press is being nasty. They're warning that he might not survive the next term. At sixty-two, they warn, he's an old man." The Republican candidate, Thomas E. Dewey, was only forty-two.

"The radical press is using the issue that six Presidents have died in office. It seems so crude," Betsy protested, "to predict that President Roosevelt won't survive the next four years."

Now Elise summoned them inside to the dining room. Grady made a point of directing the conversation into less gloomy channels. He prodded Betsy to talk about the shop.

"Thanks to my loan," she said gratefully, "I've really expanded. It was wonderful of you to see me through that," she told Grady, and remembered belatedly that Paul Jr. was unaware of Grady's part in this. Clearly he approved.

"It's great to be out here in the sea air." Grady seemed embarrassed at being identified in this manner. "I'm keeping such an insane schedule I can't take off for more than two or three days at a time, and it's too much of a project to try to run down to Nassau or up to my Vermont place. This weekend is most welcome."

"Grady, there's always a room out here for you," Paul Jr. assured him. "I don't have to tell you that."

Grady turned to Betsy. "How's Jimmy doing these days?"

"He's wonderful. Having a marvelous time out here," Betsy said. "He loves the beach—and being able to run around with almost no clothes." She laughed.

"He's the image of Paul," Paul Jr. said, radiating affection. "Every day I thank God we have him." He smiled at Betsy as though, she thought, in silent tribute to her for having given birth to Jimmy.

"Oh, compliments from my sister, Sandra," Grady told Betsy. "She fell in love with the lamp I bought from your shop. If I'm not careful she'll carry it off to her house in Boston."

"It feels so good to be out here after the heat and humidity in New York." Paul Jr. seemed to be relaxing over dinner.

"How about a brisk after-dinner walk on the beach?" Grady suggested, his eyes moving from Paul Jr. to Betsy.

"I'm bushed from the day in the city," Paul Jr. said. "I'm going to collapse on a chaise on the veranda, but don't let me keep you two back."

"Are you game for a walk, Betsy?" Grady's smile was hopeful.

"I walk on the beach every evening that I'm out here." Betsy saw his face light up. "It's one of the best parts of my day."

After dinner Paul Jr. retired to a chaise on the veranda with candid pleasure. Betsy and Grady hurried upstairs to their respective rooms to change into casual beach attire. Within minutes they were striding down the stairs that led to the beach with an air of triumph.

"I always feel as though I'm winning against the world when I walk on the beach," Betsy confided, stooping to tie the laces of her sneakers. Knowing it would be cool beside the water, she'd changed into slacks and a sweater. Grady, too, had abandoned his elegantly tailored Brooks Brothers suit for slacks and a pullover, and his city shoes were replaced by sneakers.

"When I was a kid, my parents took my sister and me to Nantucket every summer until we were old enough to go to camp. It's surprising how much Sandra and I both remember about the magnificent beach out there, even though we were so young. The summer camps—" He shrugged his shoulders. "They were just places where we went while our parents dashed off to Europe or the Caribbean. I always admired the way Alice and Paul Jr. spent their summers with Paul, the way they never sent him off to boarding school. Do you mind my talking this way about Paul?" he asked with sudden solicitude.

"Oh no," Betsy said quickly. Grady knew the other side of the coin—the children of the rich who shuttled between boarding school and summer camps. He didn't understand how Paul had been smothered by Alice's attentions—how he had longed to be just a normal boy. To be a middle-class kid, she thought tenderly, who was allowed to do all the ordinary things of childhood and adolescence. Not to have his life dictated by the state of his mother's nerves.

Betsy and Grady walked along the night-deserted beach. The sky was clear and splashed by stars; moonlight spilled a pale gold sheen over the water.

"Walking like this," she said softly, struggling against the tears that came too easily these days, "it's hard to believe that soldiers are fighting in Europe and the Pacific." Fighting and dying, she thought with fresh anguish.

"The war can't go on much longer," he said. *But already it was too late for Paul.* "In the Pacific the Americans are expected to take Guam within a few days." He didn't mention how many lives were being lost in this bloody fighting, Betsy thought involuntarily. "The Allies are making a strong drive to take back Paris." He hesitated. "I feel guilty sometimes that I've been spared active participation in the war. And I just missed by a few months being drafted for World War One."

"Be grateful," Betsy told him with a rare surge of cynicism.

For a while they strolled in companionable silence. The salt-scented night air cool and crisp.

"Are you warm enough?" Grady asked.

"Oh, yes," Betsy reassured him. He was such a gentle, caring man, she thought. Very much like Paul's father.

"Do you walk in the morning?" he asked.

"Every morning," she told him. "Very early. Before breakfast on the veranda. Some mornings I manage to be on the beach for the sunrise. To me that's one of the miracles of the world," she said whimsically. "To walk along the beach, facing the horizon, and to wait for that first faint sliver of orange-gold to rise up. I stand there without moving, just watching until that beautiful ball of fire lifts above the horizon. Then," she said, laughing to find herself suddenly self-conscious, "I'm ready to face the day."

"May I walk with you in the morning?" he asked. "To share that miracle with you?"

"A cup of Peggy's terrific coffee first," she stipulated. "I need that to get going."

For three mornings and three evenings Betsy walked with Grady on the pristine, deserted beach. He told her about his childhood, lonely after the very early years, about the pain of his wife's long illness and death. He felt a closeness to her because he understood what she was going through, Betsy thought in gratitude. He'd lost a wife and she'd lost a husband. How sad that he and his wife had never had children.

CHAPTER TWENTY-EIGHT

In Europe Allied troops had moved into Brittany, were advancing from several directions toward Paris. The French Resistance was buoyed by word that came through about the march toward the French capital.

On this August night of 1944 three men waited inside a small farmhouse, all of them dressed in the shabby attire of French peasants. The oldest of the men by forty years, Claude Laval, had been born on this farm, had seen his three sons go off to fight with the Resistance, and his wife murdered by a drunken German soldier.

When he had discovered two young American Air Force officers hiding in his fields on New Year's Day, 1943, he knew he must conceal them, somehow, on the farm. The younger of the two—the pilot of the plane that had been shot down by the Germans—spoke a fair amount of college French. The pilot explained to Claude that they had been on a secret mission—to allow a British agent to parachute into French territory—when their plane had been spotted and shot down. The three aboard had jumped clear, but the British agent's parachute had failed to open.

Ever since New Year's Day, 1943, the two Americans had hidden in the farm's root cellar. At night they emerged. On those occasions when Claude was involved in a Resistance drop, the Americans joined him. The three men lived with the knowledge that at any time the Germans might arrive and decide to burn the farm—as happened with alarming frequency. Whole villages consisting only of women and children had been annihilated.

"All right," Claude told the two Americans. "It is time."

The three men left the house and moved out into the light of the full moon. They made their way into the wheatfield. They lifted their tin-shrouded flashlights upward, prepared to flash their signal at the proper moment, knowing the light would be visible only to a plane flying above.

They waited in silence until finally they could hear the muted drone of a bomber. Simultaneously the three flashlights sent their beams into the sky.

"It will be only days," Claude predicted in triumph, "before the Allies arrive in Paris. And we will be there to help liberate the city!"

"He's jumped," one of the Americans announced after a few moments. "His parachute's opening."

"Doug, where's Claude?" the other American asked in sudden alarm.

"Right here," Claude chuckled. "Our man is on his own now."

"Each time I remember how Roger's parachute didn't open," Doug Golden said in painful recall. "Each time I worry."

"I know," his navigator murmured. "Each time I worry, too."

"No more talk," Claude ordered. "Back to the house. With Paris so close to liberation, are we to be caught by the Germans?"

"With luck on our side we could be sailing into New York Harbor in six months," Doug said softly. With Paris liberated— with the Allies taking over—they could write home to say they were alive. He flinched, imagining his family's anguish. There was no doubt in his mind that he had been reported killed in action.

On August 19 the citizens of Paris, impatient for liberation and knowing the Americans were already in Chartres, rose up in insurrection. On August 21 an urgent appeal was sent to General Eisenhower. It seemed unlikely the Paris insurrection could hold out much longer. The Americans understood they had only forty-eight—at most, seventy-two hours—to prevent a massacre.

On August 25 Paris was liberated. *Les Américains* had arrived.

* * *

On the family's return from Southampton, Betsy was startled to discover that Alice was already planning a splashy party for Jimmy's birthday in December. Out of respect for her father-in-law she refrained from comment, though she thought such extravagance was absurd at Jimmy's age. But she was watchful, determined that she, not Alice, would make the important decisions in Jimmy's upbringing.

She repeatedly reminded herself that she should be grateful that Jimmy had grandparents who loved him. She was ever conscious that he would grow up without knowing his father. But her close friends were Jimmy's family, too, she consoled herself. And *she* would guide his religious upbringing when that time came. Jimmy would know his Jewish heritage.

More often now Betsy sat down to dinner with Paul Jr. and Alice. Georgette and Carl—along with Grady—were dinner guests at the Forrest house once every two weeks. Alice entertained no one else. Each time Grady was expected for dinner, Paul Jr. made a point of making sure Betsy would be at the table.

"You and Grady keep the conversation away from morbid subjects," Paul Jr. told her gratefully. "Georgette and Carl are apt to allow Alice to wallow in her grief."

Sitting at the dinner table the evening before Election Day, Betsy upbraided herself for not being absent tonight. She knew that Paul's parents were long-standing Republicans. Now Alice—who had seldom ventured to the polls in the past—announced she would vote tomorrow.

"It's a matter of principle," Alice explained. "I can't bear Roosevelt. And I loathe his wife."

"Doesn't she wear the most ghastly clothes?" Georgette chattered. "Oh, do we need a Republican administration in this country. And a First Lady with some chic."

"You're not apt to see a Republican president next term," Paul Jr. predicted.

"You almost sound as though you're glad," Alice accused. "I come from a long line of Republicans," she said proudly. "Men in my family have been sent to the State Assembly, to the House of Representatives, and to the Senate—always as Republicans.

And if my darling son had lived, he would have followed in their footsteps."

"Not Paul," Betsy said, remembering his liberal leanings and his compassion for those harassed by bigots. "He loved what FDR stands for. He hated bigotry. He was—"

"I won't listen to this, Betsy!" Alice was pale with anger. "You knew Paul how long? Less than two years? I knew him all his life. I helped form his thinking! I—"

"It's rather chilly in the house tonight," Paul Jr. broke in. His eyes turned to Betsy in an urgent plea for silence. "Alice, why don't we have coffee in the library before a cozy blaze in the fireplace? That'll surely take off the chill."

"I don't understand this awful rationing. Never enough oil." Alice was struggling to regain her poise. "A Republican president would have known how to avoid it."

Betsy forced herself to be silent. Alice would have no part in forming Jimmy's thinking. *There was no way she could do that.*

Betsy went down to breakfast on the morning after Election Day to find her father-in-law lingering over coffee. Normally he would have been out of the house an hour ago.

"Well, your man made it," he greeted her cheerfully. "Not that it's much of a surprise."

All at once she suspected that in the privacy of the voting booth he might have discounted his wife's insistence that the family was staunchly Republican.

"What about Truman?" she asked curiously. "What do you think about him?"

"You mean the man *Time* called the 'gray little junior Senator from Missouri'?" Paul Jr. said humorously. "Nobody seems to know much about him. But that junior senator might be our next president." Paul Jr. was somber. "I saw Roosevelt for a moment the last time I was down in Washington. He looked so tired. *Wasted.* These have been grueling times for him."

"Did you hear the war news this morning?" Betsy asked.

"We know it's just a matter of time before the Allies force Germany and Japan to surrender." He seemed all at once exhausted. Betsy understood. Peace was coming too late for Paul. "American and British bombers are blasting German cities into rubble. A whole new armada of American ships and aircraft carriers are taking over the Pacific." Now he hesitated. Betsy glanced at him inquiringly. By now she knew that faint air of uncertainty meant he was about to broach a subject he preferred to ignore. "Alice and Georgette are talking with a real estate broker about a house down in Palm Beach for the last two weeks of December and the first two weeks in January. I'll probably manage to run down for a few days. Possibly for a week."

"You can use the rest," Betsy said sympathetically.

"Alice would like to take Jimmy and Miss Watkins down to Palm Beach for at least a couple of weeks." He managed a slight smile. "I'd pointed out it wasn't likely you'd be able to take time off from the shop."

"No." The word was sharper than she had intended.

"Alice adores Jimmy, of course. We both love him very much."

"I know you do." Her voice softened. But, adoring Paul, his mother had made his life miserable. "I just couldn't let Jimmy be away from me even for a few days." *How many times had they been through this?* "He's a baby. He'd be terrified if I disappeared from his life for two weeks."

"Alice felt it would be good for him to have some warm southern sun in the dead of winter," he apologized. "And you know how Jimmy loves the beach." A glint of faint hope was in his eyes.

"I'm sorry, but no. I can't let him go to Palm Beach." Betsy forced a smile. "It's sweet of his grandmother to be so solicitous of his health—but he'd be terribly upset if he woke up in the morning and I wasn't there."

Shortly after Election Day Betsy looked up from her desk to see Grady walk into the shop with a smartly dressed older woman. He was bringing her a customer, she thought. How like Grady to do something like that!

She left her desk and hurried to the front of the shop, brushing aside Della to greet him personally.

"How lovely to see you, Grady!" Smiling warmly, she extended a hand in greeting. Weeks ago he'd insisted she drop the formal "Mr. Harrison" in favor of "Grady."

With an air of pleasure he introduced his companion as his sister, Sandra. Betsy thought Sandra looked about a dozen years older than Grady, though she gathered that there were only five years between them. Betsy sensed that in a way Sandra had been his surrogate mother in the years when their parents had been so absent from their lives.

"Grady told me that you have such wonderful taste," Sandra said, "and that even though I live in Boston, you'd be able to ship whatever I bought up there to me."

"Of course, Mrs. Winthrop," Betsy assured her. So far this had not arisen, but somehow she would cope. "Did you have some special need in mind?"

Grady stood aside with a glow of pride in having brought them together while the two women discussed Sandra's living room and its unique problems.

"I want a happy air, a mood of lightness in the room. It always seems so somber. We have these enormously high ceilings and a huge bay window. The wainscotting is dark and dreary."

Betsy was amazed at how long she talked with Grady's sister, but it had been exhilarating because Mrs. Winthrop candidly admitted she would rely on *her* judgment. And the proposed project would earn the shop a huge profit.

"Betsy, Sandra and I are having a solitary dinner tonight. It's her only night in town when she isn't going to the theater," he explained with a laugh. "Of course she has a matinee tomorrow afternoon. But I was thinking, could you join us for dinner tonight? It'll be rather late," he apologized, "because I have a conference with an out-of-town client at six. But what about eight-thirty?"

"She'll come," Sandra answered for her with a persuasive smile. "We can talk more about my living room—if Grady lets us get in a word edgewise."

"I'd love it," Betsy told them.

"We'll pick you up at eight-fifteen," Grady said. "I'll make reservations for eight-thirty."

"At the Colony," Sandra instructed. "Where I can wear my black Mainbocher to its best advantage. You know, all that cerise upholstery and those masses of red roses," she said to Betsy. "What a pity, Grady, that neither of us ever had children. We each could have had a daughter Betsy's age."

For an instant, Betsy thought, Grady looked like a cornered deer. Why had Sandra reminded him how alone they were in the world? At least his sister had her husband. Grady was alone.

Not until late that evening, after their delightful dinner at the Colony, did Sandra's real meaning come through to her. She recalled Sandra's words now with fresh comprehension: *"We each could have had a daughter Betsy's age."* She was reminding Grady of the age gulf between them, as if to nip in the bud any amorous intentions he might be harboring.

But that was ridiculous! Grady harbored no romantic notions about her. They were just very good friends.

CHAPTER TWENTY-NINE

Betsy was devoting much time to Sandra Winthrop's living room. She'd made a day trip to Boston to study the room, take accurate measurements. She and Sandra were on the phone two or three times a week. Betsy understood this was a new diversion in a life that Sandra found dull. But she enjoyed working with Grady's sister. The older woman charmingly deferred to all of her decisions.

"You're the pro," Sandra reiterated at almost every step. "You'll design a room that's right for me. I'll be happy in it."

On a bleak gray morning when the previous night's beautiful snow was turning to dirty slush, Betsy was so mentally involved in deciding between two choices of wallpaper for Sandra's living room that she left the house without her briefcase. Not until she had opened the shop and instructed Della about calls to be made did she realize she had left it behind.

"Oh, damn!" She was impatient with herself for this lapse of memory. She waited until Della was between calls to tell her she had to run back to the house for her briefcase.

Finding a cab in this weather would be difficult, she realized after a moment. She could walk home faster. She glanced dubiously at her shoes. As usual, William had driven her to the shop this morning—she hadn't concerned herself about footwear.

She glanced down distastefully at the brown-tainted slush, then headed uptown. She'd change shoes at the house, she told herself, recoiling from the wet chill that threatened to invade her now. How beautiful the snow was in Central Park, she thought. How beautiful it must be in the country. Here on the city streets it was ugly.

By the time she arrived at the house, she was chilled to the bone. If William was at the house, she'd ask him to drive her back to the shop. She rarely asked—he wouldn't mind. She'd change shoes and have a cup of steaming hot coffee, she promised herself as she rang the doorbell. A moment later Elise admitted her.

"I forgot my briefcase," she said ruefully.

"You walked home in that mess outside?" Elise scolded. "I'll bring you a cup of hot coffee."

"Thanks, Elise. That'll be so good."

She hurried up to her room, kicked off her shoes, peeled off her hose, and reached for replacements.

"Jimmy," she called while she slid into dry shoes. She'd spend a few minutes with him while she had her coffee. Or was he in the park with Miss Watkins? He never seemed to get enough of the park when there was snow on the ground. No, he wasn't in the park—she heard Miss Watkins humming in the nursery.

The humming stopped. Miss Watkins knocked on the door between her bedroom and the nursery.

"Come in," Betsy called and the door opened.

Miss Watkins stood there with a warm smile.

"Such ugly weather outside," she said and smiled sympathetically. "I hope you didn't walk home in all that slush." Miss Watkins knew she loved to walk.

"There was no getting a taxi today. My shoes were soaked by the time I got here." She gazed inquiringly into the nursery. "Where's Jimmy?"

"Mrs. Forrest asked to take him off with her. She said she wanted a little time alone with her grandson," Miss Watkins said indulgently. "She's going to show him the crèche at her church."

Alarm signals shot up in Betsy's mind. All at once she was trembling.

"When did she leave?" Betsy asked.

"Just a few minutes ago. William is driving them."

"Thank you, Miss Watkins—" Betsy grabbed at her coat and purse, her mind in chaos. *What was Alice doing with Jimmy at her church?*

"Is something wrong?" Miss Watkins asked in bewilderment.

"I hope not," Betsy said tensely and darted through the door just as Elise approached with her coffee tray. "Never mind the coffee, Elise!"

Emerging from the house, she spied a taxi pulling up twenty feet to the south to disgorge a passenger. Ignoring the slush, she rushed to grab it. Perhaps all Alice meant to do was show Jimmy the crèche—but other suspicions crowded her mind.

She sat on the edge of the seat, fuming when they were caught in traffic. At last they began to move ahead. The lights were with them. At the church the cabdriver solicitously searched for a chunk of curb that was accessible to her. She spied the Forrest limousine just ahead, William at the wheel. Alice and Jimmy were here.

"This is fine," she told the cabdriver and thrust bills into his hand.

A path had been cleared to the church entrance. She charged up the path and into the church. Immediately she spied Alice, holding Jimmy in her arms while the minister smiled down at him.

"You don't have to be afraid, Jimmy," Alice crooned, unaware of her approach. "Your daddy was baptized in this very same church."

"Stop right there," Betsy called out hoarsely.

"Mommie!" Jimmy's face lighted. "Mommie!"

Alice went white with shock. The minister appeared bewildered.

"My son is not to be baptized," Betsy told him and reached to take Jimmy from Alice. "He's to be raised in my faith." She fought to keep her voice even. Alice was rushing down the aisle now, impatient to escape this scene. "I'm Jewish. His father agreed when we married that our children would be raised in my faith.

Jimmy's father was killed in action—his grandmother sometimes takes on more than is her right."

"I'm sorry," the minister apologized. "I didn't understand. Bless you. Bless you both."

By the time she and Jimmy were outside, the Forrest limousine had sped away. Still trembling from this encounter, holding Jimmy in her arms though he was demanding to be put down, she searched for a taxi.

"Jimmy, you'll get your feet all wet," Betsy scolded, but she put him down as he insisted.

"Miss Watkins made me wear my rubbers," he said aggrievedly. "See, Mommie?" He held up one small foot.

"Of course, darling. That was smart," she approved. "Now let's find us a taxi."

Clutching Jimmy's hand in hers, urging him to avoid the puddles, Betsy walked with him to the corner. She sighed with relief when a taxi pulled up.

At the house she explained to Miss Watkins what had almost happened. "Please, never allow Jimmy to go off with his grandmother." She struggled to retain her poise. But his grandmother, she remembered, paid Miss Watkins' salary.

"I'm so sorry," Miss Watkins apologized, obviously upset. "It won't happen again."

"Please, I understand that what happened was not your fault," Betsy told her.

In the taxi heading back to the shop, Betsy tried to sort out her feelings. She'd been so unnerved by Alice's efforts to have Jimmy baptized. But she should have expected something like this.

Be realistic, Betsy ordered herself. How could she continue to live in the Forrest house in the face of Alice's flagrant disregard for how she meant to raise Jimmy? The war—the horrors inflicted on the Jews in Germany by the Nazis—had made her deeply conscious of her Jewishness. She was acutely aware of the years when her mother and father had observed all the Jewish holidays, respecting the Jewish traditions. And Aunt Celia had raised her—after they were gone—in the same fashion.

She felt a rush of tenderness as she remembered Jimmy standing by her side every Friday evening while she lit the Sabbath candles. He was too little yet to understand much of what she told him about his Jewish heritage, but when he was older he would attend synagogue services—as she had with her parents before they died. He would go to Sunday school, as she had done. When he reached his thirteenth birthday he would celebrate his bar mitzvah. She would sit in the synagogue and listen with pride while he read from the Torah. He would be welcomed into the Jewish faith as a man. Paul had understood—and agreed—that their son was to follow her faith. His mother couldn't change that decision.

At the shop Della reminded her of her appointment with a new client. At the first free moment she'd focus on what she must do about their living arrangements, Betsy told herself, fighting anxiety. For now, she decided, she and Jimmy would move into the apartment with Emily. It was tiny for the three of them but they would manage somehow. Miss Watkins would stay temporarily with her sister.

Forcing herself to concentrate on her consultation with the client, she left the shop, finally flagged down a taxi, and headed for the East Side apartment of Leila Atkins. She arrived faintly breathless, only moments late but apologetic.

"Oh, that's all right," Mrs. Atkins soothed. "In this weather nobody's on time. And isn't it wild to be talking about designing my terrace in the midst of this ghastly snow?"

Pushing personal problems into a corner of her mind, Betsy threw herself into this newest project. First she listened carefully to Mrs. Atkins' own ideas—always respectful of what the client had to offer. Then she plunged ahead.

"You're absolutely right," Betsy agreed. "An awning is absolutely essential both for privacy and as a defense against city soot. But rather than the conventional kind I'd like to see an improvised awning of bamboo shades. I have a man who can set up a pulley arrangement that'll work perfectly. And with the bamboo shades," she continued with an almost genuine show of enthusiasm, "you'll have the option of changing the color whenever you like."

"I hadn't thought of that." Mrs. Atkins' face lighted up. "A bright yellow or red, do you think—for the first round?"

"You'll find white is much more comfortable for summer—or perhaps a soft blue with a lot of white trimming. White fringes," Betsy pursued.

"What about lighting?" Mrs. Atkins asked when they'd explored the subject of terrace furniture. "We do like to entertain in the evening."

"I'd suggest we install waterproof lanterns for the permanent lighting. You might like candles in hurricane shades for dining." Betsy gazed about the huge terrace, already well landscaped. "And a baby spotlight concealed in the shrubbery to highlight the planting. That can be very dramatic."

When the consultation with Mrs. Atkins was completed, Betsy hurried back to the shop. She knew she must talk with her father-in-law about her decision to move from the Forrest house. Guilty at disturbing him at his office but preferring to talk to him away from the house, Betsy phoned Paul Jr. Haltingly she explained what had happened.

"Jimmy and I can't stay at the house," she said gently. "Not after what happened today."

"I know what Alice did today was unforgivable." Betsy heard the pained shock in his voice. "But please, let me talk to her. I'll make her understand she must never try to interfere that way again. Jimmy is her life. If you and Jimmy leave, she'll have another breakdown. It's so soon after she lost Paul. Give us another chance, Betsy. Let me talk to her."

"I don't see how we—"

"Give me a few days," he pleaded. "Don't make a definite decision for the next seventy-two hours. Do this for Paul."

"Seventy-two hours," she reluctantly agreed. "But I frankly don't see how you can improve the situation."

CHAPTER THIRTY

Alice pretended to be engrossed in going through her closet as Paul Jr. struggled to command her attention.

"I don't know what you're doing home at this hour," she said with a contrived air of bewilderment. "You're not coming down with something, are you?"

"Alice, stop pretending you don't know what I'm talking about," he ordered. He saw the glass of water and the opened pill bottle on her night table. At least she'd taken her medication. "What you tried to do was horrendous."

"I'm not sure I was right in allowing Georgette to persuade me to go down to Palm Beach this season." Her eyes were overbright, her voice shaky. "It just isn't what it used to be."

"Alice, if we don't do something to change her mind, Betsy is moving out of this house with Jimmy," he warned.

"No!" She swung about to face him now. Her face was drained of color. A nerve in her left eyelid was twitching. "I was only thinking of poor little Jimmy. If he's not baptized, he'll never go to heaven! How can I let that happen to my precious grandson?" Her words tumbled over one another in her agitation.

"Alice, how Betsy raises Jimmy is her decision to make. If you want her to stay here with Jimmy, you'll have to make her understand that she makes the decisions for her son."

Alice gazed at him with haunted eyes.

"I couldn't bear it if Jimmy wasn't here—" Tears welled in her eyes. "I only meant to do what's best for him."

"That's for Betsy to decide." He resisted the impulse to take her in his arms and comfort her. "If you want to keep Jimmy in this house, you'll have to persuade Betsy you won't interfere."

"All right," she whispered. "I'll tell her. But be with me. I need your strength, Paul."

Arriving home, Betsy went directly up to the nursery. Hours later she was still unnerved by the encounter in the church. Approaching the door, she was surprised to hear Alice's voice. She was talking to Jimmy.

Her throat tight, Betsy opened the door and walked inside. Jimmy sprawled in Alice's lap while Paul Jr. smiled down at the two of them.

"And do you know what Papa Bear said?" Alice asked lovingly.

"Mommie, Grandma's telling me a story," Jimmy said happily.

"Is that all right, Betsy?" Alice asked with a startling show of humility.

"Yes, of course."

"Miss Watkins went down to bring up his dinner," Alice continued and hesitated. She turned to glance up anxiously at Paul Jr.

"Now, Alice," he told her.

"I did a terrible thing, Betsy," she whispered. "It'll never happen again. I'll swear that on my mother's Bible."

"Betsy, stay with us," Paul Jr. implored. "You and Alice and I are all the family Jimmy has. Don't deprive him of his only living grandparents."

"Grandma, finish the story," Jimmy ordered imperiously. "Tell me!"

"All right," Betsy said after a troubled moment. Paul Jr. was right. How could she deprive Jimmy of his grandparents? His only family. "We'll stay."

A few days before Alice's scheduled departure for Palm Beach, Paul Jr. told Betsy there'd be a small dinner party again.

"Not really a party," he said, as on those other such occasions. "The three of us and Georgette and Carl and Grady," he explained cajolingly. "You'll be with us, won't you?" He realized she'd been making a point of avoiding Alice at the house. "Grady will be disappointed if you're not there."

"I'll be there," Betsy promised.

"Betsy, everything is going to be all right from now on." Paul Jr. smiled reassuringly, but Betsy was conscious of his tenseness. "Alice understands."

The night of the dinner party Betsy made a point of going downstairs at the last minute. She had dawdled with Jimmy, triumphant at being allowed an extra half-hour of playtime with her, though he was already yawning.

She wore the new dinner dress she had bought at Altman's the week before: a deceptively simple forest-green velvet that was a perfect setting for her auburn hair and blue-green eyes. It was strange, she mused, how knowing you were attractively dressed raised your spirits and self-confidence. Though the dress was enormously expensive from her point of view, she knew that it had cost not a fifth of the designer dresses that Alice and Georgette would wear.

She heard the sound of voices in the library as she approached. She tried to gear herself for Alice's presence. Alice and Georgette were at one side of the room in a discussion about a coming charity ball. The three men were talking about the approaching inauguration.

"Betsy, how nice to see you—" Grady broke off in the middle of a sentence. "I talked with Sandra last night, and she's so pleased with the pieces you've sent her—and your instructions about their placements." He chuckled reminiscently. "I love my sister, but she has absolutely no sense of balance."

"She's a joy to work with," Betsy told him. Having Sandra Winthrop as a client was great for her ego, she thought, considering all the fine decorators on call in Boston.

Grady led her into conversation with the other two men. Carl was talking importantly about his Washington assignment, casting furtive glances at Betsy's slender figure at intervals. Betsy had gathered from remarks dropped by clients who knew Carl and Georgette that he often strayed from the marital bed.

"For a man based in Washington, you manage to spend a lot of time in New York," Paul Jr. said jokingly.

"I have to be in town for business on a regular basis," Carl told him with reproach. His eyes moved for an instant to Alice. He knew that no mention of the war was ever made in this household.

Now they left the library for the dining room. The seating followed Alice's usual plan for these small gatherings. Talk revolved—safely—on the coming season in Palm Beach.

"We were so lucky to find a house," Georgette said. "Complete with a full domestic staff. Grady, what are your plans for the holidays? Are you running down to Nassau?"

"No, I'll be spending Christmas day and New Year's with Sandra and her husband. In between I'll hole up at my place in Vermont."

When Georgette and Alice began to argue about what wardrobe would be best for their month in Palm Beach, Grady talked to the others about his house in Vermont.

"It's a modest little house," Grady conceded, "but the views are unbelievable. The house sits up there on a mountain—it overlooks a sweeping valley—and in the distance more mountains. The sunrises and sunsets are magnificent." His eyes settled on Betsy in a private exchange. He was remembering, Betsy thought, the perfect sunrises and sunsets they'd shared at Southampton. "One of these days," he said, suddenly self-conscious, "you all must come up to the Vermont house. There's a kind of peace I find up there that exists nowhere else."

Betsy was relieved when the evening was over. Again, she felt grateful that Alice would be away for four weeks. In the midst of the departure of the guests Grady offered Betsy a pair of tickets to *Bloomer Girl.*

"I picked them up to give to a client who'd planned to be here during the holidays. He's decided not to come into the city after all—which gives me my chance to hole up in Vermont between the holidays. I think you'll enjoy the musical."

"Thank you, Grady." Her face lighted. She'd take Emily with her. Emily preferred serious theater, but she welcomed any Broadway performance. "It's been so long since I've been to the theater."

"Perhaps you'll go with me to see the new Moss Hart play when the holidays are over?" he asked as though on impulse. "It's so much more enjoyable to see a performance with a friend."

"I know," she said softly. "I'd love to see *Christopher Blake*." This was the new Moss Hart play.

Yet a moment later she was uneasy. Grady wasn't entertaining romantic notions about her, was he? No, she scolded herself. He was just a lonely man who loved the theater. He'd referred to her as a *friend*.

Betsy was wrong. His sister was wrong.

Betsy and Emily were enthralled with the performance of *Bloomer Girl*. They emerged from the theater in a mood of euphoria. Betsy insisted on treating them to a late snack at the Stage Delicatessen. Emily had taken the evening off on annual leave so that she wouldn't have to dash from the theater to the office.

"I'm famished," Betsy confessed. "I rushed home from the shop to spend my usual time with Jimmy and then rushed to the theater."

"No dinner." Emily nodded. "I just grabbed a quick bite before I ran to meet you."

They walked swiftly through the cold night. The browned-out streets were clogged with pedestrians. Car traffic was surprisingly heavy despite gas rationing.

"Oh, a news bulletin," Emily said as they waited for a light to change from red to green. "Oliver wants me to take three days annual leave next week. Tacked on to our day off that'll give us four days to go skiing up in Vermont."

"You don't ski—" Betsy was startled.

Emily giggled.

"I may by the time we get back. But I suspect we won't spend much time on the slopes." Her eyes were eloquent.

"What's going on with you two?" Betsy was still uneasy about the relationship.

"We're having fun." Emily was all at once defensive. "Something wrong with that?"

"What about the house in suburbia and the white picket fence?"

"That'll come later. When the bastardly war is over." Emily paused. "I can't push him, Betsy. He never stops telling me he's mad about me. Oh, about the skiing trip. I told Mom that you and I—and Jimmy of course—would be going up to the ski lodge in Vermont next week. Back me up?"

"Sure."

Emily and Oliver had been sleeping together for months. What was the guy waiting for?

CHAPTER THIRTY-ONE

Early in the new year Grady called Betsy at the shop.

"How was Vermont?" she asked.

"Beautiful. So peaceful and quiet. It's a whole different world out there. I relax. Something that's impossible for me to do in the city. How have you been?" he asked.

"Working like mad," she said and laughed at herself. "But sometimes it's good to be all caught up in work."

"I know," he said gently. "This is a rough time for you. I've been there." He hesitated a moment. "Do you like Strauss waltzes?"

"Oh, I love Strauss!" she said with an impetuousness that brought a chuckle from him.

"There's a Strauss concert at Carnegie Hall next Thursday evening. Would you like to go with me? Strauss demands congenial company."

"I'd like that very much," she told him. She hadn't been to a concert in years. The last time was when she and Paul had gone with Doug and Emily and Sara to hear Benny Goodman.

Grady broke into her thoughts. "Let's have dinner first. I'll call you Thursday morning and set up the time. Do you like the Russian Tea Room?"

"I've never been there," she confessed, "but I've heard wonderful things about it." He was such a compassionate man, she told herself. He knew how she mourned for Paul.

On the evening of the concert Betsy kissed Jimmy goodnight after reading him his usual story and hurried into her room to dress. She was to meet Grady at the Russian Tea Room in forty minutes. He'd explained that he would be coming from a business conference and wouldn't be able to pick her up.

She was relieved to find a taxi as soon as she walked out of the house. Had Grady been self-conscious about picking her up at the Forrest home? she asked herself. *Was* he harboring romantic thoughts about her? But no, she reassured herself yet again. Often Nadine's name came into their conversation—and she talked about Paul. That was the bond between them—their similar losses.

The taxi deposited her before the Russian Tea Room, only a stone's throw from Carnegie Hall. She walked into the festive atmosphere of the restaurant, subconsciously admiring the colorful decor with her decorator's eye. The headwaiter led her to Grady's table.

"I'm sorry I couldn't pick you up," he said, apologizing yet again. "I had a meeting with a client who's cramming twenty hours out of twenty-four with business. Let's order quickly so we won't have to rush too much through dinner."

In high spirits Grady guided her choices. They ate the Russian Tea Room's famous blini, Beluga, sipped with caution the ice-cold Slavik vodka, and wound up with pungent hot tea.

"It's lucky that Carnegie Hall is so close." Betsy laughed, faintly light-headed from the unfamiliar vodka. "We just have to float there."

"We'll help each other," he promised with a smile.

In all her years in Manhattan Betsy had never been to Carnegie Hall, though she and Emily had walked past it on occasions when audiences were leaving after a performance and had been caught up in the magical mood that seemed to permeate the atmosphere. As they approached the neo–Italian Renaissance structure—six stories tall, with a fifteen-story tower of studio apartments, Grady told her how the great Peter Tchaikovsky had conducted some of his works at the gala opening held on May 9, 1891.

"He proclaimed the acoustics of Carnegie Hall magnificent—and of course thousands of other music greats have said the same in the years since then."

In a festive mood, they joined the throngs going into the 2,760-seat auditorium. Betsy was surprised by its almost ascetic decor, relieved only by the rose and gilt furnishings of the two tiers of boxes around three sides. She was enthralled by mental visions of the musical greats who had appeared there. Then the concert began—and she responded joyously to the lilting Strauss music.

After the performance—mindful that the following day was a working one—Grady suggested that they go to a nearby Childs for coffee. Then he would take her home. Over coffee they enthusiastically dissected the performance, both exhilarated by the music.

At the door of the house he kissed her lightly on the cheek and thanked her for going with him.

"It was fun," she said. It was pleasant and relaxing to be with Grady. So much of the time she lived with tension.

"Let's do it again soon," he said.

"Yes," she agreed. "Good night, Grady."

Betsy was working at a furious pace in the weeks ahead. She gathered that Grady, too, was caught up in business. He'd invited her to go with him to the opera, then had to cancel. He sent the tickets to the shop, and she and Emily went together to the Metropolitan. Finally, early in April, he took her to the theater. He seemed tense and tired, and she gently scolded him for working too hard.

On April 12 word of the death of Franklin Delano Roosevelt ricocheted around the world. The nation was thrust into mourning. Throughout the country Americans gathered on street corners, wept unashamedly.

"How sad that he couldn't live to see the end of the war," Betsy said to her father-in-law while they listened to the report of the progress of the presidential train, carrying the body of FDR from Fort Benning, Georgia, to Washington, D.C.

Everywhere along the route of the train mourners camped alongside the tracks, hoping for a glimpse of the coffin. On the Saturday that the train was approaching Washington, department stores across the nation were draped in black. Movie theaters were closed. When services began at four, everything ceased. Cars, buses, and trolleys came to a stop. Radios and phones were silent. In New York subway trains halted.

On May 1 the world was told by German radio that Adolf Hitler had died in the defense of Berlin. Americans waited anxiously for signs that the hostilities in Europe were over. It was clear to everyone that the Germans were on the run.

On May 7 word circulated through the country—admittedly unconfirmed—that Germany had surrendered. On Wall Street celebrants hurled ticker tape from windows. A half million people swarmed around Times Square. Mayor La Guardia's voice was heard over loudspeakers: "Please go home or return to your jobs."

On the morning of May 8 Betsy saw Jimmy off with Miss Watkins for an early morning session in Central Park. Once they were gone, she went into the dining room for breakfast. After the long years of waiting, so much seemed to be happening—and so fast. But up until formal papers were signed, Betsy thought with anguish, American servicemen would continue to die.

She rushed through breakfast, then headed upstairs to her room to collect her briefcase. As she arrived at the door of her bedroom, she heard the phone ringing. She darted inside to answer.

"Have you heard the radio this morning?" Emily asked.

"No, what's happened?"

"I came out of work and went in for breakfast at that coffee shop nearby. They had the radio on. President Truman was on the air. The Germans have signed unconditional surrender documents. The war in Europe is over!"

"Thank God," Betsy whispered. "Why did it have to take so long?"

"I'll try to make it up to the shop," Emily said. "Everybody around here is going crazy! People are running out into the street, dancing and carrying on! See you as soon as I can!"

Betsy stayed in the house only long enough to tell Elise and Peggy that the war in Europe was over. She was sure word must have reached her father-in-law at the office. He would tell Alice—or Elise or Peggy would.

She left the house, walked toward the shop, pushing past the joyous hordes that were flowing into the streets. Cars were honking in jubilation. Warships in the North River whistled shrilly.

But Betsy was conscious of conflicting emotions. She felt relief and gratitude that, at least in Europe, the shooting was over. At the same time she felt grief and anger that when the shiploads of veterans returned from Europe Paul would not be with them. Doug would not be with them.

Emily stepped down from the crosstown bus and headed for her apartment. The afternoon in Central Park with Betsy and Jimmy had been fun, she thought. The park was gorgeous in late May—everything already green with the promise of summer, flowers bursting into bloom. On afternoons like this it was hard to realize that the war was still being fought in the Pacific.

Approaching her brownstone, she checked her watch. It was a few minutes past four. She was going to Borough Park for dinner, but she didn't have to leave until close to six. Maybe—like Jimmy—she'd settle down for a short nap, she thought humorously.

Oliver was in Boston. He'd gone up the day before for his new nephew's christening. He said he didn't know what time he'd be back tonight but he'd make sure to be at the office by check-in time.

At the landing on her floor, she heard the phone ringing. God, she was glad she had managed to get a phone. It was almost impossible to get one these days unless you were a board member at AT&T. Her face alight—guessing the caller was Oliver—she rushed to unlock her apartment door, darted inside, and picked up the phone.

"Hello—"

"I'm down at Penn Station," Oliver told her. "How about meeting me at my place? I'll be there in ten minutes," he said enticingly.

"Okay, see you there. In maybe fifteen minutes," she judged, a lilt of anticipation in her voice.

She changed from slacks into one of last summer's dresses. With a light jacket it would be just right weatherwise. She tried to button the dress from neck to waist and cursed under her breath. The material tugged across the bustline. There was no way to button it at the waist.

Pin it, she told herself in a burst of impatience. Cover the safety pin with the belt. Damn! She promised herself last summer she would drop ten pounds by spring, but she'd just added another five. No more ice cream, no cake, no more French fries and potato chips, she ordered herself, reaching for a jacket. But hell, Oliver didn't mind the extra pounds—he loved her bustiness.

She hurried to the subway. A train was just pulling into the station. In three minutes she'd be at West 72nd. Another five minutes, she gauged, to walk to Oliver's brownstone on 70th near West End. Maybe this would be *the* night. Maybe tonight he'd talk to her about their getting married. She'd hate leaving New York, but wives followed their husbands.

In the foyer of Oliver's building, she buzzed his bell, the other hand already reaching for the doorknob. She was breathless by the time she'd climbed the stairs to his apartment. She heard his radio playing. He said the first thing he did when he walked in was flip on the radio. He always settled for a music program.

Ringing the doorbell, she heard the poignant lyrics of "That Old Black Magic." What kind of magic did she need to reel in Oliver? She was tired of sleeping alone most nights.

"Hi, baby—" He stood smiling in the doorway, his eyes resting for a moment on what he called his "favorite area." "I was hoping you'd be home." He reached to kiss her for a satisfying moment.

"How was Boston?" She crossed to the sofa and sat down, legs crossed high. She may have gained weight, but the legs were still great.

"Interesting," he said. All at once, it seemed to Emily, his eyes were guarded. "I had a big powwow with my brother-in-law. You know, with the war almost over—well, everybody has to start thinking ahead."

"Right," she agreed. Her smile was expectant.

"Emily, we've had some great times together—" He sat down beside her.

"I would say so." Here it came, she thought. Her heart began to pound.

"I'm going to miss you," he said ruefully. "It won't be easy, tearing myself away and moving back to Boston."

"Oh?" *What was he getting at?*

"We've had a sensational year together, but it's time to get back to reality."

"What is reality?" *Why did his eyes keep avoiding hers?*

"Sheila and me." *Sheila?* "We got engaged before I shipped out." He was gazing at the floor. "Then she enlisted as an Army nurse. She'll be coming back from Europe soon—"

"You're engaged?" Emily stared at him in disbelief. "To be married?"

"Yeah—" He hesitated, his eyes avoiding hers. "Of course Sheila won't be home for a while." Now his eyes met hers, blatant in invitation. "As long as you understand the situation, there's no reason we can't have a few more flings." He dropped a hand on her knee.

"You are scum!" Emily pushed aside his hand. "She's out there fighting a war and you're playing house with me!" Her voice was scathing. "And throwing me that line about a cottage with a white picket fence! You bastard!"

She stumbled to her feet, strode out of the apartment, down the stairs, and out into the cooling night air. Her face was hot. She felt shamed and used. *The lousy bastard.*

She paused at the first empty phone booth to call Betsy, tapped impatiently with one lacquered fingernail as she waited for Betsy to respond.

"Hello."

"Oliver is waiting for his war bride to come home," Emily drawled. "At least, she'll be his bride as soon as the war is over."

"Emily, what are you talking about?" Betsy sounded shocked.

"Dear Oliver has been playing games with me! He's marrying an Army nurse who's over in Europe somewhere. But he didn't see why we couldn't have a few more flings before she got home. Can you imagine the nerve of that son of a bitch? Giving me that crap about a pretty clapboard cottage with a white picket fence. I hope he castrates himself on that damn fence!"

CHAPTER THIRTY-TWO

Doug pushed his way across the crowded deck of the huge, three-funneled, hospital-gray ship that had been a luxury liner before the war but was now transporting almost 12,000 GIs home from Europe. He wedged himself into a momentarily unoccupied strip of railing.

The ship had been built to accommodate 1,000 passengers. Still, nobody complained about the crowded conditions, Doug thought with wry humor as he gazed up at the star-splashed sky. They were all so damned glad to be going home.

By a quirk of fate this was the same ship on which he had crossed the Atlantic in the early months of his military service. Then they had traveled in a blackout. Not a gleam of light could show. There had been none of the jovial sounds that erupted steadily aboard the homebound vessel. Then every man had known about the dangers of German subs, was subconsciously always on the watch.

"Hey, Doug! We're starting up a new poker session," a voice called to him. "You in?"

"Not this time," Doug said with a slow smile. Aboard ship the main diversions were poker and crap games. "I want to arrive home with something more than my uniform."

"Did you ever wonder if we'd really be going home one day?" a fortyish staff sergeant asked him.

"A lot of times," Doug admitted. "Of course we're just on

furlough," he pointed out. "There's still a war going on in the Pacific."

"I'm praying like hell that it'll all be over before they can ship us out again. God, it'll be sweet to be home—even for a little while." The staff sergeant's voice dropped to a husky whisper. "I can't wait to see my wife and kid." He chuckled now. "I'll tell her to let me spend a couple of hours with the kid—he's seven now— then send him over to his grandmother. I want to jump into bed with my wife and hump her for forty-eight hours! And after that I want to sit down to the biggest, thickest porterhouse steak the butcher can deliver."

"You can't say much for the cuisine here," Doug agreed. They stood in line for hours every day for rations. Most nights this consisted of dehydrated potatoes, some concoction of chopped meat substitute, and bad coffee or juice. Mom would be cooking up a storm, he thought tenderly, when she got the call from him that he was home. He'd never forget talking to her on the phone after the liberation of Paris. She'd said it was the greatest moment of her life.

"You married?" the staff sergeant asked curiously.

"No," Doug told him.

"Got a girl?" he probed.

"Not a steady," Doug said. All at once he was assaulted by memories of Betsy.

"That'll change once you're home," the staff sergeant predicted. "Christ, I can't wait to get out of uniform and to start living again. If they ship us to the Pacific, how much longer can that last?"

Long after most of those aboard were asleep—many of them sleeping on deck for lack of other facilities—Doug stood at the railing and gazed down at the summer-calm Atlantic. How had Paul and Frank and the others made out in this bloody war? He'd lost track of Paul soon after he'd been shipped overseas. But Paul was a survivor, he told himself. Paul would make it home all right.

He stared at the water—silver now in the spill of moonlight— and thought about Betsy. So many nights—in England and in

France—he'd thought about her, visualized her lovely face. He'd remembered the way she walked—with quick, small steps, body leaning slightly forward as though rushing out to meet the world. He remembered the way her face would light up when she was excited about something. His timing had been all wrong. Paul had met her first.

Now—as happened with ominous frequency in these weeks since V-E Day—his mind settled painfully on the reports he'd heard about Nazi atrocities. On board ship he'd talked with soldiers who'd been with the troops who liberated the survivors of the concentration camps at Buchenwald and Bergen-Belsen, Dachau and Auschwitz. They talked about the mounds of unburied, naked corpses, about the sick and starving and dying prisoners—and each time he felt a searing pain in his stomach.

He knew that once peace ruled the earth again, he must throw his energies into trying to help those tortured humans who were just emerging from the concentration camps. He didn't know yet what his part in this effort would be, but he knew he could not live with himself if he was not to be part of it.

CHAPTER THIRTY-THREE

Betsy felt compassion for her mother-in-law in the weeks following V-E Day. She knew that Alice—and Paul Jr.—shared her anguish, that they asked themselves the same questions she asked herself. *Why wasn't Paul coming home? Why wasn't he one of those who survived?*

Sitting in a cafeteria on Broadway, waiting for Emily to join her for a quick Saturday evening dinner before going to a neighborhood movie, Betsy reminded herself that the war was still being fought in the Pacific. GIs returning home from Europe would be sent there after brief furloughs.

She spied Emily pushing the revolving door at the entrance to the cafeteria and lifted a hand to signal her.

"Rita Hayworth's at the Loew's," Emily reported."In *Tonight and Every Night.*"

"Oh, we can't miss that," Betsy said. People often told Emily she resembled Rita Hayworth.

"A news bulletin: I'm setting up a small anniversary party for Mom and Dad on Sunday. Can you believe they've been together for thirty-five years? Anyhow, I'm making dinner for the family. The apartment will be crowded as hell, but nobody'll mind. I want you to come and bring Jimmy. Remember," she said tenderly, "you two are family."

On Sunday Betsy was amused by Jimmy's excitement at going to the anniversary dinner. He was enthralled that he would probably be allowed to stay up past his normal bedtime. He rebelled at taking his early afternoon nap.

"You nap or we don't go to the party," Betsy warned.

Dutifully Jimmy lay down on his bed and pretended to sleep. Five minutes later he opened his eyes.

"Mommie, I'm awake," he announced jubilantly. "Can we go to the party?"

"All right, we'll go." Emily would be glad they were arriving so early. She could use some help. "Come on, let me get you dressed."

Betsy and Jimmy emerged from the elevator just as Alice, Paul Jr., and Grady walked into the foyer.

"Jimmy, my precious—" Alice held out her arms lovingly to her grandson. "But you've had such a short nap. You're always still asleep when we come back from our Sunday lunch." Alice and Paul Jr. followed the same routine every Sunday, Betsy knew— morning church services, then lunch at the Colony. Today they'd been joined by Grady.

"You're looking beautiful as always," Grady told Betsy while Paul Jr. lifted Jimmy into the air in his grandson's favorite form of greeting.

"Thank you," Betsy said softly. Now her eyes turned to her son. "Jimmy's going to a party," Betsy explained. "He's so excited about that."

"Mommie, let's go." Jimmy tugged at her hand in impatience.

"William's putting the car away already," Alice said. "You didn't tell me you'd be needing it."

"We'll take a taxi over," Betsy told her. "It's right across town."

"I'll come along," Grady said. "If that's all right with you."

"That's not necessary, Grady," Betsy said, but she was touched by his solicitude.

Grady brushed this aside. "It'll be my pleasure," he insisted.

"We'll hold coffee until you return," Alice told Grady. *Grady was attracted to Betsy.* Incredibly she hadn't noticed before. "We'll be in the library."

Alice watched Betsy go off with Grady, each holding on to one of Jimmy's small hands. She felt a flicker of excitement. This was a picture that pleased her. She was upset each time Paul Jr. remarked that Betsy was young and beautiful and would probably remarry one day. But Grady was a stepfather for Jimmy that she could accept.

"I wouldn't mind a cup of coffee while we wait for Grady." Paul Jr.'s voice interrupted her thoughts.

"You drink too much coffee," she said automatically and repeated her warnings about his not taking decent care of himself.

In the library they settled themselves before one of the tall, open windows that admitted a pleasant breeze. Alice instructed Elise to bring them coffee. While Paul Jr. dissected the morning's sermon, Alice allowed her mind to follow its earlier path.

Grady would be a fine stepfather for Jimmy. She could be sure that Grady would accept her suggestions on Jimmy's upbringing. Together, she thought triumphantly, she and Grady could bring Jimmy into the church.

It was time to include Betsy in their social lives, Alice decided as she formed her plot. It would be natural for Grady to be her escort.

"Alice, you're off in space somewhere," Paul Jr. chided good-humoredly. "You haven't heard a word I've said."

"Of course I have," she insisted. "But I was thinking. We haven't seen that new play with Laurette Taylor. It won the New York Drama Critics' Circle Award. Why don't you have your secretary arrange for seats for us? For four," she said with studied casualness. "We'll take Betsy and Grady."

She didn't expect Betsy to even consider marriage for a long time. But when that time arrived, let *Grady* be her choice. She would die if Betsy married some strange man—probably Jewish—and took Jimmy away from this house. Out of their lives. *But it didn't have to be that way.*

On Friday evening Alice paused before going downstairs to join Paul Jr., waiting for her in the library. They were to leave in a few minutes for dinner with Georgette and Carl at "21." It was Georgette's birthday. There was time, she decided, to drop in to see Jimmy. He'd be asleep already, but she enjoyed just standing by his bed for a few moments each night.

A sentimental smile lighting her face, she approached the nursery on tiptoe, opened the door, and walked inside. Almost immediately she realized that Jimmy had not been put to bed yet. Frowning—because she harbored a belief that his bedtime should be inviolate—she glanced through the half-open door that led to Betsy's bedroom.

With Jimmy in pajamas and tiny slippers at her side, Betsy stood before a pair of brass candlesticks, a match in one hand. A silken scarf lay in graceful folds about her mass of auburn hair, the palm of her other hand shielding her eyes. Her lips moved in silence. Instinctively Alice knew this was the Friday-night Jewish ritual of lighting the Sabbath candles.

Trembling, Alice withdrew from the nursery. As young as Jimmy was, Betsy was already indoctrinating him in her faith! He was to be denied the faith of his father, she fretted yet again. The faith of generations of Forrests. Now, with compulsive haste, she went to join her husband. But her mind was in torment.

"You're upset," he said gently when they were settled in the limousine and William heading toward the Adams' townhouse.

"It's Jimmy," Alice told him. "I can't bear his not being baptized. I feel uncomfortable in church every Sunday."

"Alice, you must allow Betsy to raise Jimmy in her own faith," Paul Jr. said warily. "You made a promise to her. And remember, his father agreed to that."

"Maybe Paul did," she said ominously.

"Is the staff all set for the move to the beach house?" Paul Jr. sought to divert her thoughts.

"It's routine after all these years." She sighed in annoyance, knowing her husband's motives. "I must make sure Grady comes out to spend the long Fourth of July weekend with us," she pursued, her mind in high gear. "He works so hard. Like you."

She'd contrive to leave Betsy and Grady alone much of the time, she plotted. They didn't have to marry right away, but she'd feel better just knowing they had something going between them. *It would be so right for Betsy and Grady to marry.*

Betsy had just arrived at the shop on Saturday morning when Grady phoned. Already the day was unseasonably hot and humid.

"I was up in Boston on business yesterday," he said. "I wanted to tell you how much I like what you've done with my bedroom and bath at Sandra's house. She's thrilled, too."

"Grady, I'm so glad you like it." Betsy felt a sense of relief.

"How's the business going?" he asked.

"I've hired another salesperson. I'm not on the floor anymore except when a customer asks for me," she reported, appreciating his interest. She needed more space and a larger inventory, she thought with recurrent frustration. That would make life less frantic.

"Betsy, I was wondering—" Grady paused, cleared his throat. "Would you take pity on me and have dinner with me tonight? I've just heard about a great place up in Westchester that sits on the edge of a pond with weeping willows all around."

"That would be very nice," Betsy said. The prospect was enticing in this hot spell. "But not early," she added.

"I know." He chuckled. "Your time with Jimmy is precious. What about eight o'clock?"

"Perfect." Alice and Paul Jr. were going out tonight. Emily was having dinner with her family. Betsy would have been alone in the house except for Jimmy and the domestic staff.

"I'll pick you up at eight," he said ebulliently.

"I'll be waiting."

Was Alice annoyed that sometimes Grady took her out to dinner or a concert or the theater? But then it was unlikely that Alice was even aware he did.

Late in the afternoon Grady met an out-of-town client to discuss business over cocktails at the Cub Room. He was annoyed when the conference dragged on longer than he had anticipated. He wanted time for a leisurely shower and shave before he met Betsy.

Finally he was able to break away. He rushed home to his apartment. He was just about to go into the shower when his phone rang. Swearing under his breath, he reached to pick up the receiver.

"Hello."

"Grady, I'm so glad I caught you," Sandra greeted him. "Bruce and I have had a change of heart about staying in Boston for July. You know how hard it is to find a proper house at the last moment this way, but Bruce has just signed a lease on a lovely house in Newport. It's right on the ocean. Why don't you come out for the Fourth of July weekend?"

"I'm scheduled to go to Southampton," Grady told her. "With the Forrests." All at once he was self-conscious; he was remembering Sandra's remark that he could have had a daughter Betsy's age. "But I'm glad you've decided to get away from the hot city."

They talked briefly, then Grady was able to shower and shave. He couldn't wait for the long Fourth of July weekend at Southampton. He'd be able to spend all his waking hours in Betsy's company.

It would be wonderful to walk on the beach with her at dusk, to lounge on the veranda and gaze at the sea while they talked. They might even see a sunrise over the ocean together.

Emerging from the shower, Grady inspected himself in the full-length mirror on his bathroom door. He didn't look like a man past fifty, he congratulated himself with a rush of confidence. All the walking he tried to include in his daily activities plus the swimming three times a week had kept him fit. Most men his age were going to flab.

He left the bathroom and headed for the bedroom closet wall. Were his ties these days a bit too conservative? he asked himself. Too *old?* He'd drop by Brooks Brothers next week and buy a few brighter ties.

He'd been trying for so long not to admit even to himself that he was deeply attracted to Betsy. He'd told himself she was Paul's sweet, lovely widow and he wanted to help her. It pleased him that she plainly valued his business advice. She was grateful for his help in getting her loan. She *liked* him. And being with her made him feel young again.

He remembered the early years of his marriage, before Nadine was stricken with that devastating illness. He remembered his loneliness when Nadine became wrapped up in her illness, no longer a wife except in name.

His face radiated a poignant joy as he envisioned Betsy sharing his life here—Betsy as his wife. Other men had taken young wives, he told himself in a surge of excitement. It happened often in their circles.

Look at Chaplin, marrying eighteen-year-old Oona O'Neill. Stowkowski married twenty-one-year-old Gloria Vanderbilt. Hell, he was younger than both of those men by a lot of years. In time, he thought—and the newness of this made him almost giddy in anticipation—he might even have a child with Betsy. He'd have a whole new life, one that would make up for the empty lost years.

He mustn't rush Betsy, he warned himself. He'd take it easy. Slowly he would make her understand what a fine life they could have together.

CHAPTER THIRTY-FOUR

This summer Betsy planned to spend only long weekends at the Southampton house. She and Jimmy would remain in Manhattan midweek. She knew Alice would be upset, but with the way the business was growing, it was necessary for her to be in the city for most of the business week. And Jimmy would be all right, she told herself conscientiously. She and Miss Watkins had worked that out together.

Sitting down to dinner with Paul Jr. and Alice the Monday before their first scheduled weekend in Southampton, Betsy knew she couldn't stall any longer on telling Alice her summer plans.

"If it's all right with you," she told Paul Jr., "I'll send Jimmy and Miss Watkins out to Southampton with you on Thursday afternoons." He'd said earlier that he'd be leaving Manhattan around four on Thursday afternoons during the summer. "I'll take the train out early Friday afternoons so I can spend time with Jimmy before he goes to sleep."

"You mean to keep Jimmy in town four days a week?" Alice was appalled. "Aren't you forgetting the awful summer heat?"

"Miss Watkins has found a morning play group for him that has air-conditioned quarters. And he always naps in the afternoon. He'll be fine."

"But, Betsy, he doesn't have to endure a city summer," Alice said. "And all his little friends will be away."

"He'll be all right, Alice," Paul Jr. said, intervening with a reassuring smile. His look ordered Alice not to fight Betsy on this.

"Oh, I'll be going out with Georgette to Greenwich this weekend," Alice told him, capitulating to his warning. "We have some committee planning to do with her sister-in-law, who's serving with us. Why don't you suggest that Grady go out with you to Southampton? And don't you two dare spend the weekend talking business," she added. "Betsy, you make sure they don't."

Betsy felt some qualms on Thursday afternoon when she sent Jimmy out to Southampton with his grandfather and Miss Watkins.

"I'll be out tomorrow afternoon," she promised as he was settled in the limousine between Miss Watkins and Paul Jr. He wouldn't be upset that she wasn't there tonight, would he? "You be a good boy, Jimmy."

Betsy was pleased that Alice had arranged for her to drive out to Southampton with Grady. He was to pick her up at the shop at three the following day. Emily was coming in to the shop to cover for her.

A few minutes before three on Friday Betsy was waiting with her Weekender at the door of The Oasis. She was astonished to see Grady emerge from a sleek prewar white Cadillac convertible. Usually he drove a dark gray Chrysler or rode in his chauffeur-driven limousine.

"Your summer car?" she asked with a laugh as he strolled toward her with an eager smile.

"I was in the mood for something more cheerful," he said, reaching for her Weekender. "When this came on the market, I grabbed it. We'll put the top down when we get out of the city."

Grady looked so relaxed now that he was dressed casually in white slacks and a red polo shirt. He seemed younger—as though leaving Manhattan brushed aside the demands of his everyday world. There was an ebullience about him today that was new to her.

"We'll miss the rush," he told her with a broad smile as they headed for the Queensboro Bridge. "I always feel smug when I can drive out this early on a Friday."

By the time they arrived at the Queensboro Bridge they decided they'd been overly optimistic. It was a hot, humid day, and those who could leave the city early seemed determined to do so. Still, Grady approved unperturbed. His high spirits were contagious.

"Tell me how things are going in the shop," he asked while they sat stalled in traffic only a short distance from Manhattan. "Everything progressing to your satisfaction?"

"We're doing amazingly well as to the number of clients I'm picking up," she said, sorting out in her mind the problems that had been developing. "The shop has been mentioned in several of the best magazines—"

"But something bothers you," he probed sympathetically.

"My mind tells me this is the time to expand. And I learned just last week that the floor above mine is being vacated. It would be a simple matter—I think—to open up the shop to that floor with a staircase. Still, it's a huge move." She wasn't sure she could handle it financially, even by scrimping at every possible angle. "I'm probably rushing ahead too fast," she said. "I'd be almost doubling my rent. And with all that extra space"—she laughed at herself—"I'd be out there searching for merchandise I can't really afford at this point."

"Betsy, if you feel this is the time, take a chance!" His voice was electric. "Trust your instincts." He paused. "If you're concerned about financing the expansion, my bank will come forward with a larger loan."

"Grady, I wasn't hinting at that," she stammered.

"I know you weren't," he said. "But I have the greatest confidence in your ability. It gives me pleasure to see you forging ahead in your business. I enjoy your enthusiasm for your work, your creativity. We'll talk about it over the weekend," he decided. In Grady's mind, the matter was settled, Betsy understood.

"I don't even know if they'll rent me that second floor," she said candidly. "They may be afraid that I'm taking on too much."

"We'll sit down at the beach house and figure out all the angles," he soothed. "Out there my mind becomes so much clearer. I don't feel pressured. Things work out."

"I don't have the slightest idea of how much the construction will cost," Betsy confessed. "Yet it does seem a minor effort to cut through and put in a stairway." All at once the prospect of actually expanding sent waves of excitement through her.

"I have a friend who's an architect," Grady said. "He owes me a few favors. I'll have him come over to the shop and assess the situation for us, give us an estimate. I don't want you to apply for the loan until we know exactly how much you'll need. Nothing's more devastating than to underestimate your budget."

"Whatever you say, Grady." Betsy's eyes were bright with gratitude.

Betsy envisioned the expansion as an exhilarating challenge. She relished Grady's confidence in her. She welcomed his advice, as well as his helping her obtain another loan. Oh yes, Grady was a cherished friend.

At the Southampton house Betsy and Grady found Paul Jr. reading on the veranda. Absorbed in his book, he hadn't heard the car pull into the long, circular driveway.

"How was it in the city?" he asked after they'd exchanged greetings.

"An inferno," Grady told him. "I'm so glad you and Alice persuaded me to come out this weekend." He chuckled. "And have no doubts, I'll be out for the long Fourth of July weekend as planned."

"Jimmy's on the beach with Miss Watkins," Betsy guessed. She was impatient to see him.

"They'll be coming up in a few minutes. Miss Watkins knows you're due about now. You made better time on the road than I expected. I hope, Grady," Paul Jr. joshed, "that you didn't try to show Betsy how fast that new buggy of yours can go."

"I don't drive fast with precious cargo." Grady's eyes dwelt affectionately on Betsy.

"Mommie, Mommie!" Betsy turned to the stretch of beach just below at the sound of Jimmy's exuberant greeting.

She rushed toward the stairs leading up to the veranda, her arms extended. "Jimmy, I missed you! Were you a good boy?"

"He was very good." Paul Jr. beamed. "And I read him three stories at bedtime."

"Now who's spoiling him?" Betsy chided in high spirits.

Jimmy settled down on Betsy's lap to relate his activities since she last saw him. She took him into the house, gave him his dinner, prepared him for bed. By now he was yawning, but he insisted on another story when she'd finished their nightly quota.

"No more tonight," she said firmly. "It's time for you to go to sleep and for Mommie to have her dinner."

Betsy enjoyed the quiet dinner on the veranda, with the ocean providing a soothing symphony. The two men reminisced about other summers at Southampton.

"Why don't we walk off this sumptuous dinner on the beach?" Grady suggested while they dawdled over coffee. Paul Jr. had sent Elise to his room earlier to bring down sweaters for himself and Grady and to Betsy's room to bring down one for her. "It's a beautiful evening." Dusk was merging into twilight now. In the distance the lights of a pair of boats lent an exotic air to the seascape. There was a pleasant night chill to the air.

"You two walk on the beach," Paul Jr. ordered. "My most strenuous activity out here is to drop myself onto a chaise to read or gaze out at the water."

Betsy relished the emptiness of the beach as she and Grady walked in solitary pleasure at the water's edge. He talked to her about his house in Nassau and his hideaway in Vermont.

"Someday you'll have to see them," he told her while they headed back to the veranda, where Paul Jr. was listening to the radio. The sky was splashed with stars now.

"Both houses sound beautiful," Betsy said.

The weekend sped past. Betsy and Grady spent much time plotting her course in the business. She welcomed Grady's wisdom, his enthusiasm for what she meant to do with the shop. She enjoyed his low-keyed, casual companionship, his affectionate attentions to Jimmy when she took over on Sunday on Miss Watkins' day off.

"Jimmy, you come for a drive with your Uncle Grady and let Mommie go for a swim," he ordered good-humoredly. "I know a place where they have the greatest ice cream."

"Chocolate?" Jimmy asked with an anticipatory smile.

"What else?" Grady grinned broadly. "Doesn't everybody want chocolate?"

On the drive into Manhattan early Monday morning Grady worked out a schedule for Betsy.

"These are the things you're to handle," he wound up in high spirits. "I'll check with my architect, browbeat him into coming over within the next day or two to advise us. By the end of the summer," he proclaimed, "you'll be ready to move into that second-floor expansion!"

Again on the Friday afternoon of the July 4th weekend Betsy drove out to Southampton with Grady. Though tempers of motorists soared as drivers were forced to battle with monumental traffic along with overheated motors, Grady seemed unfazed by the slow exodus from the city. It was so relaxing to be with Grady, Betsy thought in gratitude.

They discussed the ongoing plans for the expansion of the shop. Betsy was amazed at the speed with which Grady was moving ahead with this. She was shocked, though, at the rent the landlord had demanded for the second-floor lease.

"Stop worrying about the rent," Grady said soothingly when she voiced this yet again as they sat in stalled traffic. "Inflation's taking over everywhere. You'll raise your prices, too." He chuckled. "Customers may complain a bit, but they'll buy. It's part of our way of life now to accept escalating prices."

"It's scary," she admitted, remembering the quotations Grady's architect friend had given them. "The costs, I mean."

"Trust me, Betsy." Grady took one hand from the wheel to squeeze one of hers in reassurance.

"Grady, I do," she said fervently.

"If I didn't think it'd work, I'd tell you. I know you'll make a tremendous go of the enlarged shop. I feel absolutely no qualms about having the bank extend a larger loan than what we'd originally anticipated."

Betsy enjoyed the long weekend at the Southampton house. She and Grady went with Alice and Paul Jr. to a cocktail party one afternoon and to a dinner party on Sunday evening. She felt faintly self-conscious that the same people were at both parties and noting that on both occasions Grady was her escort. But that was because Grady was a houseguest of the Forrests', she told herself. There was nothing romantic about his being her escort.

Still, it seemed that she and Grady were spending much of the weekend together. Alice was in a mellow mood, she decided humorously. She was constantly taking Paul Jr. off on some errand. He must help her choose a birthday gift for Georgette's husband, which became a major chore. She wanted his advice about plantings for the driveway.

One morning Grady encouraged her to go with him to watch the sun rise over the ocean. They were alone on the beach except for a few exuberant sea gulls.

"Are you warm enough?" he asked solicitously because the early morning air was cool.

"I'm fine," she reassured him, her eyes fastened to the horizon, where a pink glow told them that soon the sun would burst into view.

"This is a wonderful time of day." Grady radiated pleasure. "No one on the beach, and unless the clouds thwart us, the sun about to make its magical appearance."

"No clouds this morning." Yesterday they'd come down for early coffee in anticipation of a sunrise, but they'd been met by a gray sky and threats of rain. "Oh, there it comes!"

Together—caught up in the miracle of one of nature's most magnificent displays—they watched the ball of orange-red fire rise with tantalizing slowness above the horizon until the full sun hovered above the ocean.

"It's so lovely," Betsy whispered.

"Like you," Grady murmured. "Now let's head back to the house for breakfast on the veranda," he ordered briskly. "I'm suddenly ravenous."

Grady left his office shortly before ten on this morning late in July. He wanted to have at least half an hour with his attorney before the real estate closing this morning on his latest acquisition of property.

Leonard was not entirely happy about this purchase, he remembered. Leonard had reproached him for moving away from his customary cautious requirements in increasing his already large real estate holdings.

"Grady, what the hell do you want with that small building?" Leonard demanded again when he'd settled himself in his attorney's large, attractively furnished, private office for a last-minute discussion about the imminent closing. "Buying something like that simply isn't your style."

"I'm looking ahead to fifteen or twenty years from now," Grady lied. He was buying the building that housed The Oasis for purely sentimental reasons. He cherished heady visions of himself presenting the deed to Betsy one day as a wedding present. He mustn't rush her, of course, he exhorted himself yet again.

It was becoming increasingly difficult to be with Betsy and not pour out what was in his heart. She was so lovely, so sweet—so desirable. When he was with her, he wanted only to hold her in his arms and to make love to her. It had been so long since he'd felt this way about a woman.

"What's this tripe about fifteen or twenty years from now?" Leonard said, intruding on his thoughts.

"Land on Madison Avenue will be worth a fortune then," Grady predicted. God, it was insane—and wonderful—the way he could become aroused just thinking about Betsy. "You'll see. I'll sell it for twenty times what I'm paying for it now."

"The only good thing about that property," Leonard muttered, "is that the lease on the ground floor hasn't long to run and you'll be able to raise the rent. But there's a long lease on the second floor—and another two years to run on the third- and fourth-floor leases."

"So for once I'm speculating." Grady shrugged aside his attorney's advice. "Indulge me. I can afford to speculate now and then."

The closing was routine. Still, Grady was restless. He was impatient to declare himself to Betsy, even while his mind warned him not to rush her. Would she think him too old? No, he thought, bolstering his ego. She was always so sweet and understanding when they were together.

"Well, that's it," Leonard brought him back to the present. "Though I still can't understand your buying that building. Do you have time for lunch?"

"No, I have to get back to the office," Grady told him.

In truth, he wanted to be alone, to savor the pleasure of visualizing Betsy's astonishment when he gave her the deed to the building. That would be his wedding present to his beautiful young bride.

Betsy was recurrently unnerved by the debt she was undertaking. Grady insisted she'd make a tremendous go of the enlarged shop. He felt no qualm about having the bank extend her what seemed to be a huge loan.

But on August 6 her alarm about her financial undertaking took a back seat when she—and the world—were electrified by President Truman's announcement that "sixteen hours ago an American plane dropped one atom bomb on Hiroshima." After the Japanese government rejected a last-chance warning, he emphasized, the bomb was dropped. Within two minutes Hiroshima had lost 60,000 of its 344,000 population.

In the Forrest library Betsy and her father-in-law listened to repeated radio reports of this shattering destruction, mesmerized by the accounts.

"It means the end of the war," Paul Jr. said with a fatalistic calm. "God only knows how many American lives have been saved. Truman had no other choice."

"But to wipe out sixty thousand people in minutes?" Betsy was pale with shock. "To destroy four square miles of a city?"

"Would it have been better," he challenged, "to have killed sixty thousand Japanese in an invasion of the island and to lose perhaps as many—or more—American lives? Have you forgotten the kamikaze pilots? The armed forces know that there are over five thousand kamikazes in underground hangars waiting to die if they can take that many American ships down with them!"

"I guess I'm not being realistic," Betsy conceded. The Nazis had killed 6,000,000 Jews.

"Japan was warned," Paul Jr. emphasized. "Truman, Churchill, and Chiang Kai-shek broadcast a warning that assured them humane treatment and a Japanese 'new order of peace, security, and justice.' But they refused to surrender. The Premier called the offer beneath Japanese contempt. Truman had no recourse except to drop the bomb. Remember, Betsy, nobody warned the millions who died in the path of the German and Japanese invasions."

But Paul Jr. was wrong; it was not the end of the war. Tokyo ignored the demand for surrender. A second atomic bomb was dropped on Nagasaki on August 9. Soon after, B-29s were flying over Japan to drop millions of pamphlets that read: "TO THE JAPANESE PEOPLE: America asks that you take immediate heed of what we say on this leaflet. We are in possession of the most destructive force ever devised by man. . . ."

On August 14 Truman announced the unconditional surrender of Japan. At last the war was over. Truman declared a two-day national holiday. The nation erupted into a joyous celebration. Yet the celebration was tainted by the memories of those who would not be coming home. Of those for whom peace had come too late.

"I'll spend the rest of my life," Betsy confessed to Emily, "praying that the world never has to face another war. That somehow we'll acquire the wisdom to keep the peace."

CHAPTER THIRTY-FIVE

By mid-October the new second floor of The Oasis was about to open. Betsy and Emily, working at The Oasis full-time since shortly after V-J Day, had been at the shop since seven A.M. Now they settled down to have tea and the muffins Emily had picked up on her way in. Then they would attend to final details.

How hectic these past weeks had been, Betsy mused, tired but exhilarated. In addition to all the work involved with the shop expansion, they'd taken time out to handle Emily's move from the old apartment to the one she'd acquired last month through a friend of Rheba's. Emily was thrilled to be living just a ten-minute walk from the shop.

Grady had been wonderful, Betsy told herself gratefully. He had been in and out of the shop two or three times a week, had taken her out to dinner several times.

"Won't Mark and Eric be amazed when they see the new second floor?" Emily broke into her thoughts.

"I hope they make it into the city over the Christmas–New Year's holidays." Betsy was wistful. They were planning on that. "It's been so long since we've seen them."

"We'll have to throw a New Year's Eve party," Emily decided, eyes aglow with anticipation. "Our social lives are too bloody limited."

"It's a little early to plan," Betsy pointed out humorously. "But yes, if Mark and Eric come in, we'll have a party." But always on holidays she was conscious of Paul's absence. She was relieved when the holidays were over.

They heard a sound of someone knocking on the door. It was too early for Rhoda, the new salesgirl, to be arriving.

"It's the florist," Betsy realized and leapt to her feet. "They've got just two hours to set up before we open."

The day sped past. Betsy gloried in the admiration displayed by their invited guests. Alice had appeared with Georgette. Even Grady, despite his hectic schedule, had come in to express his approval of the new floor. By the end of the day Betsy and Emily were exhausted but triumphant.

Tonight Betsy lingered with Emily after the shop was closed. She was uneasy that Emily had begun to date an Army sergeant home from Italy only a few weeks and now discharged from service. They'd sat next to each other at a soda fountain one day and started a conversation. Betsy worried that Emily was about to throw herself into an affair with Chuck Steinberg, the former sergeant, to prove she was over the relationship with Oliver.

"Oh, what about having dinner with Chuck and me tomorrow night?" Emily asked. "He wants to take a look at the Columbia campus."

"Why?" Betsy was startled.

"He's talking about going to college under the GI Bill," Emily explained. "I figured we'd take him to the West End Bar for hamburgers, then let him roam about the campus." She hesitated, but the look in her eyes was pleading. "Go with us, Betsy. I don't think I could handle walking in there without you."

"It'll be full of ghosts." Columbia brought back such anguished memories. She hadn't been to the West End since Paul and Doug enlisted. "But all right, I'll go with you—"

On Tuesday evening Betsy left the shop a half hour early so she could spend time with Jimmy before she and Emily met Chuck at the West End. With Jimmy settled in bed, she took a cab to pick up Emily at her new apartment.

"It seems weird going up to Columbia," Emily admitted as she settled herself beside Betsy in the cab. "It's like turning the calendar back four years."

"Have you ever run into Sara since that time about a year and a half ago?" Betsy asked.

"No. It would be nice to see her again." Emily paused. "Her husband was over in England, I remember, with the quartermaster corps."

"I hope he made it home," Betsy said softly.

Betsy and Emily left the cab at the West End Bar. Chuck was waiting outside. Betsy disliked him on sight. How could Emily be dating this jerk?

She was grateful that the table conversation required little of her. She knew that for Emily, too, this was a traumatic occasion, though Emily managed flip replies for Chuck's awkward efforts at humor.

"What about grabbing a movie tonight?" Chuck asked restlessly when they had ordered and were waiting for their hamburgers and coffee.

"I thought you wanted to roam around the Columbia campus." Emily lifted her eyebrows in surprise.

"It's dark already," Chuck said with a shrug. "I wouldn't be able to see much. Anyhow, I've been thinking. Do I really want to spend the next four years with my nose in schoolbooks?" He grimaced in distaste. "I need to latch on to a job with a splashy paycheck."

Betsy was searching for an excuse to break away early when all at once her eyes focused on a young man walking into the bar with three others. She was aware of something oddly familiar about the way he carried himself. Her heart began to pound when his face came into focus. It wasn't possible. *Was it?*

"Emily—" She reached to grasp Emily's arm. Her gaze riveted on the new arrival in the bar.

"Yeah?" Emily turned to her in inquiry, then followed Betsy's gaze. "Oh wow, doesn't he resemble Doug!"

"It *is* Doug!" Betsy's face was luminescent.

"Betsy, it can't be," Emily protested gently.

"It is!" Betsy leaned forward, trembling with anticipation. "Doug!" she called loudly. The object of her attention swung about to face their table. His smile was joyous when he spied her. *She wasn't wrong.* "Oh, Doug!"

Betsy and Emily clung to his every word as Doug briefed them on what had happened since the day his plane had been shot down over France.

"I guessed it was one of you two who called Mom that day the telegram came from the War Department." His eyes were somber in recall. "You know what Mom told me? She said she was a shambles that first day, but after that she swore she wouldn't believe I was dead until my dog tags surfaced."

"My mother kept saying my brother, Bert, would show up— you remember he was reported missing in action. But it was awful, waiting for it to happen."

"You had some hope." Doug's smile was wry. "My plane was sighted going down in flames. Nobody guessed the two of us would parachute to safety."

"I still can't believe you're here!" Betsy reached out to touch his arm. "It's wonderful, Doug!"

"I never got to France," Chuck drawled, "though I was dying to see Paris and those gorgeous broads at the Folies-Bergère. Still, Italy had its moments." His smile was crudely eloquent. "And chocolate bars went a long way there."

Betsy caught Doug's fleeting grimace of contempt for Chuck before he turned to her.

"Sara told me about Paul." Now he was somber. "We lost touch once we were both on the move. I couldn't believe it—I had just taken it for granted he'd be one of the lucky ones." Betsy felt his grief. "Sara said she'd lost touch with you two. She didn't know where you were living. I tried the old apartment. There was a new name on the mail box. I talked to the super, but he was new and never heard of you."

"I moved last month," Emily explained. "I got lucky. The new apartment is a ten-minute walk to the shop."

"I even tried calling your parents," Doug said with a chuckle.

"I never guessed how many Meyers were listed out in Brooklyn. But nobody knew an Emily Meyers. And I couldn't find a listing for you, Betsy—"

"My folks have an unlisted phone number," Emily explained. "In earlier days—during the Depression—they'd been involved with a Communist group. They didn't want to be pursued with a stream of phone calls when they saw the light and broke off. They just let the phone number remain unlisted through the years."

"I'm living with Paul's parents," Betsy explained.

"I got your letter telling me about the baby." His eyes were tender. "He must be almost three."

"He'll be three in December." Betsy smiled. She remembered Doug's deep affection for children.

"I tried to locate Mark and Eric. I couldn't find a phone number for them or for Mark's shop."

"Mark and Eric moved to California. I bought the shop," Betsy explained.

"Hey, that's terrific," Doug approved. "But I couldn't find a phone listing for it—"

"It's now called The Oasis," Emily chimed in while Chuck looked bored. "That's why you couldn't find it."

Doug gazed from Emily to Betsy with obvious joy at being in their company. "You two haven't changed a bit."

"Only now there's more of me," Emily said with a sigh.

"Where are you living now?" Betsy asked, aware that his friends were showing signs of impatience at his temporary defection.

"Let me give you my address and phone number." Doug reached into his jacket pocket for a notebook and pencil, began to jot this down. "I was staying with my family until two weeks ago. You know how hard it is to find a vacancy these days. But I'm too old to live at home again," he said good-humoredly. "If I stay out all night, just walking around the city, feeling great at being back home, Mom's a nervous wreck. Anyhow, she found an apartment on West 105th Street. The woman who lived there wanted to retire to Florida. I agreed to buy the furniture, then just moved in.

Stiff key money"—he sighed—"but I received a big chunk of back pay when I was discharged from service."

"Hey, Doug," one of his companions called. "Get over here so we can order."

"I'd better go," he said. His eyes said he was eager to remain with them. "Why don't you give me a buzz later tonight? We'll arrange to get together. We've got a lot of catching up to do!"

As soon as possible Betsy contrived to break away from Emily and Chuck. She would have loved to go somewhere alone with Emily to talk about Doug's homecoming. What a beautiful discovery! Though Emily and Chuck had decided to go on to a movie tonight, Betsy suspected that Emily would have preferred to sit over endless cups of coffee with her and rehash the months between their graduation from Hunter and the attack on Pearl Harbor. What Emily called "the great days."

As Betsy prepared to leave, Chuck went in search of a phone booth to check on when the next performance at the Thalia would begin.

"I'll phone Doug later and set up something for tomorrow night," Emily promised. "Maybe dinner at my place."

"Great," Betsy whispered and left before Chuck returned.

She was caught up in the wonder that Doug was home. *He was alive.*

CHAPTER THIRTY-SIX

Betsy was in bed reading when Emily called.

"We're having dinner with Doug tomorrow night at his apartment," Emily reported. "I still can't believe he's really here."

"It's wonderful," Betsy said. "I can't wait to sit down and really talk with him."

Every hour of the next day seemed to drag endlessly. Out of deference to Jimmy's schedule, Emily had arranged for them to be at Doug's apartment at seven-thirty. And, while Betsy was eager to be on her way, tonight Jimmy was putting up a battle to stay up later. Why did he have to choose tonight to fight about bedtime? And immediately she felt guilty that she was impatient to leave.

Miss Watkins came into the nursery with a sympathetic smile. Earlier she had told Miss Watkins about Doug's return and their reunion dinner this evening.

"Jimmy, you behave now," Miss Watkins said firmly. "Mommie has to go out."

"Why?" Jimmy demanded. His beautiful little face puckered in a prelude to tears. "Why, Mommie?" he repeated in a high, thin wail.

"Because she said so," Miss Watkins repeated and gestured to Betsy to leave.

"Good night, darling." Betsy bent to kiss him goodnight and hurried from the nursery. Alice was spoiling Jimmy to death, she thought in recurrent frustration. He had to learn—as little as he was—that there were rules.

She hurried out into the unseasonably humid night, hesitated a moment, then decided to take a taxi up to West 105th. Emily had gone up earlier to help with dinner. Neither she nor Emily had slept much last night—they'd both been so excited about seeing Doug.

When she arrived at Doug's fourth-floor walkup, faintly breathless from the unfamiliar climb, she heard the lively conversation inside. She reached for the bell, rang. There was a bittersweet touch to their reunion. Paul wasn't here.

The door swung open. With a festive glow Doug pulled her inside, kissed her lightly on the cheek.

"Perfect timing," he approved. "The spaghetti is *al dente,* the garlic bread about to come out of the oven, and the sauce is bubbling. Emily's just finished the salad."

"You two sit down at the table," Emily called from the kitchenette. "I'm bringing in dinner."

"First I'll get the chianti," Doug stipulated. "We can't have spaghetti without chianti."

"Emily and I were talking this morning about how neither of us slept much last night. We were too excited about your coming home." Betsy gazed at him with a sense of wonder as he brought the chianti to the table and poured.

"Sometimes I wake up in the morning, and I'm startled to realize I'm actually home," Doug admitted.

"It's been so long," Betsy said. "We have so many questions. You're back in law school!" She spied the law books sprawled across the coffee table. "I figured you'd be."

"Law school is just as rough as it was four years ago. Maybe worse, after being away so long." The intensity of his gaze was discomforting. "Remember how it was supposed to be?" Nostalgia in his voice now. "You were going to be the interior decorator, Emily the actress, and Paul the playwright. I'd be the lawyer who'd take care of your contracts."

"You two are on the way," Emily chirped, bringing plates heaped high with spaghetti to the table. "That's a fair average."

She headed back to the kitchen for garlic bread, grated cheese, and salad.

"You always said the first year of law school would be the hardest," Betsy recalled. "You still feel that way?"

"I'm working my butt off." All at once somber. "There's little time for anything except the books. Do you realize I won't be out of law school until I'm twenty-nine?"

"That's not ancient," Betsy protested. But she understood his frustration over the lost years.

"You're in the same spot as everybody else." Emily sat down at the table now. "Half the armed forces are on college campuses now. This will be the best-educated generation in history. And the oldest graduating class," she joshed. "My father was worried about the country being swamped with unemployment again. He worried about all you guys coming home. But it doesn't look as though it'll work out that way. There are plenty of jobs to go around."

"Most people you talk to are optimistic," Doug conceded quietly, "but it'll be a long time before the memories of the war years are put to bed."

To brush aside the heaviness that invaded the room, Emily embarked on a story cherished by her brother, Bert. It dealt with what he called the "Marine barter system." In the devastating heat of the South Pacific Bert had managed, to the pleasure of his fellow Marines, to barter a PT boat for a refrigerator.

"Bert said nothing in this world tasted as good as the ice water they handed out once they found electricity for that refrigerator."

After dinner, with the table cleared away, they settled in the living room to reminisce about the intervening years.

"Tell me about Mark and Eric," Doug said. "Do you hear from them?"

"Regularly," Betsy told him. "They're hoping to come to New York between Christmas and New Year's. Mark's shop is doing very well, he writes, and Eric's working as an assistant to a top-notch set designer at one of the film studios. Mark says the future looks great for Eric out there."

"Hey, what about snapshots?" Doug asked. "Don't tell me you

dared come over here without bringing pictures of Jimmy with you!"

"I have loads." Betsy's smile reflected her love for her son. She reached for her purse on the end table at her right and pulled out a sheaf of snapshots.

"He's the image of Paul," Doug said quietly as he inspected one photo after another. "He'll grow up to find a lot of girls chasing after him."

"We'll have a real New Year's Eve blast," Emily declared. "I know how little time you have for play," she teased Doug. "But mark it on your calendar. We'll see 1946 in together!"

The weeks were rushing past with incredible speed, Betsy thought. Business was fine at the shop. She was acquiring important new clients. She was pleased that despite his heavy school schedule, Doug made a ritual of having Friday-evening dinners with Emily and her.

Often now Alice insisted that she attend social events with Paul Jr. and herself. A boom for the business, Emily kept telling her. Usually Grady was invited, too. *"He's lonely,"* Alice explained. *"He needs to be with people."*

At regular intervals Grady took her to dinner at some quiet, charming restaurant that was off the beaten track. She enjoyed these occasions—she could relax with Grady after the frenzied workday. He was like an older Mark, she thought with affection.

Emily reported that on this Thanksgiving her parents planned to be down in Miami on a five-day long-delayed vacation. Her grandmother would be with Bert and Rheba. As was their custom, Alice and Paul Jr. would be with Georgette and her family. Doug told them his parents were going to his sister's house in Connecticut, but he was remaining in the city.

"I'm not the greatest cook, as you know," Doug said with a cajoling smile, "but why don't you two come over with Jimmy for another of my spaghetti dinners?"

"Come to my place," Emily insisted. "I promise you turkey and all the trimmings."

From the moment she and Jimmy arrived, Betsy knew she would enjoy Thanksgiving at Emily's new apartment. There was a beautiful warmth here, she realized later as they settled down with second cups of coffee, leaving the piled-up dishes to soak in the sink. She relished the way Doug handled Jimmy.

"I know what I'm giving you for your birthday next month," he teased Jimmy. "Shall I tell you now or make you wait?"

"Tell me!" Jimmy prodded delightedly. "Tell me!"

"A baseball jacket," Doug said. "Every little boy should have a baseball jacket. Maybe one day your mommie will let me take you to see a baseball game. Would you like that?"

Tears stung Betsy's eyes. Doug would be Jimmy's "Uncle Doug." That would help for his not having his father.

Again Alice planned an elaborate birthday party for Jimmy. Emily scheduled a combination birthday and Hanukkah party at her apartment the previous Sunday afternoon. The guest list would be tiny—just herself, Betsy, and Doug.

Jimmy listened avidly to talk of Mrs. Meyers' rugelach plus the dreidels she was supplying for the party.

The night before the party Jimmy asked a question with an air of excitement.

"Mommie, what is Hanukkah?"

"It's a very happy holiday for Jewish people," she said softly. Jimmy knew he was Jewish. She'd made certain of that. "It's in memory of the time when the Jews were living in a place called Judea—"

"Not in New York?"

"Nobody was living in New York in those days," she explained, "except the American Indians. This was hundreds of years ago," she continued solemnly, "and for three years the Jews had been fighting the wicked Syrian tyrant Antiochus. And then at last they defeated him. They drove him and his soldiers out. Of course they wanted to celebrate their victory in the temple in Jerusalem, but they discovered they had only one small jar of oil to light their holy lamps." Jimmy was listening avidly. "But—miraculously—the jar

provided oil for eight whole days. And that's when Judas Mac-
cabaeus, the Jewish leader, proclaimed that every year hereafter at
this time Jews would celebrate the joyous festival of Hanukkah for
eight days. Each night we're going to light Hanukkah candles. One
candle for the first night, two on the second, and so on till we have
eight candles lit on the last night of Hanukkah."

Even before Jimmy's birthday-Hanukkah party Betsy and
Emily began to plan for New Year's Eve. Mark and Eric were
definitely coming to New York. Hearing that Betsy's friends
were coming in from California, Paul Jr. insisted that she have
them in for dinner during the Christmas-New Year's holiday
week. Alice was leaving for Palm Beach three days before
Christmas. The morning of Christmas Eve he would fly down
and remain until early January.

"Give a New Year's Eve party," Paul Jr. told her. "The staff will
be on duty except for Christmas day and New Year's day, so you'll
be able to entertain with no effort."

"Thank you. I'd like that very much." She knew he felt uncomfortable at leaving Jimmy and her alone during the holiday season,
and she was touched. Of course Alice had tried to persuade her to
come down with them for a few days. Alice had even invited
Grady, but he was spending that week in Boston with his sister and
brother-in-law.

Emily was enthralled by the suggestion that they have their New
Year's Eve party at the Forrest townhouse. "Honey, we'll celebrate in style. I can't wait."

Betsy tried to thrust off a feeling of unease as she went over final
preparations for the New Year's Eve party. She was uncomfortable in the role of hostess in the Forrest townhouse. It would be
different, she thought, if Paul was here.

She had insisted that the domestic staff, including Miss Watkins, leave by late afternoon. Peggy had baked one of her marvelous Black Forest cakes earlier in the day, had made a pot of
cream-of-mushroom soup that would just have to be reheated,
and had prepared a salad. An oven-ready roast and Idaho potatoes

would be popped into the ovens later. A magnum of vintage champagne, which Alice herself had offered for the party, was being chilled in the refrigerator to welcome in the New Year. A huge tray of Peggy's superb hors d'oeuvres was in readiness on the top shelf.

Before the others arrived, Betsy fed Jimmy, then prepared him for bed. He'd come downstairs in his pajamas for playtime with them, then she'd cart him off to the nursery.

"Mommie, why can't I sit at the table with everybody?" Jimmy—pajama-clad now—asked plaintively as he trailed her while she checked the table setting.

"Because on New Year's Eve grown-ups have dinner very late," she explained tenderly. "But we'll all say happy New Year to you before you go up to bed."

"Everybody's gone." His eyes were accusing. "I'll be scared up there by myself."

"All right," she said, capitulating after an instant. "You'll stay with us. I'll fix you a place to sleep down here." She, too, would feel nervous with him up in the third-floor nursery when they were on the first floor. When he drifted off to sleep, she'd put him down on the living room sofa with a couple of chairs to serve as guard rails. Later she'd carry him upstairs to bed.

Emily and Chuck were the first to arrive. She'd had to invite Chuck, she consoled herself as she greeted them. Emily was seeing him regularly. She was praying for the day Emily would admit it was a mistake and break off with him.

"Hey, how are you doing, fella?" Chuck picked up Jimmy and tossed him into the air amid his squeals of delight. "You like that, huh?"

"More!" Jimmy ordered. "More!"

"How's the insurance business?" Betsy asked, struggling to make conversation. Insurance was his newest gambit.

"It's rough," Chuck complained. "You gotta have good contacts. How about you?" he asked good-humoredly. "Thinking about buying some insurance?"

"Chuck, cut it out," Emily told him. Betsy knew she was furious, even though the question had been said lightly. "Come on, let me give you a tour of the floor."

Moments later Doug arrived. He'd brought a small toy jeep for Jimmy.

"Doug, you shouldn't have," she said softly. She knew he was fighting to survive on his government allotment checks.

"May the only jeep he ever knows be on a farm or in the mountains," Doug told her while Jimmy dropped to the floor to play with this new toy. For their generation jeeps were a symbol of war. "Do you realize this is the first New Year's Eve in five years that the country is at peace?"

"May they all be peaceful in the years ahead." Betsy fought off an urge to reach for Jimmy and hold him close. The prospect of his fighting in a war was unnerving.

The doorbell rang again. Betsy hurried to open the door to Mark and Eric, both in convivial spirits. She and Emily, along with Doug, had had a joyous reunion with them three days earlier. It was marvelous, she thought again, to have them here in New York. It was like old times.

"You said we'd be having a roast." Mark extended a package. "So I brought red wine."

"You had a head start," Emily guessed, joining them in the foyer. She leaned forward to sniff his breath. "Just as I thought. Think you can stay sober until midnight?"

"I'll give it a try." Mark reached for Jimmy, who'd trailed behind his mother. "Hey, you're all grown up!"

"I'm three," Jimmy announced.

"What about a hug for your Uncle Mark?"

"Find me a corkscrew and I'll open this bottle." Eric took the package from Betsy after a solemn introduction to Jimmy. "Let's get this party moving."

"There's a corkscrew in the bar in the library," Betsy told him, then remembered that Eric—unlike Mark—was unfamiliar with the Forrest house. "It's right down the hall and to the left. Let's settle ourselves there until dinner."

"I can't believe it's almost 1946," Emily effervesced. "But I feel so old!"

"If it wasn't for the war, I would be out of law school already."
Doug's eyes were wistful. "We've all got a lot of catching up to
do."

"I can't wait to buy a new car," Chuck said enthusiastically. "Of
course I can't afford one yet, but Fords and Chevies are due on the
market any week now."

By the time the others trailed into the library, Eric had opened
the wine bottle. Now he brought out glasses, admiring the exquisite stemware, and began to pour. Chuck went to the radio and
searched for a music program. Betsy motioned to Emily to join her
in the kitchen, on the floor below.

Betsy checked the roast, brought it out of the oven while Emily
tasted the soup.

"The soup's hot. Want me to slice the roast while you take care
of the other stuff?"

"Right. We can start getting things up to the dining room."

"Everything looks yummy," Emily crooned. "And how nice
that you didn't have to spend the day over a hot stove."

"I'm getting spoiled," Betsy said lightly.

"Enjoy it," Emily ordered and paused a moment. "Betsy—"

"Hmm?" Betsy brought the potatoes from the other oven.
"Emily?" She looked up in inquiry as Emily remained silent.

"Look, I'm dumping Chuck after today." She exuded a blend
of defiance and determination.

"When did this happen?" Betsy's relief was obvious.

"Something in my mind just clicked when he pulled that sales
pitch on you. It was weird how all at once I threw off the blinders.
I shuddered at what I saw. I don't want to spend the rest of my life
with a jerk like Chuck! We have nothing in common—"

"Thank God you see that!"

"When the next semester of evening classes start up, I'm signing up for a course at one of the drama schools—I'm not sure
which one just yet. But I mean to start 1946 with a whole new
approach to life." She shook her head in amazement. "Why the
hell did it take me so long to think straight?"

"You're back on track, Emily." Betsy glowed. There'd be no
more agonizing over the prospect of Emily's marrying Chuck.

Emily would gain confidence with a few classes behind her. She'd go after a career in theater for herself. "We'll start the new year right!"

"Now I'll just have to battle with Mom." Emily laughed. "Mom I can handle."

When she went in to summon the men to the table, Betsy was startled to see Doug on his haunches before the library fire. He was coaxing chunks of birch into a healthy blaze while Jimmy stood by blithely with a handful of kindling. Her mind shot back to the cottage at Sag Harbor, where Paul had spent so much time feeding wood into the fireplace.

"I thought it would be cozy to have a roaring fire when we come back in here after dinner," Doug told Betsy as he rose to his feet. "When I was growing up, we used to go to my grandparents' house in Amagansett for winter holidays. It used to be my job to start a fire in the fireplace on cold nights. With my two sisters as backseat drivers," he remembered indulgently.

"Thanks, Doug." *Why did she feel unnerved because Doug had a blaze going in the fireplace?* "Okay, everybody, to the table. Emily's serving the soup. She'll behead us if we let it get cold." She leaned forward to scoop Jimmy into her arms.

"Mommie, I want to come to the table," Jimmy reminded. He was already yawning but determined to remain awake.

"All right, darling." He'd be drifting off quickly, Betsy guessed. "Would you like some soup?"

"No. I just wanna sit at the table." Jimmy flashed the charismatic smile that evoked an instant picture of his father.

By the time the grown-ups had finished their soup, Jimmy's eyelids were drooping.

"I'll put him on the living room sofa," Betsy said softly.

"I'll help." Doug rose to his feet and lifted Jimmy—now asleep—in his arms. "You lead the way."

How gentle he was with Jimmy, Betsy thought in gratitude as she watched Doug deposit her small son on the sofa and position a pillow beneath his head.

"I'll cover him with the afghan," she told Doug, who was bringing over a chair to serve as guard rail. The afghan lay across the back of a club chair, as it had ever since Paul had been a baby. It was Alice's one effort at crocheting, completed during the course of her one full-term pregnancy.

Now Doug joined the men in the dining room. Betsy went to help Emily with the serving. When she and Emily returned to the dining room, they found the men discussing the war.

"Thank God," Doug was saying passionately, "that President Truman ordered that directive last week to make it easier to bring displaced persons into this country."

The others listened—Chuck blatantly bored—while he talked about the terrible postwar problems that faced the refugees, both Jewish and Christian. Betsy knew that he was involved with a volunteer group fighting to bring concentration camp refugees to this country. His was one of many groups.

"It can't happen as fast as we'd like," Doug conceded, a pulse pounding in his temple, "but I must do what I can to help despite the demands of school."

After dessert and coffee they transferred themselves to the library. Firelight lent a warm glow to the room. The birch provided a pleasing aroma. Doug strolled to the fireplace to add another chunk to those crackling in the grate.

Betsy crossed the hall to look in on Jimmy. He was sleeping soundly. She tucked the afghan about his small body with a surge of maternal love. When she rejoined the others in the library, Emily was asking Doug if he ever saw Sara.

"She's married to that guy—what's his name—" Doug fumbled in recall.

"Frank Churchill," Emily remembered. "He was working for an M.A. in library science. Sara said he wanted to write."

"God, everybody was so involved in the arts," Doug joshed.

"You were the one with his feet on the ground," Betsy said. "The strong one."

"Sounds dull," Doug said with a grimace.

"Not at all," Betsy rejected. Doug was strong, but he was also warm and sensitive.

"Do we have to wait until midnight to sample that magnum of bubbly you were bragging about?" Emily asked. Her eyes exchanged a triumphant glance with Betsy's.

"I'll get it now." Betsy rose to her feet. The others didn't know about her private celebration with Emily. "A magnum should do us for a while."

"I'll help you," Doug said and laughed. "After all, do we trust a magnum of fine champagne to one small girl?"

Restless as usual, Chuck turned to the radio to search for New Year's Eve festivities. Surprisingly he settled for the sweet swing of Guy Lombardo. Earlier he had called it "over-the-hill swing." As Betsy left the room with Doug, she saw Chuck pull Emily into his arms and begin to dance. Mark and Eric were inspecting with rapt admiration the eighteenth-century oriental lacquered cabinet that Alice said had been a gift to her grandmother by an Eastern potentate.

"The old year is going fast," Doug said, walking with Betsy downstairs to the kitchen. "In many ways I'm glad to see it go."

"You'll enjoy the winter break," she guessed. "Time off from the law books."

Betsy and Doug returned to the library with the magnum of champagne and the tray of hors d'oeuvres. The radio music was interrupted for a rundown of the hordes at Times Square waiting to welcome in 1946—barely forty-five minutes away now. The others convivially gathered around the coffee table, where Betsy had deposited the tray of hors d'oeuvres and waited for Doug to pour the champagne.

Again Betsy left to check on Jimmy. He was fast asleep. She tiptoed from the room, leaving the door slightly ajar. If Jimmy awakened, she'd be sure to hear him.

"What kind of a year do you think we'll find in 1946?" Eric was asking the others with an air of challenge as Betsy returned to the library.

"More inflation, more housing problems," Dough predicted. His smile was whimsical. "Accompanied by more television sets, more new cars, more washing machines."

"I heard somewhere that appliance manufacturers are planning to come out with an electric clothes dryer," Eric recalled.

"The age of plenty," Mark guessed. "We're going from Depression to war to the good life."

"What time is it?" Emily demanded. "How long before it's 1946?"

Now the atmosphere in the library was electric. For everybody, Betsy thought with a mixture of emotions, this was a special New Year's Eve. Farewell to the painful war years, a greeting for the first full year of peace. It was as though they were saying good-bye to an era.

A few minutes before midnight Mark made a ceremony of pouring champagne for everyone. They listened expectantly to the radio while a newscaster numbered the countdown to 1946. And then it arrived.

"Happy New Year!" the newscaster announced.

In the Forrest library there was a clicking of glasses, a merry exchange of greetings, and then a round of embraces and kisses. Betsy turned from Eric to Doug, lifted her face to his with a gladness in her heart that he was here to share this moment with their small group.

Doug pulled her close, kissed her gently. Then all at once it was a passionate, hungry kiss that triggered a matching response in her. For a startling moment it was as though they were alone in the room, caught up in unexpected emotions.

"Happy New Year," she said breathlessly when Doug's mouth withdrew from hers. Their eyes clung for a heated moment.

Her heart pounding, she swerved away to exchange a kiss with Mark. *What was happening to her?*

CHAPTER THIRTY-SEVEN

Betsy lay sleepless, aware of the first gray light of dawn creeping between her bedroom drapes. Over and over in her mind she re-created those moments when Doug kissed her with such passion and she had responded. She had been so sure she could never feel that way about any man again.

She struggled now to analyze her feelings. The love she had shared with Paul had been boy-girl love—sweet and precious but the love of two very young people in tragic times. Now she was a woman. Had those moments with Doug been real? Had it been the champagne, the sentimental occasion? How would he feel today? She must pretend those moments never happened, she told herself.

But at regular intervals between New Year's Day and the following Friday, when she and Emily would have dinner with Doug, Betsy remembered those heated moments with him as the old year rolled out and the new one came in. Had it meant more to him than a moment's arousal, created by the occasion and the fine champagne?

Tonight they would have dinner at Emily's apartment. While Columbia was in its winter break, Doug was working hard with his volunteer group. He was jubilant that the new Truman directive meant that the 1,000 refugees in a camp near Oswego, New York, wouldn't face compulsory repatriation. His group, like others scattered about the country, was urging Congress to pass a law to allow war refugees, both Jewish and Christian, to come into this country in numbers beyond the very low current quota.

He arrived at Emily's apartment almost half an hour late and full of apologies.

"We had trouble on the road just outside of Washington. First it was a flat, then some minor transmission problem."

"How did it go in Washington?" Betsy asked sympathetically while Emily brought food to the table.

"It won't happen as fast as we'd like," Doug said. It was his constant complaint. "But I think Congress will come through for us. The lives of concentration camp victims depend on that."

The two women listened while Doug talked eloquently about the situation. His enthusiasm touched a responsive chord in them. Not until they settled down over coffee did the mood lighten.

"Mom and Dad bought tickets months ago for *Carousel*. Then this wedding came up that they have to attend. They gave the tickets to my sister Karen, but her kid came down with chickenpox yesterday. So I've inherited them. They're for Sunday night. Would you like to go with me, Betsy?" He knew Emily was going to Borough Park on Sunday.

"I'd love it," Betsy accepted. It wasn't a date, she cautioned herself conscientiously. Doug just happened to inherit a pair of theater tickets. "Shall we meet at the theater?"

"Why don't we have dinner first?" Doug said. "Nothing fancy," he added and grinned. "Chinese okay, in deference to my budget?"

"It'll be fun." It wasn't a date, she reminded herself again. It would be two old friends spending an evening together.

For the rest of the evening and at intervals at the shop the next day and again on Sunday she was conscious of her pleasurable anticipation at spending an evening alone with Doug. She was troubled by this anticipation. Doug had probably forgotten those special moments on New Year's Eve. They'd just been part of the excitement of the occasion. To Doug she was a dear friend—and Paul's widow.

* * *

Alice left the kitchen after telling Peggy that she could serve dinner in half an hour, then went to make sure Elise had brought the flowers from the living room to be a centerpiece on the dining table. She was pleased that Paul Jr. would be back from that stupid business conference in time for dinner. How absurd, she thought, for a client to insist on a Sunday business meeting.

She paused at the dining room entrance. Elise had brought in the flowers and was setting the table.

"The flowers look lovely, Elise," she began and paused at the sound of the doorbell. "You go on with what you're doing. I'll answer the door." It was probably Paul Jr., she surmised, and hurried down the hall.

She pulled the door wide and stared in surprise at the young man who stood there.

"Yes?" she said, faintly imperiously. Something about the way he smiled made her think of Paul.

"I'm calling for Betsy," he said, seeming ill-at-ease. "Doug Golden. I'm a few minutes early—"

"Oh—" She pulled the door wide and gestured for him to enter. *Betsy was going out with some strange young man.* Wasn't it enough that she was seeing Grady regularly? "I'll send the maid up to tell her." She contrived a perfunctory smile and headed for the dining room. "Elise," she said at the dining room entrance, "please tell Miss Betsy there's a young man waiting for her in the foyer."

"Yes, ma'am." Elise hurried from the room. Alice hovered just within the door. Her heart was pounding. Where had Betsy met him? What had he said his name was? Doug Golden. Wasn't that a Jewish name? Her throat tightening in alarm, she pretended to be rearranging the table settings. She wanted to be within hearing when Betsy came downstairs to greet him.

A few moments later she heard Betsy rushing down the hall.

"I'm sorry, Doug," Betsy said. "I meant to be downstairs when you arrived. But you know Jimmy. He's an artist at stalling."

"How is he?" Alice heard him ask. *He knew Jimmy.*

"Great. Last night he insisted on taking that football you gave him to bed with him. You're high on the list of his favorite people."

She'd been seeing him all along, Alice thought in anguish as Betsy and Doug left the house. What was going on behind their backs? She would die if Betsy married him! She didn't want Jimmy to have a Jewish stepfather. She'd kept telling herself that when Jimmy was older and understood things, he'd want to come into the church. If Betsy married Grady, everything would be so much easier.

Alice paused, listening to the sounds in the foyer. Paul Jr. was home. She darted to the hall and called to him.

"I have to talk to you right away," she told him. Her voice was strident. "Elise, tell Peggy to hold dinner for another ten minutes."

Behind the privacy of the closed library door, her agitation soaring, Alice told Paul Jr. about Doug's appearance.

"She's been seeing him all along! He even knows Jimmy. I'll die if she marries him!"

"Alice, you're jumping to conclusions," Paul Jr. said warily.

"He came to the house to pick her up. He's given Jimmy presents. Why couldn't she be satisfied to go out with Grady?" Her face was drained of color now.

"Alice, you've got to calm down," Paul Jr. soothed. "And there's no romantic interest between Grady and Betsy. You know how lonely he's been since Nadine died. They're just company for each other. Betsy's young enough to be his daughter."

"Grady's mad about her," Alice said ominously. "Haven't you seen the way he looks at her?"

"That's rubbish." Paul Jr. had dismissed this nonsense before. "And I've told you, we have to accept the fact that Betsy's young and very lovely. We can't expect her not to remarry."

"I couldn't bear it if she married that man and took Jimmy away from us," Alice sobbed. "Why couldn't things stay the way they were?"

Both started at a knock on the door.

"What is it?" Paul Jr. called out with rare irritation.

"Peggy says that dinner will be spoiled if she doesn't serve it right away, Mr. Forrest," Elise said apologetically.

"Tell her to serve dinner," Alice called back, straining for calm. "We'll be right there."

Betsy began to relax over dinner in the modest but pleasant little Chinese restaurant off Times Square.

"When I told Jimmy I was going to the theater, he asked if we were going to see *Little Red Riding Hood*. I took him down to the Village to see a performance of that a couple of Sundays ago."

"Was he a critic?" Doug teased.

"Oh, you should have been there." Betsy's face was suffused with tenderness. "He became so involved in the play. He kept calling out to Little Red Riding Hood to watch out for the wolf. I think the audience enjoyed his performance as much as what was happening on the tiny playing area."

"Maybe I can take the two of you to *Pinocchio* or to *Peter and the Wolf* if they show up on the children's circuit," Doug said. "They were my favorites."

"That would be fun."

Doug glanced at his watch. "We'd better get moving soon if we don't want to be late for the curtain. But first let's see what the fortune cookies have to tell us."

In a playful mood each broke open a fortune cookie and withdrew the tiny slip of paper.

"You're about to begin a whole new life," Betsy read unsteadily.

"Aha!" Doug said with triumph. "That sounds exciting."

All through the performance of *Carousel* Betsy was conscious of Doug's nearness. She was upset by her own emotions. This was happening too fast. How could she react this way to another man so soon after Paul?

With the performance over, they went to a Childs for coffee. Betsy sensed that, like herself, Doug was reluctant to bring the evening to a close.

"It's a cold night but great for walking," he said. "Why don't I walk you home?"

"I'd like that." They were both fond of walking. They were alike in so many ways, she thought involuntarily. "I need the exercise." She laughed.

"I doubt that," he kidded, "the way you dash around in the shop."

While they headed uptown, the streets lively with the post-theater crowds, Doug talked about his obsession to help the refugees of the concentration camps. Betsy listened, loving his compassion, his feeling for humanity. At the house they lingered briefly at the entrance. Then, almost hesitantly, Doug leaned forward to kiss her goodnight. A casual kiss, she labeled this—far different from what they had shared on New Year's Eve.

"There's a new Jean Gabin movie coming to the Apollo next week," he told her. "Would you like to see it?"

"Yes." She hadn't been wrong about that New Year's Eve kiss, she told herself with soaring happiness. Doug was just afraid of rushing her too fast.

"I'll call you tomorrow and we'll choose a night." His smile reflected his pleasure at this new phase in their relationship.

The following Friday—according to plan—they went to a late showing of the Jean Gabin movie. They'd invited Emily to join them, but she'd diplomatically declined.

"You two go on to the Apollo," she told them after their ritual Friday-evening dinner. "I have to wash my hair and do my nails tonight."

On Sunday afternoon, Doug decided, they must take Jimmy to the Museum of Natural History.

"Jimmy's three years old," Doug said. "Isn't it about time he met his first dinosaur?"

Betsy was coming downstairs with Jimmy for his trip to the museum just as Alice and Paul Jr. came home from their usual Sunday luncheon at the Colony. They paused in the foyer to exchange greetings.

"What happened to Jimmy's nap?" Alice asked reproachfully.

"He's kind of growing out of that," Betsy explained. "And

today he has a date to see the dinosaurs at the Museum of Natural History."

"Uncle Doug said they lived a billion years ago!" Jimmy said, his eyes wide with wonder.

Betsy's face lighted at the sound of the doorbell.

"Oh, that's Doug now. Jimmy'll give you a full report on the dinosaurs later," she promised.

Alice walked in grim silence down the hall to the library. Jimmy had called that man "Uncle Doug." How could Betsy look at another man after Grady had been so good to her? Just a few nights ago she'd learned how Betsy had been able to expand the shop the way she had. Grady had arranged a ridiculously large loan for her!

"Betsy's friend seems to have hit it off well with Jimmy," Paul Jr. remarked while they settled themselves in the library. He reached for the Business Section of the Sunday *New York Times,* waiting as usual on the coffee table.

"It's outrageous!" Alice fumed. "Don't you see what's happening right before your eyes? She's going to throw over Grady for him!"

"Alice, there's never been anything between Betsy and Grady except friendship."

"She wouldn't have that business except for Grady," Alice shot back. "You said yourself—you were surprised as I was when Betsy let it slip that Grady had arranged bank loans for her."

"Because she was Paul's widow—and because they'd developed a warm friendship. There's been nothing else between them," he insisted.

Alice stared at him in frustration. How could he be so naive?

"I have an awful headache." She tossed aside the copy of *Town & Country* she had picked up a few moments ago. "I'm going upstairs and lie down for a while."

"Take one of your pills," Paul Jr. urged routinely. "You know you mustn't upset yourself this way."

Upstairs in the master bedroom suite Alice took a pill and then settled herself on the bed, pillows heaped behind her back. It was clear enough—Doug Golden was in serious pursuit of Betsy.

They'd go off to some stupid little house in suburbia, the way so many young couples were doing these days. She'd be lucky if she saw Jimmy twice a year, she told herself in a tidal wave of anguish. Her precious baby would be completely in their hands.

She must find some way to stop that marriage. If Betsy's business were in danger, she thought—grasping irrationally at this— there could be no marriage. Betsy couldn't afford to marry. Hadn't she said her new boyfriend was in law school? He had no way of supporting her and Jimmy. Without her business Betsy couldn't afford to leave this house.

Let her give Betsy something to think about besides Doug Golden. Her heart thumping, Alice reached for the phone on the night table, dialed Grady's home number. Impatient for him to respond.

"Hello—"

"Grady, we haven't seen you in over two weeks," she scolded.

"You know how busy I've been, Alice, with all those new branches opening up," he apologized. "But things should settle down in another few weeks."

Go ahead with this, Alice commanded herself. She must stop Betsy from marrying that law student—for Jimmy's sake.

"I'm so upset about Betsy," she began.

"What's wrong?" Grady broke in anxiously.

"I mean, this sordid affair she's having with that law student. Staying out with him to all hours of the night. Thank God, Jimmy's too young to know what's going on. And after the way she's led you on!" She allowed indignation to infiltrate her voice. "I won't forgive her for treating you so shabbily."

"Alice, what are you talking about?" His efforts at dissembling were awkward. "Betsy never led me on. We were—" He paused, then continued. "We are close friends."

"Of course she led you on," Alice said. "So often I wanted to warn you, but Paul Jr. kept telling me I had no right to interfere. Oh, she's the sly one. Look what she did to Paul. She managed to get herself pregnant, and Paul felt he had to marry her. Then she went after you. Grady, you mustn't let her get away with this," she entreated dramatically. "First Paul, now you. I can't bear it."

"Alice, I have to leave for an appointment." He was struggling to appear calm, she thought in triumph, but he was upset. "We'll talk another time."

"Yes, we must," she agreed. "You can't let Betsy go on hurting every man who comes her way."

"I have to run, Alice. I'm meeting an out-of-town client at my club." His voice was tense. "We'll talk."

Grady sat by the phone with his head in his hands. He felt humiliated, stripped of all pride. Alice had guessed how he felt about Betsy. Paul Jr. knew. *They'd talked about it.* How had he given himself away?

Alice said Betsy was having an affair. He'd been so fearful of rushing her. He'd never touched her. Just a fatherly goodnight kiss each time they went out together—when he'd ached to take her in his arms and make passionate love to her. It was so long since he had felt this way about a woman. It was as though he'd found Nadine again.

Had Betsy been laughing at him for being an old fool? Had she, too, known that he was in love with her? Had she talked about it with Emily?

God, what an idiot he had been! How many others besides Alice and Paul Jr. knew how he felt about Betsy? Alice was right. Betsy had been using him, taking advantage of his compassion to further her career. How many other men had she been sleeping with besides this law student?

Betsy needed to have her wings clipped—and he knew just how to do it.

CHAPTER THIRTY-EIGHT

"Betsy!" Emily called excitedly. "Phone call for you!"

"Mr. Kincaid?" Betsy hurried to the rear of the shop. She was going out of her mind trying to line up the right dining table and chairs for Amy Andrews' kitchen. He was her best hope.

"Right." Emily held out the phone.

"Mr. Kincaid, how are you?" Betsy asked and listened for a few moments to his complaints about a bad cold. "Do you have some ideas about my problem?" she asked now, a hint of wistful helplessness in her voice. To Mr. Kincaid she was that "sweet little girl who worked with Mark down in New York." Still, he was delighted by the commissions she paid him.

"Yeah, I got something lined up for you. Got a pencil?"

"Yes, go ahead—"

Mr. Kincaid had spoken to a second cousin down in Amagansett, who apparently had just the table and chairs she needed.

"It'll cost you," Mr. Kincaid warned. "My cousin's sharp. He knows you antique folks sell high."

"I'd love to talk to him."

"Call him up, maybe head out to Amagansett Sunday morning. I know we're supposed to have bad weather over the weekend, but you can't let grass grow under your feet when you want something."

"Thanks so much, Mr. Kincaid. We do appreciate your help."
And he would appreciate his commission.

"Change your mind about that cheval mirror I showed you last
time?" he asked hopefully.

"If somebody comes along who can use it, I'll certainly let you
know," she promised, always diplomatic. Mr. Kincaid knew the
mirror was a piece of garbage. "Now take care of that cold."

Betsy sat in thought for a moment before she phoned Mr.
Kincaid's cousin. A heavy snow was predicted for tomorrow and
Sunday. She hated driving when the roads were bad. Maybe Doug
would go up with her and drive. He'd said his grandparents had
a cottage in Amagansett. He knew the area.

"Sure, I'll go up to Amagansett with you," Doug said when she
reached him. Betsy thought she detected a lilt of anticipation in his
voice. "It's one of my favorite places."

"I know I'm taking you away from the books and your volunteer
group," she said, apologizing, "but I'm petrified of driving on
snow or ice."

"I deserve a day off. And I wouldn't want you driving in bad
conditions."

"I'll call Mr. Kincaid's cousin and set it up right now." Betsy
was relieved. "He's also a Mr. Kincaid," she laughed.

She got off the phone with Doug and called the second Mr.
Kincaid.

"Oh, I can't make it on a Sunday," he drawled. "On Sunday
mornings the wife and I always go to church. Then we go either
to our son's house or to our daughter's for a big Sunday dinner.
After that we just sit around and relax for the rest of the afternoon.
Make it tomorrow." She sensed his anticipation. He knew he was
in the driver's seat—and that meant he'd haggle for top price.

"All right, tomorrow," she conceded after a moment. She hated
being away from the shop on Saturdays, but Emily could cover for
her. "What time, Mr. Kincaid?"

"Oh, it don't matter much on Saturdays—" He hesitated.
"Let's make it two o'clock. All right?"

"Two o'clock's fine," Betsy agreed. "See you tomorrow."

Now she had to phone Doug to see if he was clear on Saturday.

"No problem," he assured her when she reached him. "I was just going to dig into the books. I'll do it on Sunday instead."

"The table and chairs may be dogs," she warned, "or if they're truly Early American and in decent condition, he may want a chunk of Fort Knox for them. He sounded like a real horse-trader."

"You can horse-trade with the best of them," he told her.

"I hope the pieces are authentic and in good condition," she said once more. "They're just what I need for an important client."

"We'll keep our fingers crossed. And it'll be beautiful out there if it does snow." Doug sounded enthusiastic about the trip. "Of course it might not. You know how often the weather reports are wrong."

"I'm looking forward to a few hours out of the city," Betsy confessed. *A precious parcel of time alone with Doug.* "Of course I'm not sure I'll be able to work something out with this dealer—even if he has what I'm looking for. His cousin says he's tough to do business with."

"You'll manage," Doug said with conviction.

Before ten on Saturday morning Betsy and Doug were in the shop's car and en route to Amagansett. The sky was gray with unleashed snow. Doug had phoned earlier to remind her to dress warmly.

"Did you have breakfast?" Doug asked as they crossed the Queensboro Bridge.

"Yes, with Jimmy," she told him. "What about you?"

"Not really," he admitted, his smile rueful. "I'm one of those people who settles for coffee on getting up, and then stalls on breakfast for another hour or two."

"I'll have coffee while you have breakfast," she said. "I'll watch for a place along the road."

"You'll like Amagansett," he predicted. "I remember when I was a little kid how we couldn't wait to go up to my grandmother's cottage out there. It was small, so the three sons and their wives, and the grandchildren, couldn't all go up at the same time." His voice was warm with nostalgia. "We'd get to the cottage and rush down to the ocean, and I'd stand there and shout, 'My ocean!' "

Over breakfast at a restaurant off the highway, Doug talked with fervor about the efforts of his volunteer group.

"It's heartwarming to see how dozens of Jewish communities in every part of the country are taking in the Jewish refugees from the Oswego camp. The non-Jews," he explained, "are being placed by the American Christian Committee for Refugees and by the Catholic Committee for Refugees."

"Of course, the likes of Westbrook Pegler are screaming they may all be Communists," Betsy said, shaking her head.

Doug nodded in agreement. "There's a frightening amount of relocation work to be done—and fund-raising is urgent."

"More coffee?" The waitress hovered over their table. She glanced fleetingly at Betsy, then focused on Doug. Her eyes made it clear she found him attractive. She barely acknowledged Betsy's quiet "Thank you, no."

"Please," Doug said with a warm smile and turned to Betsy. "I promise to get down from the soapbox. I'll swig down my coffee and we'll be on our way."

The waitress's blatant interest in Doug reminded Betsy of Emily's conviction that many women were drawn to him. *She* was drawn to him. He made her conscious of emotions she thought she'd forever put aside when Paul died. And she was sure that Doug, too, felt these same emotions. It was sweet of him not to rush her.

When it was clear they would be arriving at their destination at least twenty minutes early, Doug suggested they park and sight-see about the village of Amagansett.

"The Kincaid place is about five minutes out of town. Let me show you some of the landmarks from my childhood," he said nostalgically.

"Your ocean?" Her eyes crinkled in tender laughter.

"We'll see that later. Let's park right here on Main Street. I'll show you Joe's Restaurant with its marble soda fountain, where my sisters and I used to line up for ice-cream sodas on Saturday afternoons. And the Amagansett News Store, where we bought candy and magazines and Horton's ice cream."

Betsy was entranced by the quaint village, its 150-feet wide Main Street lined with magnificent elms and comfortable houses set on expansive plots of ground. She could visualize Doug as a young boy, embracing this village—another world from Manhattan—with joyous enthusiasm.

"The locals are very proud that the village has never granted a liquor license—and it was already a thriving village in 1700," Doug told her.

Betsy laughed. "Some people might have trouble with that."

"Summer visitors have learned to bring their own. Mom's a gourmet cook who loves to cook with wine, so we always arrive with a wine collection."

"Is there a large summer colony?" Betsy asked. It wouldn't resemble Southampton.

"Not large but steady. Those who come out here love it. Of course most of the local families go back to the first settlers. I remember as a kid walking through the cemetery, where the tombstones date back to the seventeenth century and bear the same names as current families." He chuckled reminiscently. "I remember Mom saying you didn't dare say anything unpleasant about anybody in town to another year-round resident because they all seemed to be related to some degree."

"It must be lovely to have roots like that," Betsy said wistfully.

Doug glanced at his watch.

"We'd better get back to the car. You don't want to keep Mr. Kincaid waiting."

Because Doug knew Amagansett, they located Mr. Kincaid's small farm with no difficulty. He immediately escorted them to the barn where he stored unused furniture that dated back to earlier generations of his family.

Betsy struggled to hide her elation when Mr. Kincaid folded back the much-washed blankets that covered the table and chairs she'd come to see. They were perfect. Amy Andrews would be delighted to own them.

Betsy realized Mr. Kincaid enjoyed dickering. It was a game

with which she was familiar. Twenty minutes after she and Doug had walked into the barn with him, she was writing out a check. She had not bought at bargain rates, Betsy conceded—but Amy Andrews would not question the price.

"You're looking smug," Doug joshed while he and Betsy walked to the car. He and Mr. Kincaid had finally managed to stash two of the chairs in the trunk of the car, two chairs on the rear seat, and the table on the luggage rack.

"That was a great deal," Betsy said with quiet satisfaction. "Thanks for rearranging your schedule."

"For you, Betsy, I'll rearrange anytime." He said this lightly, but she felt an undercurrent of conviction that she welcomed.

"Could we drive down to the beach?" Betsy asked on an impulse. Earlier he'd talked about the beautiful stretch of beach at his grandparents' cottage.

"Sure thing. We'll go to the house. It sits right on the dunes. Why don't we pick up some cold cuts and have a picnic lunch there?" His eyes brightened in anticipation. "There's always coffee in the kitchen. Sugar but no milk," he said with an air of apology. "But that doesn't matter—you take your coffee black."

"Do you have the key with you?" She was all at once self-conscious about this detour.

"We don't really need a key out here," Doug laughed," because my grandfather insists, my grandmother always locks the front door, then hides the key under a stone urn. There's no crime in Amagansett. Nobody ever steals anything. Most families—especially the ones who've lived here for generations—don't even have locks on their doors."

They drove back into town and went into the Amagansett Food Market to shop for lunch-makings. En route to their destination Doug gave her a colorful description of the damage done to Amagansett by the 1938 hurricane.

"It was the only time ever that my grandmother was alone at the cottage. She'd gone up early to prepare for a big family gathering—the last of the summer. Then, on a Wednesday in late September, all hell broke loose. The rain came down in torrents. Trees

were going down all over the place. Grandma said she looked out
the window and saw the roof of a toolhouse sitting on a laundry
line across the road."

"She must have been terrified!"

"We were all nervous wrecks—nobody could get through to
Amagansett until Friday. On Thursday the New York newspapers
carried headline stories about how all the beach houses in a new
development—Beach Hampton on Bluff Road—had been swept
into the ocean. And we were on the dunes close by! But later that
day word came through that the houses were all right, though the
Barbour Beach Club had been destroyed."

"It must have been an awful experience for your grandmother,"
Betsy said sympathetically.

"She's quite a lady." Doug's voice deepened with love. How
wonderful, Betsy thought again, to be part of an extended family.
"Nothing upsets her. She and Grandpa always battled because he
said women didn't need to drive, so she never learned. Then, three
years ago—when she was seventy-three and he was seventy-
four—he fell and sprained his ankle. He was laid up for a couple
of weeks. Without a word to any of us she went out, took driving
lessons, and got her license. Now when they come out in the
summer, she drives herself into the village."

Then they were drawing up before a small, gray-shingled cottage.

"This is it." Doug turned off the ignition and sat smiling for a
moment. "Some great memories stored away in there."

"I hope you're hungry," she said with forced lightness. They
should have driven right back to the city, she thought uneasily.
Emily and Rhoda were alone in the shop. "We bought a lot of
food."

The cottage was modest but comfortably furnished—and right
on the dunes. The ocean was a forbidding gray today, reflecting
the sky. The beach was deserted.

"Let's eat by the window that looks out on the water," Doug
said, pulling a small table from a corner of the room. "The view's
great. I'll put up coffee, bring in plates and silverware. Keep your

jacket on," he told her as she made a move to take it off. "It'll take awhile to warm up in here." He'd pushed up the thermostat the moment they walked in.

They settled themselves at the table, both relishing this parcel of time. Yet in a corner of her mind Betsy tried to deal with a growing apprehension. The atmosphere was electric with unspoken emotions.

"More coffee?" Betsy asked. "I'll get the percolator—"

"No, this is fine," Doug insisted. "I wish we could stay here like this forever."

"I have to get back to the shop," she reminded him, her voice uneven.

"I didn't mean that literally," he joshed, his eyes betraying his emotions.

"My guilty conscience was talking. I told Emily we'd be back by late afternoon."

"There'll be no traffic on the road this time of year," he said, reassuring her. "We'll make good time driving back." He rose to his feet, gazed for a moment at the mildly choppy ocean, then began to collect the plates.

"I'll wash, you dry," Betsy said, her heart pounding.

Within minutes they'd washed and dried the dishes. Betsy was ever conscious of his nearness. Doug put away the dishes and turned to her.

"So many times I've imagined us out here this way." He reached for her hand. Their eyes were devoid of camouflage now. "Betsy, I've loved you almost since the day we met. I don't know if you have other commitments—" He faltered for a moment. "But I told myself I'd get into the arena and fight for you."

"I have no commitments," she whispered. She'd die if Doug didn't make love to her now.

His mouth was warm and gentle on hers, then more demanding. Her arms closed in about his shoulders as he drew her against the hungry length of him.

"I've waited such a long time," he murmured, his mouth at her ear. "I was afraid it would never happen."

"I was afraid you didn't want anything but friendship from me," she confessed.

Hand in hand they walked into one of the tiny bedrooms. As though to seal themselves off from the rest of the world, Doug kicked the door shut. His mouth sought hers again. While the winter waves crashed against the beach and a pair of gulls cawed on a nearby roof, they sought to quench a long, long thirst.

Betsy stood at the picture window that faced the ocean. Doug's arm was about her waist.

"I feel like shooting off firecrackers," he said. "I want to tell the whole world how wonderful it was for us."

"I wouldn't advise it," she said with a laugh. "I don't think they're ready for that."

"I know I have over two years of law school ahead of me. But I don't have to stay in school," he said in sudden decision. "I can go out and get a job. We can get married as soon as I'm settled in something."

"No, Doug," Betsy said. "I couldn't live with myself if I were responsible for your walking out on your law degree."

"You'll wait all that time for us to marry? Betsy, I don't want to miss a day that isn't necessary—"

"We don't have to wait," she pointed out joyously. "Between your government allotment and my business, we can manage well." He didn't understand how successful her business had become, she thought tenderly.

"I'll be taking you away from a fancy life-style," he warned.

"I can handle that." She chuckled. "We can't get married right away—we'll have to give Paul's mother time to understand what's happening. But it won't be long," she promised. "A few weeks—"

"Oh, Lord, wait till my folks hear about us!" Doug broke into exultant laughter. "They've been scared to death I'd still be a bachelor at sixty."

CHAPTER THIRTY-NINE

Betsy was pleased when Doug found a parking spot right in front of the shop. She hurried inside to see if Emily or Rhoda was free to help with the unloading. Rhoda was showing one of their chronic "lookers" two tiny Tiffany lamps they'd recently acquired. Emily hurried out to the car with Betsy so they could help Doug with the unloading.

"It was a good deal," Emily guessed. "You've got that glow about you."

Together they transferred the dining table and chairs into the rear storage room of the shop. Then Doug prepared to take the car back to the garage—a company expense—and to head for some cramming at the law library.

"Dinner?" he asked Betsy. "My place?"

"As soon as Jimmy is asleep," she promised, her eyes bright with love.

"It's been quite a day for you, baby," Emily drawled when they were alone.

"I'm thrilled about this haul," Betsy admitted.

"I meant you and Doug," Emily said. "It happened, didn't it?" She radiated approval.

Betsy gazed at her in astonishment.

"How did you know?"

"That special glow about the two of you. It's about time." Emily reached to pull her close. "I'm so happy for you and Doug. You were made for each other."

Betsy arrived at the shop on Monday morning in a state of euphoria. In the space of a weekend her whole life had been miraculously uplifted. She hadn't said anything yet to Alice or Paul Jr. about Doug and herself. Just for a few days she needed to keep this to herself.

She settled herself at her desk to look over their accounts. She was always punctual about paying bills. She wished, she thought whimsically, that some of her clients behaved in the same fashion. Emily complained that the richer they were, the slower they paid.

"The usual Monday morning deluge of mail," Emily commented, depositing a batch of envelopes on her desk. Betsy squinted at an envelope from the real estate firm that had recently bought the building. Curious about the contents—it wasn't the rent bill at this time of month—she slit the envelope and pulled out the letter.

Her curiosity immediately spiraled into shock. Pale and trembling, she reread the letter. *This couldn't be happening.*

The real estate firm was giving notice that on the renewal of her lease the rent would be increased by 600 percent. Her lease expired in four months. She'd expected a small increase but this was outrageous!

Fighting against panic, she struggled to absorb what was happening. In the current real estate market, with vacancies being grabbed up the moment they appeared on the market, where would she find another place within four months?

"Emily—" Her voice was sharp. "Come over here!"

Her alarm was contagious. Emily rushed to the rear of the shop with an air of anxiety.

"What's happened?"

"Read this." She handed the sheet of paper to Emily.

Emily scanned the brief message. "Can they do that?" She stared at Betsy in disbelief.

"I don't know. With the war over controls are being phased out.

I expected a raise—but this—" She gestured in incomprehension. "And I have a separate lease on the second floor that has years to run," she remembered with mixed emotions.

"Could we just move to the second floor?" Emily asked. "And operate from there? I know we'll be awfully crowded, but—"

"Emily, I can't ask my clients to walk up a steep flight of stairs." They were decrepit, ugly stairs at that. "And even if we can find another shop, I'm still responsible for the rent on the second floor. We won't be able to use it except for storage. Wildly expensive storage." She was reeling from this sudden catastrophe. "I know rents keep going up—we're always reading about it in the newspapers. But six hundred percent?"

"Maybe a secretary made a mistake." Emily grasped at this possibility. "You know, added an extra zero. But even sixty percent is way above the norm."

"I'll call the office." Betsy reached for the telephone and dialed the number on the letterhead.

She was startled to reach an answering service. Perhaps it was a small firm, she reasoned. A one-person office and that person was out showing property at the moment. She left her name and phone number and asked that someone return her call.

"Isn't there some kind of ruling about rent increases?" Emily asked, trying to conceal her own anxiety. But Betsy knew she, too, was upset. "Doesn't that come under the OPA?"

"I don't know," Betsy said. "But I know how hard it is to find vacant space in good neighborhoods. I can't believe this is happening—"

"Call Grady," Emily suggested. "He's smart. He'll know how to handle this."

"I'll call him tonight at home," Betsy agreed. "I never call him at the office."

"But this is an emergency," Emily protested.

"I'll phone him tonight." Betsy glanced at her watch. "I can't reach Doug now. He won't be out of classes until five."

"You know what I think?" Emily tried to sound calm. "It must be a typo. It should have read sixty percent."

"If there was a dollar figure mentioned, we'd know," Betsy said in exasperation. "Wouldn't you think they'd mention a specific figure? All we can do is sit here and wait for them to call back."

For Betsy and Emily the day dragged painfully. Each time the phone rang, Betsy reached for it in the hope that it was the real estate office and she could confirm that there had indeed been a typographical error. Normally she read the *New York Times* in the evening—when the workday was behind her. Today she sought out the real estate section to scan the commercial rental columns.

There was nothing listed that would be of use to them, she confessed to Emily.

"We'll have to start with the real estate brokers right away." Desperation crept into Betsy's voice. "Though how I'm going to handle the rent on another location plus the second floor here— just warehouse space if we have to move out of this floor—I don't know."

"You'll manage." Emily tried to sound optimistic. "You'll be—throwing a lot of money back into the business," she conceded, "but you'll manage."

"If we can *find* another place," Betsy said. "We're going to have a wild time looking."

Five minutes later her call to the real estate office was returned.

"The letter is correct as written," a male voice brusquely informed her. "We have nothing further to discuss."

Shortly after five Betsy phoned Doug and explained what had happened.

"Doug, can they raise the rent that way? What about the OPA?"

"It's on its way out," he reminded. "It'll be dead before your lease is up. I'll start asking questions at the school in case somebody knows of a loophole."

"How can they expect anybody to pay that kind of rent?" All day long she'd been asking herself this.

"It may be that the owner wants to take possession himself," Doug pointed out. "Let me get off the phone and start asking questions," he said again. "I'll call you later at the house. This isn't going to push you out of business, Betsy." She understood he was determined to bolster her confidence. "You'll survive."

Betsy and Emily were reluctant to part at closing time.

"Honey, we'll work this out," Emily comforted.

"I'll call Grady—once Jimmy's asleep—and talk to him."

"Call and tell me what he says," Emily said.

"You know I will," Betsy said softly.

Tonight, Jimmy manufactured endless excuses to delay going to sleep. Finally Betsy refused to accept any more.

"No more stories, no more glasses of water, no more stuffed animals," she said as she turned off the lamp on his night table. "It's time for you to go to sleep." She tucked the covers about his small form, kissed him, and headed for the door to her bedroom.

"Mommie, leave the door open," he pleaded. His voice was reproachful, but already he was yawning.

"All right, darling," she agreed. "I'll leave the door open."

Within minutes Jimmy was asleep. She settled herself at the edge of her bed, and reached for the phone. Grady would come up with some way out of this nightmare, she told herself. He was so knowledgeable about business. She'd feel better after she'd talked with him.

"May I speak to Mr. Harrison, please." She was startled that his housekeeper answered his private line. Normally, when he wasn't home, this line went unanswered.

"Who's calling?" the housekeeper asked crisply.

"Betsy Forrest," she said.

"I'm sorry, Mrs. Forrest. Mr. Harrison isn't here. He was called away on business. He'll be in Switzerland for the next four weeks."

"Thank you." Betsy put down the phone. She was astonished that Grady would leave the country without some word. But she'd probably find a note in the mail tomorrow, or Alice or Paul Jr. would mention that he'd been called away.

An hour later Doug phoned to report his findings. "The landlord can raise the rent. Still, that figure sounds insane. To say the least, it's unrealistic. But you've got four months to find another place," he encouraged. "We'll cover every suitable area. There's got to be something out there for you. Look, everybody told me it was impossible to find an apartment—but I latched on to this one," he reminded her. "We'll go out there and we'll find a shop for you. There's got to be one place that's right and available!"

* * *

Every free moment that Betsy and Doug and Emily could salvage was dedicated to searching for new premises for The Oasis. Betsy saw Jimmy off to nursery school in the morning in Miss Watkins' care, then met with Doug and Emily for a strategy meeting before the shop opened and Doug had to head up to the Columbia campus for classes. Once Jimmy was asleep in the evening, she left the house for dinner with Doug and to discuss whatever leads had come up during the day.

On Friday evening—five days after the ominous letter had arrived from the real estate office—Betsy sat with Doug at the West End Bar and tried not to show the alarm that had tugged at her since she'd learned about the rent increase.

"Betsy, we've only been looking for a few days," he told her. He knew she was distraught. "We're going to find a place. We have four months," he reminded her. "Tonight we're going down to the *New York Times* and pick up the Real Estate section for Sunday's paper. That'll give us a head start on following up ads."

"How do we get that?" Her fork poised in midair.

"The Real Estate section is ready by then. If you're down there, you get it." He grinned reminiscently. "That's how I got my apartment. I was there before the Sunday *Times* was distributed."

"I'd be falling apart by now except for you." His confidence—his strength—held her together.

"Hey, we're going to lick this problem." He reached for her hand. "No insane landlord is going to mess up your business. Now finish your dinner," he said with mock ferocity, "so we can stop off at the apartment for a while before we go down to the *Times.* I've got an awful hunger—" His eyes were eloquent.

"I've got that hunger, too." Her own eyes were luminous. "Let's eat and run."

On Monday morning Betsy followed up a lead from the Sunday *Times* while Emily opened up the shop. Though the rent was considerably higher than what she paid under her current lease, it wasn't outrageous. The real estate agent was checking on renovations that would be necessary and was to call her within forty-eight hours.

"Well?" Emily greeted her with a determined smile as Betsy hurried into the shop.

"It's a possibility," she reported. "A great locale, high rent—but that's expected these days."

"With the clients you're picking up, you can afford a high rent," Emily said exuberantly.

Betsy checked her watch.

"Doug's in class—I'll call him later."

The phone rang—shrill in the morning quiet. "I'll grab it." Emily dashed to Betsy's desk, picked up the phone. "It's for you," she said a moment later. "A Mr. Ransome from your bank."

"That's the man in charge when Grady's away." Probably with some message from Grady, Betsy surmised with relief. She'd had no word since he'd left for Switzerland. "Hello—"

"Mrs. Forrest?"

"Yes, Mr. Ransome."

"I'm sorry to have to tell you," he said, his voice guarded, "but the bank must call in your loan. You have three days in which to pay it off or—"

"What do you mean?" She was simultaneously shocked and furious. "I've never once been late on a payment! I have my canceled checks to prove this!"

"If you read your contract," he pursued, "you'll see there is a provision that gives us the right to call in the loan with three days' notice if you are ever thirty days in arrears on an account."

"I'm not late on any bills!" *This was insane.* "I take pride in paying my bills on schedule!"

"I'm sorry, Mrs. Forrest, but a stockholder has notified us that you are behind on payments to a supplier. The Fair Harbor Import Company."

"I'm not behind in payment. I've not paid Fair Harbor because the wrong materials were delivered—and I returned them. I—"

"I'm sorry," he said again. "If you read your contract, you'll understand. We have an affidavit from a stockholder, and—"

"What stockholder?" Betsy interrupted, fighting for poise. "Give me that stockholder's name!"

"I'm not at liberty to do that," he said. "I can only tell you that if the loan is not paid in full by the close of business on Wednesday, then we have no recourse except to take action. The bank will file the necessary papers to take over The Oasis."

CHAPTER FORTY

$\mathbf{H}$er voice unsteady, her heart pounding, Betsy told Emily what the bank executive had said.

"They're giving me seventy-two hours to pay off the loan in full, or they'll take over the shop. How can this be happening?" Every cent she had was tied up in the shop. She'd plowed back all of her profits. Her inventory alone was worth twenty times what she owed the bank. "I'm not in arrears to Fair Harbor!"

"You returned everything," Emily recalled. "You have the receipts, haven't you?"

"The bank doesn't want to hear about that!" Again, fury surged in her. "And who's the stockholder who complained?"

"It has to be some nut that Fair Harbor knows," Emily rationalized. "Call Grady. He'll straighten it out."

"Grady's in Switzerland," Betsy reminded. She glanced at her watch. "Doug will have an hour between classes at eleven o'clock. Her mind charged into high gear. "He'll either go to the apartment or grab lunch outside somewhere. I'll run up to the campus and catch him when he comes out of class."

"Have you got a copy of the contract you signed at the bank?"

"It's right here." Betsy reached for the metal box on her desk that held special papers. "I didn't bother reading it." Why should she have read it? It was the standard contract for loans like that. "I'll take it up to show Doug."

Betsy took a cab uptown. A quarter before eleven she was

striding across the sunbathed Columbia campus, beautiful with the first signs of spring. The trees were green again, the grass was shedding its winter drabness. Here and there golden forsythia bloomed.

Should she have called the apartment first to make sure Doug was in class? she asked herself belatedly. He'd been fighting a cold. But only a disaster would keep him from class. He was so impatient to have his degree, to graduate with honors. He planned on attending summer school sessions to speed this up.

She waited at the building where Doug's class was held, checking her watch at brief intervals. How had Grady allowed her to sign that loan contract? But immediately she felt guilty at reproaching him. It was the standard bank contract. *But she wasn't in violation.* She owed Fair Harbor nothing. The materials they'd delivered were not what she'd ordered. She'd returned them.

At last she spied Doug emerging from the building. She was conscious of tenuous relief. Doug would know what she must do. Wouldn't he?

"Betsy!" His face lit up in welcome, but that joy was immediately displaced by anxiety. He knew she never left the shop during the day except for business. "You're here to take me to brunch?" he asked, with an effort at raillery.

"The sky's falling down—" She forced a shaky smile. "I need your advice."

"My favorite coffee shop is fairly empty at this hour." He reached for her hand, his face radiating reassurance. "We'll go there and talk."

While they walked to the coffee shop, Betsy explained what was happening.

"I brought along the contract. I still haven't read it," she confessed. "It's the standard deal."

"They got you in the boiler plate. That's the stock stuff that goes into the contract and that most people don't bother reading— but it can deliver an awful wallop," he explained.

"But I'm not in arrears," Betsy protested. "I'm not in violation of the contract."

"They have a creditor who's claiming otherwise," Doug explained. "You've bought from Fair Harbor before?"

"Twice. Oh, you mean they know my bank," Betsy said in sudden comprehension. "From the checks I sent them for previous payments."

"And they know somebody who's a stockholder," Doug followed up. "They're out for blood because you refused the shipment." His face grew tense in anger. "I'll cut my next class. We'll go over and talk to them together. But first let's have coffee and I'll read the contract."

As Doug predicted, the coffee shop was nearly empty. They settled themselves in a private booth in the rear, where Doug could study the contract with no distractions. He and Betsy ordered cheese omelets and coffee. Then he focused on dissecting the contents of the bank document.

"Honey," he said ruefully when he'd finished reading the contract, "never sign anything again without absorbing every word. And make sure," he added, "that your attorney has given his approval."

They left the coffee shop and grabbed a cab to take them to Fair Harbor Importers, located in a loft in the West Thirties. Doug reached for her hand and smiled reassuringly as they rode up in the decrepit elevator.

"It's right down the hall," Betsy told him, her heart pounding at the prospect of an ugly confrontation.

A girl at the desk summoned the owner at Betsy's request. From the girl's attitude they knew that Betsy had been much maligned by her boss. He arrived grim and wary.

Before Doug could finish his first sentence, the importer was on the offensive.

"I don't want to talk to you!" he yelled and turned to Betsy. "You owe me four thousand dollars for materials I bought just for you! What am I supposed to do with it now? Where do you get the nerve to send it back?" His foreign accent made it difficult to understand what he was saying.

"It's not what I ordered." Betsy repeated what she had told him in the past, in person and in correspondence. "I gave you a sample that my client approved. You didn't deliver what I ordered." She struggled to keep her voice even. She was fearful he and Doug would come to blows.

"I sue you!" he said triumphantly. "My lawyer say we win!"

"We're not going to get anywhere with this guy," Doug told Betsy in disgust. "Let's get out of here."

They left the loft and went down into the street again.

"How do I convince the bank I don't owe Fair Harbor?" Betsy shook her head in frustration. "This is unbelievable."

"You'll have to call your friend Grady," Doug said gently. "I know he's out of town, but you can't wait until he returns."

"Grady knows the trouble I had with Fair Harbor," Betsy remembered with a flurry of hope. "I told him about it when it first happened. He never thought there'd be anything like this. He didn't think they'd even sue."

"Phone him," Doug said.

"Doug, he's in Switzerland!"

"They have phones in Switzerland. Grady can straighten this out with one call to the bank. You'll be off the hook. And don't worry about a suit. You have a file on the whole transaction, haven't you?"

"Of course. I have a sample of the material I ordered, and I clipped a swatch from what Fair Harbor sent me. I have letters from the client rejecting what was delivered. The shade and the quality were way off." Betsy hesitated. "I don't know where Grady's staying in Switzerland, but Paul Jr. and Alice must know."

"There's a phone booth on the corner." Doug pointed. "Call and get Grady's address in Switzerland. Then go back to the shop and call him from there."

With Doug standing by, Betsy tried to reach first Paul Jr., then Alice. Neither was available. She glanced at her watch, ever conscious of the time element involved.

"I'll ask them when I get home from the shop," Betsy decided. "What's the time difference between New York and Switzerland?

Seven hours?" Without waiting for Doug to confirm this, she continued. "I'll phone Grady at eight A.M. Swiss time. He says he's always an early riser."

"Fine." Doug smiled reassuringly. "I have to rush back up to campus for a class. I'll pick you up at the house at the usual time. And don't look so frightened. We'll work this out."

The afternoon dragged excruciatingly for Betsy. On her arrival at the house she was disappointed to discover that Alice had not yet returned from a cocktail party, nor had Paul Jr. returned from the office. Fighting impatience, she went upstairs to the nursery.

Jimmy came rushing to her with his usual exuberant welcome. "Mommie, Mommie!"

Now she focused on her private time with Jimmy, while Miss Watkins went downstairs for her dinner.

Unless Grady was able to clear up this nightmare, she thought in despair, there was no way she could leave the Forrest house. If she lost the business, she'd have no security for Jimmy except what his grandparents provided. *She couldn't marry Doug.*

Halfway to his apartment Grady leaned forward and instructed his chauffeur to take him to the Forrest townhouse. He had struggled all day with his conscience. What he was doing to Betsy was unforgivable. How had he allowed Alice to drive him into such a despicable act? He'd go to Betsy now, tell her what he had tried to do. He couldn't live with himself if he allowed this to continue.

At the Forrest house he dismissed the chauffeur. After he'd bared his soul to Betsy, he thought grimly, he'd need to walk. Now he headed for the entrance to the townhouse.

"Grady, how nice to see you." Alice had just emerged from her limousine, directly behind his own. "We're having dinner late because Paul Jr.'s tied up in a conference, but you must stay."

"Alice, I have to talk to you." He felt sickened, humiliated by his behavior. He'd make Alice understand what terrible things they'd tried to do—and then he'd tell Betsy her nightmare was over.

All at once Alice's eyes were guarded. Grady knew she was becoming distressed. *She must understand he couldn't go on with this charade.*

Elise opened the door for them with a welcoming smile.

"Elise, tell Peggy Mr. Harrison will be staying for dinner," Alice instructed.

"I don't think so," Grady said.

"Of course you'll stay for dinner," Alice said and headed down the hall to the library. Grady followed in tormented silence.

Alice closed the library door behind them and turned to Grady.

"What on earth has you in such a foul mood?" She was struggling to appear casual.

"Alice, I can't go through with this. I've never been so ashamed of myself. To do something so rotten to someone as fine and sweet as Betsy! I shouldn't have listened to you!" His throat tightened as he recalled his actions. "I have to tell her what I've done—and make everything right again."

"*Grady, no!*" Alice's voice was shrill. "You were right. She's been using you shamefully. She—" Alice paused as Grady swung away from her. "Grady—"

"There's Betsy in the foyer," he said tensely. "I must talk to her." He charged from the library, his sole thought to make amends for his shameful actions. In shock, Alice followed at his heels.

"Grady!" Betsy stared at him in astonishment. "I thought you were in Switzerland. That's what your housekeeper told me when I phoned you."

"She lied, Betsy. That's what I told her to say." He was pale with anguish. "I did terrible things to you. I own the building where your shop is located. *I* raised the rent in that insane fashion. *I* was the one who ordered the bank to call in your loan. But it's all over," he said urgently. "Please—"

"Grady, why?" Betsy gasped, cutting him off.

"There's no fool like an old fool," he said with a sigh. "I knew you were seeing that young man. That law student. I let myself be consumed with jealousy. I felt as though I were losing you—"

All at once the pieces leaped together in Betsy's mind. Grady knew nothing about Doug. *Alice* had told him. *Alice* had pushed him into trying to ruin her business. And now—always the gentleman—Grady was trying to shield Alice.

"Grady, you know how much I value your friendship," Betsy whispered, feeling his pain. "Doug knows that, too." She didn't hear the doorbell or see Alice rush to respond.

"I want to be your friend always, Betsy—and Jimmy's Uncle Grady. If you'll let me."

"Oh, Grady, of course." Betsy gazed at him with relief. This had all been Alice's sick mind. "Now my only problem is to keep Fair Harbor from suing me," she said ruefully. "Even the threat of a suit could be damaging in the eyes of my clients."

"You have your file on Fair Harbor," Grady pointed out. "Let my attorney handle it. I'm sure he'll be able to convince the company they'll just be wasting attorney's fees if they try to sue. Betsy, you're totally in the clear in that matter."

"You've been so wonderful to me, Grady." Betsy didn't hear the door being opened. She didn't see Doug hovering in the doorway. "You're so dear to me." She threw her arms about Grady and kissed him tenderly.

"Are you surprised?" Alice said in a tart whisper as Doug gazed in shock at the tableau before him. "They've been going together over a year. *You're an intruder.*" Triumph soared in her.

"I'm a little early . . . as always," Doug said with strained politeness. Trying to ignore Alice's accusation.

At the sound of Doug's voice Betsy turned toward the door.

"Doug, everything's all right!" Her smile was brilliant. "Grady's taken care of everything!"

Betsy sat across the tiny table in the small Italian restaurant Doug had recently discovered on First Avenue in the Sixties. She was puzzled by the odd withdrawal she sensed in him. He toyed with his eggplant parmigiana, when normally he attacked it with relish.

"Grady says I'm not to worry about Fair Harbor's suing me," she said again. "His attorney will handle it for me."

"That's great." He seemed to be relieved for her, yet there was a strange wall between them tonight. He couldn't be jealous of Grady, could he? No, that was ridiculous.

"You won't mind if we break up early tonight?" Doug asked self-consciously.

"No—" Betsy was startled.

"I'm having the devil of a time with a paper," he said, but Betsy sensed that something other than a school paper was disturbing him tonight. "I want to get home and tackle it again."

"Sure." Betsy made an effort to conceal her bewilderment.

When she arrived home, Betsy walked directly to the library. The lack of sounds from the dining room told her that Alice and Paul Jr. had not sat down to dinner yet. This was one of those late nights.

Out of loyalty to Grady and Alice she had said nothing to Doug about Grady's feelings toward her or about Alice's role in this nightmare. She had just explained that Grady was clearing up the matter at the bank and would handle the exorbitant rent increase situation for her. *But she couldn't stay in this house with Alice after what had happened.*

Alice sat alone in the library, in a chair before the fireplace. She was staring into the ruddy blaze that sent warm color into the room. Betsy suspected she stared without seeing. She was lacing her fingers in that nervous way she did when she was upset.

Betsy hesitated for a moment. She knew Alice's mental state was fragile. Still, they must deal with this situation. She and Jimmy couldn't stay in this house any longer. She couldn't allow herself and Jimmy to be exposed to whatever future act of insanity Alice might commit. Paul would have understood that.

"We must have a talk," Betsy said quietly, and Alice turned toward her with a frightened gasp. "It's time for Jimmy and me to move into a small apartment of our own. I'm grateful for all you've done for us," she continued with contrived calm, "but—"

"No!" Alice broke in. "Don't do that to me! Don't take my grandson away from me!"

"I'm not taking him away from you," Betsy said. "You and his grandfather will be welcome to see him whenever you like." She paused, unnerved by Alice's stricken face. But compassion had limitations, she told herself defensively. "Doug and I plan to be married shortly. He'll be a fine stepfather for Jimmy. And you and Paul Jr. will always be welcome in our home."

Without waiting for further discussion, Betsy fled into the hall and headed for the front door. As always in a crisis Emily was her refuge. She needed to talk with Emily.

On top of all the other craziness, what was happening between Doug and her? He'd behaved so strangely tonight. Was Doug sorry he'd asked her to marry him? Was everything over between them?

CHAPTER FORTY-ONE

Alice sat motionless for painful moments after Betsy left the library. In the silence of the house she heard the front door open, then close. Betsy was going out again. Back to that Doug Golden, she taunted herself. To tell him what had just happened.

How was she to stop Betsy from moving out of this house, taking Jimmy from them? How was she to stop Betsy from marrying Doug Golden? They might move a thousand—three thousand—miles away. She'd lose her grandson. All she had of Paul.

Betsy mustn't move out of this house. She couldn't marry Doug Golden—he couldn't support her and Jimmy. If her business were ruined, Betsy would have to stay here for Jimmy's sake.

All at once Alice's fevered mind clutched at a way to destroy Betsy's business—despite Grady's help. Betsy had said that if the import company sued her, she'd be in serious trouble, that her clients might leave her.

If Betsy lost her file on Fair Harbor—which Grady said would clear her—then she would be in real trouble. Get that file. Destroy it.

She mustn't say a word to Paul Jr. about what had happened, she warned herself when she heard his voice in the foyer. They'd sit down to dinner as usual. She'd talk about her committee meeting this afternoon. But Betsy wasn't going to take her precious baby from this house. *She knew how to handle this situation.*

Steeling herself for what lay ahead, Alice left the library to greet her husband. She talked with unnatural vivacity as she walked with him into the dining room. Her conversation ranged from the afternoon's committee meeting to the coming gala for the found-ling hospital to which they contributed generously. All the while she listened for sounds that would tell her Betsy had returned.

"Alice, are you all right?" Paul Jr. asked midway through din-ner. "You're not coming down with something? Your face is flushed." He inspected her anxiously.

"I'm just a little tired from this afternoon's meeting," she told him. "It became rather heated." She had to get into Betsy's room and find the spare key to the shop that Betsy kept there. *Before Betsy came back.* "I think I'll go upstairs and read in bed for a while."

"Good idea," Paul Jr. said. "I'll be up early, too."

"You said you wanted to hear that news forum tonight," she reminded. She didn't want him coming up to their room early—that would spoil everything. "What time is it broadcast?"

"From nine to ten," he told her. It was almost nine now. "I'll hear that, then come up. I have to be out of the house by seven tomorrow morning. I'm having a business breakfast with an im-portant client."

Her heart pounding, her mind focusing on what she must ac-complish, Alice went upstairs to the nursery. She did this every night. Even if Miss Watkins heard her, she'd think nothing of it. But Miss Watkins wouldn't hear her—she was in her room listen-ing to the radio.

Alice tiptoed into the nursery, pausing beside Jimmy's bed. She was doing this for her precious baby. He needed her.

Then she walked to the connecting door that led to Betsy's bedroom. When Betsy arrived at the house, she would hear. Now to find that key!

Tomorrow morning—as soon as Paul Jr. drove off for his ap-pointment—she would leave the house and go to the shop. She'd find that file. She'd tell Amy Andrews and Millicent Roberts that Betsy was being sued by a supplier and was sure to lose the case.

They'd circulate it among their whole crowd. Betsy would be ruined.

With mounting frenzy, careful to leave no telltale trail, Alice searched for the key. When she was about to concede defeat, she discovered it at the back of Betsy's lingerie drawer. She knew it was the key to the office because of the identifying tag. At the same moment she heard voices down below in the foyer. Betsy was talking with Elise.

Alice hurried from the room, anxious to return to her own. Behind the door of the master bedroom suite she listened for Betsy's approach. Thank God she wasn't going into the library— she wouldn't tell Paul Jr. that she was threatening to move out of the house. And she wouldn't know the key to the shop was missing from its usual place.

Conscious of her highly emotional state, Alice took one of her pills, then searched for her small travel clock so that she could set the alarm. *She mustn't oversleep in the morning.* She slid the tiny clock beneath the bed, where Paul Jr. would never notice it. The alarm would go off twenty minutes after he left the house. No chance that he would linger later than that, she told herself. He was punctilious about keeping appointments on schedule.

She pretended to be asleep when Paul Jr. came to bed. She knew that despite her medication she would sleep little tonight. No matter. She had an urgent task to accomplish.

She slept at troubled intervals through the night, waking to the sounds of her husband's usual morning routine. She feigned sleep until she heard him go downstairs. William would be waiting at the curb with the limousine.

She rose from the bed, turned off the alarm, and rushed to dress. She wasn't expected downstairs for breakfast until ten. She'd be back long before then. William was driving Paul Jr. to his breakfast appointment. Peggy and Elise would be in the kitchen, having their own breakfast. They wouldn't know she'd left the house.

Alice found a taxi immediately, gave the driver her destination. At this hour of the morning Madison Avenue was near-deserted.

In minutes she stood before the door of The Oasis. She reached into her alligator purse and fumbled for the key. Her throat tight with excitement, she unlocked the door and hurried inside.

In the rear office area she began to search for the file in the desk drawers. It wasn't here. Where would Betsy keep something so important?

Lord, it was cold in here. She hadn't worn a fur coat so as to be less conspicuous, but now she regretted that decision.

Her eyes fell on an electric heater pushed against the back wall. She reached to plug it into place, hovered gratefully for a moment before the reddening coils. Searching further, she discovered a two-drawer file concealed behind a Coromandel screen. The Fair Harbor file must be here!

In a surge of impatience Alice flipped through the top file drawer. Here it was! The tab on the folder was clearly marked: FAIR HARBOR.

She concealed the folder beneath her coat and left the shop. She would make sure Fair Harbor knew they could sue and win, she promised herself in triumph. She'd give them the folder in person. Betsy wouldn't have a shred of evidence to clear herself.

After a night of troubled sleep Betsy awoke twenty minutes later than usual. Her first conscious thoughts were of Doug's strange behavior the previous night. *What had happened between the time she saw him earlier in the day and when he came to pick her up?*

She rushed through her morning preparations, spending less than her usual time with Jimmy. She'd have him with her at the shop that morning while Miss Watkins kept a dental appointment. Nursery classes today had been called off because of the death of the founder of the school.

She'd forgo breakfast and settle for tea at the office, Betsy decided, reaching for her purse and briefcase. Emily always came in with muffins for a snack break.

Now Emily's advice last night ricocheted in her brain:

"Betsy, talk to Doug! Come right out and ask him what's bugging him. I can't believe he's jealous of Grady."

She'd phone Doug, she resolved. They'd always been able to talk freely. She'd ask him why he was upset with her. But not this morning, she decided. He had an eight o'clock class this morning. She would call him later.

Up in his apartment Doug, too, after a restless night, was wrestling with his feelings. He'd acted like a jackass, he told himself. He didn't believe that garbage about Betsy and Grady that Mrs. Forrest had tossed at him. She was off her rocker.

Betsy had kissed Grady in gratitude for his efforts at saving her shop. It was the natural thing to do. How could he have reacted so stupidly?

He'd cut his early class this morning. He had to go to the shop and apologize to Betsy. At this moment nothing else in his life was so important as to mend this breach between them. She'd sensed he was angry with her. She'd been bewildered. Let him put things right.

He hurried from the apartment to the IRT, upset that he had to wait for a train. He left the train at Columbus Circle, intent on walking across to Madison and then south the short blocks to the shop. He berated himself yet again as he strode across town in the sharp morning cold. The sky was gray and foreboding, hinting at snow.

He felt relief well in him as he opened the door and walked into the shop. It had just opened for business. Betsy was at the far side, in deep conversation with a customer. Emily was upstairs, he surmised. He knew Rhoda was due in at noon.

His face lighted as he spied Jimmy, on his knees before a coffee table in the rear of the shop—and engrossed in a crayon drawing. Then pleasure in this endearing tableau turned to horror as he saw a batch of fabrics that lay across a lounge chair between Jimmy and himself suddenly burst into flames.

"Betsy, where's Emily?" he yelled across the floor as he charged toward Jimmy.

"Upstairs," Betsy said as she turned to face him. Then she cried out in terror. "Oh, my God! Jimmy!"

"Call Emily downstairs!" He stopped her flight toward Jimmy.

"I'll get Jimmy—" He grabbed at a scatter rug to protect him as he pushed past the flames. He heard Betsy's anxious voice ordering Emily to the lower floor.

"Mommie, Mommie!" Jimmy's voice was a high, frightened wail.

"It's all right," Doug soothed, reaching for the small boy, wrapping him in the scatter rug as the flames spread to a display of sheer kitchen curtains. "You're going to be okay."

He hurried toward the entrance, cradling Jimmy—sobbing in terrified gasps, in his arms. His eyes strained to find Betsy. There she was, at the front of the stairs. "Where's Emily?"

"Right here," Betsy said, her voice husky with relief.

"Mommie?" Jimmy cried. "Mommie—"

"Mommie's coming," she said, rushing toward him.

"I'll call the fire department from the extension up front," Emily said, heading in that direction.

"Emily, for God's sake, let's all get out of the shop!" Doug ordered. "Call next door!"

In minutes fire trucks were arriving at the scene. Shivering in the cold, Betsy stood with Jimmy in her arms—enveloped now in Doug's suede jacket and flanked by Doug and Emily. *What had happened to cause the fire?*

With commendable speed the firemen put out the blaze, emerged from the shop to report that the fire had been caused by a faulty electric heater.

"But that heater has been unplugged for days!" Betsy was baffled. "I was worried about the frayed cord."

"Who could have plugged it in?" Emily demanded. "Jimmy," she asked gently, "did you plug in the heater?"

"No." Jimmy shook his head fiercely. "I didn't do it."

"Let me get you and Jimmy to the house," Doug said firmly. "Emily, can you handle things here?"

"Sure, you all go back to the house. I'll take care of everything. And won't Miss Watkins be shocked when she returns from the dentist?" Emily smiled wryly while the first of the fire trucks began to pull away from the site.

Doug hailed a cab, helped Betsy and Jimmy inside, and gave the driver directions.

"Your hair is singed," Betsy told Doug in astonishment. "I was too upset to notice before."

Doug shrugged. "It'll grow back."

"Me, too?" Jimmy asked in alarm. "What you just said."

"No, your hair is fine," Betsy soothed. "Uncle Doug had you all covered up with the rug." But she felt sick in recall. Jimmy's beautiful little face was tear-stained and puffy from crying. Why hadn't she noticed that the heater was on? And immediately she understood: a customer had come in before she could do more than drop her purse into a desk drawer. There'd been no time to notice. "And weren't the firemen wonderful, the way they put out the fire?" She tried to coax a smile from Jimmy.

"I'll tell Zach tomorrow at school." All at once Jimmy beamed. "I saw the firemen put out the fire!"

When they emerged from the taxi, Jimmy rebelled against being carried. Clutching Doug's jacket about himself, almost tripping as it dragged on the ground, he walked with his mother and Doug to the entrance of the Forrest townhouse.

"You're freezing," Doug said compassionately, pulling Betsy close while they waited for someone to open the door. The first snowflakes were beginning to fall.

"I won't be in a minute." She tried to dismiss the dank cold.

Elise pulled the door wide, stared in shock at their disheveled appearances, at Jimmy's tear-stained face.

"Jimmy, where's your coat and cap?" she asked. "What happened, sweetheart?" Her voice was suddenly shrill with anxiety.

"We had a fire!" He grinned at Elise's astonishment. "Uncle Doug saved me!"

"What's this about a fire?" Alice emerged from the dining room in alarm. "Jimmy, baby, are you all right?"

"Five fire trucks came." Jimmy told his grandmother with pride while she hurried toward them. "I counted them."

"There was a fire at the shop," Betsy began, struggling to sound calm. "We—"

"What was Jimmy doing at the shop?" Alice dropped to her haunches before him, reached to pull him close.

"The school was closed today. Miss Watkins brought him to me because she had to keep a dental appointment. I don't know how it happened," Betsy said exhaustedly. "I know I left that electric heater unplugged. But the firemen insisted it had been plugged into an outlet."

"The electric heater in the shop?" Alice rose shakily to her feet. Her face was drained of color. "Oh, my God," she whispered. "Is that what caused the fire?"

"It was an electrical fire," Doug explained. "With all those fabrics around, it—"

"It was my fault!" Alice closed her eyes in anguish. "My fault! I was so cold this morning—I plugged in the heater. I forgot to turn it off. I could have killed my precious baby," she moaned.

"What were you doing in the shop?" Betsy gasped.

"I couldn't bear the thought of your moving out of the house with Jimmy," Alice whispered. "I went there to take the Fair Harbor file—I remembered what Grady said about it. I was going to give it to them this afternoon. I thought if you were sued, you'd have trouble with your clients. You'd lose the store. You'd need us—you couldn't take Jimmy away. I've done a terrible thing. I didn't mean it. Betsy, I didn't mean it," she moaned. "I just wanted to keep Jimmy with me."

Doug caught Alice as she swayed and held a protective arm about her.

"Elise, get Mrs. Forrest's pills," Betsy said, but Elise was already rushing for Alice's medication.

"Grandma?" Jimmy was bewildered, yet he understood something was wrong.

"Grandma's going to be all right," Betsy soothed. "Let's all go into the library and sit down."

Betsy was touched by the way Doug took charge of the situation. He sat beside Alice on the sofa and talked to her in soft, reassuring tones. Miss Watkins arrived, was told what had happened. She took Jimmy upstairs to be washed and changed. She signaled to Betsy that she would give him lunch and see that he was calmed down.

Betsy turned toward the library door in astonishment when she heard Paul Jr.'s voice in the foyer. From his conversation with Elise she understood the maid had phoned his office, as she must have done on other traumatic occasions through the years.

Alice stumbled awkwardly to her feet as Paul Jr. appeared at the doorway.

"I did a terrible thing," she sobbed. "I almost killed Jimmy! I don't deserve to live!"

Paul Jr. hurried to take his wife into his arms, listened while she stammered her confession.

"I was out of my mind to do such an awful thing."

"Everybody is all right," Doug said quietly. "The damage to the shop isn't extensive. In a week Betsy can reopen."

"Alice, let's put all this behind us," Betsy said gently, her eyes blurred by tears. Subconsciously she realized that she had called her mother-in-law by her given name for the first time. "When Doug and I are married, we'll live right here in New York. You can see Jimmy as often and for as long as you wish." Her eyes moved from Alice to Paul Jr. "Jimmy loves you both very much. I'm so happy he has you two. You're a very special part of his life."

"Betsy, we want to set up a trust fund for Jimmy," Alice said. She looked to Paul Jr. for confirmation. She reached a hand out for his. "We want to know that's always there for him."

"And a trust fund for you, Betsy," Paul Jr. added. "Paul would have wanted that. When the time comes, you and Jimmy will inherit the Forrest estate. Paul would have wished for that, too."

Much later, after they'd sat down to a familial lunch with Alice and Paul Jr., Betsy and Doug went upstairs to look in on Jimmy. He was asleep in the nursery—exhausted from his morning adventure.

He lay asleep on his stomach, one hand extended in a small fist. Betsy reached to caress a finger. She was conscious of a poignantly beautiful sense of well-being.

Through pain and travail she had earned what was most precious in the world to her—a loving family. No doubt in her mind that Paul's parents were forever woven into her life and Jimmy's—and now there was Doug to complete her family. To be a loving father to Jimmy.

With her free hand she reached to clasp one of Doug's. A sliver of moonlight seeped through the drapes to lend an ethereal beauty to these moments.

"Doug, do you know that quotation from the Bible?" she whispered. Aunt Celia's favorite quotation. " 'To everything there is a season—' " Betsy's face was radiant. "This is *our* season. At last."